~~~~~~~~~~~~~~~~~~~~~~~~~~~~~~~~~

"What kind of sorcery puts a wood nymph in the body of a handsome human hunk?" the wood nymph inquired.

"I'm a man, not a wood nymph," Joe retorted.

"Your soul and aura are the same as ours," the nymph maintained. "Were you changed by sorcery or did you forget your real self?"

"I was born like this. The Master of the Dead once put my soul into a wood nymph, but magic gave me back my original form."

"I see. You were a human who became a fairy. But no magic can change a fairy soul—ever. So you *are* a fairy."

"I feel like my old self. I bleed, I bruise, I handle iron."

"The flesh magic protects you," the nymph explained. "You'll live your life as you are. But when the flesh dies, you'll be one of us. Only if iron stabs your fairy heart would you really die."

It was the most unsettling certainty of hereafter Joe could imagine.

By Jack L. Chalker
Published by Ballantine Books:

THE WEB OF THE CHOZEN
AND THE DEVIL WILL DRAG YOU UNDER
A JUNGLE OF STARS
DANCE BAND ON THE *TITANIC*
DANCERS IN THE AFTERGLOW

THE SAGA OF THE WELL WORLD
Volume 1: *Midnight at the Well of Souls*
Volume 2: *Exiles at the Well of Souls*
Volume 3: *Quest for the Well of Souls*
Volume 4: *The Return of Nathan Brazil*
Volume 5: *Twilight at the Well of Souls:*
         The Legacy of Nathan Brazil

THE FOUR LORDS OF THE DIAMOND
Book One: *Lilith: A Snake in the Grass*
Book Two: *Cerberus: A Wolf in the Fold*
Book Three: *Charon: A Dragon at the Gate*
Book Four: *Medusa: A Tiger by the Tail*

THE DANCING GODS
Book One: *The River of Dancing Gods*
Book Two: *Demons of the Dancing Gods*
Book Three: *Vengeance of the Dancing Gods*
Book Four: *Songs of the Dancing Gods*

THE RINGS OF THE MASTER
Book One: *Lords of the Middle Dark*
Book Two: *Pirates of the Thunder*
Book Three: *Warriors of the Storm*
Book Four: *Masks of the Martyrs*

Songs of the Dancing Gods

Book Four of *The Dancing Gods*

Jack L. Chalker

A Del Rey Book

BALLANTINE BOOKS • NEW YORK

FOR THE DELPHI WEDNESDAY CROWD:
JANET, MARTHA, BYRON & EILEEN, CHERP,
GARDNER & SUE, PAT, CHUQ, MIKE & ROSA,
PAUL, GEORGE, BRANDON, RALPH, EVA (OF COURSE),
AND, OH YEAH, YOU, TOO, RESNICK

TABLE OF CONTENTS

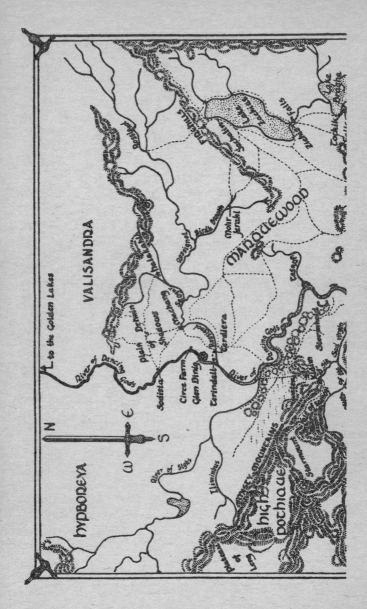

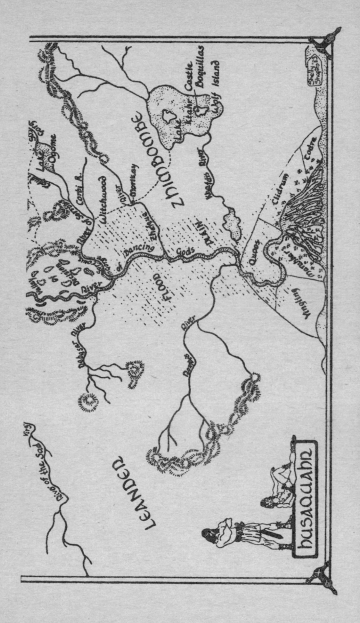

TO THOSE WHO CAME IN LATE AND
TO THOSE AWAY TOO LONG

JUST AFTER THE START OF THE PAST DECADE, I DECIDED TO write an Epic Fantasy Novel. It wasn't anything that I came upon either late or cynically; back when I was a publisher, I published the first three books ever done about swords and sorcery and I'd read Conan when Conan, let alone Arnold Schwarzenegger, wasn't cool.

I felt a little out of touch, though, in that genre; I still remembered the old stuff: Robert E. Howard, the still-going-strong Fritz Leiber, the ubiquitous Tolkien, and the like, but, aside from a couple of Moorcocks, my contemporary fantasy education was lacking.

Now, I know that reading the best science fiction of prior generations is an essential part of education, but if you read only thirty-year-old SF to get an idea of what was going on, you'd be pretty well out of it. With that thought, I went out and picked up a dozen or so major fantasies by various writers, who were now best-sellers and highly acclaimed and had their own groupies, and settled in to see what heroic fantasy had evolved into, fully expecting the same kind of revolution I knew had happened in science fiction. I won't mention the titles or the authors, because it didn't matter.

Before I was halfway through the first one, I had the eerie feeling that, although it had been written within the last couple of years, by someone far younger than I, somehow, I'd read it before. When a quick check to the end showed that it indeed went where I knew it would, I put it down and started anew.

The names were different, the points of view were shifted, the villain bore a different name, the hero was perhaps a bit nastier, but, this time, I *knew* I'd read it before—in the previous book.

Investigating this phenomenon further, I went through a ton of books, past and present, and came up with the remarkable discovery that there were really only two books there, and a hybrid constituting a third. One was an idealized quasi-medieval universe with its costumes and manners and My Lords and My Ladies and, somehow, the serfs who held it all together were mere background, unless, of course, the hero or heroine was raised as one not knowing that he or she was really Prince or Queen or something of the sort.

The other was Hyborea—whether Howard's Hyborean Age or Smith's Hyperborea, they were one and the same, focused perhaps on the barbarian adventurers as in Howard or on the upper class and top sorcerers and upper-class rulers as in Smith. Of course, the lower classes and thralls were mere background, unless, of course, the hero or heroine was raised as one without knowing that he or she was really Prince or Queen or . . . well, you get the idea.

This led to a research project to determine the truth of the matter. If indeed there really were only two epic fantasies, all the works being simple variations on common themes, or even, perhaps, just one, with the setting a choice between the time of *King Lear* or the time of *Hamlet*, then why? Was it that there were only two basic settings and a single set of heroic fantasy themes?

Rejecting straight away the cynic's concept that all these books were knockoffs of the originals, both because I knew so many writers wouldn't stay so bound otherwise, nor would such a wide audience continue to respond so enthusiastically to each slight theme and variation of the same book, over and over, I knew there had to be another reason, and, after much work, I discovered it, in an improbable place, while doing research in particle physics for another book.

There was not, as western religion tells us, a single creation, nor a series as other faiths have it. The single act of creation, the Big Bang, whatever you like, created not a single universe but many, overlapping but generally invisible and intangible and, therefore, unknown to one another. Ours is the Prime Universe, where the great and ultimate fate of all life would be decided in the epic battle of opposites, of good and evil, of powers of light and darkness.

In the backwash of this creation, the other worlds trail out, each occupying the same space but not the same space-time continuum. Because they were not fully formed, and the Ultimate Engineer was preoccupied with us, they were left for development to the Lesser Powers—let's call them Angels. The universe closest to us is the universe of the Lesser Powers. Not quite as dynamic, shaped by Lesser Powers, it has developed differently.

At the start, both universes, theirs and ours, had as much magic as natural law, and creatures evolved that were like ours, even human, and partly human, and some intelligent races that were not human at all. On Earth, the humans became dominant to the point where they slew the others, out of fear, out of competition, or out of ignorance, driving the few remnants further and further underground even as physical law was locked into near immutability. Ultimately the others, the creatures of magic, of faërie, of centaurs and unicorns, pixies and leprechauns, passed into the realm of legends and stories, until there are none left here now who truly understand the magic or know its capabilities, and even fewer who truly believe. Without belief, the magic bends more to physics, so that even the powers of Darkness must battle through surrogates and hard technology in more hidden, mundane fashion.

In Husaquahr, which is the name of that other world, this did not happen. Natural law exists there, but it is of a more rudimentary and pliable nature than our own here and now. A master engineer designs a Great Pyramid, a Stonehenge, that lasts the ages; lesser engineers allow compromises and design flaws and their work eventually wears away or collapses. A Master Engineer designed our world; Husaquahr was designed by lesser lights. And from that came uneasy chaos which lasted for millennia.

An ironclad contract is one drawn up by a great lawyer; the contracts with all those loopholes are drawn by lesser legal talents. Ultimately, there arose a very few, a mere handful, of powerful magicians who were also master lawyers. Together they formed an uneasy but necessary alliance, the Council of Thirteen, and with their combined powers they began to fill in the loopholes in Husaquahr's Creation, imposing logic, rules, on all the world, its denizens, its very stones, and codified these as the Books of Rules for the guidance and training of future generations.

Order was imposed, but at the price of stagnancy. Things were as they were in broad terms because they were mandated to be that way by sorcerers so powerful, so much closer to Creation, that they were immutable.

Over the great span of time, though, even those great ones passed on, either through death or transmigration or in ways of which we can not even dream, leaving only the Rules to reign.

The Council, however, remained, filled by increasingly lesser individuals, lacking some of the power and all of the wisdom of the founders. Great sorcerers, yes, by comparison, but mere wisps of smoke compared to the ones who had once held their positions. Not, of course, that *they* thought so; generation after generation of Councils have worked hard to keep plugging more and more loopholes, adding on Rule after Rule, binding the whole of the world as tightly as rôles in a never-ending stage play.

The inheritors from the greatest of the great and the wisest of the wise had evolved, if you want to call it that, into that most fearsome of the creatures of civilization.

The inheritors of greatness were bureaucrats.

Of course, such a horrible fate could not befall us in our own world. Look at the ones who established the great nations of the world and those inheritors who run our world now. Right?

Beyond Husaquahr still is another world, a world that did not even have the luxury of a coherent creation, let alone the great and wise minds to impose order upon it. A nightmarish world without physical laws at all, a universe of chaos and disorder so terrifying that none can comprehend it and the few that have been there neither discuss what they saw nor wish to return. To those of Husaquahr, that is known as the Land of the Djinn.

These three universes, however, the only ones with anything we might even comprehend as sentient life, are not connected and are in the main ignorant of one another, save in our dreams.

Physicists might have many names for it, but to Husaquahr, the barrier between us and them is simply the Sea of Dreams, for only the dreams of one may generally pass to the other through that detachment of the soul called sleep. All of us intercept some of Husaquahr when we sleep, when we dream, whether we are aware of it or not. Most of us are not aware; a few of us who are *too* aware provide incredibly comfortable livings for legions of psychiatrists. A *very* few of us awaken with little conscious memory of the impressions we gain from Husaquahr, but we sit down with pens and pads, or typewriters, or word processors, and we write out great accounts of the things that happen there and we call it heroic fiction and we really believe it is. Those of us who do so have always been around; the storytellers and shamans of ancient times, the Homers and others of ancient literature, were all such, which is why they have a certain consistency.

Naturally, since both their world and ours is a *world*, we intersect different regions, so the creatures and demons of the East are different than ours, as are those of the African and the Amerind. But, commonly, our myths, our legends, our heroic sagas, are dream-linked accounts of that other place. The rest of you, the audience for these, whether reading or hearing them, respond because there is a suspension of disbelief induced by your own dream-links as well.

That is why we seem to be reading, and writing, the same book. We are not writing fiction at all; we are writing subjectively filtered accounts of the history of this other world.

There is a way through; a physical passageway across the Sea of Dreams. A few find it by accident, by unnatural convergence of being at just the wrong spot at the right time, vanishing there and becoming mysterious disappearances here, lumped with all the mundane, and more evil, fates of the bulk of the disappeared. A few go through, one way or the other, due to the rare dabbling in supernatural agencies that still goes on in back rooms and upper-class conservatories. Only one man, a sorcerer of great power in Husaquahr, can do it at will, and when and with whom and what he chooses.

He's been around a long time—nobody knows how long, not even the others on the Council—and he's had many names, both here and there. A decade ago he needed a hero not so bound by the Rules to combat an army of evil, and he chose, by means we will never know, an interstate trucker on the skids, a man in whose veins flowed the blood of the ancient Apaches, snatching him at the last moment from a fatal accident on a lonely west Texas highway. With him came an unexpected addition, a young woman hitchhiker who had education and once had promise, but whose life was so broken and mangled that she was just looking for a decent place to commit suicide. Together they battled the forces of Darkness, and vanquished them—for a time, for even the Rules mandate that no victory is without costs, nor may good or evil totally triumph.

Their saga was the one that came into my dreams, and which I told in three books before this one, including their discovery that the longer they were in Husaquahr the more they, too, became entrapped and bound by the Rules. Marge, the once-suicidal young woman, became that most classic of creatures who cross the Sea of Dreams in stories and legends, a changeling, becoming a beautiful winged fairy, a Kauri, while Joe, the truck driver, truly became a hero and at one point a king, marrying the buxom Tiana and ruling in peace, until evil again reared and threw them out of power and eventually out of bodies, so that Joe once again became his old trucker self in appearance while Tiana found herself now in the small but stunning body of what must charitably be called an exotic dancer. Together with the little Husaquahrian thief who had shared their adventures, Macore, and the enigmatic adept, the Imir Poquah, they had journeyed back to Earth to save it from the exiled Dark Baron, who was ready to do Hell's work upon us.

When we left them, they were victorious, preparing to return across the Sea of Dreams to Husaquahr, with a new pair as well—the pixie Gimlet, finally finding a way to the place where there were still more of her kind, and Joe's son Irving, whom he rescued from a promising career in a Philadelphia street gang. There was still a villain back in Husaquahr to vanquish; the zombie armies of the evil Sugasto, now calling himself the Master of the Dead, were still on the march. But the archvillain whom they had been forced to fight again and again, and whose evil had even brought them here, Esmilio Boquillas, the Dark Baron, whom they thought killed, they discovered had used his soul-swapping trick and entered the body of a third newcomer, the beautiful Mahalo McMahon, high priestess of the Neo-Primitive Hawaiian Church. The great and good sorcerer, however, who now called himself Throckmorton P. Ruddygore, was onto him/her. The Baron was stripped of his true powers and couldn't even switch again without help of a master magician. Ruddygore intended Boquillas to lead him straight to Sugasto, whom he was certain he could best in a sorcerous showdown.

If you'd like to renew your acquaintance with this saga, go back and find your copies of the previous *Dancing Gods* books and do so. If you don't have them, you'll be able to get along with just this summary, but you should still go back and find those first three books, stocked by any good, intelligent, competent bookseller.

It has been five years for my own dreams to come and sort themselves out into coherency, for time is different there than here, but now I have it. When we left, everything looked bright, everything set, and what hadn't been resolved before was clearly working its way to the end. Joe and Tiana, not looking as they did when they reigned, were free to travel and enjoy life and show the new land to Irving. Macore had some minor mental problems due to his sudden exposure to our culture, but, once back home, he'd straighten out. The saga was drawing to a close.

Alas, the Books of Rules covered more volumes than the Tax Code; not even a Ruddygore could remember them all. Still, he should have remembered that most basic of Rules governing the ultimate battle between good and evil, for it was one that had saved all of their necks at one time or another.

Those who are familiar with the past adventures of our band may find the going here a bit more serious, a bit more adult, than past volumes, perhaps because that, too, is a Rule for sagas that are continued by tellers of tales who inevitably, alas, grow older themselves. But, bear with it; Destiny's threads are interwoven, and one can not weave a tale until all the threads are in place. Our tale begins in madness, and descends into humiliation, debauchery, and degradation, yet all leads to a climax of pure, unabashed lunacy.

All beings whose deeds might alter or affect the course of history, regardless of side or motive, who are faced with absolute defeat and impending doom, must always be provided with at least one way out.

—The Books of Rules, III, 351.5

CHAPTER I

ENCOUNTER ON A LONELY ROAD

Epic quests for which circumstances set no deadline shall take at least seven (7) years, although exceptions may be made in rare circumstances if the quest just seems like seven years.
—The Books of Rules, XV, 251, 331(c)

SHE WATCHED HIM COME FROM HER HEIGHTS, FROM HER SHADows, but then she had lost sight of him in the gathering gloom. And so she summoned the wind, and whispered softly to it in the silence.

"Bring him to me," she commanded, as the wind whipped around her and played with the folds of her cloak. "Find him and bring him to me."

The cold wind wailed a reply, then crept down into the hollows and sped across the barren hills of Mazra-dum searching for the one tiny figure below in the wastes and finding him, as a chill wind always could.

The tiny, gray-clad traveler on the weary roan horse looked even smaller against the majestic background of the badlands landscape, a place of rounded mounds cut into the land and colored in dull candy stripes of all the various shades of rust and decay and where even the thin ribbon of water that snaked through its bottommost canyons was not clear or even mineral brown, but rather a milky, alkaline, and poisonous chalk white.

Here and there, the traveler and his long-suffering steed passed dull and slowly dissolving skeletons of many an animal who had attempted this place before and failed or, in desperation, had sipped from the white death that was at least something that moved in this place. The traveler pulled his cowl up to protect

9

against the chill wind whose eerie moans and shrieks seemed like the trapped and hopeless cries of the lost souls who had never made it through the route he now attempted.

Now the trail hit a point where one could go either way, but there was no way to tell from the ground, hard as steel, which was the right way and which was the wrong, if there was such, and he stopped a moment, his face coming up from its weary downward cast. Eyes far older than the years of the traveler scanned the choices; the face was weathered and lined and covered with a full beard that obviously had just grown rather than been cultivated and had, for its trouble, been ignored by its wearer. The beard, like the tangled, shoulder-length hair revealed when the cowl slipped back, had been black once, but it was now tinged with gray bought by hard experience, not comfortable old age.

The man frowned, unable to decide which trail led to somewhere fruitful and also unable to decide at this point if it made much difference which route he chose. Yet he had not lost hope of attaining his goals; the eyes still burned with a fire only fanaticism brought, and the soul was still fueled by a singleness of purpose that said, *success or death!*

The sun was but an hour from the horizon; already the shadows grew long and the wind bolder, the temperature dropping fast under brilliantly clear skies. The horse seemed suddenly nervous and made a nervous sound as the wind came around and seemed to be speaking to its master.

"Which way? Which way? We know the way. We know the way . . ."

"The way to what?" he asked, rather sardonically, but without fear, his voice breaking the silence and echoing here and there, although he did not shout over the wind, speaking as he was to it—or what was within it.

"The way, the way . . . The way to safety, to warmth and comfort, to clean water and lush green fields . . ."

"You'll not buy me that cheap," he retorted. "Think you that I would be out here in this miserable place for lack of such things? I am the richest thief in Husaquahr! All those things were not enough!"

"To safety, to safety . . . Where neither man nor god will find you . . ."

He drew himself up straight in the saddle, pride dispelling his weariness of body and spirit. "I am the greatest thief in the history of Husaquahr!" he retorted in a regal tone. "I fear neither man nor god, having stolen from both, and never caught!" That was not *quite* true, he knew, but if one spit into the wind, better it blow back praise than cold spittle.

"A quest, a quest . . . He is under a geas *and embarked upon a quest . . ."*

"No *geas,* not for such as I," he told the wind. "I quest as I steal, not for others, but for my own pleasure and interests."

"We can lead you there, lead you there . . ." the wind asserted. *"The wind goes everywhere and sees all things . . . The wind can find who or what you seek . . ."*

"Persistent, nagging spirit! You are not even powerful enough to know in advance that I am on a quest, let alone for what it is that I seek! I, who have stolen the sacred jewels from the navels of gods themselves and plucked the rings from demons' noses, will not be taken in by the likes of you! Now, be gone or be silent!"

"Who can silence the wind?" the wind mocked. *"Who can banish it when it wants to caress? The wind which grinds the very rock to dust, which gives strength and power to fire or blows it out as only the wind chooses, who stirs the water and cools it and uses it to batter the shore? Who are you to command the wind?"* it mocked in its screaming, eerie voice.

"Well, someone commands *you,*" he responded. "You speak as a cat but you obey like a dog. Whose big-mouthed puppy are you?"

"Follow the wind," it responded. *"Follow the wind to that which you seek."*

He thought a moment, seeming almost amused by all this despite the grim setting. "All right, then—lead on. I might as well be *somewhere* before dark." But he reached under his woolen robe to his tunic and touched his blade just to make certain it was ready.

It wasn't difficult to tell the way, although it was the opposite of following just about anything else. You just headed the one direction that the wind was *not*, in this case to the left and up a bit, away from the deadly little white river.

It was near dark when he came to her, but she was not hard to find for all that. She sat there, crouching before a welcome fire, a delicate and mysterious figure in azure robes. His horse started a bit upon seeing her, but the traveler calmed him, then slid off the saddle and approached the lady at the fire.

She looked up at his approach, and he was struck by her dark beauty almost at once, as he'd suspected he would be. He was not certain how much of that beauty was real, but the fire was, and that was enough for the moment.

"Come, good sir, and be warmed by my fire," she invited, in a soft, very sexy voice.

He seemed quite relaxed. "I thank you, Madam. It feels good after the chill your pet sent to me upon the sunset."

She was puzzled by him, and by his casual manner, as if he knew not only her own secrets but all the secrets of the world. He was a small but very strong-looking man, with a big hawk nose and small, almost beady little black eyes that seemed to reflect the dancing flames perfectly.

"You do not seem at all curious about me, or how I came to be here," she noted.

He sighed wearily. "Well, Madam, if you be here alone in this accursed place, then I take you to be either an enchantress or dead or of the world usually unseen—or perhaps all of them together. Whichever, you build a *mighty* good fire."

That drew from her a bemused smile, and perhaps a hint of wariness in her eyes, for clearly this was no lost and innocent pilgrim, nor did he fit the mold of great hero or wandering adventurer. "Are you then a sorcerer who walks the land without fear?"

He chuckled. "As I told your blowhard puppy, I am—I *was* a thief. The greatest in all the land. That does not mean, of course, that I am without skills in the magical arts, but they are of a specialized sort. One cannot last long in my line of work without being able to beat *all* the systems, as it were."

"And yet you do not fear me? Or is it, rather, the thrill of danger that propels your life and gives you energy and meaning?''

''That last is true for ordinary thieves,'' he admitted readily, ''and once, when I was young and did not know how very good I was, it was true for me. No longer. I have outgrown fear because it is a weakness that interferes with thought at the time one needs it most. I do not fear you, Madam, because I have already looked into the faces of horror far worse than even the undead can comprehend and it reams the soul of such inclinations. Nor is it that I have a choice. Better to sit here in the fire's warm glow and speak with you than to wonder where or what you might be in the darkness. No, I cannot afford to fear you. Let us say, rather, that I respect your potential.''

That brought a slight smile to her lips. ''Are you escaping, then, the pursuit of your latest escapade? Or are you, rather, going between here and there?''

''Onc is always going between here and there,'' he responded lightly. ''I have been on a quest for a very long time; a quest for a kind of magic that no one else can or will offer me and which is beyond my power to steal. It is quite frustrating, particularly for a master thief, to discover that there is something that you want and need that is beyond the power of the greatest thief to steal. I, who can beg, buy, borrow, or steal most anything any mind can imagine in this world, cannot have this one thing, so I must go searching for one who can supply it.''

''What is such a thing as that?'' she asked, genuinely curious.

''I have been to the Other World and found it a world where magicks far greater than any dreamed of in Husaquahr are taken for granted even by the poorest folk, who buy miracles at a discount and never even think twice about it. Their magical devices are beyond number in kind and abilities and do things even the greatest of our sorcerers would find impossible to imagine. I have such devices, brought back with me from that expedition, but I soon discovered that they are not sufficient in and of themselves. The sorcerers of that Other World dispense their miracles on the cheap, but they retain the ultimate power, in that the magical spells required for their devices to work their miracles are transitory and need frequent or constant renewal.

There one merely pays gold and the spells leap from the walls into the devices, but here there is no such thing. In my ignorance, I believed that the devices I have would retain their spells even away from such sources, but even there the sorcerers of the Other World are clever. The devices ultimately consume and devour the magical energy themselves, over time and use, and I can get no more here. Only a very few of our greatest sorcerers could even synthesize such things and they will not. I search for one who can and will.''

"These must be devices of great power for you to come so far and surrender so much to gain their powers," she noted.

He sighed once more. "They deliver something of insubstantial value, really. The images of a great epic quest, possibly the greatest epic produced by the poets of the civilization of the Other World. It is long and magnificent, each act a work of unparalleled brilliance, mixing humor and pathos to a degree unknown here by our finest poets and bards. Once any mind capable of appreciating its genius beholds it, that mind cannot rest until it beholds the saga once more. The saga is *there*, as if the actors come out and perform their great play only for you and at your command, but beyond my power to view. Such frustration has driven me near madness. I *must* see it again, and it is *there*, yet beyond my sight!''

She seemed genuinely fascinated. "Go, tend to your mount, make camp here for the night, and when you are ready you must tell me of this great saga," she said softly.

Whether witch, ghost, or creature, he was delighted to have an opportunity after brooding alone upon it for so long to talk of his great passion with someone new and eager to listen. Next to himself, it was the subject he loved to talk upon most of all. And, like the subject of himself, it was a subject almost nobody else wanted to hear him speak about.

She seemed very patient and understanding, even *interested*, and he was so very, very lonely. He knew not if she be nymph or goddess, demon or sorceress, but she was something right now that he needed very, very badly; the one thing he could not even steal in these trackless wastes.

She was an *audience*.

The wind which had been constantly swirling and twisting and screaming through the wastelands paused as well; the very air seemed impossibly frozen, the night still, yet oddly expectant. Although incredibly weary, his voice echoed from the dark walls unseen beyond the firelight with the strength and vigor of youth as the very experience brought forth his last reserves of energy, saved for just such an occasion as this.

And yet, there was still enough of the gentleman in him that he paused, after telling the Forty-Seventh Tale, realizing that he was getting so carried away he was not only imposing upon her hospitality, he was, worse, starting to *improvise* the tale after so long a time. And so he reached for his water flask, drank, and said, "But I have imposed far too much, and you have been gracious to hear me out beyond measure."

"I do not mind," she responded quietly, sounding very sincere. "This is not a place where interesting company often travels through, and, after you, it may be long until I hear a man's voice again—and perhaps never one with such wondrous sagas to spin." She paused a moment, staring at him. "But in truth it is I who have imposed. You are weary; the way from here is long and harsh. Rest if you like. Sleep and dream great dreams."

He was mad, even he knew that much, but he wasn't *crazy*. The quest, all the sacrifices, all the loneliness and travails, would be for nothing if he slept here now and failed to awaken the next morning; even worse if he *did* awaken, but undead, stranded here to serve her as slave forever, knowing he would never be able to fulfill his grand ambition.

"How come you here?" he asked her, the weariness which she noted now coming to him full as the energy stole quickly away. "What is your name and who and what are you?"

She seemed to shimmer slightly in the firelight, and the wind stirred a bit.

"I am cursed to be here," she told him. "Once my people reigned over a great kingdom, but we were overthrown by treachery and sorcery, expelled and cursed forever to reign over waste and desolation, commanding none but wind and barren rock. We had great power," she added wistfully, "but, obviously, not great enough."

The weariness kept creeping over him; he felt himself nodding off in spite of his best efforts, his storytelling having drained him even more than the travel. "What was this kingdom," he asked her, "and where? And what is your name?"

To know the name of an entity was to gain some power over it.

"I can be whoever you want me to be," she responded evasively. "I can be the one who you desire most."

She stirred, then, moving more into the firelight, and pulled back her veil, and he gasped and stared in spite of himself, and his jaw dropped.

"Mary Ann . . ." he breathed.

For a moment all defenses were down, all rationality fled, as she came closer and closer to him. She was more beautiful even than he had remembered her, more sensuous than the fantasies that had gotten him through this much of his quest.

Now she was to him, and they were in an embrace, and for the briefest moment it was the closest to Heaven he would ever come, but there was something wrong, something that triggered all those defenses that had kept him alive all this time.

Through all that exotic perfume, she smelled like warmed-over horse dung.

He broke free of the kiss. "You—you're not Mary Ann!" he gasped. "You—you're *all the rest*!"

Where the strength came from he would never know, but he lashed out hard and shoved her away, unbalancing her for just a moment. As she staggered and tried to retain her balance, the wind began to swirl and then scream around him.

"I tried to make this pleasant," she snapped. "Now we'll have to do it the hard way. Look, how about you just relax and don't fight it? After all, you have no strength left, and I *did* sit here and listen to that interminable crap for hours and hours!"

The wind began to swirl and scream at him.

It was as if all the gods suddenly supercharged him with energy. *"Crap!"* he exclaimed. *"CRAP!"*

His new energy and his sudden rage loosened her grip on his mind; the girl seemed to blur and fade out in the firelight, and a new, more sinister shape slowly emerged from the mass: *A*

*skeletal body covered with coarse brown fur; thin arms linked
to leathery wings, and a ratlike face with eyes of burning coal
and a mouth with pointed teeth designed only to rend flesh. . . .*

Because he was small and seemingly fragile, enemies always
underestimated his fighting skills. He was a thief, but not *merely*
a thief—the greatest of all thieves, the King of Thieves. His
timing was always perfect, his instincts always correct.

Even as the creature launched itself at him, he did the most
unexpected of actions and, instead of backing up into the darkness, off the cliff or against a rock wall, he leaped forward at
the thing, drawing his short sword with one and the same action.
They met virtually in the air, the creature totally unprepared for
anyone to attack *it*, and the sword blade came up and made
contact. The creature and the wind screamed as one, and the
thing dropped back to the ground.

He didn't let things go with that kind of blow. Instead, he
leaped upon the wounded thing, and with strength that belied
his size and his condition pushed back taloned claws set now
not to tear his flesh but just to keep him away.

"Crap, huh?" The sword pointed down at the thing's chest.
"I'll show you crap!"

The creature's eyes widened. *"No!"* it screamed. *"We can
make a deal! Anything! Anything!"*

"Ah, no! I know you now for what you are! *Critic!* The only
thing worse than blasphemers are critics!" he snapped back.
The sword came down. If the creature were of faërie, the iron
in its blade would be pure poison to it; if it were of flesh, however foul, it was so solid a blow that it would almost be a coup
de grace.

The fire flared like a torch, the ground trembled, and the wind
seemed to go mad as the sword pushed through the creature's
chest as if through air itself, the thing's flesh hissing as it passed.
He rolled over and, catlike, was on his feet, wary, prepared to
do more if it were necessary.

It was not, although the thing was rolling around and screeching horribly in its death agony, and the elements seemed ready
to join in. Suddenly, the creature stiffened, its back arched, its
wings sprawled, and, for a brief moment it almost looked as if

it were gaining new strength, but it was the last brilliant blast of energy before it collapsed into a stinking, smoldering heap.

Wind and fire seemed to rise into the air, and a bright ball of energy suddenly sailed skyward and was quickly gone. A wind swept through, forming something of a whirlwind over the still smoking body of the creature, then seemed to pause in the air.

"You . . . you killed her . . . killed her . . ." it moaned to him.

He stared at the secondary creature that had led him to her. "And what of it, elemental? Would you avenge her, you bag of hot air?"

The whirlwind seemed suddenly agitated. *"No, no!"* it responded. *"We like the saga, we do, we do . . ."*

"Then you shall pledge yourself to me through these wastes!" he shouted. "You shall bind to me, the killer of your mistress, until I leave your domain!"

"We bind . . . we bind . . ."

"Very well, then. Stand watch, while I sleep, and let no harm come to me or my horse while we rest, or you shall die the true death of dissipation!"

"We obey . . . obey . . ."

He moved as far away from the stinking body as he could and prepared his bedroll. He settled down, but still could not quite rest.

"Elemental! A gentle breeze away from me, so I do not smell the odor of that carrion!"

Instantly a very light but steady breeze came from behind him and the air cleared. He was impressed. Air elementals were more useful than he would have thought. But he was still too keyed up, perhaps too overtired to sleep. He needed to relax himself after the events of the evening.

"Well, blowhard, you say you *like* the saga."

"We do . . . we do . . ."

"Well, then, follow along, sing the great ballad with me."

There was no response.

"Just sit right back . . ." he started, then stopped. "You're not singing along!"

"We know not the words . . . the words . . ."

"Well, listen, then! And we'll serenade each other on the 'morrow!"

"*We obey . . . obey . . .*" the elemental responded, sounding resigned.

Now, at last, he leaned back, relaxed, and closed his eyes, and a smile grew upon his face. Yet, in spite of the hopes of the elemental, he did not quickly fade to sleep, but, instead, started again to sing the ballad that was prologue to the object of his sacred quest.

He drifted off to sleep, and the elemental, too, seemed to relax, perhaps more because the saga would not have to be endured further that night.

He slept soundly, the sleep of the dead, but, occasionally, through the night, he would stir, that smile would return to his sleeping face, and he would breathe a line of the refrain: " *'Twas Gilligan, the Skipper, too . . .*"

CHAPTER 2

ON DANCING YOUR HEART OUT

Unless contravened by magic or other Rules, an individual's rôle in life shall be determined by destiny and circumstance. However, once fixed in that rôle, only those things necessary to perfect one's rôle may be learned, acquired or retained. In this way is social and cultural harmony and stability maintained.

—The Books of Rules, II, 228(c)

THEY MADE A MOST UNLIKELY LOOKING GROUP AS THEY SLOWLY made their way down the road away from the mountains, toward green fields and rolling hills.

In the lead was a big man with bronze skin and tight muscles, the kind you would never doubt could carry the horse he rode as well or better than that same horse carried him. His skin, darkened and weathered by the elements, was, nonetheless, bronze to begin with; his finely chiseled face was barren of facial hair unlike the local customs, yet seemed as if it had never known a razor, and his thick black hair hung below his shoulders like a mane. His high cheekbones marked him as an Ostrider, a continent weeks from Husaquahr over dangerous seas, yet he had never been to that fabled continent. He wore only a strange, broad-brimmed hat, a loincloth, and swordbelt, and from the latter one could see the hilt of a massive and elegant sword. He looked at once exotic, strange, and dangerous.

The woman was fairly tall, with extremely long, muscular legs; fair of skin, although tanned by the sun, her hair lightened by exposure to the sun, she had delicate, sensual features and an athlete's thin, firm build, without fat or loose areas. But a head shorter than the man, she had perhaps half his mass, perhaps less, and seemed almost tiny by comparison. Although she wore a thin, shielding cloak of light brown tied at the neck, otherwise she wore strings of woven beads that barely hung on her slender hips from which strings of more varicolored beads protected what little there was of her modesty. Another such assortment of beads strung together barely covered but hardly concealed her small, tight breasts. A faded, thin, golden headband, worn more for decoration than utility, sat upon her head, a slight bit of ornamental work extending below it in a triangular shape extending down almost to eye level. Matching bracelets and anklets completed her wardrobe, the bands holding tiny enclosed bells that sounded when she moved.

The third of the company was a young man, possibly not much past puberty, dressed much like the man. His skin was extremely dark, the deepest of browns without going to full black, like the Nubians of the Southern Continent, a trace of whose common features could also be seen in his face, yet his steely black hair was straight and long, like the big man's. He was dressed in dark brown leather briefs and chest straps of the same, studded with ornamental bronze bolts, and matching leather boots.

"Man! This place is *boooring*!" the lad muttered, loud enough for the others to overhear. "I'm hot and sweaty and smellin' like a stuck pig. This whole *world* smells like a horse's ass! And this damn outfit's rubbin' my skin *raw*."

"We've heard it all before," the big man responded, not looking back. "As for the outfit, *you're* the one who picked that out, remember, against our advice. Most of this world's a lot warmer than back home."

"Yeah, I know, I know, but it look *baad*!"

" 'Looks,' " the woman corrected him. "It *looks* bad. How many times do we have to drill that into you?"

"You ain't my mother!" the boy shot back. "You got no place speakin' to me like that."

"No, your mother let you run wild on the damned streets," the big man responded. "Now I *am* your father, and I didn't carry you away—you came yourself when I gave you the chance. Your real mother, for what she's worth, is so far away from us that she, or you, might as well be dead. Tiana's my wife and your stepmother, and I'll have no more of that. Unless, maybe, you want to take me on and show me who's really boss, like last time?''

The boy glared, but did not immediately respond. He was still getting to know his father and unsure that he ever really would, deep down, but he sure as hell knew that the big man was the meanest, toughest dude he'd ever run across. He'd quickly learned that much the hard way and didn't want to push it. Being a full-blooded Apache trucker was bad enough, but a guy who'd spent the past several years in this world as everything from mercenary to adventurer to ruler of a kingdom and seemed none the worse for it wasn't anybody you wanted to screw around with. He decided to switch familiar gripes.

''Yeah, but where's all the fun in this hole? I thought there'd be dragons and monsters and all that Conan stuff. What we seen most of is proof that white folks can live even worse here than black folks in Philadelphia.''

''They're here,'' the big man assured his son. ''You're just not ready to take them on yet.''

''That's what parents always say, ain't it? *You're* ready, and you say you got all them big connections, but we're movin' 'round here and livin' like runaways and eatin' worse.''

''I've had my three big quests,'' the father responded. ''I'm a little tired of nearly getting killed every ten minutes. I needed a break. You wait until we run into something nasty. Then remember your complaining.''

''Yeah, well, it—*it's* got to be better than *this*. Man! What a place! No electricity, no runnin' water, no flush toilets, no cars, no guns, no rap, no rock, no soul, not even no TV!''

''You want out? Back to the streets? Back to running drugs for some street gang until somebody didn't like the way you looked at him and blew you away? No future but death at a real young age? You didn't have a future, Irv—you didn't even have a present. The way you whine and complain, somebody in that crowd you ran with would've knocked you off within a year or so, anyway. You know it, and I know it.''

The boy looked sullen. ''So?''

"So cut the crap! In a couple of days, we'll reach the river, and not long after that we'll be at Castle Terindell. Still nothing supermodern, but comfortable. Lots of good food, featherbeds, and the like."

"Yeah? Why we goin' there, though? Just for laughs or what?"

"Uh-uh. Time you went to school, son."

"*School!* You ain't said nothin' 'bout no school!"

"Not the kind you're thinking of, although, God knows, you sure could use one. The same kind of school I once went to at Terindell. Survival school, you might call it. Learning how to survive to my age around here."

The boy was suddenly interested. "You mean *fightin'*? Like swords and knives and shi—er, stuff like that? O-boy!"

"I mean stuff *exactly* like that. Don't get your hopes too high, though, tough boy. We're gonna see just how tough you really are. And if you wash out, you might have a real future as a stablehand shoveling horse shit for the rest of your life."

"Hey! Wait just a damn second! You sayin' if I flunk out of this hero school I'm a nothin'? I might just not like it."

"Oh, I *guarantee* you won't like it, at least at the start," his father assured him. "But nobody flunks out. You keep at it until you get it and you pass—or you get killed trying or you quit and walk out. The only one that flunks you is *you*. If you can't hack this, then you can't hack it anywhere on your own in this world, and anybody—I mean *anybody*—who can't handle himself out here on his own winds up practically owned by somebody else. You've seen that already. There are only three kinds of people here. The rulers, maybe five in a hundred folks; the ruled, which is ninety-four point nine of the rest, and that tiny one in thousands who's an independent like me. You weren't born royal and you haven't shown any talent for magic, so being independent or one of the ruled is all you can get. And of the ruled, if you can't fight, can't read or write the chicken scratches they use here, and have no skills, you shovel shit. Hell, son, *somebody's* got to do it."

"Not me!"

"Yeah? Well, you prove it. Because if you walk, that's the

best you can hope for and I won't stick around to help you do it. Do that or you're dead. Those are the choices if you walk. Remember that.''

Irv seemed to have lost a lot of his confidence all of a sudden, but he still maintained a brave front. "*You* got through it, didn't you? If you can do it, I can do it!''

"Wagons coming, Joe,'' Tiana cut in.

Joe pulled his horse up and looked at the oncoming traffic. It was less wagons than a wagon train, coming single file, pulled by massed teams of horses.

"Man!'' Irv swore. "Whatever they're carryin', it's heavy as gold and big as a subway!''

The boy wasn't far off the mark in his comments on the load. When they got right up to the lead wagon, they could see the eight-horse team straining, the driver and brakeman working constantly to keep them straight, balanced, and in line.

"Hello!'' Joe shouted to them. "What are you hauling?''

"Sorry! Can't stop to chat!'' the brakeman shouted back. He gestured at the load in back of him. "*Rules* change sheets! If we stop, there'll be two more revisions of *these* right in back of us!''

Irv looked at the wagons. Five . . . six . . . seven of them. Each the size of a locomotive, or so it seemed. He knew what the *Rules* were—the crazy books of laws that governed everything and everybody in this nutty place. But—"What're *Rules* change sheets?'' he asked, genuinely puzzled.

"You know the history,'' Tiana replied as they made way and watched the huge train go by. "In the Creation, Husaquahr was created in a kind of backwash, with the leftover energy from the creation of *your* world. The Creator Himself took charge of Earth, but He delegated Husaquahr to the lesser angels who weren't as thorough or competent. They mated with the ones here and produced the first in the line of sorcerers, people of great power who were half human, half angel.''

"Yeah, yeah, I know all that. You told me. But—*change sheets*?''

"In the beginning,'' Tiana explained, "the incomplete universe which contained Husaquahr was basically chaotic. Even the basics, like gravity, only worked *some* of the time. The Founding Angels rushed in to do what they could, establish a basic set of Angelic Laws to supplement natural laws where they were weak, creating stability out of the chaos. Being lesser, they still took a number of short cuts, creating much imitation of Earth but often not *quite* like Earth. Given a core number of souls by the Creator, early experiments produced strange results, in which the soul itself took on physical reality and mated with those things of animal and plant which imitated forms from Earth. The offspring of those created the thousands of races of faërie.* Essentially immune to age, they were made very slow to breed, and set to supplementing the angels in their establishing tasks, from climatological management, like the legendary Frost Giants, to the mineral management of the dwarves, the flower-tending of the pixies, and the husbandry of the nymphs and satyrs. The basics were maintained by the least of the souls, the elementals.

"After the Great Upheaval on Earth, some of the fallen humans were given to the angels of Husaquahr to establish their dominion here and duplicate the basic system. But since they were already stained by sin, these humans had a hard time from the start and even less wisdom. To compensate, the angels mated with men and produced a hybrid race. Half retained more of the angelic powers and began the line of sorcery; the other half gained higher wisdom, and became the founders of the royal lines. The sorcerers then became the finishers of the work, as the angelic powers had to withdraw, and, from experience living in this new world and from their own humanity, wrote the *Books of Rules* to bind and control and shape the subsequent history of Husaquahr for both faërie and human.

"That, of course, was close to the dawn of human time. After a while—who knew how long—these first founders felt their job done and went on to some higher, perhaps angelic plane, them-

*Faërie refers to the heritage, magic nature, power, and "realm" of fairies in general; it has a connotation of that which is withdrawn from human ken. Fairy refers in more specific manner to individuals, races, traits, and abilities of the fairy folk; its connotation is more that of a normal, day-to-day existence.

selves; *their* children now became the sorcerers. But, although sorcerers tended to live impossibly long lives, as each generation of them grew and the elders eventually tired and went on to wherever sorcerers went on to, the angelic blood was diluted more and more with humans. The powers of sorcerers of five generations before were only shadows of what their ancestors could do; those today mere shadows of that generation. And yet, each generation, generation after generation, kept on finding loopholes or specifics not addressed in the Rules and, as such, amended them. They couldn't really change what their more powerful predecessors had decreed, but they could keep adding, keep 'plugging in the holes' as time passed. And the less power and the less wisdom that they had, the more holes they found and the more new Rules they wrote.

"By now, the sorcerous bureaucracy was incredibly well organized; it only remained for that huge assembly to get out the amendations and hair-splitting new Rules to all those magical folk and royal, temporal powers throughout the world so that they would know what was being done."

"There's probably a Rule in this batch regulating the length of nose hairs," Joe muttered.

"Oh, no," Tiana responded sourly. "They would have addressed something *that* major generations ago."

Irv looked at the last wagon to pass and imagined the mountain of paper contained within. "Is there *anybody* who knows even *half* of what's in them papers?" he asked.

"Probably not, not even among those that create them," Tiana responded honestly. "It doesn't make any difference. Once the Rules are properly distributed, they go into force and we're stuck with them. They're not like laws, you know. Those are made by governments, which we also have plenty of. Everyone, even nonhumans, will be bound by whatever is in there as if it is natural law, like breathing or what goes up usually comes down."

"And you ain't worried? I mean, that somethin' buried in one of them wagons won't suddenly change the way we look or talk or think or act?"

"I was born here," she reminded him. "I sort of take it for granted."

"You just learn to forget that it's going on," Joe told him. "You can't do anything about it anyway, and by this time everything really nasty that they could do has either been done or been stepped on by some prior rule so it's canceled out anyway. I wouldn't worry about it."

The boy frowned. "But if all them papers don't make no difference, then why do it at all?"

"Oh, they might make some minor differences," Tiana told him. "Still, you are right—it's mostly harmless at this point. But, you see, constantly revising and perfecting the Rules takes a huge bureaucracy, larger than the kind that runs most governments. Thousands upon thousands of people and fairies, all employed in everything from proposing the additions to arguing for them or against them, helping adopt and implement them, printing and delivering them—it's a massive undertaking."

"And yet all them people do all that work and nothin' much happens because of it?"

"Essentially, yes."

"Then why do they do it? Seems like a total waste of time."

"Oh, their positions are essential," she responded matter-of-factly. "If they didn't do what they did, then all those masses would be unemployed, and, being bureaucrats, most of them couldn't *do* anything useful. Why, they wouldn't *survive!*"

"Or, worse, they might get together and try to do something really useful," Joe added. "That *would* be a disaster. So, don't worry much about it, and particularly not yet. You're still not quite within the Rules. So long as you aren't physically changed here by some magic, you're still outside the more specific rules. Unless you're a changeling, which I seriously doubt, since we'd have noticed by this time, you'll just slowly come under more and more the longer you're here, without even noticing it."

"Changeling. Yeah. Like that sexy broad with the wings we met on the boat."

"Uh-huh. Marge. She came over with me and at the time was as human as Tiana or me. She changed into one of the fairy races after she was here. It happens. But I doubt if you qualify.

I seriously doubt if your mother had that trigger in her genes, and I sure don't. And, judging by the time she took to change, I think you'd have done it by now if you were going to, anyway."

"What do'ya mean by trigger in my jeans? I ain't got no jeans on."

"In your blood," Joe told him. "If you'd ever gone to church back home, you'd know that it wasn't just here that angels mated with people. That was so long ago, though, back before Moses' time, that it's even more diluted back there than here. But some folks have a little of that blood, either from the angels or from demons, too, or early fairy-human matings, passed down in them. If you do, you become a changeling when you get here."

"Jeaz . . . I think that'd be kind a neat," the boy said. "Maybe growin' wings and gettin' magic powers and all that. Uh—did you say *demons*?"

Joe nodded. "There's some pretty mean fairies, too. Pray you don't meet them, believe me!"

"But being one of the fairy folk isn't all it's cracked up to be," Tiana pointed out, glad that the boy was at least interested in *something*. "Our souls are eternal; they do not die with our body. In the fairies, the soul is made flesh and *is* the body. They never really grow old, although experience gives them that look after a long time, but as they are flesh, they *are* mortal. Iron, for example, is deadly to most of them, except gnomes and a few other special races, and they are also subject to some forms of accidents and even murder. If they die, they're *dead*. To kill a fairy is to kill its soul as well. They don't even have the option of dying. Their only chance is to remain alive and well until Judgment."

"Un-huh," Joe put in. "And they're sort of one-dimensional. Stuck. Remember, son, the fairies were shaped to do particular kinds of things and nothing else. They can't change, can't learn or do other things, outside what they were basically designed to do. They can't quit and try something else. It's got to become either boring or frustrating after a while, maybe after a few hundred years, no matter what you're doing, particularly if you're smart and curious and ambitious. They can no more change than a horse can decide one day it would rather be a cat."

Tiana nodded in agreement with him. "Yes, sometimes I feel rather sorry for Marge. Even more, now that I have a similar if more mortal situation. Her changeling race was dictated by her own soul at the time and was what she needed to be at that time, but, now . . . I'm not so sure. She's intelligent, educated, adventurous, and could have been someone really important."

Joe looked over at Tiana. "Do you feel frustrated?"

"No, not really. I admit that some days I'm still not used to being this small and light, but when have you ever heard of a woman complaining of *that*?" Tiana's original body had been as large as he was, and as massive. Thanks to the body and soul snatching techniques of the Master of the Dead, her soul had wound up first in the body of a mermaid, then this dancer's.

"Yeah, but what about bein' somebody real important?" Irv asked her.

She shrugged. "I *was* somebody important. A queen, in fact. And, by sorcery, your dad at the time looked like some northern barbarian instead of his old self."

"And your body got stole?"

"Well, in the end, I could have had it back," she admitted. "But, then, you see, I'd have to have come back to being Queen. And if your dad had gone back to the way he was most of the time here, he'd have been King."

"Hey! What's wrong with that? All the best, no work, and—wait a minute! That'd make me a prince!"

"It's luxury, all right," Joe agreed, "but it's also a trap, a prison, and, believe me, if you think *this* is boring, you haven't been a monarch. Your job is to cut ribbons and preside over boring meetings and stay apart from the common folks. That was the worst. Not even being able to walk down the street in my own city, go into a good pub and have a beer, talk to who I wanted, do what I felt like."

"Yeah, maybe I'd hate it, but I didn't even get the chance to *try* it. I mean—like, I thought kings and queens could do pretty much what they felt like."

"Less than the stableboy," Tiana told him. "You can't change the system and you are what you are and you have to play the part. We couldn't even sneak out for a night. The society decided we were demigods, half human, half divine. They erected thousands and thousands of huge statues of us in the nude in practically every public place. Everybody knew us—in the most intimate detail you can imagine. You've seen some in the towns we passed.''

The boy was thunderstruck. ''*Those* two was *you* two?'' He laughed.

''Uh-huh. And that's why we decided to stick to the way we are now,'' Tiana told him. ''It wasn't a radical change for your dad. He's still big and handsome, just in a different way.''

''I'm in much better condition than Ruddygore found me,'' Joe noted. ''But, yeah, I'm still classed as your typical barbarian hero. That's why he picked me off that road seconds before I would have died in a crash. Tiana, though, was born here to a royal family. I think she's even prettier and sexier now than she was before, but it's a very different life for her. From royalty to commoner, and inheriting the baggage the Rules placed on the new body before she had it.''

''I don't mind if you don't,'' she told him sincerely. ''In fact, because I was Ruddygore's ward and educated on Earth, I had some feeling for what it was like among the common people. I haven't missed it nearly as much as I thought I might. The only frustration I really have sometimes is that I used to be strong as an ox. Now I couldn't lift my own shadow. I'm not used to having to depend on others to protect me, even in so simple a thing as walking down a street. Strange places, dark places, strange crowds all seem somehow *threatening* now. I guess most women grow up with that, but I didn't, and I'm still learning how to cope with it. I'm still learning to be tough again, in a different way. That's also been part of this trip. Not just for you to learn, but me as well.''

At the City-States, where they'd docked after crossing the Sea of Dreams, Joe had decided Irving needed experience. So he'd taken a long vacation while he, Tiana, and the boy rode up through Leander and High Pothique on horseback. During that time, Irving had turned thirteen. And now they were nearing the end of the journey.

The boy seemed puzzled. ''I don't get it. You say the fairy

folk got problems 'cause they're locked in to doin' one thing while we're not, then you say you're just as locked in by them Rules as they is—*are*."

"He's got you there," Joe said, somewhat approvingly of his boy's debating logic.

The argument disturbed her. "No, we have more *potential* before we're locked in. We don't *have* to turn out the way we do. We set out upon a path and only when that path is certain do the Rules specifically kick in for us."

"Yeah, like Dad had a choice of whether or not to be a fighter, maybe? Or did you set out all along to be a dancer?"

She sighed. "No, but I had a choice of dancer or queen, at least. And your father's personality, his mind and body, likes and dislikes, modes and inclinations, made him a mercenary when he came here. With an education, with skills, you can become all sorts of things."

"Uh-huh. Like the *law* says 'cause I was born in America I could be president, but the *real* life said I was born poor and black with a choice of choosin' up gangs or bein' carved up by both of 'em. Uh-huh."

Joe took pity on Tiana and decided to rescue her. "You just said it, Irv. Not too many people get choices no matter *where* they are. But some do—they're smart enough or maybe they just luck out. It's hard to say for sure. It's lots of things we can't control, from race to brains to breaks. But even folks who have all the right things sometimes wind up in the mud, and sometimes folks who have nothing really do wind up with it all. Not many, but some. Right now you're coming up on that point. You can be a fighter if you have the guts—I know you got the makings in you, since you're half Apache—or you can chicken out and become a laborer. That's more choice than you were heading to back home. But when you're locked in here, you're locked in. The system depends on that, on nobody rocking too much of the boat, so they made sure nobody could rock it but so much."

"Sounds *just* like back home," the boy responded.

A little before midday the next morning, they went up high on a bluff and looked down on the river.

It was incredibly wide, perhaps more than a mile wide at this point, and swift-flowing; within its broad expanse you could see currents and small whirlpools and eddies. It was the aorta of Husaquahr, the source of its power and wealth and riches and of life itself. Virtually every drop of rain that fell for a thousand miles in any direction wound up in it; all other rivers and streams were its servants, its arteries. The people, both human and fairy, of this land thought of it less as a thing of nature than as something nearly divine; it was their mother, their companion, the one factor that linked them all together, no matter what their race or job, no matter their nationality or culture.

Even Irv was impressed. "Man! That's *some* big wet sucker!"

Joe chuckled. "Can you swim?"

"In *that*? You *got* to be kiddin'!"

"Don't worry—you won't have to. Not that we could, anyway. That current is strong enough to sweep you miles downriver before flinging you against the next bend, and it's plenty deep."

"What they got then? A bridge?"

"Nobody here could possibly build a bridge that would stand up to it," Joe replied. "Maybe way, way upstream, where it's a lot narrower, they could, but they wouldn't."

"Huh? Why not?"

"It's kind of—well, against their religion, you might say. Oh, they'll bridge most any other river or creek and dam up the others and do all the usual things, but not the River of Dancing Gods."

"So how do you cross it, then? I see some small boats out there but I don't think none of 'em could make it regular here to there without no engine."

"You're probably right," Tiana agreed, "but the river bends and twists like a snake for all its length. Where it bends, it slows and deposits its loads as well, which often narrow it. Just above those narrows it seems almost still, and at those points boats can cross without much problem. We'll have to go up till we find such a point."

"Yeah? And they take you across for nothin'?"

Joe looked at Tiana. "He's got a point there. We're back in civilization now—these are all farms and preserves and freeholds. No living off the land here. And we don't want to blow half a year if I land a commission.''

She shrugged. ''We both know the area here. We could reach Samachgast by nightfall. It is the kind of river port suited to my talents.''

''The kind of place where you can get yourself killed or worse,'' Joe responded worriedly.

''Do you think I like it? Remember where I came from and how far I have come down. But, as the boy said, it is the Rules. In spite of it all, I am nearly driven to do it. Besides, I have my two protectors with me, do I not?''

She turned and kicked her horse to action, and they followed, going up the river road toward the distant town.

They were the typical rabble who worked ports and the sea; not nearly as rough or mean as ocean men, but a rough enough looking bunch to give anybody pause. Now, as they gathered around the torchlit posts and watched her dance, they gave the usual lewd and salty comments and obscene suggestions as she whirled.

Irving had early displayed a real talent for the drums; the ones they carried weren't exactly first rate of their kind and were less than great as instruments in any event, being somewhat limited in range, but he got everything out of them that they were capable of.

The only thing Joe ever remembered being able to play well was a stereo system, and those were pretty far away right now, the only remnant the Peterbilt logo on his incongruous but ever-present trucker's cowboy hat. He just stood well back, almost in the shadows, as always, having more than a few mixed feelings about all this, and nervously watching the men in the crowd.

Tiana was not merely any old dancer; her body was essentially built and honed to that one function above all others, and she could twist and turn in ways that would put most people into hospitals or homes or at least traction. Any part of her seemed capable of bending in any direction independent of the rest and, without thinking, any part of her could be rubber or steel as called for. It seemed as if there was little in the way of acrobatics she could not perform with those legs, and, as a performer, she was spellbinding, even hypnotic. It was all done essentially without thinking; when there was a rhythm she could dance to, some kind of switch just got thrown in her brain and from that point it was totally automatic, the routine always skilled but improvised, the pace increasingly frantic, timing and balance absolutely perfect.

If that had been all, Joe still wouldn't have minded as much, but she wasn't merely a great acrobatic dancer, either. She was almost pure animal, catlike, savage, magnetic. She was an *erotic* dancer.

One of the Books of Rules had something like two chapters strictly on erotic dancing, and that didn't count the inevitable supplements and addenda they'd never seen or gotten to. Naturally, as soon as they'd hit a town, they sought out the library and looked it up. Trouble was, that was the first inkling of problems. He'd never learn to read that crap—they had a pictographic writing, like Chinese, only with even *more* symbols—and Tiana, who always could, had discovered now that she could not. A friendly librarian, used to the problem, read it for them.

Dancers danced. Period. The Rules removed or prohibited all things that might interfere with that function. Dancers did not need reading, writing, or the like, so that was simply eliminated as a possibility. Dancers *could* read and write music, however, if they desired to learn it. Yet they had quite an innate mathematical sense, something Tiana had heretofore lacked. It appeared that dancing involved a whole lot of instant, unthinking calculations.

Erotic dancers, in addition, turned people on. It did not necessarily mean lust for her, but that was certainly a factor and a possibility, even a probability in a crowd like this, already uninhibited, probably drunk, and out for a night on the town.

Irv had learned by now not to let her go on too long or it might cause riots. The idea was to give the crowd a real thrill so they'd toss money for more, then give them a little more, and so forth. She wouldn't, maybe couldn't, stop until he did, and he brought it to a close and ended quickly, leaving her with a perfect split.

There was a momentary silence, and then a lot of clapping and yelling and cries of ''More! More!'' They, however, knew the traditions, and coins started being showered from the crowd all around her. Irving, with long street experience in his still short years, wasted no time in gathering them up so expertly they seemed almost to be vacuumed from the ground.

They weren't quite that fired up yet; they wanted more and they'd paid for more. At this point, Joe was less worried than he was amazed, as always, that with all that leaping and whirling and twisting, Tiana wasn't even breathing hard and had barely raised a sweat.

The second set was no mere repeat of the first, but a whole different routine, far more elaborate, erotic, and somewhat inflammatory. If she really was in control of herself when doing this, she could manage it better; but once she got started, all bets were off, and it had been some time since she'd danced for an appreciative crowd. The Rules didn't just make you a dancer; you *had* to do it, all out, to the best of your ability, and hers was pretty damned good. The longer she went between shows, the more it built up inside her, like a tightly coiled spring, and when it was let out it was intense after this kind of layoff.

Hell, Joe didn't think it was a big deal to turn on a bunch of drunken male river rats, but at this stage she could turn on almost *anybody*, and even the *women* with some of the men were showing real signs of bodily desire. He shifted his sword to the ready and moved into a better position.

Irv knew the dangers, and kept the second set short. This time the coins came faster and more furiously; this time they were demanding she go on and on. Between dances now, he could see Tiana's face begin to pale as she sized up the crowd, many of whom were beginning to press closer to her, and she was already encircled. They had rehearsed a maneuver for this kind of situation, since it proved not that uncommon; a particular cue, a particular signal that Irv would make with the drums that would command this sort of finish. It depended, though, on her having the strength of will to break through that emotional trancelike dance state, to make the old Tiana control the new.

The one time they had tried it before, she'd managed it, but that spring inside her wasn't totally uncoiled as yet, and it was no sure thing in this bigger crowd and rougher environment, either. He gave the signal to Irving, hoping the boy would catch it or have the sense of the crowd to do it anyway.

Irv did, but this third set was a humdinger; the crowd was joining in to the same rhythms, which were, after all, more street Philadelphia than Husaquahrian to begin with and thus had an extra impact, and Tiana was outdoing herself and leading them on. The situation was rife with the potential for, at best, a mass open-air orgy or, far worse, a violent and dangerous frenzy. Joe pulled his sword out of its sheath and held it so that the flat could be used, almost clublike. Tiana had already missed a couple of exit opportunities, and he feared the worst.

However, just when he thought he'd have to wade in and get her out, she did a tremendous series of twists and leaps and then, with the crowd giving almost awestruck room, she dashed for the crowd, then gave a mighty broad jump and actually cleared the heads of the nearest spectators, landing with a three-roll up to the edge of the buildings, then quickly running into the nearest doorway and out of sight of the crowd, which, momentarily stunned, now galvanized as a mob and stormed after her.

Joe stepped back, sheathed his sword, and let them charge the open doorway to the small bar into which she'd run, and, when the last were inside or milling just outside, made his way to Irv, who was already packed and ready.

"Pretty good haul," the boy remarked. "Man! If I only had a guitar, maybe a sax, I could lay down a great rap and they'd *never* come down!"

"Come on," Joe snapped. "We better make sure she made it out the back way. It sounds real mean in there right now."

"Don't it always?"

They made their way to the back of the buildings, which were virtually on the river itself, and Joe tried to get his eyes accustomed to the sudden darkness. "Watch your step," he warned the boy. "This wood's old and rotten here; one false step and you go right into the river."

A dark shape moved from beneath the stairs in front of them.

"It's about time," Tiana said nervously.

"We're here as fast as we can move," Joe responded. "Why? Trouble?"

"A couple of filthy types in that bar made grabs for me," she told them. "I had to kick one of 'em in the balls and the other one in the face."

"You're learning fast," the big man said approvingly. She might not manage a sword, but legs powerful enough to make the kind of leap she'd made, combined with her timing, were lethal weapons in and of themselves. "You delayed a long time, though. I was afraid you weren't going to make your break."

"Too many people. Too many *tall* people. I had to wait until there was a thin spot with shorter men. Even then I kind of back-kicked one as I went. I'm still not used to looking *up* at most men. Still, I have to admit I haven't had this much fun in my life."

She wasn't being sarcastic with that last remark and he knew it. She was quickly developing a taste for living on the edge, for taking last-second chances and, he knew, she relished the power and attention and near mystical effect her dancing and athletic skills could have on people.

"Yeah, well, one of these days there's gonna be too many tall guys to jump over and too many for me to fend off, too," he warned her. "If you survive that, it'll take most of the fun out of it."

She came up to him, put her arms around him, and kissed him. "God! I'm really turned on!" she whispered. She always was after one of these things.

At that moment a door crashed open, flooding the back area with light, and a big, bearded man shouted, "There she is!"

"Scatter!" Joe shouted. "The usual places!" He held out his hand. It was time to call upon the great magical sword named after his son. "Irving, to me!"

"Yeah, Dad?"

"Not you," he growled, as the men streamed out with blood in their eyes. "I said for you to scatter! *The sword*, damn it!"

"Oh!"

Frustrated, he drew his great sword just barely in time as the first of the men came at him. Using mostly the flat, he banged heads and sent men sprawling. Some fell back and there was the crack of rotting wood and then yells and splashes.

A knife whizzed past his ear and he decided it was time to beat a retreat himself. He waited until they surged forward, then quickly backed up, causing the mob almost to fall over each other. Satisfied, he turned, there was a cracking sound, and in a few more seconds he felt himself fall into the river.

It wasn't terribly deep right in there, and he hit the mud bottom and kicked off, encumbered by his necessary grip on his sword. The river water here was static, due to the piers and construction, and smelled like raw sewage, which was what got dumped into it by the town anyway. Struggling, he made his way in under one of the piers to where his head and shoulders were above water when he stood and managed to sheath the sword.

As much as he wanted out of that river at that point, he decided to stay in and try and make his way down, away from the port itself, cloaked by darkness and by the natural unwillingness of anybody up there voluntarily to jump in this fetid mess. He didn't like it, either, but anything he was going to catch from it he most certainly already had.

Like almost all river ports, the town was situated at a bend where the river slowed and deposited its silt, creating a flat, swampy land mass that none the less allowed for the docking of boats and the laying of foundations on pilings in the muck. At the far end the harbor stopped, as the water was far too shallow to be useful, leaving a good quarter of a mile of broad mud flats. Here, untouched by man's attempt to control the land, was a slippery quagmire that, nonetheless, he could manage, although the scabbard of his sword dragged in it and occasionally made him lose his balance. By the time he reached firmer land, he was totally covered in sticky brown mud. He hauled himself up and sat in the harder mud near shore and coughed a bit. After a few minutes, he heard someone else, a woman, coughing as well.

"Who's there?" he challenged.

"Joe? Is that you?"

"Ti? What the hell are *you* doing here in this mess?"

She made her way over to him. "Same as you, I guess. I tripped over something on the pier and the next thing I knew I was in the water. This seemed like the only way out."

He laughed and soon she laughed with him. Finally he asked, "Irv?"

"Oh, he went in between the buildings. He'll be fine. He knows where the camp is and he's pretty street-wise, so I don't think he'll get in any real trouble." She chuckled. "God! I must look a fright. As bad as you do! It'll take me a *week* of washing to get this gook out of my hair!"

"Yeah, it's almost a shame. Here we are alone together and free for the first time in a long time, and look at us! By the time we got anyplace decent the mud would dry us into statues."

She thought about it. "Then maybe the trick is to make sure the mud doesn't dry."

"Huh? You mean—over there? In the mud?"

"Why not? Kinky, huh?"

He thought about it. "Well, why not? We can't get any muddier."

He was definitely wrong about that.

Still, it was a night to remember. Caked with the gooey stuff, they made their way to the edge of the flats, where the river made the full curve and began to pick up again, cleansed now. They were able to swim about and get as much off as they could, and it turned into one of those rare magical nights when it felt good to be alive.

Finally, they made their way back to the area just outside of town where they had been forced to camp, not then having the money to stay in town. The boy was sleeping there, and they stood there a moment and looked at him.

"You know, it's kind of odd," Joe commented. "You take the average person from Earth and stick them here, the kind who mows his lawn and works in an office nine-to-five and maybe goes to singles bars, and he'd be dead or enslaved in no time at all. But you take a kid forced to live in a nasty neighborhood, surviving by his wits, facing danger all the time, like him, and he adapts pretty damned well. We could probably make a lot of folks happy if we could work it out so those kids in the street gangs got over here and some of our better people who just can't hack it here went back there in their place."

She shrugged. "He's still just a boy."

"Not here. Not anymore. But he'll make it. He'll do better here than he would back home, that's for sure."

"Of course he will," she assured him. "He's your son."

Joe looked around at the quiet scene. "Yeah, he is. That's what's got me to wondering."

"Huh?"

"He was on his own, in that town, with a fair piece of change, and since he's the only one now who knows how much, we'll never know if any of it was spent. I wonder how long he's really been back here? I wonder how long he's been asleep? I wonder how old and gray I'm gonna have to be to find out the answer to those questions? If ever," he added.

CHAPTER 3

HARD ANSWERS, BIGGER QUESTIONS

If, by sorcery, any citizen, of whatever rank or station, shall find him, her, or itself in the body, form, or husk of another already bound to these Rules, the Rules governing the actual body, form, or husk inhabited by soul or spirit shall prevail and be binding.
—The Books of Rules, II, 412-9-11(d)

DUE TO THE LONG NIGHT, THEY HAD SLEPT UNTIL PAST MIDDAY; even so, when Tiana awoke, she saw that Irving was still asleep. Clearly while his father's suspicions were confirmed by this, and it was something she, too, worried about, she decided that it was best if it be kept a minor mystery from the big man. Joe still sprawled on the blanket, snoring away, so she gently awoke the boy, put a finger to her lips, and gave him a knowing wink.

He sat up fast, looked around, saw his father still asleep and relaxed. "Thanks," he whispered to her.

"You've had your little fun, now go to work," she whispered in reply. "You still have most of the money, I assume?"

"Yeah, sure. Right here. I didn't use much. Uh—you think this is enough?"

She poured out the haul and looked it over. In among the masses of copper were a number of coins of silver and gold. "Oh, yes. More than enough, I think. Enough, too, to buy a decent breakfast."

The boy started to pack up, working around the still sleeping Joe, and Tiana rummaged around in her pack and found what amounted to little more than a string bikini made of colored beads, then slipped it on so it hung on her hips. Then she started doing her normal routine of exercising, which included just about

41

every bend and gyration even her body was capable of doing and repeating it over and over. It was unsettling to be talking to a woman who, seemingly without effort, balanced on the toes of one foot while raising the other leg almost straight even with her body against her head, over and over. It hurt just to look at it. The fact that she could also hold a normal conversation while doing this sort of thing was, well, unsettling.

The boy turned away and continued packing up the camp. "I still can't get over how little most girls are dressed in this place. There's more skin and tits here than a skin flick," he remarked.

"It's vanity, mostly, based on one of the Rules," she told him. "It goes something like, *'Weather permitting, all beautiful women will be scantily clad.'* The thing is, 'beauty' is nearly impossible to define, even for a bureaucrat. Some women whose looks are beyond question fall under that compulsion, but most do not. On the other hand, most women like to *think* that they are under that compulsion, and even those who don't also tend to follow it, including many who shouldn't."

"Huh?"

"Otherwise, you're sort of going around advertising that you think you're plain or ugly," she explained. "And, frankly, many women don't really have the body for it. They need some well-placed clothing to look their best—but most won't, anyway."

"And that's every place?"

"Oh, there are lots of places where the rule has no practical effect—cold climates, high places, places with lots of nasty insects or cutting vegetation. In those places, you undress for formal occasions! But in this broad region, which covers much of Husaquahr, it's subtropical or downright tropical, and that's the way things are."

"Man! That's still weird! It almost seems like you all are puttin' up ads sayin', 'Come and get me.' "

"It's not *that* bad, mostly because almost everybody does it. It's normal, and whatever's normal, no matter how different or strange, people get used to and take for granted in a hurry. It's sort of like some ancient cultures in your own world, where a woman who was overdressed and usually veiled was a prostitute, since the clothing was used to hide her identity and maybe titillate the customers. Most original tropical cultures wore few clothes unless the missionaries or conquerors got to them. And, like them, there's the sad fact of being in a world without science or machines governed by Rules that keep things as they are.''

"Yeah, this place could stand some fans and some television.''

"That's not exactly what I meant. You're lucky to be his son and not his daughter here. Unless a woman has magical powers, or is of royal blood, she usually doesn't count for much here. For most folks here, life is short and hard. You need a lot of babies here, because most babies die before they get a chance to grow up. Most girls are already married and having kids by age thirteen or fourteen. Women get no education and are mostly wives and laborers in homes and fields. It's mostly that way on Earth, too, even now, although those who live in countries where women have some freedom like yours forget that. Of course, most of the men don't get educated here, either. Here, some sort of trade for them, however menial, is all-important.''

"You got educated," he noted.

"I was of royal blood. The Rules are different. And, with my parents murdered, I was hustled off to Earth for protection by Ruddygore. I had the best education, the best schools, the best things money could buy. It was only by happy chance that I could marry for love rather than politics.''

"Yeah? So what did it get you? You can't remember half the schoolin' you got—you keep sayin' how more 'n' more just slips away, and you're goin' around this place barefoot and close to bare-ass naked, dancin' for coins thrown by horny geeks.''

She shrugged. "I think about that sometimes, but, the fact is, I think most street dancers dream of being princesses or queens, and most princesses or queens find the life so boring and so meaningless they fantasize about being dancers. Right now I'm having more fun than I ever did the other way. It might not be the life I'd pick, but it's better than the one I had.''

"Yeah, for now," the boy responded sagely. "But, sooner or later, this life's gonna go sour, and there ain't gonna be no way for you to go back to bein' queen again. One of these days you're gonna wake up and suddenly see that you ain't slummin', you ain't playin' poor, that's what you *are*."

Joe stirred. "Huh? *Wuzzit?*" He groaned, rolled over, tried to sit up, made it on the second attempt, and opened his eyes blearily. "Don't you two ever *sleep*?"

"Sure, and we did," Tiana told him. "It's not morning, love, it's afternoon, and if we want to make any time at all today we'd better pack up and get started."

"Huh? No breakfast?"

"We'll have to get some on the way. We're cleaned out as it is, but we've got a little money now."

Irv frowned. "You sure it's safe to go through that town again?"

"Sure, so long as we skirt the riverfront," Joe answered, still half asleep. He rummaged in his pack and pulled out a small cloth satchel. Opening it, he removed four identical-looking loincloths, picked the one that looked cleanest, and put it on.

Tiana did not mount or prepare her horse. She usually finished up her morning routine with a brisk run of eight to ten kilometers. She wouldn't have that much this morning, so she was taking what she could get, and at a real run. Those extremely long legs were pure muscle, and she meant to keep them that way. They actually had to urge their horses to a trot to keep up with her.

The port town looked different by daylight, but not improved. It was pretty seedy, really, with buildings of ramshackle wood and well-worn adobe intermixed with no thought or plan. It also smelled of garbage and feces and collective human sweat and was thick with all sorts of bugs, most particularly flies and roaches.

Through it all, the population was about. Away from the port and markets, the hard-packed dirt streets were filled with human traffic; carts going this way and that, donkeys, and lots of bare-chested women in colorful slit skirts, often with one or two small babies strapped to a front halter or carrier on their backs and other naked, dirty-looking toddlers bringing up the rear, carrying huge loads on top of their heads this way and that, trying to avoid the omnipresent horse dung that was always in the streets. The centers of each neighborhood were the communal wells with their pumps and pools held by crumbling adobe masonry. The women there *all* had kids, and it seemed like every other one was pregnant, even the ones with small crying babies.

It had taken Irving weeks to stop gagging every time he was around places like this. Somehow, all those sword-and-sandal epics on TV had never gotten to what those places smelled like. Now, though, he was almost getting used to it, and, in fact, he was no longer ogling every bare breast he saw, either. Tiana had a point about what was normal one place or another. The amazing thing was that it took so little time to get used to a new normality.

Most of the cafes and bars only opened during normal mealtimes, but they were able to find a small place off one of the squares with a big well that had some leftover stuff from lunch and was willing to let them have it cheap. Without refrigerators, you couldn't keep much long around here. A trio of girls, the oldest of whom looked to be ten or eleven, seemed to do most things. It had also seemed odd to Irv at first that kids his age and even younger got served beer or wine, but, early on, when he saw a couple of little kids pissing in one of the wells, he understood and didn't touch regular water again if he could help it.

Of course, when they had come over, Ruddygore had worked some sort of magic that had given him the immunity he'd have if he'd been born and grown up here, and that helped, but there was still a lot of sickness and a lot of young deaths here, and nobody was immune from the galloping runs.

Tiana, at least now, was a total vegetarian; she didn't even drink milk or eat eggs. If it didn't grow in the ground, she didn't touch it. Fortunately, his father had no such problems, and in that, he most certainly decided, like father, like son. He, for one, didn't know how the hell she got all that energy off cow fodder.

The proprietor was a fat little lady named Esaga who looked a lot older than she probably was. She wore only a rope tied loosely about her waist, with modesty coming from a utilitarian towel hanging over the front and another in back. She had the biggest boobs Irv thought he'd ever seen, and, even though she was really roly-poly, there was no question that she was pregnant and well along in it, too.

"I see what you mean about the ones that shouldn't," Irv whispered to Tiana.

"Oh, I doubt if that's the reason," she responded in the same low tone. "Most likely she's got fires going for cooking in back and, considering how hot it is even out here in front, she'd drop from heat back there if she wore much more. The big thing to remember is, here, it doesn't *matter*."

"Madame," Joe called to Esaga. "How far upriver is it to the ferry across? Do you know?"

"Mercy, sir, I couldn't tell ya," she responded in a deep, rich voice. "I been borned and riz right here and never had no time t'go no place else. Keepin' this place stocked and a-goin' every day of the week and seein' t'my kids keeps me too busy fer much else. There's a prefect house a block down and to the left, there, though. They'd know if anybody does."

Even Joe had never quite gotten used to that, and Irving thought he never would. Nobody gave you anything here, least of all the government. You worked or you starved, and your kids did, too. Those had to be her daughters working here—they looked like sisters. How many kids had she had, and from what age? And how many survived to grow up? And what did their old man do other than knock up his old lady?

It didn't seem right, somehow. Worse, it seemed pretty damned *rough*.

Joe's soft heart made him try to overpay the very tiny bill, but they would have none of it. To them, tipping was charity, and if they had nothing else, they had their pride and their honor.

And that, of course, was what made this screwy world work in the end. They might not have much or be much, but they took pride in what they did have and what they earned, and so did most others. It was the one noticeable thing that seemed everywhere here, standing out even more because of the lack of such a sense back home. Hell, even the crooks had a code of honor here. In a way, it was the one thing about them that was superior to anybody he'd known back home. Finally, they did manage to give them a little extra money for some extra leftovers and an urn of wine; provisions for the journey north to the ferry.

The prefect house was like a small police station—*very* small, it turned out. The one guy on duty, sweltering in his threadbare but perfectly maintained fancy uniform, was pretty helpful. Yes, there *was* a ferry, about twelve miles north if you followed the river road. There were certainly others farther up, but even *he* hadn't been farther than the first one and had certainly never ridden on it. No, he didn't know where it went, but it was definitely somewhere in the Kingdom of Marquewood, since that was all the other shore, and it had to go *somewhere* worth going or they wouldn't have a ferry there. He had a map of his own of High Pothique, or at least the coastal section, and all that showed was that they were farther south than they thought they were.

Admitting the point, Joe asked, "Any dangers or warnings about the route come down?"

"No, not close to here. There are reports of problems near the northern border, but you will not be going anywhere near that far. As for Marquewood, I cannot say. They say there's lots of fairy folk along the river over there, and you never know about *them*. We haven't had an incident along the route in either direction for a day or more's ride in—well, since the War."

"Suits us fine," he told the prefect, and left. "He says it's clear riding," he told Tiana and the boy. "Let's head 'em up and move 'em out."

They set out right away, and soon left the town far behind.

"The way the sundial in the square back there pointed, I don't think we've got much more than four hours more of sunlight, thanks to our late start," Joe said to them. "I'm not too thrilled trying to take this river road at night, the way it twists and turns. I say we make what time we can, then camp and get an *early* start tomorrow. No telling how long a wait it'll be to get on the boat."

Every couple of miles along the road there was a small spur leading down to a flat, mossy area almost at the river. These in fact were rest stops, so to speak, where you could use the river to relieve yourself, build a fire to cook and to eat, or make camp if you were caught short on the trail by sunset. Sunsets came very quickly in this part of Husaquahr, and the nights tended to be very, very dark.

After their first pit stop, Tiana said, "No telling how much standing around we'll have to do tomorrow, so I'm gonna run the distance today. Too much riding makes me stiff."

"Well, we're not in any real hurry, so don't get too far ahead," Joe warned her. "You never know who or what's around on roads like this."

"Don't worry so much," she scolded him. "If you're that nervous, keep up with me!"

"Man! I'm tired just watchin' her go!" Irv said bemusedly. "How can anybody get that way on lettuce and fruit salad?"

Joe laughed. "I don't know. She was never like that before. She was like six-two or -three, two hundred and sixty pounds. You saw the statues. She was something of a fitness nut even then, though. Hell, I think she could'a lifted *me*."

"She ain't all that short now, for a girl."

"Talking averages, no, five-six isn't short, but it's three-quarters of a foot shorter than she was. And, of course, the body's totally different. It's still her inside, though, and I'd trust her judgment most of the time, except when she's dancing, anyway."

Irving looked out at the broad river, more majestic-looking than ever, the distant green shore showing little detail. Suddenly he frowned, stared, and looked again. "There are girls—women—out there!"

Joe turned and looked, not seeing them at first, then finally catching what the boy had seen.

"Holy Hell! Did you see that?" Irv cried. "A big fish just jumped out and right on top of one of them!"

Joe laughed. "No, it only looked that way. Those aren't women, they're river mermaids. Contrary to the old legends, mermaids are mammals like us and breathe air. River mermaids mostly have that bluish cast to their bodies and light underbellies, kind of like dolphins. Ask your stepmother about mermaids sometime. She was one of the salt water kind once, in between then and now."

Irving could just stare for a moment. "Jeez! Just when you

start gettin' used to this place, somethin' like *that* pops up and hits you in the face! *Mermaids!* Wow! Uh—are there any mer-*men*?''

"Not that I know of, but I couldn't be dead certain on that. I think they mate with regular men, like you or me. They're supposed to be able to hypnotize you or something so they're irresistible. But they only have daughters and they're always mermaids. Don't get any bright romantic ideas at your age, though. They do it in the water, and it's even odds the guy drowns in the end."

Irving gulped. "Uh—thanks for the warnin'.''

"There's all sorts of things that live out there in and beneath that river," Joe told him. "A lot of 'em aren't that pleasant, and even the ones that *are* might have little flaws like that. You run into any of the nonhuman races, never make the mistake of thinking that they're just funny-looking people or people with odd abilities or powers. They're not. They think different, live different, and have a whole different way of seeing things than we do, and most of 'em haven't got a lot good to say or think about humans. Our people pretty much wiped out their people back on Earth, and they know it, and since death to them is final, they don't ever want to give us much of a chance here."

There was little traffic on the river road; they passed only a few people going in the other direction, mostly men on horseback, looking as if they were heading home from someplace, and some folks with carts heading in with produce for the town they'd left. Each one reported seeing Tiana and that she was in good shape.

One fellow had come off the ferry. "Yeah, it's decent," he told them. "Pricey, though. The next crossing's almost seventy miles north or fifty miles south and they know it. A Marquewood boat and fairy-run. That means only gold."

"A *fairy ferry*?" Irv laughed. "What kind?"

"You wait and see, youngster," the man responded.

Joe ignored the exchange. "What's the rate?"

"Two gold apiece one way, three round trip. That's with horse, of course. One and a half and two without, but I wouldn't advise it. They charge plenty for horses on the other side, too, and it's a long walk to anywhere else."

Joe whistled. "We're short, then."

"There's some brokers at the landing, but they'll steal you blind," the man warned. "Best if you can sell something ahead of time."

"Any towns between here and there?"

"No, it's only about an hour and a half ahead of you. No use hurrying there, though. They don't run at night and they're on their last trip of the day by now."

"Where's it go?"

"Daryia. Nice little town, but just inland is a main junction for most anyplace in Marquewood."

"Huh. If it's as costly as you say, and we're this far down, I might be better going the extra two days' distance north and taking the shorter run. I've taken that one before."

"Wouldn't recommend it," he responded. "Not much government authority up in that area, and a lot of nasties lurking around. Still got those damned zombies about, you know."

That got Joe's attention fast. "Zombies? You mean the Master of the Dead is still going?"

"Sure. Where have you been? His advance stopped about six months ago, and he actually withdrew a bit, consolidating his gains, but he's still powerful and nobody's been able to take anything back yet. It's a miracle he stopped his advance at all, but he's sure to start up again sooner or later. Rumor has it he reached the limit of how many of the walking dead he could control or maybe how big an area of 'em he could control. Sooner or later he'll make a deal with some principalities or others and get what he needs, though, mark my words! I sure wouldn't be going *north* right now!"

They pressed on, but Irving wanted to know the details.

"His name is Sugasto, and sooner or later I've got a score to settle with him," Joe told the boy. "I met the dirty weasel on our first quest here. An oilier traitor I don't think I've ever met. Even the old Dark Baron was a gentleman compared to this guy. Ruling over corpses is only one of his tricks, but a good one. Hard as hell to kill somebody who's already dead. His other little trick of snatching your soul from your body and putting it in a jar is one reason why Tiana's in the body she's in and caused us all sorts of problems. That was a trick he even taught the Baron. If you get close to him, your soul will wind up in one of his wine cellars and he'll be free to play games with your body. Funny. Old Ruddygore said he would be easy to take care of with the Baron out of the way. I don't like the sound of it."

"Why not?"

"Well, that second ferry's just below Castle Terindell on the Marquewood side. If Sugasto's got control down about to the other side there, that means he's only stuck because of Ruddygore, and *that* means that he's pretty much got our old patron in a stalemate and he's trying to figure a way to break it before going further. I don't want to run into him just yet. The last time I was out for the count in a bottle, and when Marge found the bottles of all of us, they didn't have any labels on them. We wound up being poured back into the wrong bodies, and the one I drew was one I don't want to have to detail."

He worried about Tiana being out of sight ahead, but just before sunset she came back to them down the trail, breathing hard but not looking out of sorts at all. They took the next turnout to the river, and set up camp for the night. While doing so, Joe gave Tiana the news from the traveler.

"Well, then, we must take this ferry," she told them. "We don't dare get near his territory now, particularly if somebody recognizes us, and we must assume he's got a pretty good intelligence service."

Joe sighed. "Well, converting the silver and the copper, we've got maybe four gold pieces. We're two short, and if those traders at the landing are the kind that usually are at places like that, we'll get no more than one for a horse, but pay three on the other side to get somebody else's horse, and it's another sixty or seventy miles easy to Terindell once we get over."

She thought about it. "Well, if we sell them one of the horses, and with the silver converted, we should make it. I can run part way and double up with Irving, here, for the distance. Of course, there's usually a bar or cafe at these landings, too. Maybe I could dance."

"Uh-uh. Not on this side, anyway," Joe responded quickly. "No chance of a getaway if things get wild. We might take our chances over there, but not here."

She shrugged. "Well, we'll see what the situation is when we get there."

They built a small fire and had some of the provisions, and Joe was already yawning. "Damn! Too big a night last night and not enough sleep after. I'm ready to fall over right now!"

"You go ahead, then," she told him. "I want to wind down a little more yet, then I'll join you."

By this time the entire region was in pitch darkness; there was no moon, and the stars provided very little decent illumination.

Joe was soon snoring away as usual, but Irving was having problems getting to sleep. He was just starting to drift off when he heard something and came awake. Dimly, by the thin light the dying fire gave, he could see Tiana putting a bridle on her horse. He got up and went over to her.

"What's up?"

"Shhh . . . Don't wake Joe. If I'm lucky he'll never know I've gone and I'll be back long before he wakes up."

"But where are you going?" he whispered.

"Up to the landing. It's only about a half-hour by horse. I know—I saw the boat leave before I came back from the bluff just ahead."

"You want me to come with you?"

"No. Stay here. Get some rest, and watch over the provisions."

"But—what you gonna do?"

"Never mind. I'll make a deal with you. I didn't go anywhere but to sleep tonight, and you came straight back to camp *last* night. Period. Okay?"

She had him there.

"But—"

"No buts. I want to get a move on. I've just been waiting until he was out. Don't worry. This is my turf, as you say."

Irving watched her ride off, not quite knowing what to do. The fact was, this *wasn't* her turf; she didn't know that place ahead, but he knew the kind of people most likely to be around there at night. They'd run from them *last* night. She was off doin' some fool thing with nobody to protect her at all.

It felt, well, dishonest, somehow. Sure, he'd had his little thing last night, but it wasn't the same. He was a *guy*, and she was, well, *married*.

Now he had three choices: follow her on the quiet and see what was what and be there to bail her out if she needed it, do as she said, or wake Dad and betray her—and himself. He'd rather not face his father on that, even if he was an adult by Husaquahrian standards at thirteen, so the last one was out. Besides, he might be pissed off at her, too. But he couldn't just, well, sit here, even if he didn't like the idea of riding this road in the dark.

He got his horse, put on a bridle and blanket, and headed off in the direction of the landing as quietly as possible.

She beat him by a fair amount of time, of course; he was *very* cautious, knowing he didn't have much experience in riding and yet wouldn't be much good to her if he fell off the road and in the river and killed his horse or maybe broke his own neck. Her horse was tied up at the landing when he approached it.

It wasn't all that much. A few small buildings, hardly a big deal. The biggest of them was apparently the pawn shop or whatever the equivalent was here; it probably also sold souvenirs. The other place was lit up, though, and from the sounds it appeared to be some kind of bar or nightclub. He tethered his horse away from the landing and crept down to it, then peered inside.

It *was* a bar, or, rather, what they called an inn here—a small bar and restaurant area, with a few rooms for rent either in back or upstairs. She was in there all right, and she was having a good old time with three or four guys, both doing some playful dancing and getting real suggestive with them. She was lying there at one point, real suggestive and seductive on this table, and one guy was feeding her *grapes* and stuff!

He knew now exactly what her Majesty was doing, and he didn't know what to do about it. If Mama could be believed, which was always a question, she'd broken up with Dad after finding out he had a whole string of girls on the road. Of course, she wasn't no slouch in that department, either, but the only memories of her like that was after the split. Dad had kind of admitted some of it, but claimed Mama was never a one-guy woman and they both knew it straight out at the start and that she'd taken up with this guy who was superjealous and she'd taken the new guy's side in things and that led to the split. He wasn't sure, but he sure never liked it the way it was while he was growing up.

He was so mixed up in his feelings he didn't know quite what to do, so he went back to his horse, sat down on a rock, and just waited. Finally, he got so bored he dozed off, and only woke up when he heard another horse neigh. He jerked himself awake and saw her out there getting on her horse and turning it back toward him. He might have beaten her back to camp if he wanted to risk the ride, but the questions inside him forced him to wait.

She was startled to see him, but instantly she knew the whole story without his saying a word.

"Well," she sighed, "I *could* say it was the Rules for me, and I think it might well be the truth, because I really do love your father deeply and yet I have no guilt or shame about this at all. It might also be something inside me wanting to get even with him."

"Huh? He cheated on you?"

"Many times, when we were ruling together. It was nearly impossible for him to keep his hands off all those pretty young things who are attracted to strength and power, and with all the scheduling demands it wasn't that hard for him, either. I'm not so sure that wasn't one reason I wanted to end that phase of our life."

"But you never cheated on him—then?"

"Eventually. Not right away, but, after a while, I started playing the same kind of games, partly in revenge, partly because he was getting such a workout with them he had little energy left for me. The difference was, I knew not only that he cheated, but with whom and when. He didn't know about me. His male ego wouldn't let him in any case unless he caught me in bed with somebody, and I was much too discreet for that. After a while, I got to like it. The variety, no complications, that kind of thing. But I was always, as you say, hung up with others then. I'm not any more. The other thing is, as I discovered tonight, I can't just give it away, except to him. That's some Rule someplace, no question.''

"You been doin' this all along since we got here, then?''

"No, I'm in full control of myself. This was the first time. I'm not so sure about him, though, although he's probably been good because you're with us. I'm just sorry you had to find out, particularly like this. I guess I must not seem much of a change to you, and certainly not a good example. *That* I feel bad about.''

"Well, I dunno . . . What if he finds out?''

"He probably will someday, and then I'll pull the Rules on him—everybody does it because nobody knows what the Rules really *say*—and he'll feel free and that'll be that. But I'd just as soon not right now. I don't plan on this as a regular habit unless he forces me. I did it for just one good reason—pure practicality.''

"You did it for money.''

She nodded, holding out a hand. He reached out and into his outstretched palm dropped two gold and two silver pieces. "Jeez!'' he said. "That's two and a quarter horses! Was that all of them or are you really that good?''

"Never mind, smartass. Let's get back and get some sleep. Tomorrow you can find the extra pieces you didn't notice, maybe hidden away in a fold of the bag or whatever.'' She grew very serious. "Look, it's *important* to me that you understand this. I love your father. I would never leave him, and I wouldn't want to be with any other man like this. I don't know what happened between him and your mother because he never talks about it except in vague terms, but if *we* split up, it'll be him taking the walk out of male ego, not me. I'm sorry, but the situation's just different here.''

"All right, I'll shut up about it,'' he assured her, "but only this once. You keep sneakin' off with these strangers in strange places with no backup and sooner or later somebody's gonna get you good. People just ain't that different over here as you like to think they are.''

Not too different at all, he thought, as they rode back in silence, except that these folks have a ready excuse for the wrong things they do. Except that at least these two *cared* what *he* felt, and that was something. Something he very much needed, and didn't want to lose.

When Irving had asked what sort of fairies ran the ferry, the man had told him to wait and see. Now, as it came in, he *still* wasn't quite sure. It was a big thing, flat but raised up, with a real hull, and there was a huge single sail on a mast in the center controlled by some kind of rope-and-pulley system that extended to the sides of the ship and seemed to go down into the water. There seemed to be lots of some sort of large fish, maybe dolphins, ahead of it in the water as if scouting the way, but, aboard, there appeared to be no wheel, no wheelhouse, and no apparent crew!

As it drew closer, it was clear that the big fish or whatever they were in front were on lines, like a team of horses attached to a big wagon, and that they were in fact steering the boat that way, although the main propulsion came from the manipulations of the single sail. And there was someone, or *something*, atop the lead fish, almost invisible from any distance because the creature's coloration seemed to match or reflect the water.

Now the boat was angled so that the current would take it into shore, the sail slowly folded inward so that it was no longer driving the boat, and, for a moment, the rider was against the dark background of the boat hull rather than the water. The outline was of an impossibly beautiful girl, almost a cartoon of a sexy girl, only her skin seemed weird, as if she were somehow made of glass or plastic and filled with water.

"A water nymph!" Joe exclaimed. "I never knew they did *any* work they didn't have to!"

Tiana nodded. "But what's pulling and steering? Mermaids?"

At that moment the "fish" team, freed of its tension for a moment, sounded as one, and from the water emerged the ugliest, most fearsome, monstrous heads Irving had ever seen, almost a cross between a lion's head and maybe the Creature from the Black Lagoon. They roared with a terrible sound that more than fit their horrible visage.

"Hippogryphs!" Joe exclaimed. "Nymphs who never did anything in their lives riding and guiding a beast that I never knew could be tamed! They've *got* to be tame, though. She wouldn't have the strength to guide them against their wills!"

The water nymph stood atop the lead beast, reins in hand, like a performer in some big water show, pulling this rein and that until the beasts were to one side, out of the way of the boat, which then passed them. The team moved in and started nudging the boat into the landing.

There was no dock as such; just a mud flat that went gently down into and under the water. The boat ran right up on the flat and seemed to dig a little trench as it stuck fast in the shallow mud. Now a couple of human boys, maybe eight or nine years old, who had been sitting on a piece of wood, ran up and started unfastening the front end of the boat, which dropped with a crash onto the mud and created a ramp from the exterior. As soon as the people, horses, and carts inside started to come off, all sorts of adults seemed to pop up from all over the place hawking just about everything and keeping an incessant set of pleas to buy this or that or, "You'll need this," as the travelers disembarked.

"It'll be interesting to see how they collect the fares," Tiana commented. "Water nymphs must be pretty much in contact with the water at all times or they'll start to dry out."

If Joe had been at all aware of the previous night's activities, he did not let on to either of them, and seemed perfectly happy to accept Irv's contention that there was more in the purse than he'd thought. He really began to wonder about his Dad, though; he knew that Joe had lightning reflexes and could pop up out of an apparently sound sleep, sword in hand, at the merest sound of danger. For the simple life, the boy thought, things were sure getting complicated, with everybody keeping secrets from everybody else.

Now it was their turn to be besieged by the vendors as they loaded back on. It was kind of the honor system on who got on first, but it wasn't much of a crowd and the line was pretty much self-enforcing.

Irving looked inside and wasn't sure he liked it. "Hey! This tub's sinkin'!"

An old guy with a thick gray beard taking a cart aboard chuckled. "Don't worry about it none, son. *They* decide if the water comes in or stays out. Just you wait!"

The small boys who'd unfastened the ramp now waded into the water and got hold of ropes floating there on the surface. Then they ran back and attached hooks on the ropes to an assembly at each end of the ramp and gave a shout. Something pulled on the ropes from the sea, raising the ramp, which hit a wooden catch at the top of each side and clicked into place. The boat lurched this way and that, and suddenly was floating free. The deck had only a few inches of water in it, but now the water seemed to coalesce in clear spots and from those spots arose, almost oozed, the shapes of two of the water nymphs. They had an unnerving, Other-Worldly perfection to them, and they looked exactly alike, each about four feet of total feminine sensuality.

"Don't touch the hair, boy," the old man cautioned in a low tone. "It's like sea nettles. Stings like crazy."

"Welcome to the Daryia ferry," they said in unison, in truly musical, singsong voices. "Please give us your fares now as we pass among you. After we are squared away, the water will recede and there is fodder in the forward hold for the animals which is included in the fare."

"I wonder what happens if you don't have the fare?" Irv mused.

"Then they take *you*," the old man replied.

That was not a comforting thought.

Even up close, the fairy nymphs seemed weird, like beautiful but extreme sculptures made of glass. Irv, like all the other men, couldn't really take his eyes off the creatures.

When one got to them, Joe, who'd appropriated the money pouch, fished out six gold pieces and dropped them in the nymph's palm. The pieces sat there a moment, then seemed to sink into her hand, and you could watch the golden coins go down through her into the water and then to who knew where?

"I've never heard of nymphs running a ferry before," Tiana commented. "Nor tamed hippogryphs, either."

The nymph shrugged. "It beats lying around all day being seductive," she responded. "It's an old troll ferry that was abandoned during the War. We looked at it and decided that sitting around looking sexy for a few thousand years had grown kinda old, so we did it. The hippogryphs are not tame. They're partners."

Joe thought some reply to that was called for, but, for the life of him, he couldn't think of one. Finally, Tiana commented, "It's nice to see some independent businesswomen here for a change."

As soon as all the fares were collected, the nymphs melted into the water, and, true to their word, the water itself began to drain out somewhere, until the deck was as dry as a bone.

From what was now the front came a series of splashes and an eerie, hypnotic siren song, and the boat began moving in earnest.

Although the crossing should have taken no more than twenty five or thirty minutes, it was tricky in the crosscurrents of the big river, and there were constant adjustments this way and that.

Finally, Joe muttered, "What I want to know is what they do with their money."

"Perhaps it is best not to know that one," Tiana replied. "Even nymphs might like pretty baubles, and who knows how they live under the water, but what and where does a *hippogryph* go to spend it?"

Irv just shook his head in wonder. Maybe this place *wasn't* so much like home after all.

He went over and jumped up on some of the side-bracing so he could look out at the passing scene. The ferry landing was already receding in the distance, and they were about to clear the bend and go out into the mainstream of the river itself.

As soon as they did clear, he could look back and up and saw, or thought he saw, the point near the next bend where they'd spent the night. Looking the other way, Marquewood still wasn't much, although, beyond the trees, he thought he saw the roofs of some buildings that perhaps marked the town.

The river itself was amazing, both as a main highway for the entire continent and for supporting lives and livelihoods of both humans and nonhumans. It had an abundance of fish; he'd watched some being caught from small jerry-built piers near the landing, and while the fish looked, well, pretty strange, they were still fish and it was still pretty much what would be expected.

Just in front of them, a small school, or whatever they'd call them, of mermaids popped up out of the water and shouted and waved, not to him or the passengers, but to the strange nymph who was both captain and teamster up ahead. Up close, the mermaids' skins did have a rather bluish cast not evident from shore, and their hair was a much darker blue, but they still looked remarkably like a bunch of schoolgirls out in the river for a swim.

Part of the reason the trip took so long was the number of small islands that had been built up by the river's deposits near the bend, forcing them to thread their way through small inlets separating the mounds. And yet, even the small islands were covered with trees and bushes and the nests of exotic tropical birds. Some mermaids were sunning themselves on a big rock at the end of one of the islands, and on shore a number of dark shapes seemed to writhe and then go into the water. Alligators, maybe? Or something else as weird as barking, bearded fish.

Here and there some water nymphs would rise to the surface and seem to walk on or even slightly above the water, shouting things in their operalike singsong voices to those handling the boat. Somehow, it drove home just how *vulnerable* land-dwelling humans like him were on this thing. Not only did this river have all the dangers of any tropical river or even any deep river, except maybe the ton of pollution Earth added, but it was also home to a number of races as intelligent in their own way as humans were, but as different as night and day from humans as well. There might be whole civilizations living beneath these waters, with who knew what powers and what kind of lives?

Finally, they began to come in to the opposite shore; the one they left now seemed eerily lost in a late morning mist. The town itself was still mostly masked, starting on a bluff well up from the river landing and sheltered by thick, almost junglelike vegetation.

He wanted to see how they came in, but a yell from Joe ordered him down and he reluctantly obeyed. He quickly saw why; the bumps and jolts of the operation might well have shaken him off the side or, if he'd leaned too far forward, into the river itself.

"We've still got a little money," Joe told him, "so we'll catch a bite to eat here and get what news we can of the route. I want to find out if there's anything nasty between here and Terindell."

"We're not stayin' here tonight, then? I figured it might be time for another dance," the boy responded

"It might be, but it's still fairly early, and we can make it halfway there, if we keep on, and all the way by tomorrow night. Five or ten miles north and I'll be in country I know well, which helps a lot."

"You still worried 'bout that zombie guy, huh? He's way over on the other side now."

"He's on both sides—bet on it. And he's been down farther than this and a little inland before, so I don't want to take any chances. Not too many years ago, a demon-led army was literally at the gates of Terindell, and not too long ago, some of the towns between here and there were under Sugasto's control. If he had to pull back because he was reaching his limit, then we're still within his limit now. I don't underestimate the S.O.B. I keep doing that and almost dying or worse as a result. And he's got a particular set of scores to settle with us, just as we do with him. Last time he controlled things; the next time I want to set the conditions."

The town, like the vegetation, *was* rather different than the High Pothique ones he'd been in, but the basics were the same. Gone was any trace of adobe; buildings here were of stone and wood, with thick straw or bamboo or even, in a few cases, red slate roofs. The people seemed a bit more prosperous, although that was like going from zero to almost one on a scale of ten, and had a different look about them. It wasn't a big difference, but the folk of High Pothique looked more Arabic, while these looked more European, their complexions more tan than olive, their features more like the typical white folks he knew back home.

The men tended to wear white cotton in a uniform, baggy style, often with soft leather boots, and about half tended to wear broad-brimmed, rounded white hats. The women, on the other hand, made those of High Pothique seem almost over-dressed, most of them wearing little more than varicolored cotton string bikini bottoms or petite cotton loincloths. They tended to be fatter, or chunkier, on average than those of High Pothique, and most all of them wore oversized earrings, bracelets, and the like of bone or copper or something else, and almost all of them tended to cut their hair real short, almost in a man's trim cut. Like those of High Pothique, they tended to carry huge amphoras or boxes on their heads, and, also like High Pothique, most seemed to be pregnant, carrying babies as well, and having lots of naked kids around.

It didn't smell much better, either.

Most of the small cafes were just preparing for lunch, though, so it was possible to get hot, thoroughly cooked food, which always made Irving feel a bit better. Cooking still killed little nasties that wanted at your insides. As usual, he let his father order; he wasn't sure he really *wanted* to know what some of the stuff was. At this level of cooking, anyway, it all tasted pretty much like whatever it was cooked in, anyway.

Joe picked up his tankard and looked at them. "Two days to real beds and decent food," he said. He gestured in a sort of a toast. "To the end of the road,"he added, and drank.

The proprietor, over here a man, told them that they'd have to clear border entry at the crossroads; the only road out of town led to there, so it was the border station, to avoid crimping the town's economy more than any other reason. Travelers who cleared the border here might tend to hurry on past; those who knew they would yet have to usually stopped and spent something. And, of course, going the other way, travelers to High Pothique tended to come here and spend the night before the journey.

The border people would have information on all the roads and routes.

Unlike High Pothique, which seemed pretty loose about its guards and such, this station was almost like a small military stockade built of formidable stone. The blue-and-gold flag of Marquewood flew atop a large pole, and the bordermen were dressed more like soldiers, in uniforms that matched the flag.

Irving looked over next to the flag and tried unsuccessfully to suppress laughing. Standing just beneath it was a huge marble statue of a nude man and woman, bigger than life, looking back at them.

"No wisecracks," Joe warned. "Besides, we're going to have enough problems remembering that we're suddenly nobodies here."

A soldier, with a trim, brown mustache and military bearing, came up to him. "Do you have any papers?"

"No, sir, although we are all citizens of Marquewood. Although my parents were from a far-off place, I was born in, and am going home to, Terdiera; the lady is of Sachalin origin."

The soldier nodded, then looked at Irving. "You, young sir, are not of Marquewood, surely."

"My son," Joe answered hastily. "I travel a lot in my work."

The soldier looked at Joe, then the boy, then shrugged. "Apparently so. And from where did you journey?"

"High Pothique, entirely. A well-earned holiday, you might say. Now I am returning to my employer."

"I see. And who might that be?"

"Ruddygore of Terindell, of course."

The soldier started a bit. "You work for the sorcerer?"

"Legally, no. But he has first claim on my services."

The soldier nodded and went to Tiana. "You are of Sachalin?"

"I was born in that city, my lord."

"And what are you to these two?"

"My lord, I am his slave and mistress," she responded, pointing to Joe.

The response startled Irving. Hell, she was his *wife*, wasn't she? But it seemed to satisfy the guy. Maybe it was an image thing, he decided, or one more of them damned Rules.

"Name and family?"

"My lord knows that upon becoming a slave I gave up my name and family. I am called by whatever name my master chooses, and for now he calls me Ti, after the Blessed Goddess."

"You were acquired in High Pothique."

"No, my lord, in Marquewood."

He nodded, then asked a few specific questions about the far-off city, which she answered perfectly and without hesitation, knowing the place well. He seemed satisfied. "Very well." He wrote something and handed it to Joe.

"This is your customs entry for the horses and slave," the border guard told the big man. "She seems to be of Marquewood and her accent is right, so I will allow her in free of duty. However, if you plan on leaving the kingdom again with her and returning, you should have her fitted with a nose ring to validate her country of origin or you could wind up paying duty."

Now the borderman walked back to Irving, who had been watching all this with increasing horror. At least he had been properly briefed for his own questions.

"You are not born here?"

"No, sir, first time. I am of age, and my father is taking me to be trained by the one who trained him."

The border patrolman walked back to Joe. "All seems in order, sir. Left to Terdiera. You are cautioned that most of the route is Royal Preserve—no poaching."

"Any problems?" Joe asked him. "The last time I was through the Master of the Dead was working down almost past here."

"He withdrew his forces northward as far as we can tell upon the sorcerer's return," the soldier told them. "Your route should be safe, although there are reports of hidden enemy encampments in these parts and occasional bits of nastiness— cemeteries getting up and taking walks, that sort of thing. Stay on the road and camp only in and around the towns and you should have no trouble. The Majin fairies have been moved in between Hotsphar and Terdiera as they are loyal and have proven resistant to the enemy's powers, but from a few miles north of here until perhaps the old tollhouse at

Grotom Wood there's been reports of firesprites and possible banshee presence, so don't camp in there even after dark. Otherwise, no problems.''

Joe nodded, and they moved through the opening to the crossroads and turned left.

"I wonder what that guy considers a problem?'' Irving asked no one in particular.

CHAPTER 4

ON CHANGES AND UNCHANGES

Fairy flesh is essentially immortal (except under Sections 7 and 16 and provisos in Volumes IV and VI as amended) and, once fixed, can never be changed in its character. It is outside the purview of magic.

—The Books of Rules, III, 79(b)

THE ROAD TO TERINDELL KEPT GETTING CREEPIER AND CREEPIER as they went.

The road was in excellent shape, and obviously was well maintained, but the landscape quickly became a jungle, with huge trees rising almost too high to see the tops of them, so close together that they tended to block out much of the light and form almost a rooflike canopy over them.

"So this is home sweet home?" Irving asked, looking nervously around. He could believe zombies or almost *anything* in this place.

"Marquewood's a huge country, one of the largest in Husaquahr," Tiana told him. "There are rolling hills and beautiful glades and mountains and river valleys and just about anything you can think of. It's just that this area, for the next twenty-five miles or so, is swamp and rain forest."

"Yeah, but it hadn't occurred to me that we'd be on *this* route," Joe said a bit nervously. "I'm never gonna be really thrilled with this region again."

Tiana dropped back and said to Irv, in a low tone, "It was elsewhere in this region that Sugasto had an encampment. Our souls were snatched from our bodies and taken here and stored

66

there. The changeling Marge was a key to them finding us, but there was no way to tell who was who."

"Yeah, you told me that. Around *here*?"

"Farther south, but the same sort of place. What he'd never tell you was that he was placed in the body of a wood nymph and bound by her Rules. It took powerful magic much later to restore him."

Irv suppressed a loud laugh. "Dad? A *girl*?"

"Worse. A wood nymph. They are compulsive hussies with the brains of a banana peel. There's no real memory of our time in the bottles, but he still has nightmares about his time as a nymph. Don't rub it in."

Irving felt a shiver creep up his spine. "Man! I hope that don't happen to me! I don't never wanna be no girl!"

She stared at him. "Why not? I happen to like it just fine."

"Yeah? Would you like to be a man instead? Really?"

"No! I like it the way I am!"

"See?"

"What're you two whispering about?" Joe asked, turning.

"I just filled him in on why you really want to get even with Sugasto," she told him. At his expression, she added, "He had a right to know."

Joe shrugged, but he was clearly angry at her for doing it. He was just realistic enough to know that you couldn't undo something once done.

Irving thought it would be a good idea to change the subject.

"Hey—back there you said you was Dad's mistress and *slave*, even. You're his wife, ain't you? Why the other line?"

"Not only under the Rules, but under the law, we're not married anymore," she explained. "We just consider ourselves married. The one who married him is different from me. Officially, legally, and under the Rules, I'm somebody else. So is he, for that matter. That dizzy nymph ran off in his old body and this one, which looks the way he originally looked, was actually a magical transformation. Under the Rules, I'm of the underclass—the class of the masses, like the people in those towns, and serfs, and slaves. I was not married within my class in proper fashion, but instead I am a dancer who dances before crowds for money. That places me in the same category as a trained animal who performs in the square for coppers for its owner. An animal has no rights at all, let alone the right to marry. An animal can only be wild or owned.''

"Yeah, but—*slave*! You ain't no animal! You're just a person bein' treated like an animal!''

"Joe has explained to me how terrible that idea is to you, which is one reason we never brought it up, but it is like the thing we discussed about women's dress here. This is not only a different world, it exists stuck in a different, earlier time and way of thinking.''

"But keepin' slaves is *wrong*! It's *evil*!''

"There is a lot of evil in both our worlds, some practiced by very good people. You must learn to think differently. There will be no revolutions here to change things like this. Not ever. Things can only become worse. Now that you know, you should be aware that I will be telling everyone here that I am Joe's slave. It is vital to me that I do so. Being someone's property is the only protection I have here.''

"Come again?''

"Otherwise, you see, I am nothing at all, without status or position of any sort, and, therefore, anyone could do anything with and to me that they felt like. As his slave, I am protected under law and the Rules because of *his* property rights.''

This kind of thinking made Irv dizzy. Still, it suddenly occurred to him that this put her indiscretions of the night before in this new light. "But, if he gets mad at you or somethin' he could *sell* you or even just *give* you away!''

"That is so,'' she admitted, "but we are married in our own minds, and I think I know him better than that.''

"Couldn't he just give you your freedom?''

"No, that's not permitted. If he freed me, renounced me, or sent me away, I would still be without status and unable to be anything other than I am. I can only survive as someone's property. It is the only way I get some measure of independence.''

"Come again?''

"He is my owner, not my puppeteer. I am as independent as I can get away with.''

This was too much for the boy. If they weren't married anymore, then she wasn't cheating on him last night, and, likewise, he could have all the flings he wanted and not be cheating on her. But he still didn't like it. Slavery was evil; when it was the good guys who kept slaves, what did it take to be a bad guy? He had been with them many months now, and he was only discovering what they already knew.

"What was that bit about a nose ring?" he asked her.

"He means a small ring that would be inserted through my nose, of course," she told him. "Each nation has its own unique alloy for making them, all done by fairy folk, of course. In addition, it carries a spell which identifies the owner and all previous owners. They're usually not worn unless ownership is transferred—sort of a bill of sale, as it were. You notice how the guardsman barely questioned the two of you but went to some length to determine I really was of Marquewood?"

"Yeah. So?"

"Because I had no ring, he wanted to make certain that Joe wasn't smuggling me in. I hadn't even thought of it before, but I'm very glad he was so easy on us. A stickler for the law might well have confiscated me!"

"You gonna get one of them rings put in?"

"I'd rather not," she replied honestly, "but I think I'll have to. I don't want to take a risk like that again. I tried not to think about getting one, since the idea of having something in my nose sends chills through me, but, all of a sudden, I keep thinking about all the nasty possibilities without one. Without Joe around, I have nothing to prove that I am his. Slavers could steal me and sell me to anyone with impunity! And the law would back them up!"

They rode in silence for a while, and that wasn't much better, since he wasn't getting things sorted out at all, and the lack of conversation made the dark, junglelike swamp even darker and more menacing. Aside from the noise of the horses moving along the road, all other sounds came from the dense forest, and those noises included strange hoots, weird screeches, growls, grunts, and other sounds hard on the nerves, made all the worse because you couldn't see what was making them.

He noticed that Tiana wasn't anxious to get her run in around here, either.

"Let's pick up the pace a little," Joe suggested. "I'd like to be out of here before dark."

This was good for a while, but horses couldn't be pushed forever without some water and breaks. As the afternoon went on, the low light that filtered down angled lower, causing a sinister, creeping dark to pervade slowly, the hot, humid air as still as death. It was also nearly impossible to tell what time it was; they didn't seem to have watches in this world, either, and under this jungle canopy it was nearly impossible to tell where the sun was in the sky. In these latitudes, the sun went down like a stone somewhere around six-thirty.

"What happens if we don't make it out of this mess by dark?" Irving asked nervously.

"It's too damp to find anything useful as a torch," Joe replied, frowning and looking around. "We'll be blind as bats once the sun sets if we don't clear it, and the only thing I'd rather not do than spend a night here is ride blind. We're just gonna have to push the horses and hope."

But within another twenty minutes, it seemed to grow darker still, and from the tops of the great trees there came a rushing noise as some strong winds picked up, and then there was the sound of thunder.

So dense was the canopy that for quite some time no rain fell on them, although the air was so thick and heavy it made them wet just riding through it. Finally, though, it filled the upper reaches and began running off, not as rain but more like the buckets of giants being emptied on top of them. They were forced to stop, not only because of their own problems but because it was dangerous for the horses, and they could only find as dry a place as they could up against some big trunks, hold the horses, and wait it out.

The storm itself was over in perhaps half an hour, perhaps less, but the runoff continued for almost as long as the rain made its way down below. By the time they were through, they were in a muddy, wet steambath. Worse, they had lost an hour and it would be slow going for a while from this point as well.

"What do we do now?" Irving asked his father miserably.

"Well, all those in favor of camping here, in ankle-deep water and smelly swamp, have a seat. I'm for pressing on. We may not make it out, but the closer we are to out the better; at least, it'll give things time to dry. There's not a prayer I've got anything dry to put on, either, so I'm gonna shock you all and go bare-ass on a wet horse blanket and hang this loincloth on the side to dry as we ride. Irv, I'd suggest you do the same with your leather, since, when that stuff dries, it's gonna cut right into you."

"But—suppose we meet somebody on the trail?" the boy responded, embarrassed.

"Have we met anybody yet? And we're not likely to meet anybody, either, at least not anybody who's here for honest purposes. We're more than halfway, I'm pretty sure, and only nuts like us would start in on this route after sunup."

Ti was busy wringing out her hair, almost to no avail, but she commented, seeing the boy's nervousness, "Come, come! I have seen much worse than you and lived!"

The leather thongs were already starting to irritate his skin, so he knew he had no choice, and finally stripped. *Seems like this place is hell bent on gettin' everybody stark naked,* he thought sourly.

The horse blanket was also soaked through and felt like a wooly sponge, but there was no getting rid of it. Bare-assed and truly bareback on a horse was an open invitation to saddle sores, as he'd learned early on in his experience here. Until Husaquahr, he'd never been on a horse that moved unless you stuck a quarter in the slot first, but his father had been a good teacher and he a quick learner. It no longer even hurt like hell to get off anymore.

The problem really was, it didn't seem to get any dryer as they went on slowly through the muck that had been the road and was still better than what was on either side of it. Instead, the rain forest took on an even more eerie cast, with fog forming just above the ground and thickening as they went. Irving couldn't help noticing that his father was still wearing the sword that was the boy's namesake, and in a position where it could be easily drawn while mounted.

The fog grew thicker, as did the silence of the land, with only the drip, drip, drip of water making its way down to join its whole at the base of the great trees. What sunlight remained created only a grim, ghostly gray, and it seemed that it was getting darker and darker with each passing minute.

Joe had given up any idea of getting out before full darkness; now he was looking at every place that gave any potential for both safety and protection. Cursing himself for not allowing for any variables and maybe waiting until morning for this passage, he spotted an area that might just have to do.

"We'll have to camp there," he told them, gesturing to an area on a slight rise about twenty feet off the right side of the road. "The trees are close enough to give us some protection for our backs, and there's fallen logs and thick wood shavings all over. It's not much, but it's the best I've seen since we took this road and I don't expect any better if we keep on. On the other hand, I'd rather be there than in the swamp."

Tiana looked it over. "This is almost like a fairy circle," she noted. "Are we certain we're not going to camp in the middle of trouble?"

He shrugged. "Maybe, but it's suddenly almost dark as pitch, and I don't think we have much choice." He couldn't explain it to them or to himself, but this place *felt* right, felt, somehow, safe and secure. It was a mystery, and he didn't plan to trust the feeling absolutely, but he *knew* this was the right place.

When the darkness fell, it *fell*. There was no light at all, anywhere. Irving had thought he'd seen darkness out on the trail under cloudy or moonless skies, but this was the darkness of a cellar, or maybe the grave. Tiana tried the flint, but there was nothing around dry enough to set afire, and the brief sparks, hardly noticeable in other circumstances, briefly lit the scene like flashes of lightning on a dark night.

"We're lucky it's midsummer here," Joe said, trying to sound optimistic. "That means we've only got eleven hours of this instead of thirteen. Now if I can find the pack—ah! Anybody want some soggy, half-stale bread and some warmed wine?"

They managed to eat something, although none of them had a lot of appetite. Nerves made it nearly impossible to sleep, either, although Joe suggested a guard rotation, but being wide awake and seeing nothing but darkness while sitting in back of logs against great trees and on soaked wood chips wasn't exactly thrilling. It seemed, somehow, even risky to be talking, but there wasn't much else to do. Even so, they all found themselves whispering, although none could really say why.

"Hey, I been here a pretty long time now," Irving said, trying to make some conversation, "and mostly it's been gettin' the horses, goin' off into that plains area and campin' out and learnin' how to ride and doin' a little huntin' and fishin' and all, but how come it ain't 'til we're in this pesthole that this slave bit comes up?"

"It's the Rules again, kicking in, most likely," Joe replied as they huddled together. "They can be pretty cruel sometimes. And tremendously inconvenient."

"I'm sure of it," Tiana agreed. "This body was not even fully defined, I think, when I became it. I was from the upper classes; I *thought* in those terms, even when I didn't realize it. It never occurred to me that I would drop in class or could. But almost from the start, everybody kept commenting on how I had an athlete's body, then a dancer's body. I'm native to here; the Rules bind me always. Even I began thinking of athletic dancing, idly fantasizing as a dancing girl, that kind of thing. I was defined by that. Slowly, the Rules under which I had unconsciously lived slipped away as no longer relevant; the Rules that replaced them were the ones I and others defined without even thinking about it."

"That don't seem fair."

"It's not," Joe agreed, "but it's only a kind of legal thing of what we both already knew from Earth. People always looked at me, particularly in the east, and they started defining me. At first they thought I was Hispanic, and when I told them I was a full-blooded native American, the real jokes began. I was called 'Chief,' talked to in mock-Tonto, everything. That's one reason I grew up tough. I had to take it or fight. I fought. That's why I wound up driving a truck instead of getting a decent education and maybe going on to college. I always thought I would be some kind of sports superstar. Jim Thorpe, a full-blooded native American who was also born in Pennsylvania, was a sports superstar and my big hero. But I never really worked at it and I got passed over. Wound up doing some bare-knuckle boxing at truck stops and doing repairs of big rigs. Everybody remembers those dumb cowboy movies and figures, hey, he's an Indian. He's got muscles and all that but no real brains. Pretty soon, you find yourself thinking that way, too.''

"You mean like the way white folks looked at me back home. First they saw black, and then they saw kid, and all of a sudden there was some kinda wall between us, even if we was friendly. Only the black kids, they saw the high cheeks and straight black hair and they started callin' me 'Geronimo' and stuff like that. It was like nobody could see *me* in here.''

"Uh-huh,'' Tiana responded. "Only *there* there's at least a *chance* of breaking out of it. Here, once, even for a short time, you get that in your or other folks' heads, the Rules grab you and define you and you're stuck. It seems to be human nature that everybody tries to define and pigeonhole everybody else. Here, though, once you're defined, even incorrectly, that's *it*. I started doing the exercises to get in shape, then the dance stuff, and it just started coming naturally to me. The erotic part I guess was my fault, for fantasies at the wrong time. Each time I was defined a little more and a little more. When we started the dances for money, that finished it. I was defined. People who do that are slaves. Slaves have more Rules. Today, without even realizing I'd changed, I found myself *thinking* like a slave. The responses I gave the guardsman just came naturally to me. When I was explaining the situation to you earlier, I was really also explaining it to me. I know, we had the Rules read to us, but they were abstract and didn't cover the half of it.''

"You mean you're gettin' to *like* it?'' the boy asked, still confused.

"No, I never have to like it, but *accepting* it is something else again. I *have* to accept it or go crazy or kill myself, because I've got no choice but to be that way.''

Irving thought about it a bit. "Am *I* gonna be trapped by them Rules?''

"Eventually,'' Joe told him. "Not right off. That's part of the idea of taking you to be trained at Terindell as I was. I didn't realize it at the time, but Ruddygore wasn't just providing me with training; the training and my success at it defined me, so by the time I finally was put under the Rules they only made me what I already had become. You think about that if things get tough. There are male slaves here, too. Here, nobody will be prejudiced because of your looks or color. They'll think you look downright exotic. Because so much is always the same here, differences are admired, even envied, not looked down on. Right now you're still a clean slate to the Rules, and you even have some resistance because of that to magic—but I wouldn't count too much on that in a pinch. But if you wind up a loser here, you'll have done it to yourself.''

Tiana yawned in spite of herself. ''Some of us should get some sleep,'' she told the others. ''I think I might be able to drift off now.''

''I slept the latest; I'll take the first watch,'' Joe told them. ''When I get too tired, I'll awaken the one of you who goes to sleep first. That second one does the same for the third. It's the best system I can think of.''

''I don't think I'm gonna be able to sleep all night,'' Irving muttered as Tiana settled down beside him. ''But I'll try.''

The fact was, he almost beat her into slumber.

Joe didn't feel all that tired, but if it was boring to sit around staring at nothingness with two others, it was much more boring to do it alone. Still, he prayed for a deathly boring night.

Some leader I've become! he thought sourly. *I'm as scared of this place and this darkness as they are.* Worse, he'd gotten them into this partly out of emotion. He hadn't stayed alive this long by letting two people get on horses and ride out of camp while he slept. He knew she'd gone and probably where and for what and where the extra money had come from. The thing was, he hadn't stopped her, although he easily could have, and he wasn't sure why he hadn't, particularly after the kid had gone after her. Now Irving knew, too, and was keeping a Big Secret from Dad. The worst thing was, considering his real mother, he probably was getting a very weird idea of women. Some father *he* was!

And now here he was, sticking the kid in this kind of danger, just because he couldn't bring himself to leave Tiana free in that town for a night.

Not that he was a great shining example of fidelity, either. She, at least, could tell herself it was the Rules, and maybe be right. She was not the same woman he had married and was becoming less so as time passed. He was the poor dumb Injun who wound up marrying the highly educated and cultured princess like some fairy tale and it had really fed his ego. Now he was the same poor dumb Injun with a dancing whore for a slave and mistress.

He didn't blame her for that. It was nobody's fault, as she said, and even this beat the boring hell out of being reigning gods. The thing was, he'd reached the heights of society and acceptance and found out that it was less fun than driving a truck. Now he found himself wondering if he'd married her for love or lust, the same as he had the first time, or just because some of her blue blood and education might rub off on him and cause all those other educated blue-blooded males to turn green with envy.

It still wasn't fair to her, though. He *had* to give it up; he was strangling as ruler and lived again only when they had to go into action. She, on the other hand, had given it up for his sake. He was back where he wanted to be, but she was lower than her worst nightmares because of him.

He knew well how absolute those Rules were when they all kicked in, too. He'd never been aware of them as a barbarian, a warrior, but when he'd been dumped in that wood nymph's body, he'd slowly *become* a wood nymph—at one and the same time becoming two hundred percent seductive fairy female and forgetting his knowledge, his experience, his common sense, just to go with the flow emotion. Joe de Oro had literally ceased to exist; it took a wish from that most powerful of magic things, the Lamp of Lakash, ancient product of that third world beyond even this one, the Land of the Djinn, where only magic, no natural law at all, applied. But for that, he wouldn't really exist; there'd just be some sexy, curvaceous, light green, barely thinking bimbo living inside a tree and thinking about nothing but seducing all and sundry until Judgment Day.

Irving had been forced to grow up too soon; maybe it was time *he* did, too. He couldn't really help Ti, but he owed her, and particularly he owed her protection, loyalty, and a *very* loose leash.

He had started to doze in his musings in spite of himself, but something suddenly stirred him awake. His hand went automatically to his sword, but he did not draw it or wake the others, not yet. It might just be nerves or a figment of a dream.

It might be, but it wasn't.

There was definitely something out there. Many somethings. He heard the horses stir nervously and, slowly, he withdrew the great sword from its scabbard. The great sword had a life of its own and, awakened by being drawn, pulsed with energy, as if eager to be put to use. He felt its power, as if arm and sword were one, and he was never quite sure who was boss.

Well, they weren't firesprites or they'd light up the night; and they weren't banshees, because they weren't howling, but that only left a few million other possibilities. He feared zombies the most; you had to hack zombies to pieces and, even then, get away from the pieces. *Damn* him for thinking with his emotions and not sorting out this business with Tiana when no harm could be done! How *dare* he put Irving in such danger?

Filled with rage at himself, he stood to face his attackers.

Suddenly he made out a figure, about the size of a small child, over to his right. It was odd, but he wasn't actually *seeing* the creature; rather, he was seeing a kind of glowing soft, green outline of it. It looked, somehow, familiar, as if he'd seen it somewhere before, but he couldn't place where or when.

Now, suddenly, he could see other figures in front of him—two, three, no, four of them, all nearly identical as only fairies might be, yet, somehow, he could sense a very slight difference in each one.

Wood nymphs! They were being surrounded by wood nymphs! And that was why this spot had attracted him, had somehow sent a signal that it was safe. The great sword in his hand changed its humming pitch to sound much like a disappointed, metallic Bronx cheer. There were things to fear from wood nymphs, but the most threatening was dying of exhaustion.

He sheathed the sword, literally feeling its irritation, and stepped forward to meet them halfway. He didn't want his son to meet a bunch of wood nymphs in their usual full heat right now. Still, he found going to them and meeting with them more unnerving than fighting a horde of homicidal zombies. The sight of them brought back memories he'd been trying to forget, and it unsettled him that he could not only see their fairy auras even now but also tell them apart, something virtually no human could do. As he drew close he could make out their full form and detail, although he was still not seeing in a normal sense. They stared at him, wide-eyed, looking less their insatiably lustful selves at the sight of a naked human male than completely confused.

"What manner of fairy are you, who has the husk of a human man and handles iron, yet glows inside with the aura of our Sisterhood?" one asked in that cute, sexy, seductive voice they all had.

He stopped. "I—what?"

"What kind of sorcery puts a wood nymph in the body of a big, handsome, human hunk?" another asked.

"I'm a man, not a wood nymph," he retorted, not knowing why he suddenly felt so cold in the damp heat.

"Your soul and aura are as ours," a third maintained. "It burns through the oversized husk."

"This *husk* is my body."

"The soul is hid real good," the first one agreed, " 'cept'n it's plain to us. Were you changed by some sorcery or did somebody make you f'get your real self?"

"I was born like this. The Master of the Dead took my soul once and put it in the body of a wood nymph, but the most powerful magic of all wished me back in my original body," he told them. "I really don't like to discuss it."

"Oh, I see," the first nymph replied. "Your soul was in a husk of the Sisterhood, and it didn't get put back the same way. You were a human who became a fairy, not by nature or Rule or birth, but it happened. You were fairy. You *are* fairy. No mere magic or sorcery, no matter how strong, can change a fairy soul, only hide it like the leaves hide the ground."

"Wait a minute. Are you saying that, deep down, I'm still a wood nymph? I don't *feel* like a wood nymph. I feel like my old self. I bleed, I bruise, I handle iron, I like girls, and I don't want any time in the grass with any man."

"The flesh magic protects and shelters you," she replied. "The magic is *real* strong, too. It made you a body like your old one and gave you all that you knowed 'n' felt 'n' should feel. But it couldn't change the fairy soul inside. Your flesh makes you look 'n' think 'n' act like a mortal man, but only to mortals. You get turned on by *us*?"

He didn't want to hear any more of this, but he had to, and he had to answer honestly. "No. Not a bit." And come to think of it, Irving had his tongue hanging out for those water nymphs on the ferry, but he'd felt nothing at all. These living refugees from a *Playboy* cartoon would turn on almost anybody, but, somehow, to him, it would be like, well . . .

Like kissing your sister.

"Are you telling me this is all a fake? That I'm not really a human man?"

"Oh, no. The magic is real strong, strongest I ever seen, and I been around a couple thousand years. You'll live your life as you are. But when the flesh is gone, your soul will still be of us. Only if iron stabs your fairy heart would you really die—and forever."

Although it was close to his worst nightmares, he knew, somehow, that it was true. He was Joe de Oro; nothing had changed about that. And he would be Joe, in every way, until death. But when death came, he would not pass on, or be reincarnated, or whatever happened to human souls; instead, he would be one of *these* once again, forever until Judgment Day.

It was the most unsettling certainty of a hereafter he could have imagined.

This was something to take up with Ruddygore, if they ever got there.

Unfortunately, it also explained some of his own changes since returning here. His sudden liking for the outdoors and outdoor living, for one thing. His strange, unsettling dreams, for another, and his otherwise uncharacteristic lapses in self-control such as the one that got them stuck here now. If Ti wasn't Tiana anymore, he wasn't—quite—Joe, either.

Still, he felt anger at finding out this way, in the middle of nowhere, in a situation still fraught with dangers. "Who other than wood nymphs could tell this about me?" he asked.

She shrugged. "Of course, any of the Sisterhood right off. You can't hide from your own. Any other fairy *could* see it, if they was lookin' for it, but most wouldn't. Most times folks see what they expect to see, not what's there. Same as fairy sight. You could see like we see if you knowed you could and really wanted to."

He tried to dampen his emotions as best he could, though, become Joe the Barbarian. There was nothing at all he could do about this now, and, at least, he was no longer ignorant of it. The fairy soul might panic at this news, but Joe would accept it as something to be dealt with later and, for now, something to be used. If wood nymphs saw him as one of their own, then they were potential allies. Not in a fight—wood nymphs were totally passive, as he well knew—but that wasn't what he needed right now. And this head nymph, while no Einstein, talked smarter than any other one he'd known. Maybe if you lived long enough you had time to learn *something*. Or, possibly, the clan leaders were always a bit smarter. Although he'd been one of them, he'd never lived among them, and he was totally ignorant of their ways when they were among one another. No matter now.

"All right—*sisters*—can you help us with some information?"

The nymph leader shrugged. "Maybe. We don't go far from our trees, you know."

"What's in this neighborhood that we have to worry about?"

"Nothin' much right 'round here," she told him. "But there's hundreds of them walkin' dead all holed up at the edge of the forest, run by some witches workin' for the Master of the Dead. We dunno what they're doin' here. There's lotsa firesprites up another coupl've miles, but they don't come near here and they sleep days. 'Round here there's just the usual snakes 'n' lizards 'n' stuff like that."

"How do you know about the sprites and coven and zombies if you never go far from this spot?" he asked, genuinely curious.

She shrugged. "Oh, we heard it through the great vines."

He let that one pass. Some things it was better not to know.

"Can you do me a favor, then? As one of you to another? Keep a watch out tonight for anything that might harm us and awaken me if it draws near before sunup?"

"Yeah, sure. But can't you wake up the young one, there? It's been a real long time for most of us."

He stiffened. "That young one's my son, and he's still not ready for the likes of you yet."

That seemed to amaze them. "Your kid," one breathed, almost in awe. "Ain't none of us ever had a kid. The only time one of us is born is when one of us dies, and ain't none of us ever died yet. Wow. . . ."

"Will you do it, then? And keep out of his sight if he wakes up?"

The leader sighed. "Oh, well, what the hell. Sure."

He bid them a good-night, then realized he was well away from the glade and it was still pitch dark. Something in him didn't want to admit to them he couldn't see out here, but what was that they'd said about having fairy sight if he really believed in it?

He let his mind go and stared into the darkness, and he found that it was oddly easy. How many times could he have used this, if only he'd known and believed in its existence? But he'd spent nights when his mind continually refused to admit what they had now told him was true, and now he knew.

The scene came alive. Not with normal sight, but truly *alive*, magically so. He was seeing not reflected light but the auras of a forest teeming with life. Each tree, each weed, had its own unique pattern. About ten feet from where he stood, two forms blazed brightly.

He walked confidently back and lay down beside them. Now that he knew the truth, it really wasn't that hard to deal with. If a nymph could walk off in his old barbarian body and become mortal, then he could eventually find a way to fix his own unique problem. In the meantime, use it, and try not to get killed or stabbed through the heart with iron, two things he was earnestly trying to avoid in any case. Don't fight it, *use* it.

In the midst of a dank rain forest, naked and undefended against all sorts of things that lurked, he had his best sleep in months.

When Ti awakened it was false dawn. The sun still hadn't come up, but there was some light from its reflections from over the horizon, and the forbidding scene around them was dimly glowing. It was sufficient to keep from breaking your neck, but it was kind of eerie, with wisps of ground fog about and a deathly silence.

She looked down at Joe. Why hadn't he awakened her? Irving didn't look as if he'd been up for hours, so Joe had simply decided to go to sleep. She didn't like the thought that they'd been undefended, without guards, through that night, but, on the other hand, they seemed to have lucked out. Still, it disturbed her.

I should have had the watch, all night if necessary. It was my duty to do so, and I have failed my master.

She caught herself with the thought and analyzed it. That wasn't a thought she'd have ever had before. Joe was husband, lover, equal, or just plain Joe, but never her "master." And yet, somehow, the thought, the *attitude* it represented, felt *right*. Intellectually, she still rebelled at the mind-set, but the mind-set remained stubbornly there, none the less

She went off a ways and relieved herself, then checked the horses, who all seemed well rested and even able to have munched on some of the vegetation. Joe's loincloths were still damp, but they would do. Likewise, the horse blankets and gear were drying out, but would need to get out of here and into full sunlight to get right. In places like this there was always the danger of jungle rot on clothing.

Irving's leather outfit wasn't in very good shape as it was, and she decided that it was time he stopped being the tough guy and suffering with it and maybe trying one of his dad's loincloths for a while. It would be oversized, but she could adjust it to protect his manly modesty.

The food was also not in good shape. She got a knife from Joe's pack and trimmed off some of the mold that was already creeping in, keeping what was edible, and laying it out on a blanket, but, although she was quite hungry, she ate none of it.

Slaves eat last.

It was something she'd known, of course, but she'd never thought of that with herself as the slave. Defiantly, she reached out and picked up the stump of a carrot, as if to show that she was still in charge of her life, but, somehow, she just couldn't bite into it.

So it had happened. After slowly building one step at a time over a period of months, she was now so thoroughly defined by the major Rules that all the minor ones just tumbled in at once, filling in the gaps.

She recalled an incident, forgotten until now, when she'd asked one of the maids at the palace if the girl, who was bright and intelligent, resented being a slave. "Oh, no, my lady," she had responded. "It is much like being a housewife, only you don't expect your husband to say thank you and, while you owe him your loyalty, you do not owe him fidelity. It all works out. There is nothing dishonorable about being a slave, and it is necessary work. I would certainly rather be living this way, in such a fine place, than as my mother did, living in a small place where meat was a luxury we rarely could afford and her dying of complications in the birth of her fifteenth child at age twenty-eight."

It was a sobering thought, particularly when thinking of all those women at the town wells and small cafes.

There were other compensations. She would much rather be out in the world and in adventurous circumstances than being cooped up in a satin prison. And Ruddygore had estimated the physical age of her body at possibly fifteen, certainly no older than sixteen, which meant she had lost more than a decade in physical aging. Physically, at least, she was closer in age to Irving than to Joe.

"There is nothing dishonorable about being a slave, and it is necessary work. . . ."

It would be hard, but that was the way she had to think, had to look at it. As she had told Irving, it wasn't a matter of liking or not liking it, it was a matter of *acceptance* and *adjustment*. The only alternative was to wage futile war against the reality and dishonor herself by doing it badly as a result.

She went over and quietly nuzzled Joe awake. He came to with a sweet smile, stretched, looked around, and saw at once all the work she'd done. "Impressive."

"You're my master now, remember," she said softly. "It's part of my job."

He looked at her strangely for a moment, then smiled. "That's the biggest turn-on statement I can think of."

At that moment, Irving stirred, spoiling the mood.

Joe sighed. "Well, it looks like the sun's coming up and we shouldn't have much trouble getting out of here this morning. You know, I had the oddest dream last night. . . ." He looked around at the still forest, and let his mind run free for a moment; somehow, in the larger stand nearby, he sensed friendly presences. *Or maybe not a dream,* he added to himself.

"I should have taken the watch," she said flatly. "That, too, is part of my job. If anything had happened to us last night it would have been my fault."

"No," he responded enigmatically, looking at the grove, "we were okay. Don't ask how, but we were well defended."

She wanted to get elaboration on that cryptic comment, but she sensed that she'd get no more out of him.

Irving arose in the same lethargic fashion characteristic of his father, and said, "Well, I guess we made it, huh?"

"Yeah, we made it," Joe replied. "Let's finish off what's still edible and hit the road."

They finished it off and tossed what was left into the brush, then packed up the last stuff to go. Ti had very little trouble talking Irving into the loincloth, and she managed to get it so that it stayed. It *did* look more like a giant diaper on him than the romantic he-man image it gave his father, but she didn't make the comment, and Joe seemed to understand and kept his mouth shut, too.

They mounted up, and Joe took one last look around, then focused on the small grove and mentally said, *"Thank you,"* in their direction. And from them, although it might have been the wind in the trees, he thought he heard, *"Any time."*

If it wasn't a dream, if it *was* real, then their information was reliable as well. The dangerous creatures of faërie were mostly of the night, at least around here, but if there was an outpost Sugasto's people maintained with zombies protecting it, they were a threat any time. He wouldn't feel reasonably secure until they passed the tollhouse at the edge of Grotom Wood.

He couldn't help thinking about his old enemy. "I wonder why Sugasto stopped?" he asked aloud. "Nobody was able to hold him off for long, he had an endless supply of new recruits from among his own victims, and he had enormous power."

Ti shrugged. "Possibly he had something more important to attend to first," she suggested. "Or, perhaps he was ill. Perhaps he still doesn't feel he's a match for Ruddygore. Who knows? It is enough for me that he *did* stop."

They came upon the old tollhouse, now a roofless stone ruin encrusted in moss, lichen, and creeping vines, looking like some sinister gateway to Hell, and almost immediately the country-side started to change its character and things brightened considerably. Now there were rolling hills and fields with farms and forests that looked more charming than threatening. To Joe, it felt like home.

By midmorning they reached Hotsphar, a small town built on a thermal region, with hot springs and hissing holes in the ground the locals used for everything from cooking to bathing. The idea of a hot bath in one of the small bathhouses was irresistible, particularly when it cost only a few coppers. They were running pretty low on money, but they no longer had that far to go.

They had the place almost to themselves. "The nearby wood still frightens many good folk in these troubled times," the proprietress explained. "And, of course, it's the off-season."

The bath in the crystal clear water of the hot springs was *wonderful*, and the thermal-heated sauna not only relaxed but did a nice job of drying out the clothing and blankets. Ti was methodical in getting them washed and even combing their hair. After, she was even able to borrow some scissors and thread and make a decent loincloth for Irving. She was quite pleased with her handiwork and the praise it invoked.

The change that had come over her was remarkable, Joe thought. She not only had completely stopped nagging and complaining about things, but she actually was doing a lot of stuff on her own initiative that, not long before, she would have thought beneath her. She was solicitous, cheerful, and even deferential. That last was hard to get used to, since it went a little against his grain, but he went with the flow. He felt rotten about feeling the way he did, but, the fact was, he liked it. He just kept telling himself that, if the situation had been reversed, with him the slave and she the mistress, she would have liked it, too.

They blew the last of their money on a hot meal and some basic snacklike provisions. It was now nearly certain that they would get to their destination by nightfall. Joe was anxious to see Ruddygore again, in any event. The master sorcerer would know the situation on Sugasto and maybe have a job or two for him. He also had another little matter to take up with him in private.

In the very late afternoon, they passed the trail to the upper ferry and reached the bridge over the Rossignol, a major tributary of the Dancing Gods, at Terdiera. Beyond, overlooking both the town and the confluence of the two rivers, could be seen the massive spires of Castle Terindell.

It was a troll bridge, of course, and Joe suddenly realized that they were flat broke, and that even the town was across the river from them.

Irving stared fearfully at the trolls, who seemed to be all big, glaring eyes and sharklike teeth, sort of like Muppets from Hell, but the lead troll recognized Joe.

"Ah! You are prepaid, barbarian, and your company," he growled. "Lord Ruddygore's cadet came down three days ago. Until you showed up, we thought we'd gotten a freebie."

They were delighted to hear it, but puzzled. "You say they came down and paid three days ago? But they didn't even know we were coming!"

"Obviously they did," the troll responded. "They know most everything hereabouts before anybody else does."

The town looked pretty much as he remembered it, but they didn't linger there, instead heading straight on up the one additional mile or so to the castle on the point. Joe couldn't help but think back many years ago to the first time he and Marge had come through these huge outer walls and gates and across the drawbridges. It seemed like a lifetime ago.

Like most castles of the region, Terindell was actually a series of buildings, one inside the other, and the interior contained a hollow, rectangular courtyard. Tiny brownies tended to the elaborate gardens that encircled the open area, and elf grooms appeared to help them down and take their horses.

Irving was awestruck by it all, gaping at all and sundry, but unable to say a word. They walked up to the main entrance as the sun set. Before they could knock, the huge wooden door opened, revealing a slender, dangerous-looking fairy dressed in a gray robe with golden tassels. He was nearly six feet tall, and there was something at once cold and menacing about him. That was the mark of the Imir, one of the few warrior races that the faërie had.

"Hello, Poquah," Joe greeted the creature.

"Jeez! Mister Spock!" Irving muttered under his breath. "What next?"

"You're late!" the Imir snapped. "It's about time you showed up!"

"I didn't know we had an appointment."

"Humans!" the Imir sniffed. "You probably still think you just got the idea to come here. You were *summoned*!"

"What's the rush?"

"Oh, nothing much," the Imir responded a bit sarcastically. "Only that the Dark Baron slipped our leash and is free once again and that, perhaps not coincidentally, Sugasto seems to be getting his act together once more."

Joe shook his head in wonder and returned a wry smile. "Back to normal," he sighed. "Nice to see you, too, Poquah."

CHAPTER 5

PLOTS GO WRONG, AS USUAL

*Anyone, whether hero or villain, human or fairy, whose life or death
would in any way change the course of destiny, shall always be
given a way out, no matter how certain the doom or absolute the
trap.*

—The Books of Rules, XXII, 102(b)

THROCKMORTON P. RUDDYGORE LOOKED HIS OLD SELF AND
none the worse for wear, almost out of place in his grand sorcerer's robes, which he favored in Husaquahr. Of course, he
also looked out of place in his characteristic formal wear on
Earth. Frankly, he looked as if he should be wearing a red suit
with white fur trim, for there was not one from Earth who met
him who didn't immediately think of him as the perfect, perhaps
the real Santa Claus.

"Joe! Tiana! And, oh yes, the young master Irving as well!
Welcome, welcome to my humble abode!"

Irving looked around the sumptuous great hall, with its ornate
gold on almost everything, its finely polished handcrafted fur-
niture, thick, plush rugs, and all the rest that shouted the height
of luxury, even back home, and sniggered a bit.

"Come, now. Have seats! Anywhere at all, please. How was
your vacation?"

Joe took one of the chairs and Tiana sat down cross-legged
on the floor to his left without even thinking about it.

"Restful, until the last week or so, "Joe told him. "Irving's
gotten pretty good on a horse and shows real potential. We had
a pretty rough trip until the last day, though. Short on money,
long on problems. It was worth it, I think, to get back into some

kind of trim, and, of course, to get to know my son a little bit more.''

The old sorcerer nodded. Irving had just sat down in the plushest, most comfortable chair he'd ever experienced in his whole life when the host said, ''But, come, come! I'm forgetting my manners. You must be starved after such a journey! Come, let us sup, and then we'll have time to talk!''

Irving was suddenly torn between leaving the most luxurious seat he'd ever sat in and the idea of real, decent food. It was no contest; food won. Besides, he thought, this joint is so big, if I don't follow them now, I may never find my way out.

They walked for what seemed like a mile, then entered a huge banquet hall, with a long table and plush red chairs and a kind of screened-off area where, it appeared, the food came from.

''We'll just eat in the small dining room tonight,'' Ruddygore said almost apologetically.

Showoff! Irving thought. But the old geezer really did have things to show off, he had to admit that. Now *this* was the way to live!

''Take any seat,'' Ruddygore told them. ''We don't stand on formality here most of the time.''

Joe took a seat to one side of the far end and Irving the other. Ruddygore went around to sit at the head, then noticed that Tiana was just standing there. ''Come, come, girl! Sit!''

She looked almost in tears. ''I—I *can't*. I just *can't*, that's all.''

The sorcerer got up and walked around to her and looked her over with a gaze so fixed and concentrated that it seemed as if he even looked inside her and inventoried the atoms in her structure.

''Oh, my! The Rules have been rather vicious to you since we came back, haven't they, my dear? Oh, my! I *must* be growing old and senile. That possibility simply never entered my head. Well, there are no slaves at Terindell—fairy folk work for peanuts and have a much lower overhead than humans. And I'll not have any guest in my house serving here. Tell you what— you go into the kitchen and eat what you like and gossip with the help, and we'll talk together, you and I, privately later. Okay?''

She nodded, looked at Joe, who seemed a little confused, but shrugged, and she walked back behind the screen and presumably into the kitchen.

''What's *that* about?'' Joe asked him. ''We all ate at the cafes together.''

Ruddygore took his seat and nodded. ''True, but that's a different situation. Those sorts of places are within her allowable social range. In this setting, she could serve us, but she could not *join* us. How long has she been fixed in this level?''

''A couple of days. Oh, it's been little changes all along, but this way, just maybe two, three days tops.''

''I thought as much. She's going to have a tough time because she's smart and strong-willed and used to equality, at the very least. I've seen minds snap under that sort of strain.''

''Can't you unslave her?'' Irving asked him. ''I mean, you're a superpowerful wizard, right?''

''True, young sir, but I am bound by the Rules just as much as she is. She may not like it, but she understands that as well. The only two ways I know would be to use the most powerful of djinn magicks, which I will not do unless there is no alternative, so dangerous is it, or, alternatively, to switch her soul to another body with different Rules.''

''You can do that?''

''No, that's one outside my knowledge. I could put one *into* an empty vessel—that's simple. It's getting it out, and maintaining the empty vessel, that's the problem. It's one that Sugasto somehow solved, or probably either appropriated or got from Baron Boquillas.''

''I keep hearin' 'bout this bad dude the Baron. What's his problem?'' the boy asked.

''He's a throwback. The most brilliant mathemagical mind in ten thousand years. There's probably not a single thing we can imagine that he couldn't figure out how to do if he wanted to do so.''

''Yeah? So how come you beat him, then?''

Ruddygore sighed. ''The Baron suffers from several flaws

without which he would have been invincible. For one thing, he suffers from an admirable lack of imagination. He's predictable to a degree, and his mind works in narrow channels. That doesn't mean he doesn't come up with highly innovative new ways to cause trouble—that television preacher business he tried on Earth was highly creative—but he is obsessed only with Earthly power over others. He is unshakable in his belief that out of Hell can come all of the solutions to all of the problems of the universe. He was taken in by that idea, just as many others were and continue to be taken in by it, and because he knows he is brilliant, he is incapable of believing that he can be taken in. It's a nasty little mental circle common to megalomaniacs."

"And you *lost* him when you had him?"

Ruddygore sighed. "Alas, yes. I should have known better, but after what happened back on Earth when he was loosed there, essentially powerless himself, I didn't dare allow him to remain there again."

"Then why not just kill him? I mean, he kills lots of folks, don't he?"

Ruddygore nodded. "The Rules again. They gave him his chance, his way out, by seducing me with the idea that I could use and control him to get at Sugasto. It's an arbitrary Rule, but it's not one we can hate, either. Your father's escaped death more than once because of the same regulation." There was a commotion behind him, and he paused and brightened. "Ah, but I think the food has arrived! Business and hard thinking can wait until we've done."

And arrive it did. Short, plump fairies who looked like a cross between the Munchkins and the Pillsbury Doughboy began marching out with platter after platter, course after course. It was an impeccably cooked feast for twelve, and even after Joe and Irv had eaten their fill and Ruddygore had eaten six times theirs, there was plenty left over.

And when they'd protested over and over that they couldn't handle another thing, Ruddygore signaled the end to it. Finally he got up and said, "Joe, why don't you take Irving down and show him around? I suspect he'd enjoy the games room in particular. We'll speak in a little while."

Joe nodded, glad to have an excuse to walk some of this off and knowing already that he was going to regret this overindulgence later, but knowing, too, that it was worth it.

Ruddygore watched them go, then gave a signal. An elf in household livery appeared almost instantly.

"Has the girl finished eating?"

"Yes, sir. She ate pretty good."

"Very well. Give me five minutes and bring her to my study."

The elf bowed and vanished.

Ruddygore's study was smaller than the great halls, but it was no tiny room. It couldn't be, since, among other things, it had to hold the complete Books of Rules. They rose there, from floor to ceiling, in custom-made, built-in bookcases, covering every wall and allowing only for the door. A sturdy ladder on rails that would hold even the sorcerer's great bulk went completely around the place. Ruddygore studied the seemingly identical thick, red-bound volumes for a moment, then pulled the ladder around, got up to one particular shelf, and pulled down a volume. He checked to see that it was the right one, then went over to his desk, fished around in a crowded drawer, and came up with a small case from which he removed a brilliant lavender jewel whose one outstanding feature was that it was totally flat on one side. He placed the jewel on the book, his hand on both, and concentrated.

It was a convenient gimmick for looking up things in a hurry or impressing others that you knew everything in all those books. For a while, perhaps a couple of hours unless he used it again, he *did* know every single word in that one book. It would fade, of course, but he didn't want to retain it. An intelligent man didn't know everything, he simply knew how to look everything up quickly and efficiently.

There was a knock at the door, and he said, "Come in." The door opened, and Tiana walked in, hesitantly. The elf closed the door from the outside, leaving them alone.

Ruddygore settled back in his chair and she stood in front of his desk. He didn't offer her a seat because he knew, particularly now, that she could not do so alone in his presence.

"I *am* really sorry," he began. "I was preoccupied. I'd spent all that time with the djinn, which is an unnerving experience for anyone, then the quick hustle out, and all those loose ends to attend to—I should have thought to safeguard you before you returned.''

''My lord, it is not anyone's fault but mine,'' she responded. ''My ego blinded me. Even so, with this build I could hardly have been an Amazon warrior. Joe belongs out and free to do what he does best. Given this body, there is nothing much else I could have become when I chose to go with him.''

''But you still had the romantic view of it all, didn't you? It is only now, when all the strings are finally tied, that you realize all the implications of it, and it is very hard on you.''

''Yes, my lord. Very hard.''

''You do know why the system exists here. I know you do. I ran into an Earth phrase that catches the very essence of life: 'There is no such thing as a free meal.' Somebody always pays. You live in a hot climate, you have bugs upon bugs and tropical diseases. You live in a house and you have high costs. Live in a flat and you have horrible and noisy neighbors. Every positive has negatives. To be in the upper classes means to be virtual prisoners, unable to see and do anything you really wish, dressing thus and so, attending this and so, and having a totally regulated life. If everyone were rich and nobody had to work, there'd soon be no one to maintain the roads, guard the wealth, build the buildings and tear them down, cook the food, grow and crush and age the wine, and so on. Money is meaningless in itself. It gains its meaning from the blood, sweat, and toil, the labor, materials, services, and skills that it took to get us things.''

''Yes, my lord. I understand this.''

''Earth has a dynamic system, ours is relatively static. The Rules and the laws under them guarantee inequality without much change, but we accept it as the price for the meal. Here, no one is involuntarily unemployed or homeless against his or her will. Here the system provides the basics to everyone, and in the process we have rid ourselves of many of the social tensions, the hatreds, prejudices, and fears, that bring out the worst in Earth society. That was built-in the moment the Founders decided upon the supremacy of magic over technology. Tell me—did you think slavery was so bad, so evil, when you were on the other side of it?''

"In truth I did not, my lord. Not really." *It is not dishonor-able. . . .* "But also, in truth, I did not wish ever to become one."

"Well you are and you will probably remain one. In a sense, you're lucky. Your master is your husband, if not in law, then in fact; and, since you both still bear the infection of the were, you at least get to be somebody and something else every full moon. You may be the only slave who gets three days off a month."

"I know," she said quickly. "But it is the other twenty-seven days that I dread."

"It's still driving you nuts."

"Yes. Some of it, anyway. The fact that I could not even eat a meal with all of you, or that he is no longer my husband nor I his wife. Even the common women have some sort of lives of their own. We met one with a cafe, and there are others who do other things, even help plant the fields. A slave, on the other hand, exists only to serve a master. It is my sole activity and interest. To serve him. When he was short of money, I did not hesitate to sneak away and sell my body to two crude and filthy men I chanced upon. On my own—but to serve him. And not *just* him. It was all I could do to keep from jumping up and doing the dishes in the kitchen."

"That's what a slave does. It's not like slaves of war or con-quest. I could, however, make it easier on you. Easier for you to adjust to and accept this."

"Yes, my lord, but I—I don't know. If that were to happen, the last of me would be gone, like the last of him finally went when he was the nymph. And I fear, too, the loss of whatever love or affection he still feels for me."

"Oh, it wouldn't be like that. You'd still be you. You just wouldn't be in as much agony. It would be a little thing to help you and to help him. If he loves you now, it wouldn't change. But it might make it easier on him, too. He feels for your situ-ation. I see that he does. And the both of you may have to go into some danger ahead. If that happens, I want you unhesitatingly at his side.''

He got up and came around the desk and stood in front of her. His enormity made her seem and feel even smaller than she was.

''Are you willing?''

''I—I guess so. We've always trusted you.''

''Do so now. Just clear your mind, relax, and do not resist me.'' He waited a moment, then put his huge hand on her forehead and the top of her head. She swayed, then he let go and she caught her balance, blinked, and frowned. ''I—I do not feel any different.''

''You won't,'' he told her. ''But you'll sleep better and worry less. Now go, and my man will show you where your quarters are. You can get unpacked and get things ready. We'll have a busy time coming up.''

She bent a knee and bowed slightly. ''Thank you, my lord.''

The door opened, although he hadn't given a signal, and the elf in livery was there to take her away. ''See that the boy is kept amused and bring up the mercenary,'' he called to the elf, who nodded and shut the door.

He still felt badly doing it, but he'd known that someday this was coming. It was too bad, really, but it couldn't be helped. He couldn't avoid wondering if he shouldn't have just gone the whole way with her. Well, he'd have to sleep on that.

By the time she reached the room, she wouldn't even remember that they'd ever spoken in here. What he'd done was simply to use his speed-learned knowledge of the Rules on slaves to analyze those that bound her, then did a process known as backweaving to the magical trade. She would still be much the same, but now her perspective would be different; the slave reaction would feel the normal and natural one to her, the Tiana perspective more abstract.

Having such power—and much more than this mere trifle—always bothered him, and he wanted to make certain that it *always* bothered him. He had become an adept and worked as hard and as long as he could to become the best in his trade because he had seen such power used for evil or, worse, for its own sake. Only by becoming the best could he protect himself. Those who had not the blood and the talent for it he felt a special responsibility toward, viewing the world as filled with potential victims. No one, not Sugasto, not Boquillas, was ever going to best him at this game. Never. Sugasto was powerful, but impatient, unwilling to take the time to learn the nuances, the little tricks of the trade that made one sorcerer that hairs-breadth better than the others. Boquillas had a mind he could not hope to match, but the Baron was like the mathematician who memorized every possible combination of cards in a poker hand and played by strictly mathematical rules. Put him in a game with amateurs and decent players and he won every time. But put him in a game with a master of psychology and bluff who didn't even *care* what cards he was dealt, and Boquillas could always be taken to the cleaners.

There was a knock, the door opened once again, and now Joe was admitted.

"Have a seat, Joe," he invited. "Cigar? Chocolate bonbons?" The sorcerer grinned. "My secret ultimate vice."

"That's okay. I'm still digesting dinner. Now what's this about losing the Baron?"

"Well, you remember that we returned to the City-States, since I had business to take care of there and you wanted to get away. At the time, the Baron was in the body of Mahalo McMahon and thought it the perfect disguise. I had her—or him—or whatever under my spell, and I wanted to give Boquillas enough leash to lead me to Sugasto without slipping away. It didn't happen. The Baron was kidnapped off the streets in broad daylight by men none of my people had ever seen before, and almost immediately my psychic link was broken. That meant somebody with a good deal of power made the snatch, and that meant they knew who was in that body."

"Sugasto?"

"Possibly. Possibly not. It's uncertain whether the Baron would work *under* Sugasto. With, yes. And by my own doing Boquillas had enough protections to be able to wriggle out of most binding spells of others, anyway. It's even possible he had those spells to ward off even me cast upon him before we ever got to Earth. He was always quite cautious.''

"Who, then?''

"Hard to say. Boquillas took his instructions from the demons of Hell themselves, and they cannot be underestimated, no matter what their alleged limitations in the here and now. Hell borders upon all points in space-time simultaneously, so they almost certainly knew what went on back on Earth. It wouldn't take more than a demonic message to a competent coven to pull this off. In fact, I could *almost* swear that he pulled this off himself.''

"I thought you said it was impossible for him to get his powers back!''

"It is. Everything I've ever been taught says so. But I just can't shake the feeling that, somehow, he found some sort of opening to regain at least *some* power. I've been spending as much time as I can spare poring over the Rules, trying to find some way for it to be possible. It's not really my intellect speaking, I admit, but gut instinct, combined with the knowledge that, if there *is* a loophole, however minute it may be, somewhere in this vast assemblage of verbiage, Boquillas would find it.''

"That's all we need. And what about Sugasto? He was going great guns when we left, then he's suddenly well back of where he was before.''

"Sugasto was part of an overall plan directed from Hell to take over both Earth and Husaquahr simultaneously, forcing Armageddon. When we thwarted the Baron, somebody, probably some dumb demon, let it slip. That is hardly what Sugasto wishes. He wants to rule all Husaquahr and, instead, he finds he's being used to end the world. He put on the brakes, severed his direct ties with the Underworld, pulled back, retrenched, and he's been trying since to figure out what to do next. I believe he was unnerved. Of course, Hell didn't really want Armageddon yet, either. It was the plot of some ambitious lower demons, remember, to impress the boss. One wonders where rebels against Hell are sent? Oh, well.''

"So it's a loss of nerve?''

"More likely a change of tactics. Now he's been trying to do it with alliances and promises, Boquillas style. He's got some interested parties, but not enough. The others who might join with him wish first to see a demonstration that he or he and others can deal with *me*. Until then, he's stalled, but that's not good enough. He has more than twenty million people under his control. That cannot, *must* not, be a permanent condition.''

"*That* I go along with."

"And, of course, I have my own nightmares. What if Boquillas *does* somehow strike a bargain with Sugasto? *That* might be the catalyst to drive those malcontented forces to him. With Sugasto's powers and Boquillas' knowledge, it might even be enough to finish me. The last time I faced down the Baron it was a near thing. With the two of them combined in power and with their armies and lands, the Council would not hesitate to go over to them again as well just to protect their own turf, for all the good it would do them with Esmilio *or* Sugasto calling the shots.''

"So what can I do about it?''

"I need intelligence. I need to know what it's like comfortably behind Sugasto's boundaries. What he's doing. What the rumors are. What foreign faces might be about.''

"Surely Marquewood, High Pothique, and Leander, not to mention the others, have people in there.''

"Indeed they do. And if you were still running the empire, I might even trust what some of them are giving me.''

"Surely Marquewood is dependable!''

"Indeed? My native land is also our greatest danger and might well fall soon without a single act of war unless something can be done. Think of *that*!''

"Come again?''

"When you and Tiana ruled, you were deities. They made you demigods and built statues to you all over, even in other lands. You were literally *worshiped*.''

"Yeah, I know. It was embarrassing as hell.''

"Well, did you think that stopped when you left? You went back to Heaven, right? But what would be the effect if you both reappeared?''

"Hey! Hold it! You said both our bodies were dead!''

"In Sugasto's hands, the term is meaningless. We feared at the time that he might have gotten them. He removed the souls of the mermaid and the nymph, probably bottling them up somewhere, and he used his spell to keep the bodies alive. I have reason to believe that those bodies are about to be reanimated with the souls of henchmen fanatically loyal to Sugasto. Think of what would happen if both of you—the old pair—suddenly descended into the main square of the capital. They would again be the divine rulers of the land and even gain the loyalty of those outside the old empire who joined the cult. And Sugasto would rule them. The rest of High Pothique, then Leander, would be child's play to knock over. The City-States would have to knuckle under or face economic ruin and siege. In one grand gesture, he would control the River of Dancing Gods from the source to its mouth, and all its primary tributaries. The one who did that, which no one has ever done, would be considered truly divine, a living god, by the entire continent. You know that."

It was so damned simple. "We really blew it, didn't we?"

"Well, things sort of grew of their own accord, remember, far beyond our own plans."

Joe thought a moment. "So what do you want me to do?"

"Just producing the animated bodies wouldn't do. It might impress the boondocks, but it certainly wouldn't be accepted as the two of you in the palace and capital where they knew you so well. They're going to have to walk like you, talk like you, act like you in every way. They're going to have to know your Earth background, Tiana's education, likes, dislikes, and do it flawlessly. There is now in Marquewood intensive research into just that sort of thing. But they can't absorb it by magic, either. Any spells on your bodies would be immediately detected. By definition, demigods can't have binding spells. We've got some time while they learn all there is to learn and then rehearse, rehearse, rehearse until they are perfect. If they are not believed and accepted, they'll be converted to figureheads and be unable to make the key changes needed."

"You know where they are?"

"The area, yes. It's deep inside enemy territory, Joe, as it would be, and quite secluded. Far up in the Cold Wastes of Hypboreya, where Sugasto goes to plot."

"But if you know this, why not use the Lamp of Lakash? Irving's never used it. He's safe."

"Well, first, because it wouldn't work in this matter."

"Why not?"

"Remember, its power is localized, which is why we can't stop a war or solve all the world's problems with the damned thing. To use the Lamp against those bodies we would have to take the Lamp close enough to them for it to work. And I am not about to risk getting the Lamp into Sugasto's hands! Never! Even if I could."

"What's that mean?"

"It means I have become so fearful of it getting into the wrong hands since it was once stolen that it is now put even beyond *my* reach."

Joe sighed. "I see. But, then—what exactly are you proposing?"

"Assassination. Find those bodies and kill them. Destroy them utterly so that they can never again be resurrected or used in this fashion, even on a local level."

"Ruddygore—that body of me was your creation. I don't give a damn about it. But you're asking me to kill Tiana's body, too."

"Not just kill. Utterly destroy. Burning, acid, that sort of thing."

"That's the natural body of the woman I married. The woman whose mind and soul is now trapped in the body and mind-set of a slave."

"I know. But unless you can find out how in the hell they swap minds and souls so effortlessly and have somebody there to do it, it doesn't do anybody any damned good anyway. But, alive, it can do horrible damage."

Joe thought about it. He was uneasy enough at anybody else doing it, but he didn't want this job at all. "Doesn't it seem stupid to send up the only guy they can get all the details from to make their Joe real?"

"Ordinarily, yes, but I suspect you're going to be more of a target here than in there. Also, you have certain advantages.

There are few guns here, and no silver bullets, to my knowledge. As a were, without silver in your bloodstream, you're essentially immortal. That's a rather good edge in a fight. You're resourceful, and you're used to working in the enemy backfield. As a barbarian with a face as yet unknown to the enemy, you won't be out of place in a militaristic state girding for conquest. And, frankly, you above all others have at least some stake in saving your adopted country from, essentially, yourself."

"What about Tiana?"

"That's up to you. She has many of the same advantages as you. She's still tough, she's as smart as she ever was—don't ever forget that!—and she'll do her duty. I think, in fact, she above all should have the right to be there."

"Have you told her yet? I assume you talked to her."

"I did, I didn't tell her, and she won't remember we talked."

Joe started. "What did you do to her?"

"Nothing much, I assure you. She is the way she is for the same reason that you became fully and completely Joey the wood nymph, not due to my sorcery. I gave her some protections. She will no longer answer to Tiana. That's an essential one, I think. She will answer to Ti, or any other name you want to give her, but if you call 'Tiana,' she will not respond. Since no one but Boquillas knows what the two of you now look like, it is a safety precaution. I might suggest a total name change if you can keep it straight. You, too, at least temporarily."

"It's her body, damn it! Why didn't you tell her of this, or at the same time as me?"

"Because she would be incapable of making an honest decision on it, and because slaves do not discuss matters of import with their betters. They tune them out. *You* tell her, as master to slave, but she cannot be here as a coequal, even in this."

"If I take her, and they capture us both, they'll have everything they need," he pointed out.

"That is not exactly true. She has a very strong memory of a slave she once knew, the daughter of a dirt poor serf who wound up a palace maid. I built on the memory, fusing it with a bit of imagination and other histories I know to give her a complete background from birth to now. She's protected better than you in some ways.''

"I still don't like it.''

"Tell me true—do you still love her?''

"I—sort of. Not in the way I used to. I know that sounds terrible, but it hasn't been quite the same since, well, she went from being a mermaid to this current body. But I *do* care for and about her, a lot.''

"Don't blame yourself for that. Tiana did it when she used the Lamp to wish you back.''

"Huh?''

"The mermaid's spell. Men who make love to mermaids always consider it to be the greatest emotional and sexual experience they ever had. When she wished you back, when she was a mermaid, she wished you'd return as the perfect mermaid lover and make love to her. She thought it would insure your fidelity. It did—but no longer to her.''

"Well I'll be damned!'' Joe breathed. "And I been thinking I was a dirty skunk!''

"Does that make it easier?''

"It does and it doesn't. Damn, Ruddygore! This means I can never really be totally satisfied by any woman ever again!''

"Everything has its price.''

"Easy for you to say! And while I'm at it, I've got another problem along those lines.'' Quickly he told the sorcerer about his encounter with the wood nymphs.

"I'm afraid it's true,'' the sorcerer told him. "There didn't seem much point in bringing it up, since at the time I could do nothing about it. When I had Boquillas/Mahalo under my spell I tried to get the mechanism, but he had cleverly laid the same sort of mental traps in himself as I use. The moment I demanded it, the formula and its concepts erased. Dacaro wasn't much more help. He performed them, sometimes, but it was far too complex for him to understand, let alone remember. He only said that it was strikingly different every single time, as if each switch required its own independent spell. I've worked and worked on it and I can't understand how it's even possible.''

"So I've got to watch out for silver *and* iron.''

"No, it's more complex than that. Iron is only a threat if it kills at the same time both body and soul. Silver is fatal to the body; it will release the soul which will form its husk. *Then* you would be vulnerable to iron alone. The were curse goes when the body goes. In effect, the odds are that you're as close to unkillable as anything short of angel or demon."

"Great. So I'm an almost immortal guy who can never be lucky in love again, but if I *do* get potted with silver or burned to a crisp, I become a wood nymph."

"That's pretty much it," Ruddygore admitted. "I wouldn't take it all that hard. Fairies are immune from the Lamp. You knew that. If we'd brought you and the Lamp together early enough, we might have stopped it before your soul completely transformed, but by the time we did, it was already totally changed, and, of course, we also did it from a slight distance. The Lamp was faced with a dilemma and it did what it could. It formed the old 'you' as modified by Tiana's wish around the fairy core."

"Isn't there any way to unmodify it?"

"Fairy flesh? I sincerely doubt it. Even if your soul was removed by whatever trick Sugasto uses, it would still be fairy. But is it so horrible? Marge seems to enjoy it."

"Marge is not a brainless bimbo living in a tree!"

"Well, I can't do much about the tree, or the bimbo part whatever that is, but Tiana's wish at least insured that you won't turn brainless. She also wished your mind restored with all of its memories. The Lamp's magic supercedes the Rules of Husaquahr. That is why it is so dangerous."

"Wait a second. You're saying that even if my body were destroyed, I'd still have my memories, who I was and what I was, and be as smart as I ever was?"

"I guarantee it. In fact, even now, you're a very rare breed indeed. You're a hybrid. Your invocation of fairy sight shows that. The wood nymph is one of the most common creatures of faërie, and all will consider you one of them, since they see the inside first. If you really reach, you've probably got all the powers a wood nymph has, although there are, admittedly, fewer of those than with some races and the majority of those powers I'm sure you'd rather not invoke. Still, you should never reject something in the arsenal."

Joe sighed. "Yeah, and the only one I can think of that might be useful isn't gonna be much good in the Cold Wastes. No trees."

"You'll do it, then?"

He looked at Ruddygore. "All right. Against all my instincts and better judgment, I'll try. But I have a very bad feeling about this one, and the last one was something of a disaster. Most of all, I hate leaving Irving, but he's not ready by a long shot to get into this sort of thing and, in a bad situation, he'd be a club over my head."

"I agree. But if he's in Gorodo's capable hands and learning how to be as great a fighter as his father, I think he'll be okay."

"Gorodo! Oh, he'll *love* Gorodo! On that son of a bitch's final exam, I got turned into a horse!"

"Oh, that Circe's a setup. Didn't you ever figure that out? *Everybody* winds up a horse or cow or pig or something. If you can't face that kind of problem and still make it back, then you're not going to make it in this world as a mercenary, are you?"

"Well I'd be damned!"

"Not before Judgment Day, if you're cautious and lucky."

Joe got up to leave, then hesitated. "What about Macore? I could use a master thief on this kind of job."

Ruddygore sighed. "I'm afraid he's gone mad, and I'm not certain *where* he is now. Again, fallout from that last unpleasantness. It started that first night, when he was exposed for the first time to that infernal cable television and wound up watching one hundred and twenty-two consecutive episodes of *Gilligan's Island*."

Joe chuckled. "I remember."

"If there's a better argument for keeping technology out of Husaquahr, this is it. On the way back, he bought, or more likely stole, a battery-powered television, a battery videocassette player, and, somehow, he got all of the hundreds of episodes of that infernal show. Naturally, being from here, he never really understood about batteries, and it didn't take long for the batteries to run down. He was frantic! He offered all and sundry

anything, slavery for life, any theft of anything, you name it—
anything—for a battery recharge. *I* could have done it, of course,
but I thought that, if it seemed impossible, he'd eventually give
it up! Instead, he set out on a quest for someone, anyone, who
could put more 'magic energy' into his batteries. When he was
asked where he was going, he responded . . ." Ruddygore
coughed apologetically. "He said he was going on a three-hour
tour . . ."

Ti was very pleased with the way she had unpacked and laid
out the room, although, truth to tell, there wasn't much to un-
pack. Well, traveling light made for easy work, and she never
minded that.

She wanted to do her exercises, but she wasn't certain if she
should. She'd been upset about something, although she wasn't
sure what—oh, yes, they wouldn't let her clean up in the
kitchen—and then that elf came to take her to the room and she
had some kind of dizzy spell. Probably due to overeating that
rich food after so long on short rations. It really screwed up the
system. Well, she'd skip it one more day. After sleeping a night
in a damp forest on wood chips, she felt as if she hadn't slept at
all.

She went over and stared out the window. It was dark, but
there were torches all along the outer wall reflecting eerily on
the river below. It was kind of pretty, really. She imagined herself dancing along that wall, beneath those torches. It would be
kind of neat to do it. She still felt a bit confused, almost as if
she were two people, one Ti the slave girl that she felt was her
true self, the other the grander figure of some other time and
place and world, which she remembered but somehow could no
longer quite comprehend.

Joe came in, looking tired and oddly bothered, and she said,
"Is there anything I can get you, Master?"

He started to tell her *never* to call him "Master," always
"Joe," then stopped. Even though it made him feel that he was
trapped in an old episode of *I Dream of Jeannie* as much as
Macore was hung up on *Gilligan's Island*, it was the proper slave
response here. If he was going to be using an alias in enemy

country, and if she was what she now was, it was far better if she *did* call him "Master" and went through the rest of the rigmarole as well.

Instead he said, "Yeah, Ti, it's fine. Come, sit here. I have to talk some important things over with you."

She came over and sat on the rug at his feet, looking up at him.

Briefly, but spelling out as much of the implications as he could, he told her the situation with their old bodies, Sugasto, and what Ruddygore was proposing. She listened attentively, but couldn't conceal from her face that she didn't like what she was hearing very much at all.

"Any comments?" he prompted. "Speak freely and honestly. It's your old body and your neck."

"My neck belongs to you," she noted, "along with the rest of me. But I cannot say that the news that my old self still lives does not fill me with longing, and the idea that we are to destroy it, well, it is *very* hard. When I thought it dead, that was that, but to find that it is alive, and that we are to *kill* it . . . If it lives, there is always *some* hope. If it dies, then I am a slave forever."

"I know. The odds are we won't get the chance anyway. We're taking a journey through lands we don't know, held by people we *do* know and who hate us as much as we hate them, toward a goal we really don't want to reach, and even if we do would most likely put us in the hands of our worst enemies." He paused. "You do not have to go, you know. I know you're not supposed to make big decisions for yourself, but this is one you *must* make. You can remain here, in service of Castle Terindell, and look after Irving for me."

"But you are going, regardless?"

"It was put to me in Ruddygore's usual democratic fashion, which is basically, 'You don't have to do this, it's your choice, but, remember, if you don't, evil will win, millions will die, and it'll be all your fault.' Yes, I have to go."

"Then I go."

"You're sure?"

She looked up at him. "If you go, and never return, then all of this was for nothing. If you go, and fail because I was not there when you needed me, it will be even worse. Perhaps this is why destiny has bound me to you. In the past, sometime, you have needed me before in such matters.''

"We'll probably be killed. Or worse, caught by Sugasto.''

"Then we go opposing evil, and that has meaning. And we might just beat them, as before, which would make everything worth it.''

There was more of the old Tiana beneath this servile veneer than he'd thought or feared. It made him feel better.

"Okay, then. It means starting out again in just a couple of days. We have a long journey, and the clock is running, and we don't know how long the clock runs.''

"This Sugasto is a coward at heart or he would not have stopped his war,'' she noted. "There are only two bodies tha' will do. He will not risk them until he is very, very sure o' them.''

"Good point,'' he agreed. He looked over near the window. "What's that on the floor?''

"A straw mat,'' she responded. "It is for me to sleep on.''

"Bullshit! Blow out that oil lamp and come sleep in this big featherbed with me! Who knows when we'll get the chance to be this luxurious again?''

She grinned happily and blew out the light.

Joe was walking across the great hall on his way outside when a firm soprano voice suddenly said, in English, in a solid West Texas accent, "Hi, sailor! New in town? Want to have a good time?''

He stopped dead, turned, and there, sitting on a fur-covered stool, was a creature of faërie. She was small, perhaps a bit over four feet in height, and quite sexy; almost a deep red variation of a nymph, to whom her sort were closely related, but with big, varicolored wings that seemed to catch any light and throw back a beauteous, changing, yet butterflylike appearance.

"*Marge!*'' he shouted, and she ran to him and gave him a big hug. He hesitated to return it for a moment because of the wings, but she said, playfully, "You ought to know by now that these wings can't be damaged by hugs!''

"What are *you* doing here?" he asked her, happy enough to see her in any event. "Did Ruddygore send for you?"

"No, he doesn't have to. I'm kind of tuned in to you folks and I just sort of know when things are wrong and trouble's brewing, and that always brings me like a wildcatter to oil. So, how are you?"

"Not good," he replied honestly. "Everything's going the wrong way, as usual."

"Nasty job? I assume the Baron slipped the noose."

"How'd you know that?"

"I've just been around here long enough now to figure things like that out. The moment they brought that bastard back here I knew we'd eventually be in for it."

"Well, that's part of it, but not the main job. And there are—well, complications."

"C'mon. Tell Auntie Marge about them. She's a very good confessor."

Marge was a changeling, one of those very rare individuals who arrived in this world with just some long-unsuspected single gene or trace of ancient faërie in her that caused the Rules to change her outright to her ancestral race. A former English teacher in Texas who'd lost her job and wound up a battered wife, she'd been running away and contemplating suicide when Joe had picked her up as a hitchhiker on a lonely stretch of West Texas highway just before being picked up himself by Ruddygore. She had, in effect, unknowingly hitched a ride to Husaquahr, where she'd turned into what she was now: a Kauri, a flying fairy race with a rather unique function.

Like almost all members of the nymph family, the Kauri were natural, near compulsive seductresses, but, unlike most of the rest, who had some role in the management of one or another aspect of nature, the Kauri "weeded people" as they called it. Natural empaths, they could sense and were attracted to deep depression and other black moods in others, and, through seduction, they could take on and remove those heavy emotional loads, converting the energy into food. Because they had to absorb whatever came along, they tended to be the most intelligent of the nymph family, so Marge, in fact, had lost none of her memory or IQ; because part of their talents came in a sort of hypnotic hold over mortals, they could seem to look like any female the subject desired, so Marge had lost none of her personality and cunning. Like all nymphs, however, they were passive by nature, and rarely even able to defend themselves against an attack, although Marge had managed it, briefly, on one or two occasions. When you're being grabbed by a rotting corpse, even instinct can sometimes be overcome.

And, alone among the nymph family, they could fly.

Joe told her about Ti, and what they had been asked to do.

She whistled. "Wow! That's as mean a kick as this world's thrown yet."

"It's like a pact with the devil, though," he noted. "Don't destroy the body and she's still a slave but Sugasto wins. Destroy the body, and she's lower than nothing forever. They're not going to pull any more soul snatches with her even if they find out about her; being as she is would suit them just fine."

"There's still more, though, isn't there? I can tell, remember. Your emotions are an open book here."

"All right," he sighed. "You alone would understand *my* problem. But I don't want anyone else knowing, not even Ti."

"My race always keeps its secrets."

"Use your fairy sight. Look inside me, down to my soul, and look very hard for something unusual."

"I can no more see a human soul than you can."

"That's what I mean. Look and don't just see what you expect to see."

She looked, and, for a moment, frowned, then saw it and gave a slight gasp. "You went fairy! I'll be damned! Even the Lamp can't change a fairy soul!"

He nodded. "So you have the package. Mum on that last part. Not only is it damned embarrassing to me, considering, but I don't want any enemy finding it out and getting ideas. Silver, the right sorcery, and burning could do it. And," he added hesitantly, "I particularly don't want Irving to ever know. I just don't think he could handle it."

Marge sighed. "Man, you're taking so much baggage on this trip you're half whipped before you start! It's a good thing I showed up when I did. No *wonder* you've been sending out those distress vibes!''

"Where we're going to wind up it's pretty cold,'' he warned her. "You sure you're up to that? You've never been in that kind of weather before.''

She shrugged. "We're a hot race; plenty of warmth to spare. Just keep that dwarf-forged steel sword of yours away and I'll be fine.''

"You really don't have to go just for us, you know.''

"For you? Don't forget, I'm the one who had that zombie horde sicced on me, and had to ignore that bastard's sniggering laugh. It seems like we're gonna have to endure that damned Baron to Judgment, but maybe we can send Sugasto straight to Hell!''

"Glad to have you as always. All we lack is Macore, but he's off somewhere searching for *Gilligan's Island.*''

"Oh, no! I always used to warn my students that TV could rot innocent minds, but I never really thought it went *that* far!'' She paused. "Where's Ti now?''

"In Terdiera with one of Santa's elves getting together initial supplies and such for the trip. It's going to be a long journey and much of it could be ugly. We don't know what a Sugasto administration might be like, but I can guess.''

She nodded. "We've heard all sorts of rumors. A lot of *bad* fairy folk have gravitated to him, not to mention people, and he's got a near lock on the dwarf kings, being able to blockade their trade if they don't play ball with him, as well as gnomes, trolls, you name it. And, of course, he's got two-thirds of the witches and warlocks in Creation with him and who knows how many overambitious magicians with real or imagined grudges. When a land comes under the control of evil here, it even takes on an evil life of its own. It's in the Rules, I think. This won't be any picnic, and you're the only sword arm we've got.''

"Don't you think I know it,'' he told her. "Come on—I'm going to introduce Irving to Gorodo.''

"Oh, joy. He'll just *love* that,'' she responded, following him out.

Love, joy, awe, and all the other such descriptives did not

begin to describe Irving's first reaction to Gorodo. Abject terror, perhaps, was closest.

For one thing, someone who is nine feet tall, about five hundred pounds of pure muscle, and also has nine-inch fangs and a body covered with blue fur wasn't exactly anybody's idea of a teddy bear.

Joe was never sure just what Gorodo *was*; a member of the troll family, most likely, but in all his travels he'd never seen another like him. There were all sorts of stories about Ruddygore's Master Armorer, most contradictory, all totally unbelievable, and all admitted to by the huge creature, but he remained the meanest, solidest enigma in Marquewood.

A long, taloned finger pointed at Joe. "You've really let yourself go to seed since I last had you," the creature rumbled in a voice so deep it seemed to shake the ground. "You oughta let me get you back in *real* shape."

Irving looked up at his father nervously and said, "I think maybe being a farmhand's a real neat idea . . ."

"Nonsense!" the blue giant roared. "Ain't nothin' free in this world, boy, or the next, neither! No pain, no gain! But you stick with me a few months and really work at it and I'll have you able to outrun and outfight anybody here. You stick with it, and there's no place in Husaquahr you'll fear to go and no enemy you won't vanquish, and all the turd-wallowers will turn and wish they was you!"

"His bark's worse than his bite, right?" Irving whispered hopefully.

"No, they're about the same, son," his father replied. "But he's right. You've seen Ti. You want to be a male version of her?"

"Hell, no! Ain't no way *this* boy's gonna be no slave!"

"Well, there's the only insurance you have right there. You know I've got to go away for a while, and why you can't come with me. Imagine armies of *him*, only not on your side but out to get you. You want to be free and independent in this world, there's the price of admission."

"You plucked me outa Philly for *this*?"

Joe thought of the neighborhood, the gangs with their cocaine runners and needles and the rest, the number of potentially good kids living in squalor and dead in their teens, born and raised to lose. "Yes, son, I did."

"Your father survived me and all I threw at him and came out a real *man*," Gorodo said. "Then he went out and eventually married a princess and took over an empire, then threw it away when he decided it wasn't no fun anymore. *That's* the kind of freedom I give, boy! The kind most folks only dream about. Lion or antelope, boy, there ain't but two kinds. Be a turnip— that's easy! Or be the one what eats turnips for lunch!"

"This," Irving breathed, "ain't gonna be no fun at all."

CHAPTER 6

DON'T IT MAKE MY BROWN EYES BLUE

Alchemy is the science of coming up with what one needs when one has foreclosed all other possibilities.
                                    —The Books of Rules, XVIII, 21(a)

"I HAVEN'T DONE THIS SPELL IN, OH, SEVEN, EIGHT HUNDRED years," Ruddygore commented. "Had to look it up, in fact. The Rules allow more latitude than normal on how a slave is marked, with at least three dozen possibilities. However, the ring method is the only one recognized internationally and throughout Husaquahr, since it's the only one with permanence. You see, once the ring is inserted and the spell given, it cannot be removed or altered by anyone—the Rules are quite strict on that."

Joe frowned and looked at Ti, who had actually asked for this to be done prior to their journey. He didn't like it, not a bit. "You *sure* about this?"

She nodded. "Master, it is the only way I can gain any real freedom, as odd as that may sound. It marks me instantly, not only as property, but as *your* property. It is the only security I may have."

"She's right," the sorcerer assured him. "If she'd had this, she wouldn't have had to have been accompanied into town to pick up things for you, tend to things, that sort of thing. Theft of a registered slave is punishable by reduction to slavery status yourself almost everywhere, and purchase of a stolen one the same. Nor can she be transferred to another without the owner's consent and be bound to serve. You might as well just kidnap and imprison *any* lowborn. It's not worth the risk when there's so much easier stuff to lift, and she becomes nearly impossible to market.''

''Yeah, that's true here, now, but when we get into Hypboreya, what will they care?''

''Oh, you'll find that an evil regime is even more a stickler for law and order than a benign one, as a rule, since they trust no one and are inherently paranoid. Indeed, there's nothing poor and oppressed people seem to like more than having slaves about. It's a cruel streak in human nature, but, the fact is, no matter how poor, how miserable, and how oppressed you are, you can always point to a slave and say, 'At least I'm not a *slave*.' That attitude also serves the ruling regime's interest, obviously, since no matter how much they lay on the people, there's one lower rung. No, she'll probably be safer than you, although, my dear, even the common folk will treat you like dirt.''

Joe shrugged. ''Okay, then. Go ahead. What do we do?''

Ruddygore removed a small bronze-colored ring from a box. It looked quite ordinary, and had an opening which, with a bit of flexing, fit into her nose. ''This will sting for just a moment,'' the sorcerer warned her, grasping the ring between two fingers. He then shut his eyes a moment, and there was a surge of energy into the ring that went around it and into her nose. She flinched, then relaxed. Ruddygore opened his eyes, examined his work, nodded to himself, and then actually moved the ring around. There was no sign of a hole or joint, but it wasn't in stiffly. You could turn it, as if she were born with it and with the proper hole inside her nose.

''Hmmm. . . . Yes, blood from the incision mixed with the ring quite well. A pretty fair job, if I do say so myself. It actually looks quite . . . exotic . . . on you, my dear. The only problem I know from one of these is head colds. It's hell to blow your nose with one of them in. But, of course, I've already given you both enough immunization spells to cover anything I could find in the books.'' He turned to Joe. ''Final phase. Take the ring like I did. Yes, that's it.'' He reached out and put his fingers on Joe's, and the big man braced for a shock or something, but nothing happened. "That's it," the sorcerer said, letting go. "You can release the ring now."

"I didn't feel anything," Joe said, thinking something went wrong.

"You lose thousands, maybe millions of cells, every day," Ruddygore told him. "Only a couple are needed here and the few off your fingertips were plenty. The ring now has, well, for want of a better word, your genetic code in it. You alone can alter the record. Anyone touching it with you will know instantly she's yours. A transfer can only take place if you do what we did with someone else, your fingers where mine were, and you tell it you want to transfer title. It's quite elegant. The same system is used on prized livestock all over the world. Bigger rings, of course."

"What happens if we're separated? Or if the worst happens and, well, you know."

He nodded. "If the worst happens, and you do not get the chance to make a transfer, the ring's memory will clear. The first person to hold it as you did will own her, just as you can claim unbranded cattle on the range. On the other hand, if you're merely separated, no matter by what distance, but your body still lives, it holds. She'll either be on her own initiative to find you, within her class limitations, or she'll be taken as a ward of the state and put to work, pending your location, if any. Since nobody ever looks, then the initiative's on your shoulders to find her."

Ruddygore looked at Ti. "You're dying to see what it looks like, I know. Go ahead. There's a mirror over there."

Joe nodded, and she went over and looked at herself. It *didn't* look ugly or disfiguring, as she'd feared. She'd seen some rings in some slaves that were awful. In fact, it really locked in the exotic dancer image. And she really did feel much better with it in. She was now defined to the world, and she felt oddly as if chains that had been holding her were suddenly cast aside.

"Master, may I go back down into town?" she asked Joe.

"Why? Just want to test it out?"

"Partly. But I also beg permission to buy something I saw earlier. There is a merchant in the marketplace who has among his wares castanets. I have been *dying* to try some dances with castanets and without the drums. . . . *Please?*"

He shrugged. "All right, go ahead," he said, then thought of something. "Wait a minute! From this moment on, and forever after, until I tell you different, if anybody demands to know who your master is, you tell them you are owned by—" He thought a moment. "—the great warrior chief Cochise, who won you in a fight. Got it? Get used to calling me that, even in private. We won't know who's listening and we don't want the name 'Joe' to pass either of our lips if we can help it."

She grinned. "Yes, Master," she responded. "Can I go now?" He nodded, and she was off.

"She'll do," the sorcerer said. "The one thing that didn't change a whit about her was her drive for self-perfection. Even in her situation, she wants to be the perfect dancer, the perfect slave. The only thing I did yesterday was to give her some armor, so she can take all the crap that will be dished out to her. She still won't like it, but she'll be able to handle it better. She's got more self-confidence now, too. She spent time this morning before she went into town down in the armory, practicing leaps and jump-kicks. She's also got quite an eye with a knife at short range, and might well handle some other weapons she was previously good at. Not swords, or battleaxes, but, well, what some call 'women's weapons.' And I'd hate to be on the receiving end of a kick from those runner's legs! Her carrying a weapon is out, both for propriety and for her own protection, but I'd keep some at hand just in case."

"That's good to know. Marge is the best scout and spy I can think of, but she's only good in a fight as a diversion."

"There's one more thing, and I think perhaps it should be reinforced with Ti and explained to Marge as well, who might not understand. You've made a good start in letting her call you 'Master,' which, by the way, she doesn't mind, and which is natural to her, said without thinking about it, and your idea of using a pseudonym, even in private. The thing is, you're going to have to go even further. You're going to have to stop thinking of her as your ex-wife and think of her totally as your slave and property, no matter how unnatural that feels on personal and moral grounds. And I mean *think* that way, not playact. You may have to reign her in harshly, even treat her roughly, and I mean that. She has the absolute best possible disguise to go into that country. As I said, even the Baron, who knows her appearance and *might*, just *might* recognize her, although I think even there the chance is slight, would disbelieve his own memory at seeing the mighty Tiana as Ti the slave. Still, if he's at all involved in this business or going to be and gives a description, that's where the attitude you display toward her becomes most important. They'll be looking for a wedded couple—partners. They'll see a slave. They must believe that's all she ever was, and that part's up to you. Your lives and others depend on it.''

''You mean yell at her? Make her grovel? *Beat* her if she doesn't do something? I'm not sure I *can*. The whole idea of slavery is repugnant to me.''

''Remember, once inside enemy lines, you must be what your son would call a 'badass' or 'tough dude.' The one thing an evil society does best is spy on itself. There will be eyes on you constantly, sizing you up.''

''I'll try. I hope *she* understands.''

''Joe—there is *no way* she can get her old body back. Even if, by some impossible good fortune, you secured it, there's no way to get it back alive and no way in any event I could do it. And even if, by some unbelievable occurrence, you got the spell as well, you couldn't make hide nor tail out of it, let alone remember its complexity. Not even Dacaro could, and he's a pro.''

''Maybe if you'd use the Lamp to wish for the formula, I'd risk it anyway,'' he told the big man.

''Joe, it wouldn't help. The Lamp's magic is djinn magic. It can no more tell me how to do it in *this* universe than it could suddenly give you a total grasp of quantum physics. That Lamp's a curse, because those who see what it *can* do assume it is somehow godlike. It's not. If it were, I could use it to become a god and end all this foolishness. The only way is the hard way, Joe. Face it.''

It was impossible to argue with the logic. The bodies *had* to be destroyed.

"And, I'd suggest a new name for Ti as well. It will not only remove the last link in the identification chain, but it will help you divorce the woman that was from the girl that is. Tell her no longer to answer to 'Ti.' She won't. It'll be gone. Then tell her to answer to and think of her name only as 'Mia.' Got it? Mia."

"Mia?"

Ruddygore nodded. "To protect her from having her old self revealed, I told you I took elements from her. Her second, rudimentary slave personality and background I took mostly from her own memories of a palace maid whose name was Mia. If you tell her that's her name, it will seem to her as if it really is. Understand? It's consistent."

"Yeah, okay. Mia. That closes the disguise on her, but everything you say makes me the weakest link in this. Not just how I behave and how I treat others, but we know how these things always go. Somehow, sometime, I'm going to bump into the Baron, even if he's *not* involved, and probably at the wrong time. If he's got any freedom at all, he's probably given those descriptions out just for revenge. I might not last ten seconds up there, and you know it."

Ruddygore nodded. "I've been thinking about that. And he knows you're an Amerind, which is rather distinctive here. I cannot transform your body or do much magic on it. You're locked in as a twenty-year-old Joe. We can, however, make use of the Baron's knowledge that you're what they call back on Earth an Indian or Native American. That's why I asked Doctor Mujahn to drop by this afternoon. He's the best alchemist Husaquahr ever produced—he actually *has* turned gold into lead."

"I thought the idea was to turn lead into gold."

"He's halfway. Don't knock it. Pure science is often unprofitable. At any rate, I want to see what he can do for you. Strictly chemicals, potions, and nostrums, of course. But he can do some startling things in cosmetology, and they stick, unless you have the antidotes. And," he added, "he's so absentminded in day-to-day things he won't remember he was even here, let alone you, ten seconds after he leaves."

"Uh—I assume he has the antidotes to anything he tries on

me? That he's not so absentminded that he'll forget how to reverse things?''

"I assume so, too, yes.''

"Well, if he can do anything, I'll try it. I want to come back
alive from this one if possible. What about Marge, then? Sugasto's seen her, and a man and woman traveling with a Kauri
will strike a few folks as familiar.''

"I doubt if that's a real problem, if you and Ti aren't recognized. All Kauri look absolutely identical except to another
Kauri, the same as all members of the nymph family. Remove
her wings and color her leaf-green and she could be any wood
nymph in the world—sorry. But you get the point. It's only by
your total familiarity with her personality and manners that you
know it's her and not another. I'm not concerned about her being
recognized at all.''

Doctor Mujahn looked like a bumbling, middle-aged accoun-
tant in dark brown monklike robes, complete with small mustache and thin, slicked-down hair and glasses. He also looked
like the kind of man who'd forget his head if it wasn't attached.

He poked and probed and took some skin and blood samples
and cooked up a whole bunch of weird stuff, and he often had
to be reminded that a subject was there and he wasn't doing
research in his laboratory.

"Bleaching the skin is out, but we can tint it, going from the
more olive cast to bronze,'' he muttered, not really to anybody
else but himself. "We've got endless options on the hair, but
because of the skin bath I'd recommend a medium brown. Poor
contrast but it'll have a slight reddish tint, and it can be cropped
and thickened, yes. Hmmm . . . Brown eyes . . . Let's see, let's
see.'' He fumbled through a case full of vials. "Red . . . blood-
shot . . . black . . . pinkeye . . . Ah! This one! Can't tell for
sure what exact color will come out, but it should be somewhere
between emerald and turquoise.''

"Wait a minute. You can even change my eye color?'' Joe
asked him.

"No problem. Simplest of all, really, except for making everything black or albino. That's child's play.'' He puttered around

some more and came up with a vial that seemed made of polished obsidian. "Ah! Yes, the final ingredient! I find it fascinating that your people don't have much in the way of facial or body hair."

"What is it? Hair-growing formula?"

"Yes. We looked to give one fellow a hairier chest once. Poor man looked like an ape at the end. *Tsk-tsk.* Blew my demonstration. Oh, don't worry! It was a simple mistake—I used one part per *thousand* when it should have been one per *hundred thousand*. I was always better at working out formulas than following them. Once baked a loaf of bread that rose so dramatically it blew the roof off the house. Not as bad as the fireworks mixture I did once. You can still see the crater where the town used to be . . . Hmmm . . . All right. Now I have everything worked out for you *exactly correct*. At least I hope I do."

Joe felt much like Irving had felt being introduced to Gorodo. All he wanted was out of there.

He had Ti—no, Mia now, he'd have to remember that—in the room with him. Poquah was also there, looking over the alchemist's shoulder, and that was the only reassurance he had. The Imir was one of the few known adepts who was of faërie, and he was pretty damned good. Ruddygore said he'd never be as good as a human adept with the same talent, simply because he was of faërie, but that he was already the most knowledgeable and powerful of the elf family in all history. The Imir were also one of the rare warrior races of elves, and were great in a fight. But Ruddygore had proclaimed that his adept was needed here, particularly if Joe failed.

First the alchemist used a bathtub that could only have been Ruddygore's—it was the largest even Joe had ever seen—and, after elf servants filled it with water, he began mixing and stirring various potions in there. Joe grew more nervous when he saw that no exact measuring devices were being used; it was a pinch of this and two drops of that.

Finally, Doctor Mujahn proclaimed the mixture correct. "You must get in and submerge completely," he told Joe. "Eyes and mouth shut, but once under, turn your lips out in a pucker, as if about to give a big kiss. That's quite important. Don't worry if you swallow a little bit. The worse that will do is turn your urine green for a few days. Stay under until I tap you on the head. Then you can come up. That, too, is important.''

"Uh—you're sure I'm not gonna come out purple or something?"

"Reasonably sure. Of course, I could always *test*, I suppose, but it's such a waste of time."

"Test!" Joe ordered.

He sighed. "Very well, very well. Let's see. Ah. This leather patch will do fine.'' He picked up a small patch of dark brown leather, stuck it to the end of a pair of pliers, and dipped it into the bathtub. Then he waited, and waited, whistling a bit as he did so.

"Hey! How long does this take?" Joe asked nervously. "I have to *breathe*, you know!"

"Oh, almost done. Another little bit . . . yes . . . there!" He pulled the patch up.

The leather was a yellow orange and most unattractive.

"I don't want *that* color!" Joe protested.

"Oh, don't worry about *that*. It's matched to your current skin color. Naturally, it's going to have a different, but predictable, effect on ordinary brown cow leather. It will work. This is the expected result. Come, come! Your turn!''

Joe sighed. "All right, all right. If it goes *too* wrong Ruddygore will have to cancel this whole thing and send other people.'' He slipped off his loincloth and sandals and went over, hoisted himself up, paused a moment, took a deep breath, let it out, then took in another and held it, then slid into the tub. He submerged all the way, eyes shut, as instructed, but only at the last minute did he remember the pucker. A little did come in. It tasted like cream soda.

His whole body tingled, and he was *very* uncomfortable. Besides, the water might have been nice and warm when they poured it, but it was at best lukewarm now. He began to fear his lungs were going to burst, and he could hold his breath a pretty long time. As long as he had to pucker, why the hell didn't they give him a breathing straw? Just when he decided he could hold it no longer, that he was coming up anyway, he felt a none too gentle blow on his forehead and he immediately broke through the surface, gasping for air and coughing.

"Out! Out! Get out quickly or you won't stay even!" the alchemist shouted, oblivious to his discomfort. He managed to lift himself out and stood there dripping on the floor.

Mia brought him a towel and he wiped his face and eyes and opened them, then looked around. "Well?" he asked, then looked down.

For the first time in his life, Joe de Oro was truly golden. Not bright gold, but the natural kind, the kind you saw in those California and Hawaiian surfing films.

"I want to do the hair before the solution dries," the alchemist said, busily mixing. "Here. Just soak your hair completely in this bowl, then come up and we'll dry it off."

He was suddenly forced over a large bowl full of foul-smelling stuff, rotten egg stinking stuff, and his head was dunked in it. The doctor used a small ladle to apply it to areas that couldn't be totally submerged, then said, "All right, out. Take this towel and dry your hair as thoroughly as you can. Quickly now! Delay too long and your hair will lose all its color."

That got him moving, with Mia's help. His whole scalp tingled, and it wasn't comfortable at all.

"That's sufficient," the alchemist pronounced. "Now come sit in this chair. Girl, you take those scissors and comb and trim his hair nicely in back!"

"Can you do a haircut, Mia?" Joe asked nervously.

"I shall do my best, Master," she told him.

"Go to it, then."

The alchemist was still moving fast. "Wait. Before you cut, let me put these drops in his eyes. It will sting a bit. Close them, and keep them closed until I tell you to open them. In the meantime, I'm going to apply the hair paste."

The guy was as quick and good with drops as an eye doctor, Joe had to admit, but that stuff *burned*. Not the paste that was being applied over a lot of his face and to his arms, chests, and legs, though. That itched like crazy instead, but every time he went to scratch at it Doctor Mujahn slapped his hand.

Mia's combing wasn't too great, either. Actually, it wasn't so much her as it was the tangles he obviously had in abundance. She kept running into them, trying to comb them out, and, in most cases, wound up cutting them out. It felt as if she were doing a lot of cutting back there, and that made him almost as nervous as Doctor Mujahn did.

"Open your eyes!" the alchemist ordered, and he did.

"Blurry as hell," he said.

"That will pass. Close them again, though. Not quite there yet."

Now he felt the itching paste being washed from his body with very warm water. The water felt good, but the itching didn't stop.

"Open your eyes again!" Mujahn ordered. He did, and it was even blurrier. The alchemist studied them, frowning, then he nodded. "All right. Stop the haircut, girl. I'm going to wash his eyes."

He was given another set of eyedrops, and was told this time to keep blinking. He did, and, slowly, his eyesight began to clear. Mujahn gave him two more flushes, then pronounced himself satisfied.

"Finish the hair now, girl! Well, big fellow, how do you feel?"

"Itchy," he responded.

"Quite natural. You've never had hair there before. Give it a few more days and you'll have several month's growth. There! My own mother wouldn't know you now!"

"Your mother is not the one I'm worried about," Joe responded. "Mia, how much longer is it gonna be?"

"It is mostly done, Master. I hope you will be pleased."

"I want to see what I look like, damn it!"

Poquah looked him over. "Actually, since I know your visage well and watched the process, I recognize you, but I doubt if anyone who did not look very closely and very well with great suspicion would, sir."

"Damn it, Mia, when will you be done? I'm not going to the ball, you know."

"Just another minute, Master."

"That's what you said before."

"Not too much longer . . ."

"Finish it, damn it! Now!"

She stiffened, then did two more snips and a comb. "Yes, Master."

The very instant he regretted the tone he also realized that this was exactly what Ruddygore was talking about. An apology was stopped before it began. You never, *never* apologized to a slave.

He got up and stalked into the other room, which was a dressing room of sorts and had a full mirror. He stopped, looked at himself, and hardly believed what he saw. Yeah, okay, his face and body weren't really changed. He was still the same guy. But the changes, all entirely superficial, were as dramatic as a sorcerous transformation.

The most startling were the azure blue eyes. Geronimo had blue eyes, it was said, but he'd never expected to see it. The hair was thick and slightly curly, more beach-bum stuff, and a sandy reddish brown. The eyebrows were a slightly darker brown, probably because he'd wiped his eyes, but it looked natural at least. And the complexion change, for all its discomforts, was actually quite subtle, which made it, in combination with the rest, all the more effective.

But most dramatic was his face. He actually had a thick stubble! Not the occasional wispy hair he'd known, but *whiskers*. Not yet a beard, but certainly even now at the stage where most white men would be if they hadn't shaved in a week. Nice and full, too. And hair was also growing over much of the rest of his body! He hadn't had this sort of hair since he'd returned from that body Ruddygore and his pet demon had formed for him long ago, the same body he was now supposed to destroy.

He turned and saw Mia standing there, looking at him. "Well? Am I a new man or not?"

"The change is—dramatic, Master."

"You don't approve?"

"It is not for me to approve or disapprove. But it wears well on you, Master. No enemy is going to recognize you now."

And that, of course, was the real point.

"It's a very good haircut," he told her, unable to resist.

She was about to respond when Doctor Mujahn came in. "Would you like your voice altered? Wouldn't be much of a problem to raise or lower you an octave, you know, since your baritone's about in the middle range. Give you a sore throat for a few days, but after that, fine."

"No, this is more than good enough, Doctor. In fact, it's positively brilliant. My apologies for doubting you." He hesitated. "Ah—this beard and body hair is growing at a fantastic rate. It *will* slow down, won't it?"

"Oh, of course. Give it a week and you'll have enough to trim. After that, trim it every couple of days for another week, then it will have slowed to the normal body rate of about a quarter of an inch a month. The body hair will reach its own length and pretty much stop, but it won't be replaced very quickly."

"But it won't fall out, or the colors wear off?"

"Oh, over many years, perhaps, but not otherwise. After about a year, the hair will have a tendency to go gray, but it can always be dyed. The rest—no, not without more treatments from me."

He nodded. "Mia, fetch me my barbarian outfit and let's go meet the critics."

Marge was absolutely stunned. "It's *perfect*!" she assured him. "And when the beard comes in, you could go up to Bo quillas himself and spit in his face and he wouldn't know you!"

"That, my dear, is the whole idea," Throckmorton P. Ruddygore put in. "I have had my staff work up a past history for you, by the way, as a cover story. It will hold up if you practice it. We've also worked out a route, of sorts, although circumstances might alter it. I'll discuss it with you later."

Joe nodded. "I just wish I could stop this damned hair from *itching* so much!"

"Oh, when it comes in full, that stops," Ruddygore assured him. "Then it's simply a matter of a trim. You're just out of practice."

Irving was even more amazed by Joe, not even recognizing him until the big man spoke.

"Oh, wow! You look like Conan of Hawaii!" he exclaimed. Then his face fell. "I guess this means you're goin' soon."

"We leave tomorrow morning," Joe told him. "I wish more than anything you could come with us, Irv, but it's just not time yet."

"I know. I just . . . well, I just have this crazy . . . Oh, damn, I'm afraid you won't come back!"

"If I'm alive, I'll come back. That I swear," Joe assured him. "But there's always that possibility. There was that possibility every time I climbed into a truck for a run or crossed a street."

"If they get you, I'll get them," Irving said firmly. "I promise you that."

"Then you think you can stick it out with Gorodo?"

The boy grinned evilly. "Oh, him and me are gonna get along real fine. He don't know 'bout karate!"

Joe laughed and hugged him and held him close.

It was dark; they had all eaten, and Marge had gone into Terdiera for her own needs with a promise to be back by ten. Kauri were by nature nocturnal; they *could* function in daylight, but always in a slight stupor, almost a jet-lag feeling of being up at the wrong time. But nighttime was when they needed a flying sentinel most in any event.

Joe was spending the last hours with Irving and would also not be up until the meeting. Mia was going around, seeing to the last minute details, and was now heading out to the courtyard to practice a dance with her new castanets.

In truth, she still worried Ruddygore the most. He had gotten the report from Poquah of her reaction to Joe's anger, and he knew she was hurt, that she'd conveyed that hurt wordlessly to Joe, and he'd softened because of it. The half measures he'd taken clearly weren't adequate. Only a clean break, at the risk of her ego, would do the trick after all. There was no other way open to him.

He stepped out quickly from behind a pillar just in front of her and she jumped a bit, startled. "I—I am sorry, my lord. I did not see you there."

"My fault entirely," he responded, then lifted his hand. She immediately stiffened, in an immediate trance.

"Mia," he said softly, "I am going to tell you some things about yourself and you will believe them and know that they are true."

"Yes, my lord."

"You are not, nor have you ever been, the highborn and demigoddess Tiana," he told her. "The memories you have of the parents and siblings of Mia are true. You were, however, Tiana's maid and slave in the palace. All of your memories and impressions of that life, of Joe *and* Tiana, come from that. The Dark Baron had you kidnapped and brought to Earth in order to learn intimate details of his enemies, Joe and Tiana, and, as you were under his power, you did so. When he captured Tiana, he first interrogated her, and from that you learned the other details, and then he killed her. Then he cast a spell so that you believed that you were Tiana. He was going to use you to get at us, but he was defeated and so could not use you and his hold on you was broken. You returned as Tiana, and basically fooled yourself that you were really Tiana, the details you knew and your own worshipful devotion to Tiana making you refuse to admit that she was dead and, thanks to the new body and the Rules that gripped you, convincing even Joe that you were really Tiana.

"But when you returned to Husaquahr, you became the slave Mia once more, since that is who you were and the only person you can be. You love Joe, have since your days in the palace, but you know you can never be more than his slave. You now truly realize that you can never keep up the pretense of being Tiana and you are going to abandon it. But you won't stop loving Joe, no matter how cross he is, no matter if he even beats you, no matter if he has a hundred other women. To be Joe's slave is your highest aspiration. You are proud to be his slave and proud that for so long you were taken as Tiana's equal. That is the true source of your own pride. You now know that, were you not a slave, you might have been her equal. You have proven as smart, as tough, and as resourceful as she was. But even as you know your duty, you will ever after know and accept your status and your place."

He paused, sorry it had come to this. If she survived this—if *he* survived this, if they couldn't pull it off!—and if he ever figured that body-switching trick, he promised himself that he would make it up to her, get her out of this body and into one commensurate in status with her intelligence and skills. Until then, this would have to do.

"You remember that you once told Tiana that you did not mind being a slave, that it was better than many alternatives you could think of, and that it was honorable and necessary work," he continued. "As the truth that you are truly Mia comes to you, you will remember that and believe it all the more. You are *proud* of being the slave of the greatest of Husaquahr. To serve such a noble one in such a noble cause fills your heart with joy. To be a slave on such a great quest and perhaps aid in its outcome gives you pride, meaning. In a crisis, when you are needed, you will do as Tiana would have done, had you truly been her.

"These things will not come upon you all at once when I let you go, but you will suspect them, feel their truth deep down, and, over the next few days, you will know and understand all of them and it will actually make you happy to know that you are truly Mia, the best and luckiest slave girl in all Husaquahr."

Once she made that leap, and truly believed that she was Mia and had never been Tiana or anyone else, her mind would sort itself out. All pretenses of Tiana, including particularly the pride and her sense of shame, would go as well. She would accept herself entirely as Mia; her whole ego would be redirected.

He raised his hand and she suddenly came awake.

"I am sorry, my lord! I did not see you there!" she said.

"That's all right, Mia. My fault entirely. Go wherever you were going. You've got a big day coming tomorrow."

"Thank you, my lord," she said, doing the partial bow and slight knee bend and then continuing on her way. She was glad that he didn't need her for anything and that she had no more duties for now. She was all mixed up in her mind and she needed to sort things out, and dancing really helped do that.

Ruddygore watched her go, then reached into his robe and took out a huge old gold-encased pocket watch with *Great Western Railway, Ltd.* written upon its face. He flipped it open and saw that it was just after nine. So much meddling to do, so little time . . .

He caught Joe just as he was coming up the stairs from the armory area and had him in the same sort of trance in seconds.

"Joe, what I'm going to tell you is true and you will believe it is true." Quickly he sketched much the same scenario as he had for Tiana. "You will not know this immediately, but will come to suspect it, and she will finally tell you, if you ask her," he concluded, spelling out a few of the implications.

Joe, too, would not remember the encounter nor the conversation, but by the time he had his beard he would believe it, and he'd interact with her accordingly. Not as his former wife and love, but as this little slave he'll now vaguely remember. She would then go from being someone he still considered his equal and for whom he retained, no matter what, some real love, to a near total stranger, and a masquerader, however unconsciously, at that. He would still never consider selling her; the sorcerer had seen to that. But the master-slave status would be absolute, convincing, and believed and accepted by both.

If, of course, Marge didn't screw it up.

Marge *was* late, but only by a few minutes. Ruddygore had anticipated it, but also knew she could go out afterward, and that, while it took some time to walk or ride to the town, she could fly it rather quickly.

Joe was already there, looking over a map with Ruddygore and Poquah.

"I'd head north across the Plain of Shadows," the Imir, a military advisor at this meeting, told them. "Cross into Valisandra, which our reports say is not under Sugasto directly but is scared enough of him that he essentially has them neutralized and in no way interfering. Trust no one, rely on your cover story. You really *did* fight at the Battle of Sorrow's Gorge, and you truly do have the sort of experience you will be claiming, including a knowledge of the Dark Baron no one who hadn't met him and been with him for a stretch would have. As a mercenary among so vast an army, there is no one who could tell that you were on the other side."

He nodded. "I like that. I particularly like using the Dark Baron, curse his seemingly indestructible soul, as a way in. It's justice, somehow."

"So long as the Baron doesn't actually show up," Marge pointed out. "For sure, he wouldn't know or remember you at all, and it would take him about an hour mentally to undo the disguise and finger you. And if he fingers you, we're *all* undone."

Ruddygore sighed. "I hesitate to say that the odds of you two meeting the Baron again are one in a billion because I know damned well that your destiny has been entwined with his and what the implications of that really are. The only thing I can say is, you've both been in his clutches before and you've both beaten him more than once. If it's his destiny to find you, then it's yours to keep screwing him up. Frankly, after all the previous adventures, if I were the Dark Baron, and I figured out who you were, I'd run like hell."

"But he won't," Marge noted. "And there's a question of how many times we can screw up that kind of power and not pay a real price for it. I know how this crazy place works now. Somewhere down the pike there's a cashier we don't want to meet."

Joe looked up from the map at her. "Cold feet? Sorry you came now?"

"Cold feet, yes. Sorry, no. Not yet, anyway. Hey, what's the fun of being in a world of swordplay and sorcery if you can't have thrills once in a while? Besides, I really want to get this bastard. I've owed Sugasto a knife in the back since that first business with the Lamp. Now it turns out that the slimy, double-crossing weasel is the Master of the Dead and that he's gonna make a grab for the whole ball of wax. Uh-uh. We Kauris make love, not war, but we *Texans* have a different idea!"

"Bravo! Well said," Ruddygore approved. "Remember the Alamo and all that!"

She looked up sharply at him. "Everybody *died* at the Alamo and the bad guy won. No, remember San Jacinto, and Santa Ana found skulking under a bridge disguised as a peasant. Oh, no. I'd rather be a live Houston than a dead Bowie."

"Point taken," the sorcerer responded a bit apologetically. "I'm not totally versed in the fine details of the history of your native lands."

"At any rate," Poquah said with some irritation, "I'd use Valisandra to find out all you can about the conditions and situation in Hypboreya. Cross when you have to or when the door of opportunity opens, not before. Get an invitation. You might well have to prove yourself to do it, but be resourceful."

"And the bodies?"

"Here, beyond the Golden Lakes, in this somewhat blank expanse known as the Cold Wastes," Ruddygore answered. "It's vast and glacial, and this region is essentially uninhabited. This area here, in the shading, was the site of a mammoth battle of ancient times, the times of heroes and legends. It's sixty miles across and your most dangerous area, since that war threatened the very existence and stability of Husaquahr. There is a legend that the powers of Heaven and Hell convened while it raged, and decided that it was so terrible a thing and had such a disastrous potential, that they agreed to halt it, freezing the entire battle and both forces, from great sorcerers to majestic warriors and fairy kings of old. There they allegedly remain to this day, under the ice. People are scared to cross it because they believe that they're still somehow alive down there and can influence those who come near."

Joe looked him in the eye. "Is it true?"

Ruddygore shrugged. "I haven't the vaguest idea, but it sounds wild enough and the story has lasted long enough to have at least a grain of truth in it. Just beyond is this area, an oddity caused by volcanic activity. It's warm and lush and essentially inaccessible. It's where all the royalty of Hypboreya is crowned and is their retreat and fortress. Now, if *you* were Sugasto, and you now ruled Hypboreya absolutely with the royals as mere puppets and virtual prisoners and you had two bodies that would be instantly recognizable throughout Husaquahr and you couldn't blow your plot or their existence until you were ready to unveil them, where would *you* put them? Where would you train them? Almost any other place you can think of on this continent risks premature exposure, and then you'd have armies marching on them with religious fervor to free their captive deities from the clutches of Hell. Any other continent would remove his trump cards too far from easy access. No, they're there.''

"You're sure they actually exist?" Marge asked him.

"Now I am. It was hard-won information, I assure you. I actually had to free a demon who was bound to me indefinitely to get it.''

Joe frowned. "Then that means Sugasto's probably been tipped that you know. Oh, boy!''

"We have to assume it. At least, a few days ago the word started going out to find and capture you and Tiana at any cost and offering any reward. You can see why I'm so paranoid about you avoiding all detection. The fact is, though, they'll soon be combing every home and tree for you down here, while you'll be up there. That is one reason I decided that it might as well be you that goes for it. That, of course, and the fact that you have the long-standing grudge and are the best qualified. And you alone really have the right to do what must be done. Remember, the Rules bind bodies, not souls, as we all know. Higher law applies in that area. Even though the souls are wrong, the bodies stolen, this is still regicide.''

He had a point. If Ti was a slave because her body said she was, and he was a warrior-mercenary for the same reason, then whoever was Tiana's body *really was* a highborn, qualified to be a monarch! As was the guy wearing his old body, by right of marriage and deed.

"He'll think of that, too," Joe pointed out. "And he'll know that nobody entitled to ice them is capable of it, except us.''

"Sugasto won't think of it," Ruddygore said. "He's always been sloppy on that sort of detail.''

"But the Dark Baron would think of it," Marge noted.

"Yes, he would. But, remember, the Baron betrayed him the last time they formed an alliance. I feel certain that Sugasto would never trust the Baron again. Not on equal terms, anyway. Can you imagine Esmilio willing to subordinate *anything*, let alone something as monumental as this, to *anyone*?''

"He'd be plotting to overthrow the little twerp and take over this operation himself," Marge agreed. "Okay. Point granted. But I still don't like him loose."

Joe yawned. "I think we pretty well have what we can get at this point. I'd better get some sleep if I want to make any time tomorrow."

"Yes, Joe, good-night," Ruddygore said in a clear dismissal.

"I'm heading back for town," Marge told them. "Joe can protect *me* tomorrow morning!"

Ruddygore caught her eye and gestured for her to linger. She understood, nodding, and they wrapped up everything. First Joe, then Poquah, left. Marge went over and closed the door behind them, then turned to the sorcerer. "So what's the conspiracy?"

"No conspiracy—now. I'm afraid I've just had to undo one in a good cause. What would you say if I told you that Mia is not Tiana? That Tiana actually died at the hands of the Baron back on Earth?"

"I'd say you were feeding me baloney to try and keep Joe and me from being pissed off at the destruction of one of the neatest women this world ever produced."

He sighed. "I can prove it to you rather simply. Tiana could read Husaquahrian. Not merely the formal language, but many of its dialects and several other languages as well. She also was schooled, as you may remember, in Switzerland. She spoke, read, and wrote German, French, and Italian with ease and English rather well, too. Mia is totally illiterate now in *any* tongue, has a reasonable speaking knowledge of English because that was supplied in the plot, but none of the other languages, and she can't really read English, either."

"Big deal. The Rules account for that."

"No they don't. Ask anyone. Not just my staff, *anyone.* Marge, *there is no Rule prohibiting slaves from learning to read or write.* Some, although not very many, can. And Mia was illiterate from the start—she couldn't handle looking up the relevant passages on herself shortly after they returned here, long before even the Rules would have wiped it out, if such Rules existed. Mia doesn't know how to read or write or any of those other languages or an awful lot that Tiana knew because Mia is not Tiana, she is really Mia, a former palace slave to Tiana." Quickly, he sketched in the same scenario that he'd given to an unknowing Mia and Joe.

"Wait a minute! She sure as hell seemed like Tiana to me back on Earth, and she sure convinced Joe!"

"I know. I'm afraid I was partly responsible for that. I spotted it right away, of course, and in the course of removing the Baron's nasty little time bombs inside her, I realized that she could pull it off, allowing for the nature of Husaquahr and the Rules. I warned at the start that she'd be a dancer or courtesan, the former usually and the latter always slave jobs. I knew even then that the moment she returned to Husaquahr the Rules would take the path of least resistance and return her to her former status. Everything else they would blame on the Rules. Even *she* thought she was Tiana, and I helped that out a bit. Joe needed the time, he needed Tiana, for the wilderness period with Irving. Now I have started the unraveling. Within a few days, a week at most, both she and Joe will realize the truth."

"But—*why*?"

"Because at this point Tiana is the last person Joe needs. Not merely to avoid slipups, but suppose they *do* have a chance at the bodies? Could Joe really destroy the body of his wife, the woman he loved? Could *she*? There was no other choice. I've been letting it come off in stages, and I held off the full impact of the Rules with her as long as possible, but what was once a positive is now a negative. She *is* a very bright, talented, capable woman who is still an asset. But she is not the one anyone, even she, thought she was."

"Wow! If you're not pulling another of your scams, that's heavy stuff!"

"Marge, I am not. I just wanted you to know ahead of time. It will make things easier later."

"Yeah, well . . . Wow!"

"Remember, too, by the way, that she's still a were. They both are. Joe saw to that. They had it on the road. I understand that Irving was, in his vernacular, pretty 'freaked out.' That's an occasional problem, but, as you know, a valuable tool if used.

Keep it in mind. Joe will have enough to handle, so I'm counting on you as guide and adviser.''

She nodded, still stunned. "Yeah, I'll do what I can, as always. Still, I *said* we couldn't get away with it forever. Now you're telling me that Ti's paid the bill, and Joe's got his own curse down the pike. Why does that make me feel like target number one in this business?''

Ruddygore shrugged. "These things pile up over time, but things like that are not inevitable. You have the same odds now you always did. You know about Joe, then?''

She nodded. "He told me. I guess he had to tell somebody.''

"Well, he might not have told you that, if and when it happens, he wouldn't lose his mind and his memory any more than you did. It's not as bad as that. It won't be like the last time.''

"Yeah, but a big macho male stuck as a wood nymph isn't gonna have a happy time. At least he'll do damned near anything to stay alive as he is.''

"But that is also his Achilles' heel. He might hold back, he might hesitate when he should strike. That's another thing to watch out for.''

"Boy, you're really loading the dice on this one, aren't you?'' she said glumly. "And, it seems to me, you're loading it against your own side.''

CHAPTER 7

ON THE ROAD AGAIN

Places shall take on the atmosphere and attitude of their rulers.
Evil pervades the very rocks and trees and air where it resides.
And, if allowed to fester, killing the good, it will remain so long
after the rulers have departed.

—The Books of Rules, III, 97(a)

SAYING FAREWELL TO IRVING WAS GUT-WRENCHING, BUT JOE at least had the honest conviction that the boy had not been in better hands in his life.

They were barely out of sight of Terindell, though, taking the northern river route, when he realized how much he missed the rest of the old company and how, for the first time, really, on one of these missions, he was essentially alone. If it weren't for Marge's happy appearance, he thought, it might drive him nuts, but the Kauri wasn't any company to speak of during the day. Instead, she just sprawled out on top of the bedrolls on the packhorse, sound asleep, mostly concealed under a thin wrap so that the sight of one of the fairies out cold didn't attract too many curious stares or, worse, give the wrong impression.

The road went almost immediately inland, skirting places like the Circe's lair and the Glen Dinig, domain of the great witch-queen Huspeth, heading first to the city of Machang on the River Rossignol, from whence roads went in all directions.

Joe missed most of all the company of the old Tiana, who had been more than wife, but also companion and equal, lover and confessor. The change in her had bothered him about as much as it had seemed to bother her, and now he couldn't keep from wondering just how much of a change there was and how much he'd overlooked. Even in the months in the High Pothique wilderness, he'd been preoccupied with Irving and had tended to overlook things that now seemed to leap out at him. He'd blamed much of it on the Rules, of course, but now other things started bothering him. How had she learned to dance so well so quickly? Even he had needed to be trained by Gorodo; only the fairies got their skills by instinct. The fact that he was inclined to enjoy swordplay and combat skills hadn't meant he hadn't had to learn them and practice, practice, practice. Tiana had always been clumsy, even at *formal* dances; who had taught her those erotic moves and gyrations? For that matter, she'd lately shown some skill as a seamstress, barber, maid, and other such jobs that she'd never shown any knowledge of or interest in before.

The Baron had Tiana briefly on Earth, hadn't he?

The thought came almost immediately, and he could not get it out of his head. *What if this girl really wasn't Tiana at all?*

For Mia, riding behind him on her horse while keeping the packhorse in the rear in line, the same logic and questions had gnawed even further at her. More bothersome than the skills she did have were the memories she did not. Tiana had gone to school on Earth, in Switzerland, one of the countries there, but she had no memory of the schooling, or the country, or even where it might be. She didn't even remember being a mermaid, as they'd reminisced, or anything between the palace life and the night they defeated the Baron. Even the palace memories were odd, as if she were someone else, watching Tiana rather than being her.

Memories long suppressed, strange memories but familiar ones, now came to the fore. Of all those kids jammed in a one-room hovel, of playing naked with other dirty kids in a town square, of running away at age eleven when her mother died in childbirth, determined that it would not happen to her. Of reaching a big city and being befriended by a man who was at the start very nice, but who later taught her to dance with the other girls for crowds of leering men, renting out her young body to some of them, and, finally, being arrested, where a kindly woman Procurator listened sympathetically to her life story and sentenced her to be a slave, ward of the state, and trained as a maid . . . Of being in the palace *after* Joe and Tiana left, of men in black who'd seized her, to awaken in a strange place on a strange world . . . Of seeing her Highness helpless, in some room . . .

It hit her all at once with a force that almost knocked her off the horse. *By the gods! I have been mad! I am not Tiana! I am the slave Mia!*

After the initial shock wore off, though, the realization brought not horror and regret but a sense of peace in her mind. She was not forced into slavery, she was simply now returned to her proper role and self! It was all right, then! No more inner struggles, no more anguish. Instead, she felt great pride in herself, that she, a mere ignorant whore turned slave, had managed to fool even Joe into thinking she was of the blood royal. And, for those few months, she'd had him, essentially as an equal, something beyond even the most impossible, wild dreams of one such as her. It was over now, she knew, but if she died tomorrow, it still would be enough.

The trouble was, how to tell *him*? She decided that she could not; it would embarrass him. But, if he suspected at some time, if he asked, then she would admit the truth.

It took ten hours to reach Machang, a pretty big city by Husaquahrian standards, teeming with life and busy people, its huge bridge at the northern end dominating the skyline and marking the end of navigation on the Rossignol.

They selected a low-rent hostelry near the riverfront for their night's lodging, first going into a back alley and awakening a still slightly groggy Marge, telling her where they'd be, and letting her manage to fly up to the rooftops to finish her slumbers.

Mia helped unload, then unpacked, got the room ready as much as she could, then went back down to arrange to stable the horses. She felt buoyant, giddy, almost supercharged, like a whole new person, free to act and think like a teenager again.

Joe plopped down on the bed, feeling tireder than he knew he should, simply because of the monotony of the ride. And there were weeks and weeks of this to come, with the climate, both real and political, turning worse as they went.

Marge tapped outside his third-story window and he got up and raised it fully to let her in. He was glad to see her. "Any trouble finding me?"

"Naw. Really freaked out a couple folks who saw me peekin' in, but most of 'em were doin' anything but lookin' out the window." She grinned evilly. "You may be the only person in this joint who's here to sleep."

"I think I'd be a little too conspicuous staying in one of the fancy places. Besides, I couldn't even dress for dinner."

"Mia's not back yet?"

"No, she just left to stable the horses a few minutes ago."

"You're down in the dumps about something, I can tell. Just what's ahead?"

"Well, that, but not really. I just never really been this alone on a long trip since I drove a truck, and then I had a CB and the stereo."

"What you're really saying is that you can't relate to Mia as you could to Ti and you can't just take Mia as Mia."

He nodded. "That's part of it."

"Joe, I think maybe I oughta tell you something. I checked it out last night after Ruddygore told me and it holds up, but it's a big shock. I wasn't supposed to tell, but I'm exercising that judgment the old boy thinks I have."

"I'm listening."

She told him the whole thing, beginning to end, including how she'd run into this lonely half-baked magician in Terdiera who'd looked up the literacy thing in the Rules for her and confirmed it. Joe listened with so little expression, saying nothing even after she'd finished, that she had to prompt him. "Well?"

"I—I was beginning to suspect as much, but it's still a shock to find out the woman you thought was your wife is some sixteen-year-old slave girl I don't even remember. It also means I've been had and living a lie for many months, and, most of all, it means Ti's really gone."

She hadn't thought of that last one. "Oh, Joe. I'm so sorry! Damn me!"

"No, no. You were right to tell me. It's better to know. The question is, does *she* know?"

"I think so, now. Fairy intuition, maybe. This was supposed to take a week to kick in, but I can't stand it. Ask her when she gets back. Ask her if she knows the truth about herself."

"And if she does and admits it? What then?"

"Then I'd tell her it's okay, that it's good to know, and that it's closed. And then I'd blow out the light and make love to her. Not as Joe and Ti, but as Joe and slave girl."

"Huh?"

"Trust me. Do that and all the ice will melt. After that, you can relate to her and she to you as people in their relative positions. The feminine fairy nose knows. How would you guys ever survive if you didn't have women to tell you what to do?"

And, it turned out, she was exactly right.

The next day dawned as clear and warm as the one before; good traveling weather. Mia was like a different person—which, in a way, she was—up and about before dawn, getting things packed and ready before he awoke and without awakening him, somehow even finding hot water for the basin and giving him a morning wash. To himself, guiltily, he had to admit grudgingly that he liked such treatment and could easily grow used to it.

She refused breakfast, saying she'd eat something later, and, while he ate at a dingy riverfront cafe, she went and settled the livery bill, got the horses and packed things away, then brought it all to him.

"That's a hell of a girl you got there, Mister," the grizzled proprietor of the cafe noted as she arrived. "You want to sell her?"

"Never," he responded. "She's absolutely essential to me."

They picked up Marge in the alley, and she crawled in her "hidey hole" as she called it and was soon off to dreamland, but feeling a little smug. She still didn't care for this slave girl bit; it went against her grain. But if she had to see it, then it was a lot easier to accept a little slave girl raised to this level, at least, rather than a Tiana sunk to it. After all, Tiana hadn't given a thought to slaves waiting on her hand and foot, both male and female, as being anything other than her due. That didn't make it right, but Marge had been around long enough to lose, if not her ideals, at least her hopes that one could cure the evils of the world without also inventing totally new ones.

Mia was still rigorous about her exercises and her running, but she also begged for some regular training in defense that might be useful, and Joe stopped at least once every day in a relatively uninhabited spot to help her out. She was really good with a knife, and could handle a bow at relatively short distances, but what surprised him was her karatelike kicks, which, with her powerful legs, dancer's agility, and toughened feet, managed to break a small log in half.

"Where'd you learn those moves?" he asked her, genuinely impressed.

"Irving taught them to me, Master," she responded. "It was a new kind of fighting, perfect for me to defend myself."

"Huh! And I thought he was just play-acting out Kung-Fu movies. I'll be damned!"

Mia was pretty good as it was, but much was improvised. If she could only have taken classes in it, he thought, she'd shoot to black belt in no time.

They stopped at a roadhouse just before the Valisandran border. By now Joe's facial hair had developed into a full, thick beard, and it so dramatically altered his looks while retaining his image that he was willing to overlook the few gray streaks. It gave the beard character, aged him gracefully, and spoke of hard-won experience. Although he never got used to getting stuff in a mustache, or found a way short of regular trims not to eat some hair, he wasn't about to get rid of it, particularly after the roadhouse.

Mia came up to him quietly while he relaxed outside. She had a paper in her hand, and said, "Master, I think you better look at this."

He took it and immediately saw what she meant. He couldn't read a word of it—in fact, none of them could—but the two woodcuts, while somewhat crude, were unmistakable. Lean, hard face, high cheekbones, long black hair . . . It wasn't very flattering, but, when taken with what was probably a physical description, it was recognizable. The other cut wasn't nearly as much help; he knew it was supposed to be Mia, but it could have been about every fifth girl in Marquewood, and the picture certainly had no slave ring, the one thing about her face that everyone focused on almost immediately.

At the bottom was a symbol that resembled a nasty, black falcon's head, only a falcon out of the dark side of faërie, superimposed over the outline of a crest that appeared to be a cyclops on one side and a dwarf on the other. "The Hypboreyan imperial seal, I'd bet," he commented. "I wonder if I can find anybody inside to read it to me?"

"Oh, no, Master! You *can't*!"

He grinned. "Sure I can. Just remember, those aren't pictures of *us*! Who knows, we might come across this pair and collect a fat reward. Don't worry. I want to know whom you deliver them to if you capture them. Who, and where."

The barman looked at the flyer and frowned. "Says this pair are fugitives from a treason charge in Hypboreya—not that that's unusual. Seems like most anything over there's treason now. They must want them pretty bad, though. The usual's ten gold pieces a head. These are *ten thousand* a head!" He whistled. "And twenty-five thousand for both! Man, I'll settle for just one of 'em, guilty or innocent. With ten thousand I'd walk away from this place, get myself a yacht, and just sail the river and loaf."

"That's why I wanted the details. What happens if you catch one or both? What do you do then?"

"Bring 'em here and I'll split with you!" the innkeeper responded. "No, seriously, it says they must be alive, but condition's not important, and to notify any Hypboreyan legation or trade representative, or to notify the Witches' Guild!"

"Surely all witches and warlocks aren't working for Hypboreya," Joe responded. He knew some pretty nice folks who were witches—and, of course, a ton that made the fairy-tale ones look like saints.

The barman shrugged. "Who knows? You figure they got somebody in almost all the locals. Probably got some kind of magical reward for them as a processing fee the likes of this cash so that few witches could turn it down. Most any of 'em around here are in league with the Dark One anyway. It was real creepy when this was occupied territory, you know, but they pretty well left us alone. Too busy pushing south then. They're still around, though. Just kind of low key, if you know what I mean."

"You do business with them?"

He shrugged. "I ain't never been very political. Besides, it's a long ways to the nearest Marquewood army, and, with Ruddygore off the Council, we ain't got the privileged position we once did. I guess we got enough strength to protect the big cities, which is why they ain't done nothin' more and made the truce, but that don't cut beans around here. Where you heading?"

"Valisandra for now," he replied. "Still, I figured there might be some work coming up for somebody in my profession."

"Yeah? How come them instead of south?"

Joe tapped the paper. "Because they pay better, for one thing. And because I've seen the south and tested the winds, and I like to be on the side of the winner. Winners pay. Losers run or hang."

"Yeah, well, there's something to that, I guess. Still, this bunch could stab you through the heart and then you'd *still* fight for 'em—for free!"

"Those zombies are formidable," he agreed, "but you can't win a war or even a major battle with them alone. There's no substitute for thinkers; men who can hold their own in the midst of battle and instantly size up the situation and the move and countermove. They're okay as infantry, but a good fire line could destroy them and have them marching in to be consumed before they could get the order to turn. Then your cavalry could leap right through and behind them and get at the ones who direct them. Remove the controllers and the zombies are just so much rubble."

"You sound like you know your business, all right, Mister ah—"

"Cochise."

"Interesting name."

"All barbarian mercenaries have interesting names," Joe responded lightly. "Book Fourteen, page one hundred and sixty-one."

"Well, you just watch your back, Mister Cochise, when you cross that border, 'cause over there the blackest sort of magic rules unchecked."

"I fought with the Baron at Sorrow's Gorge," Joe responded menacingly. "It'll be just like coming home."

He only wished he'd meant that.

"You get many going north these days?" Joe asked him, curious.

"Some. Salesmen, tradespeople, officials, that kind of thing, and some I'd rather not discuss. Been a ton of real mean fairies headin' in, too, I hear, but most don't come near here. A few nuts, too. Had one guy through, not long ago, crazy as a loon. Said he was on some kind of epic quest. Little guy. Just kept singin' this dumb song in some foreign tongue. Claimed he was lookin' for some desert island. Desert island! In Valisandra! Can you beat that?"

Joe grew suddenly interested. "How long ago did that little fellow come through?"

The innkeeper shrugged. "Couple weeks back, I think. Glad to get rid of him. Gave me the creeps, he did."

Marge, like all faërie, recognized no human borders and particularly not their formalities. She flew over to Valisandra that night, arranging to catch up with the other two when they cleared and were well inside the country.

The border crossing looked pretty standard, if a bit more elaborate than most; the uniforms were different, the accent on the border guards was a bit off, but it hardly seemed the gateway to Hell. They were a lot more officious, though, and they did more touching of Mia than a border guard should.

"She'll have to get down and come inside," he said at last.

"Huh? Why?" Joe was suddenly defensive and suspicious and his hand almost went to his sword.

"She's got to have her head shaved," the guard said. "It's the law here, no exceptions."

Joe was surprised that Mia didn't recoil from that. *He* sure did. "How long has *that* been the law?"

"It used to be a custom among certain of our people and

those of Hypboreya," he told them. "Now it's the law. Absolute. No exceptions."

Joe looked at her long, beautiful hair. "And if I refuse?"

He shrugged. "Then she don't get allowed in. It's your decision, Mister. She's *your* property. I don't make the laws, I just have to enforce them."

Be cold, be tough, he reminded himself. "Okay, but only in my presence."

"Okay with me."

She got down and went inside and sat in the chair they indicated. One of the guards brought these big, sharp scissors and started cutting. It didn't take very long to have a mound of hair on the floor and a scraggly mess on top. Getting the scraggly mess down was more involved, but finally they had it very short. Then they literally shaved her with foamy soap and a straight razor. He was surprised when that wasn't the end of it; they shaved her underarms, her arms, legs, even her pubic hair, leaving only her eyebrows. Then they finished it by applying a greenish liquid over not only her scalp but every place they'd shaved. But for the brows, she was totally hairless. It looked *very* strange, with her bald as a cue ball, but she did have the head for it, and it made her look rather exotic, statuesque.

Joe felt his own still unfamiliar beard and said, "I guess I'm going to have to buy a razor."

"No, the potion we finished with kills all the roots," the guard said casually. "I'd get her a hafiid as soon as I hit my first town. A collar with loop is also required. Until then, the earrings, bracelets, and anklets are okay, but she can't wear anything else. Understand?"

"Uh, yeah," Joe responded, still in a state of shock. They walked back outside.

Finally, the head man tore off a piece of paper and handed it to Joe. "Can you read?"

"No."

"All right, then. This is a conditional entry into the country for you and your property. Carry it with you at all times and don't lose it. You'll be asked to produce it for almost anything, from purchases to rooms to even using the roads. Failure to produce it can result in immediate arrest. It's good for seven days and must be renewed at a constabulary every seven days to remain valid. Travel only on main roads and only in daylight. Use or entry to any posted road or building is prohibited. Camping is prohibited without permission. That's for your protection, believe me. You understand?''

Joe nodded. ''Yeah. What, you don't want me to give blood every day, too?''

''Don't be a wise ass. That's the way to get in real trouble here.''

''Take it easy! I'm just looking to see if there's any work for my talents up here.''

''Yeah, well, could be. That's up to you. Go along, now.''

They went through the border and entered Valisandra. Almost instantly the landscape seemed a little meaner, a little more threatening, and the atmosphere seemed thick and menacing.

There was no real physical difference, nothing you could put your finger on or put into words, but it was tangible none the less. There was the smell of evil about, and it was unmistakable and unpleasant. Even the horses sensed it and grew a bit more nervous.

''Jeez! I'm as pissed off as you are about the hair,'' he told her.

''I am only sorry you no longer find me pleasing to look at, Master,'' she replied. ''I was warned of this back in Terdiera, when I suggested to the Imir that the alchemist might wish to dye my hair in disguise as well.''

''You *knew*? Why didn't you say something, then?''

''There was no purpose to it. We had to come, so it was inevitable.''

''Well, for the record, I don't think you look bad at all. Incredibly different, but I guess I'd look different with all my hair off, too. But it makes you look sexy and exotic. On some people it would be a disaster.''

''You are kind to say so, Master.''

''I can see that it bothers you, though. When we get back, we'll have the good Doctor Mujahn put it back as good as before. If he can grow hair on an old Injun like me, he can sure do it for you.''

"Thank you, Master. I do not know how it looks, but it makes me feel, oddly, naked in a way I have not ever felt before.''

"Well, we're going into colder climates pretty quickly now. The only direction other than north is up. What the hell is the *hafiid* they talked about? *Sheesh!* Seems to me like you'd want *more* hair in a place like we're going, not less!''

"I believe the idea is to insure a slave is always under control," she responded. "The hafiid is a garment, much like a robe, usually of wool, and a headdress of sorts. One wears it with boots or barefoot while outside. There is also a mask and gloves for when it is *very* cold. When a slave enters a warm place, she surrenders it to her master, or to the person in charge of the place, and gets it back when she leaves. You are unlikely to go outside or into places you should not when you are like this and it is cold out.''

"Huh! What do they do with the guys?''

"I, too, was curious about that. Much the same, although they are allowed a codpiece. Their garment is a hooded black woolen robe, tied at the waist.''

"Huh! They get shaved, too?''

She nodded. "All over. The same. They are often, but not always, neutered as well. I believe when Valisandrans speak of geldings they are not speaking of horses.''

He felt a twinge in the vital areas there. "This has been a custom in Valisandra?''

"No, Master. It is a custom in most of the tribes of Hypboreya, the only land left in all Husaquahr where the child of a slave is a slave as well. Some of the same tribes lived across the river here and practiced Hypboreyan customs. Clearly those customs are now becoming the law here, until both countries are the same. What you see here is what would be extended to Marquewood as well, if they win, and High Pothique, and then all Husaquahr.''

"Well, it certainly puts new juice to do the job and do it right here." He shook his head. "And they call *me* a barbarian!''

In most of Husaquahr slaves were always regarded as people; they were just *legally* domestic animals. Here, or at least in the customs that had dribbled over and were now law, slaves were regarded as animals, not human at all. Somehow that sounded like a nice distinction, but for the life of him he couldn't figure out exactly what it was. Maybe it was mostly in the fact that in southern society slavery at least wasn't inherited.

Of course, back home once, millions of men fought a bitter war to end slavery and they won, so now the descendants of slaves had the right to sharecrop a farm or get hooked on drugs or live in squalid ghettos as welfare wards, right? And high-sounding academic types could go on talk shows and blabber about liberation and equality while thousands more kids got hooked on drugs or put in a pimp's "stable" and forced to work the streets, and those high-sounders could forget that most of the rest of the world lived not much different than Husaquahr. Maybe it was only different by degree after all. He broke off that reverie since it got him nowhere and did nobody any good. But, man, it was tough not to get real cynical when the good guys weren't really good, they just weren't as all-out bad as the bad guys.

At least they'd passed the first hurdle, the first real test, and if the truth about Mia hadn't come out, both of them would have flunked, and he knew it. Tiana, no matter what, would have killed herself rather than allow them to do to her what was just done to Mia, and he'd have turned around and said the hell with it rather than sit back and watch it done.

"How'd you find out so much about this?" he asked her.

"I, too, had my briefing, Master," she replied.

"Oh, yeah? Anything else you know that you're not telling me?"

"Nothing of importance."

He looked around. "I wonder where Marge is? It's pretty late for her to be up, but I hope she didn't go to sleep in that forest waiting for us. There's something just, well, *dangerous* about this place."

Marge, however, finally did appear, sleepy but aware. "Oh, boy!" she said, looking at Mia. "They really do a job, don't they? Hey, it doesn't look so bad! Just wear the big earrings to set it all off.''

"What took you so long?" Joe asked. "I was beginning to get worried.''

"When I saw you hung up at the station, I took the time to do a little scouting of the land. It's real oppressive. Can't you feel it?''

He nodded. "You can cut it with a knife.''

"Even the forest's ugly. The trees are starting to grow weird and twist around, and there are lots more ugly weeds.''

He stared emptily into the trees for a moment, then said, "It's because the wood nymphs are sick. They can't do their job properly. If this keeps up, they'll eventually die, and the satyrs who husband the animals will turn wild and vicious.''

Now, how did he know that? Not by learning, but *instinctively*. And he felt it, the nausea from the trees.

Marge frowned, knowing how he knew what he did. "So maybe there really *is* such a thing as an evil wood. If this is the way it is just inside the country, and a country that's only *controlled* by the bad guys, I'm not anxious at all to see *their* land.''

He nodded. "You watch it. There's a lot of evil fairies ascendant in this land. Maybe as bad or worse than evil humans. And some of *them* can fly, too.''

"Uh-huh," she responded, settling in for her sleep.

Mia looked around. "It is as if there is a great shadow on this land, darkening all that live within it," she said. "Is that not what we are to try and lift?''

"Yeah, that's the idea, but we've got a *long* way to go.''

Just a few miles farther on, though, came the second test. Someone had built an ersatz gate of logs across the road, and that someone was six of the meanest-looking guys he'd seen in a long time.

He came up to just in front of the gate and stopped. "What is this about?" he demanded to know.

Their leader, a big man, dressed in black jerkin and leather boots and carrying a crossbow under his arm stepped forward. Joe could swear he could count the fleas on the man.

"This here's a tollgate," he said in the light tone of a man who is totally in charge. "You got to pay a toll to go on."

"I see. And you are with the government?"

Several of the men sniggered at that.

"Yeah, we collect for the guv," the leader responded, and there was more sniggering.

"Uh-huh. And how much do you collect?"

"All we kin git," one of the others said, chuckling evilly.

Joe slid off his horse in a casual way, at one and the same time shifting his swordbelt to the proper position.

"Now, why don't I believe you?" Joe mused aloud, almost taunting.

"You can believe this, foreigner," the leader responded. "There's six of us and you got just you and the bitch."

Mia slid off her horse to the other side, coolly reaching into a saddle pocket and picking up a small throwing knife, which she deftly palmed. Even this naked, without even the hair, it was possible to hide things if you just stood right and moved right.

Joe looked them over. The leader was fairly near; no problem. Three of the other five looked pretty relaxed; they would waste precious time bringing any kind of weapon to bear. The one with the loaded crossbow aimed straight at his chest was the immediate problem. He calculated position, trying to insure that he had the proper angle and that nothing else would be in the way. Mia had moved closer to the men but out of the line of fire and stood there kind of sexily, but tense.

"Six is a problem," Joe admitted. "Five is much simpler. But, of course, you give me no choice. It is give you everything and live, or refuse and die." He had his hand on the sword hilt now, and he could feel Irving's anticipation, its energy, even sheathed, feel its power uniting his arm and its dwarf magic.

"That's the choice."

"I think I choose that you all die," Joe responded, and the answer caught the leader off guard for a precious fraction of a second. Joe leaped and the great broadsword sang and sliced clean through the leader's neck, sending his head, still with a bewildered look on its face, high in the air.

At the same moment, Mia smoothly threw the knife into the chest of the man with the cocked crossbow. He screamed and bent over and the bolt shot harmlessly into the ground several feet from anybody.

Reacting to a two-pronged attack, the remaining four split, three fanning out against Joe, swords drawn, while one, with a maniacal leer, came right at Mia. She waited patiently for him, then, at almost the last second, leaped and kicked him straight in the chest, sending him backward while she whirled and retained her balance. The man she'd struck was hurt badly, probably with crushed ribs, but he was getting to his feet. She ran at him and gave him a kick to the side of the head; then, spying the crossbow bolt in the ground, she reached down, pulled it out, and plunged it into the man's neck.

Joe faced the trio, waiting for one to get brave enough to close.

"Come on, come on," the big man invited them. "I haven't got all day. I want to be in town by dark!"

"Big talk!" one snapped. "There's—"

"*Three* of you now," Joe finished. "We're halfway done and I haven't even had any *fun* yet. If you stay like this too much longer, my girl's going to have an easy time plugging each of you in the back and I won't even get to fight!"

There was a sound like a giant rubber band being sprung at high tension and the middle man screamed, then pitched over, a bolt in his back.

The other two backed up nervously. "Okay, Mister, okay! Call it off!" one of them cried. "No toll for you!"

"You don't get off *that* easily," he told them. "You insulted my girl. She doesn't like anybody calling her a bitch but me. And I don't like ragtag bandits."

They both threw down their swords. Mia, who'd had enough time to reload and recock the bow, looked very disappointed.

"All right! All right! We give up! Just let us go!" one of them pleaded.

Joe sheathed his sword but called, "Mia, keep them covered. Shoot the first one who so much as scratches his fleas and I'll have time to take the manhood from the other one!"

"Your wish is my command, Master," she responded, never enjoying that line more than now.

Methodically, never taking his eyes completely off the pair, he rifled the headless corpse of the leader, coming up with two small bags. Straightening up, he quickly looked into them and found, as he'd expected, one had coins, the other gems. He turned to the pair. "Now, the first thing you are going to do is tear down that barricade," he told them.

"Yes, sir! Yes, sir!" they both said, going to it with a vengeance. Within minutes, they had it reasonably cleared.

"Now—where are your horses? *Your horses! Where?*"

They pointed to the trees, and he went over to Mia and took the crossbow. He never liked them; one shot and then you had nothing, but if he couldn't take one of these idiots barehanded he didn't deserve to be out here. "Mia, go get the horses and any belongings you find that won't have to be burned," he ordered. She went, and soon came back, leading the horses two at a time.

"See if you can tie off all six to ours," he told her.

"You ain't gonna leave us with no horses!" one of the robbers wailed. "We couldn't get no place afore *dark* on foot!"

"Two grown men afraid of the dark," he mocked. "If you're that scared, you can make the border before sunset with a good pace. Do you good. And, by that time, you'll have no problems thinking up a good story for the nice men there. And it'll be a doozy, I bet. Take off all your clothes!"

"Why, you can't ask us to do that! It's against the Rules or somethin'!"

"Ain't fair," the other agreed.

He laughed. "You boys want a code of honor, you better head way south," he told them. "Haven't you got it yet? *I* am robbing *you*!" He uncocked the crossbow almost inviting them to come at him, and tossed it away, then went again to his sword. "Now, which is it? Your clothes or your manhood? I wonder if a man could make it back to that entry station that way without bleeding to death?"

They raced each other to get it all off.

He gestured at the two men, who looked even worse in the

buff than they looked in those clothes, then at the road back the way they came. "Now, *run!*" he ordered. "I'm going to count as high as I can, then I'm gonna pick up that crossbow and fire it right down that road."

"How high kin you count?" one asked.

"I don't know. Let's see, I got one finger, two fingers . . ."

They were off like a shot, making a hilarious sight running down that road, and even Mia laughed at them as they quickly were out of sight.

"Anything but the horses?" he asked her.

"Saddlebags, Master. A couple of crossbows, extra bolts, and a fair amount of Marquewood silks. Also two dead men. It appears we were not their first victims of the day."

He nodded. "Well, pack up what you can. Can you tie up the horses so we can take them all in? They're pretty average looking but they ought to bring some money."

She went to do that and he looked around at the four dead bodies. He felt *terrific!* His old confidence was completely back. And yet, he realized, he'd only been responsible for one of them directly and another by misdirection. Mia had done most of the work and as good as any fighter he'd ever seen.

Mia was soon back. "All set?" he asked her.

"But for one thing, Master," she responded, running to the first man she'd killed and removing the knife, then cleaning it on his tunic.

"You were amazing," he told her honestly. "Tiana could not have done any better."

She beamed. "I was sure about the first one, Master, but not the second. It is very odd, but I had never been able to do that sort of kick before. I think my hair always got in the way or threw me off. This time I did not have to allow for the hair. Perhaps this is not such a tragedy, after all."

"Well, don't get too cocky!" he warned. "These guys were dangerous, yes, but they were common thieves. Professionals would have reacted without thinking, and they would not have taken you for granted."

She spat on the ground near a body. "That sort of man always takes girl slaves for granted, Master." She ran lightly back and jumped atop her horse, then gathered what reins she could and tied everything off. They looked now like horse-breeders on their way to market.

Joe mounted his own horse and started past the former barricade. *"On the road again,"* he sang. *"Can't wait to get back on the road again . . ."*

Marge stirred from under her tarp and peered out fuzzily. "Huh, wuzzit?" She looked around and suddenly saw a whole lot more horses around her. "Where'd *they* come from?"

Joe laughed. "Poor Marge! Go back to sleep! A robbery and a fight can't wake you up, but my singing does it every time!"

Marge peered blurrily at the horses, then at Mia and Joe, frowned, shrugged, and crawled back under her tarp.

It wasn't much of a town, but it was clearly seeing better days because of the proximity of military units. There had been a lot of new and obviously slipshod construction along its one main street, probably to serve the military forces who had first passed it by, then returned in the truce and remained nearby.

The stable manager was taken aback at the number of horses. "They're for sale," Joe told him. "Cheap."

The livery man, a stout, middle-aged man, with gray hair and mustache dressed in brown, who looked and smelled as if he'd been born in the stable, looked them over. "Ain't much," he commented. "Serviceable, though. You got clear title?"

"The men who owned them won't be coming to claim them, if that's what you mean," Joe answered. "They made a serious mistake of trying to rob me."

"Well, I'll be swaggered! I *thought* that was Stirt's horse there!"

"Scruffy man, fleas, dirty gray clothes?"

"The very one!"

"If he returns, he'll be carrying his head under his arm," Joe told the liveryman. "If he does and still wants his horse, I'll refund your money."

The liveryman looked suddenly frightened. "You shouldn't oughta joke like that, son. Not 'round *here*. It ain't all that improbable!"

"Was he a friend of yours?"

"Nope. Real backstabber. Bad from the start. It's just that he owed me money. Not that I was gonna get it anyway, but . . ."

"Thirty for the lot and you put up my three for the night," Joe told him.

"Ain't possible! I'll be lucky to resell the lot for twenty-five afore some nosy somebody from the military district comes in and confiscates them as necessary for the defense. Ten plus the board and feed of yours."

"I'll sell them on the street for more than that." They went back and forth in traditional fashion, finally settling on seventeen gold pieces and the livery service. With the still uncounted booty from the thieves' stash, he was beginning to take a certain liking to Valisandra in spite of its rottenness.

"The military are near here?" he asked the liveryman.

"Couple miles. Lots of trainin' and stuff, lots of noise and marching and all that other soldier crap."

"All Valisandran?"

He nodded. "All except some of the officers. I ain't sure what *they* are. Might not even be human for all I know. There's a Valisandran Volsan detachment, too. Big suckers."

"Volsan—they're of the centaurs, right?"

"Yep. Wouldn't want to face any of *them* in a fight. Kinda all in one cavalry. Drink harder than a thievin' barman, too. Mostly humans be in tonight, though. Full pack workday; won't be many. You up here to sign up?"

"I am up here to see if there is anything worth my while to sign up for," he replied. "Any of the stores open? And how available is the hotel?"

"Most of the stores'll be open for a while yet, just in case the soldiers come in and want something. Used to have lots of folks here on their way to deal with the dwarf lords in the mountains. Even some tourists, believe it or not. Now, it's just soldiers. If they hadn't come back and stuck here, we'd 'a dried up and blowed away. Hotel's always half or better empty because of it. The guv puts soldiers up."

Joe nodded and left the stables. Mia joined him. "Let's get you your whatever it is," he told her.

"Hafiid, Master."

"Yeah, hafiid. Best to pick up what we need now."

The general store wasn't exactly overflowing with hafiids. "Not much call for 'em down here, at least 'til fall," the proprietor told him. "Still, got one or two."

The hafiid turned out to be a loose-fitting, pleated robelike garment of beige-colored wool that was essentially of a single piece, with a neat knitted hole in it and two sleeves. It was essentially a one-size-fits-all kind of thing that came down to her ankles. The loose, robelike sleeves were much too long, but could be trimmed to fit. The other part was a burnoose thing the same color, made out of stretch wool, and had a six-inch flap that hung down the back. Optional was any pair of boots, midcalf or lower, that were some shade of brown or tan. She tried out a few, clearly uncomfortable with any kind of footwear, but settled on a midcalf model that wasn't that easy to get into or out of but, she said, provided the most support.

"She will also need a neck collar," the proprietor said. "Another of the new regulations, I'm afraid. The next thing you know, they'll require them to have *leashes*. It really has gotten that odd."

She picked a bronze collar that pretty well matched the bracelets, anklets, and earrings she already had, but with evenly spaced oversized rivets that came to broad points spaced around it. In place of one rivet was a loop through which something, perhaps a chain, could be attached. Maybe the proprietor wasn't far from the truth. The proprietor fitted it carefully, then put a protective leather patch in between it and the back of her neck and pulled a series of tiny seals. There was a hissing and some smoke rose from the collar, making her flinch, but none got through and he soon removed the patch. The collar was fused, as if welded.

With the complete outfit on, Joe thought she looked like a slightly punk, tan-colored nun.

"Used to be we saw no slaves down here, and the ones we saw were all Marquewood, and there was never any problem," the storekeeper told him apologetically. "Now, though, you can be declared a slave for spitting on the boardwalk. It hasn't happened yet, but the rumors are all these new slave regulations are in preparation for making just about all the lower classes slaves. The government denies it, but you can't trust *them* these days to tell you much. Even many of the fairy races are being rounded up and forced into work gangs. It's not like it used to be."

"I can see that," Joe responded. He could see Sugasto's grand social vision clearly and it made him sick. The masses would be enslaved to the state, fed, cheaply clothed, and housed *en masse*, forced to do all the menial labor at the end of a lash until they dropped. Otherwise, there would be soldiers, a trading class to supply the necessities and maintain trade and commerce, but a rather small one, and, of course, the top one percent who would control everything. It was an ugly picture, but it explained all the harsh slave measures.

Only a small percentage of people could be truly of the slave class anywhere; he knew that. The Rules mandated it, and the ways you reached that status, and what sorts of labor were under it. If Sugasto and his cronies turned their domain into nothing more than a slave state, they wouldn't really be within the Rules but rather outside of them. Since the masses wouldn't be true slaves, bound by the Rules of slaves like Mia, they would always be a potential danger. You couldn't really turn your back on them. Hence, the collars, the chainings, all the rest. The hairless rule was equally obvious; if any of those ersatz slaves had the opportunity, they might escape. Dressed in uniforms or some such or foreign clothing, they might well cause a lot of harm. If you were hairless, though, you kind of stood out in the crowd. Back in the earliest Colonial days in the US, he knew, blacks had often been treated the same as indentured servants. They became permanent slaves because their skin made it easy to spot them anywhere. The false justifications came later.

This place felt on the verge of being the victim of a grandiose and evil experiment. Indeed, this might be regional, only one of many such, to test out what worked and what didn't and sort of get the bugs out. The one that had the highest gain and least losses and problems would be the eventual fate of all Husaquahr.

Mia took charge of helping outfit him, suggesting a buckskin sort of outfit with dark brown fur trim and a droopy, broad-brimmed leather hat. Her eye was perfect; she unerringly seemed to choose only the things that fit him.

Almost on impulse, he added a forked leather bullwhip. He used to be fair with one, but hadn't bothered with it much. Somehow, though, it fit the image.

They left for the hotel, Mia carrying her boots and, in fact, her slave outfit. She would wear them when she had to.

"I want a room, directions to a decent meal, and arrangements for a bath," he told the clerk.

"Just the one night? Heading south, then?"

"No. North."

The clerk stiffened. "Then you will be with us longer than that."

"Why? Problems?"

"You don't *know*? The zombie masters are gathering on the plains just north of here for the next three days and nights. I wouldn't go a hundred yards north of this town for at *least* one day longer!"

"Zombies, huh? Sounds like something's up."

The clerk shrugged. "These days, sir—who knows?"

He signed in and had Mia square things away in the room, then went over to the cafe. They were short on food, shorter on cuisine, but they remembered the days when wealthy Marquewood merchants would pass through on the way to the dwarf lords, there to negotiate for the exquisite craftsmanship only dwarf magic could create. They often brought their personal slaves along. There was no objection at all to Mia serving her master, and then eating anything he left on his plate. Of course, there *was* a slight hitch.

"I'm sorry, sir, but everything's rationed these days," the waitress apologized. She was one of the typical cafe-types, short, fat, and brash. "We'll soon be out of business if they don't let us get *some* regular deliveries back. All the ranch produce has been pretty much taken by the army, and nobody makes deliveries from Marquewood no more."

He was sympathetic, and managed, with serrated hunting knife, to cut what was supposed to be a steak and get it down. They were doing the best they could. At least the strictly vegetarian Mia could have her fill; local gardens were deemed too minor for the authorities, and so the locals at least had some vegetables for now, even pastries of beet sugar and bran, although they weren't sure what would happen when winter came.

If the steak was representative of the future, though, he might well go vegetarian himself, he thought, a sour taste in his throat.

Marge was waiting for them when they got back.

"It *did* look pretty hairy out there," she admitted. "I'm really tempted to try and see what's going on up there."

"You watch it!" he cautioned. "You don't know what's around here, including things that might fly and eat Kauris for dinner."

"I've always been able to take care of myself," she replied confidently. "You worry about yourself. Still, I noticed this evening that this might not be a bad time for a few days' break."

"Huh? What do you mean?"

"I'd say the moon will be completely full sometime tomorrow evening."

The curse! He'd been so preoccupied that, even though he was usually very good about it, he hadn't given it much thought.

He started thinking hard. "You know, it *is* tempting, in light of that, to see just what's what. You keep away from the dangerous parts tonight, but maybe tomorrow night we'll be able to work something out."

"What're you thinkin' of?"

"Taking a few risks. The fight today made me realize that Gorodo was right: I *have* been soft, not in the body, but in the mind."

She shrugged. "Okay. It seems like we're gettin' nowhere fast doin' what we been doin', anyway."

She left, and he knew she'd not be nearly as cautious as he wanted her to be, but, as she said, she had proven herself capable before.

There also had to be a way to speed this up, somehow; she was right about that. It would be possible to hug the river almost to the Golden Lakes district. The River of Dancing Gods wasn't all that navigable that far north, with lots of falls and cataracts, but he actually considered something like a canoe, finally rejecting it as making him too vulnerable. And, of course, horses would be harder to come by the farther in they went. Still, there just *had* to be a way to make better time. They were barely inside enemy territory, and he was impatient, and there was still such a long way to go.

He had to wonder, though: if this was the sorry state that Valisandra was reduced to, then what in *hell* must Hypboreya be like?

CHAPTER 8

ZOMBIE JAMBOREE

All important matters of evil sorcery shall be done at midnight whenever possible.

—The Books of Rules, XIX, 12(a)

"ARE YOU *REALLY* A SLAVE? A *REAL* SLAVE?"

Mia looked up at the young soldier who was gawking at her and thought, *No, of course not. I'm naked and hairless and wearing this ring in my nose just to make a fashion statement.* But, aloud, she replied, "Yes, my lord."

"My lord," several of the young soldiers responded, giggling, and the boy said, "I ain't never been called no 'lord' before."

"My lord, since all people are above me in status, you are as worthy of respect as a prince or king. There is no difference to a slave."

"You mean—you got to do what we say?"

"My lord, all people are my superiors, but I have but one master."

These weren't actually bad kids, she thought to herself, somewhat surprised. They were quite typical of the kind of young men you'd find anywhere in a city or an army. Young men from typical peasant and worker backgrounds who were probably away from home for the first time in their lives. It was in some ways a disturbing concept for her. You always thought of the "enemy" as something mean and nasty, an evil force composed of evil men. Instead, they were very much normal folks, just as on the "good" side, who were either in the service of evil or

161

the tools of it, with no more choice in the matter than she had. Nothing more brought home what a waste wars truly were.

"How'd you get this way?" one of them asked. Being from the poorer classes, they had never really seen a slave up close before. "You do something really bad?"

"My lords, my crime was to have been born too poor and to have fallen into evil company. The only proper way to make a slave is if it actually makes things better for that one."

"That ain't the way the Hypboreyans do it," one of them remarked. "They *breed* 'em."

She found that idea *most* unpleasant to think about.

"So what d'ya *do*?" another one asked.

"My lords, I attend to my master. I do all the little things so that he need not bother himself about them. Anything he wants or needs, I try and do."

"I got a want and need I could use somebody for," one of the boys muttered to the chuckles of the others.

"And," she added, "I dance."

"Yeah? Will you dance for us?"

"I would need my master's permission. Wait, and I will ask him."

She ran up to the room, where Joe was lying down, feeling the effects of the day's activities all of a sudden. "Master, some of the young soldiers wish me to dance for them. I should like to do so."

He looked at her. "I'm not gonna be there to bail you out this time."

"I feel I can take care of myself with *those* boys."

He didn't like it, but Marge had predicted to him that, sooner or later, Mia would ask just such a thing, and had promised to watch out for the dancer if things got out of hand.

"Okay, but if this goes bad and you come back all beat up, don't expect sympathy."

"Oh, thank you, Master!" she cried, then hunted for and found her castanets and rushed back down again. It wasn't just her need to dance, which was strong enough that it stopped just short of a compulsion, but also something she didn't quite understand on a conscious level, but which Marge did.

The liveryman had predicted that few soldiers would be in town, and he'd been right. There were only eight boys, the members of a squad that had escaped rigorous field training by drawing some kind of cleanup detail.

They went to the edge of town, at the livery stable, where there was a fair amount of room and good torch lighting. Above, on a nearby roof, unseen to them, Marge landed and perched to watch and watch out for her companion. She understood well the real reason Mia wanted to dance for these strangers, the reason Mia wanted what heretofore she had shunned.

The slave had examined herself in the bathhouse mirror, and had seen someone reflected back so different and strange-looking that she hardly recognized it. The shaving had chipped away a central core of her ego, as, of course, it was designed to do. Mia's dancer's body was lean and trim, but her breasts were quite small and rock hard; in spite of a perfect curve at the pelvis, she was very much of a neuter as those things went, particularly in a world where bare breasts were common. Shorn of her long hair, the neuter effect was reinforced, particularly in her eyes.

Mia needed to know if she was still a woman in the eyes of others.

She started slow, but quickly picked up the pace, using the castanets to give not merely rhythm to her moves but emphasis to her major ones, and she held the onlookers spellbound. Marge too, was fascinated. That girl could *dance*!

The whistles, claps and *very* male reactions from the small group of soldiers was just what Mia needed, and she reveled in it. Marge, reading the emotions of the group, understood Joe's reluctance to allow this, but she also read Mia's supercharged emotional state. The way she was dancing right into them, charging them up, made Marge realize that, this time, she didn't *want* Joe to rescue her, nor Marge, either. She finished right at the entrance to the stables with a big finish and ducked inside. Easy enough to get away at that point when they ran after her, but she did not come out.

All of the soldier boys would wind up being punished for being late checking back into their camp.

Mia was in fact bruised and sore the next morning, but she didn't seem to mind it a bit. Joe was somewhat concerned; but, apparently, however she'd come by them, it hadn't been against her will or her wishes. He could have forced her to tell him, of course, but he decided he'd rather not ask, not only to preserve what dignity she still had but also because he wasn't sure he really wanted to know.

In spite of some soreness and stiffness, Mia was in an extremely upbeat, confident mood, possibly as good as he'd ever seen her. And, why not? The previous day had been a banner one for her. She'd proved herself more than capable in the fight with the thieves, and, later on, she'd proven herself in the only other area that was important or even relevant to her. She had nothing left to prove to herself, and that made her spirit soar.

"It's a good thing we're laying over, though," Joe commented, looking at some of those bruises. "You wouldn't be much good in a fight *or* on a horse at this point."

"I can do anything you demand of me, Master," she responded. "You know, if you do not mind, I may remain like this even after we return. Not having to wash or fool with that hair makes things much easier."

He shrugged. "If you like it, great." He wasn't going to press her on it. "Uh—tonight is the first full moon, you know."

She stopped. "I had not thought of that, Master. What shall we do about it? We should not become each other. It would not be right, nor fair, at this time."

"Yeah. Disregarding the slave part, I don't want *those* bruises. But, I have an idea if you don't mind skipping some sleep tonight. I've done it before and it wasn't so awful, and it might give us a way to find out what the hell is going on around here. This is too close to the border. I wouldn't like to be stuck up north and discover that everything's happening down here."

"What do you have in mind, Master?"

He reached down and pulled a crumpled blanket away. Marge was asleep under it.

"I'm going to give instructions that our room is not to be entered or touched today," he told her. "That'll keep Marge from having nasty interruptions."

"I can do the clean and make up, Master. I used to be a maid, you remember."

"Good." He looked down at the sleeping Marge. "How would you like to fly?"

It felt kind of silly and looked sillier, all three of them there sitting on the floor, Mia to the left of Marge and holding her left hand, and Joe to the right of the Kauri, holding her right hand.

The curse of the were was a curse of the blood; by blood was it transmitted and by blood was it carried and held. Almost all of such curses were specific to some animal or demonic form, but there was a very rare form in which the last part of the curse's spell had somehow been miswritten or garbled when first applied. Upon the nights of the full moon, such a one was transformed until either morning or moonset. But, since only half the curse was truly operable, at this mystic moment, both Joe and Tiana would turn into the nearest living animal, and remain that way until either moonset or dawn, whichever came first.

Although the faërie were neither human nor animal in the scientific sense, they qualified under the curse, as Joe had discovered more than once.

"It's getting pretty boring," Joe said grumpily, "and it's pretty dark out there. Are you *sure* about this night, Marge?"

"I'm sure. Moonrise is a little late tonight. Any time now."

"I truly hope so, my lady," Mia sighed. "I am sitting on a particularly painful bruise."

"Don't worry about that. Weres are particularly fast healers," Marge noted. "I remember hearing about one who had his head chopped through with an ax. The ax went through and came out bloody, but aside from a scar that faded in a few days and a bad sore throat, he was no worse for wear. Scared the bejezus out of everybody and made a legend."

"Did he get away?" Joe asked, not having heard that one.

"No. Somebody found an ornamental pole with a silver tip. Drove it right through him, poor guy."

Joe was about to say something as soon as he could think what it was, when, suddenly, as the moon cleared the horizon opposite the window, it happened.

Joe felt a sudden dizziness and blurring of vision and thought, then a series of strange sensations as parts of him seemed to grow or contract or do other such things.

And, on the floor of the room, now sat three absolutely identical Kauris, holding hands. So identical were they, in fact, that not even another Kauri could tell them apart, save that Mia's collar hung loosely around her neck. She let go of Marge and shook her wrists, and the two bracelets fell to the floor, then did the same with the anklets. Her collar, however, would have to remain uncomfortably on. Her head just wasn't sufficiently smaller than her normal one to permit that.

And although her pierced earrings fell through the flesh to the floor, the ring still remained in her nose.

They hadn't thought of that, but it seemed logical. Ruddygore said that, once in, nothing save death could remove it.

Marge looked at it critically. "Huh! The only Kauri slave in all history! I hope that doesn't set a precedent."

"It won't," Joe responded, in a voice absolutely identical to Marge's. "I think at least we'll find that the ring has no effect."

"You are right!" Mia said, delighted. "You are not my master or mistress or whatever it means for now."

"Only temporarily," Joe reminded her. "Jeez. The last time I was turned female I was embarrassed as hell. This just feels like a different suit of clothes. Maybe I'm finally getting able to handle almost anything."

"I—I have never been of faërie before," Mia commented. "It does not feel all that different. I wish I could keep these breasts, though." She reached up and touched the back of her head. "And *hair* again!"

"You want different?" Joe responded. "Try a whole new set of muscles along your back you never had before."

"Well, we can all sit in here and gab, or we can have a little fun," Marge said. "Let me put out the light." She went over and blew out the oil lamp.

"But it's so dark—" Mia began, then stopped, her words ending with a gasp. It *wasn't* dark. Everything was so clear, so sharp, so detailed! And the other two, they were softly glowing, a beautiful pastel reddish pink.

No, there *was* a difference, but very slight, in Joe's glow, almost as if there was some green which the reddish glow did not quite mask.

"Been so long, I've forgotten what it's like to see human," Marge commented. "The main thing to remember, though, is to think only about those things that need thinking about, like where you're goin' and what you wanna do. Let the body do what it does naturally and don't fight it. Guide, but let the body do the work." She went over to the window. "Everybody ready?"

"But I have never flown before—on my own wings!"

"Just get up on the windowsill, look where you're goin' —that's the important part—and kick off!" Marge said, disappearing out the window.

"Go ahead," Joe urged her. "It's just your mental conditioning getting in the way. I was the same way once myself." He got her up on the windowsill, but she looked out and got really nervous.

Suddenly, Joe pushed her behind, and out she went. For a moment, she felt as if she were falling, but, suddenly, she felt the flap of the wings on her back and soared upward.

Marge was suddenly beside her. "Relax, let the wings do the work," she cautioned. "Don't even *think* about them. Just *fly*."

Now Joe was beside her, too, and they were up, up in the night sky, far over the town.

Once she learned to let go and relax, it became almost second nature to fly. It was *wonderful*, one of the greatest feelings she'd ever known!

The landscape spread out all around her, but it looked quite different, not only because of the aerial perspective but also because of additional sights and information she was now receiving. Somehow, she instantly knew where she was in relation to anything else she could see, and just exactly how far it was to any point from there. While it was clearly dark, everything was easily visible in great detail, and much that was not seen by human eyes was visible, too. The very air had slight, subtle coloration and texture, and tiny sparklies of varying colors moved along, saying exactly where the air was moving, and how fast.

Areas of forest and field and far-off mountains also had their own strange patterns. Complex patterns, mostly, like tiny spiderweblike strings of every color, intensity, and hue, and in and around areas where nothing should be there were patches of various pastel blobs in a variety of sizes.

It was beautiful.

"Fairy sight," Joe told her. "The strings are spells, magic and sorcery of some sort. The blobs are living things, creatures mostly of faërie. Although we're a sort of soft red, in general watch out for the reds and yellows and whites. They tend to be on the darker side of faërie. The blues and greens tend to be almost always to the good, the rest sort of in-betweens. Don't take them for granted, though. As the Kauri are reds, and not evil, so, too, are there exceptions to all the Rules."

"The reason why they call the darkest magic black is that it *is*," Marge told her. "And black strings and blobs blend in and can't be so easily seen until it's too late. If you ever see any sort of blackness and suspect it might have moved, ever so slightly, stay away! Don't depend on fairy flesh or the were curse to save you—there are things far worse than death. Just imagine something eating you alive . . . forever."

The point was well taken, although, in truth, as weres they were better protected than Marge.

"Let's go over to the military encampment first," Joe suggested. "It's likely to have fewer defenses from ones like us than the other place where the bigwigs are, and I want to see just what the hell they're training for."

It was becoming easier by the moment. You just picked some sparklies that were going in the general direction you wanted and got into their flow. Only when you had no lifting aid from the air did you work at it, and it quickly was becoming automatic, even at that.

"Remember," Marge warned, "we're just about incapable of an offense, so, if you run into anything, fly or run like hell. If you can't, let me handle it and go along with whatever I do, no matter how idiotic it looks to you. There are a few things only experience can tell you.''

From this height, you could see the military camp clearly, even at this distance. It was *huge*, with tents and temporary structures all over the place, some going all the way out to the horizon.

A lot of the Valisandran army was there, much of it bedding down for the night, but both Joe and Mia were struck by the enormous waves of feelings coming from the camp. Enormous waves of loneliness, unhappiness, even despair, and, over all, an atmosphere of terrible fear you could almost see. It was almost too much for Mia to handle, and she fought back tears. ''Those poor guys,'' she sympathized.

''Yeah, you really get the weight of the world as a Kauri.'' Marge sighed. ''After a while, though, you get to handle most anything. To me, that's the biggest banquet hall I ever did see.''

''Yes, but how do you feed on it?'' Mia asked, and, almost immediately, her body told her. ''Ohhh . . .'' she managed.

''Yeah, well, you shouldn't feel hungry right now,'' Marge told her, ''because I've had no problems getting energy around *this* place and you got what I got. Maybe tomorrow night. It just seems normal only you get a whole extra body kick to it and, instead of being tired at the end, you're rarin' to go.''

Joe ignored the interchange, far more interested in the lay of the land. ''There's the centaurs there. Big, mean-looking suckers, aren't they? They'd be like mounted archers that could hit a target at a couple of hundred yards, I bet. And over there, off by themselves . . . *Bentar*! I *knew* those bastards would be here someplace!''

The Bentar were the fiercest race of fighting fairies, totally without mercy, conscience, or any moral sense at all. Their tall, grim visages were at once like a bird of prey and yet oddly reptilian, with mean eyes that reflected the light. You didn't need fairy sight to know those were real sons of bitches down there.

''I don't understand it,'' Marge said, shaking her head. ''It looks as if they're assembling something the size of the Battle of Sorrow's Gorge, yet where's the heavy stuff? The big catapults and siege machines and all the rest and the second army on wheels with all the supplies?''

Joe thought it over. "The only reason you'd have something like this without those things is if you didn't think you were going to need them," he replied. "That's not an army of conquest being assembled down there—it's an army of occupation."

Mia looked out over the assemblage and to the stars beyond, and, quite suddenly, a few of the stars winked out, then on again, then others did the same.

"Black shapes!" she warned. "Coming in fast from the plain! Flying!"

"Scatter!" Marge shouted. "Rendezvous back on the hotel roof!"

The concept of being eaten alive forever hadn't lingered far from Mia's consciousness. She was off like a shot.

The Kauri, it was true, had no offense at all, but they were by no means helpless. In addition to Marge's bag of illusory magic tricks, they were very light and very, very fast when they needed to be, and had a flight instinct second to none. There were some birds and tiny fairies, like pixies, that could match them in speed, but for both speed and distance they were virtually unequaled.

Mia rose, caught a fast current, and made six or seven miles from the military camp to the hotel roof in no more than seven minutes, a sprint that, she suddenly realized, meant she'd made something like *sixty miles an hour*! And she'd done it without really thinking at all!

Incredibly impressed with herself, she was equally amazed to find that Joe had beaten her.

"It's the collar," he said. "Probably slowed you down a bit. And, yeah, I'm impressed, too. I never knew she could do *that*. And we're not even breathing particularly hard!" He looked around and frowned. "But where is Marge?"

They waited worriedly for several minutes. Finally, the real Kauri arrived, but not from the direction of camp, flying low.

"Sorry, but I figured I'd give 'em something to chase in the wrong direction. They're pretty slow, relatively speaking. I had actually to slow down so I wouldn't lose 'em until I was ready to."

"What were they?" Joe asked, looking around at the sky.

"Nazga. All leathery wings and teeth and hard as a rock. Not too bright on their own, though, and one of 'em had riders. Odds were they were just told to patrol for flying intruders as a routine thing."

"I'm not so sure about that other gathering now," Joe said worriedly. "They'll have a lot more security there than at the camp, and it's possible they may be warned about us."

"Aw, I doubt if those flying stomachs will bother warning anybody. They have enough trouble remembering their own names," Marge replied. "But, you're right. They'll have a lot more security. I'm still game, though, if you are."

Joe sat back on the rooftop and sighed. Mia looked at him and couldn't get over how naturally *feminine* the moves and manner of the big macho man were as a Kauri. The fact that it was still his methodical fighting man's mind speaking actually just gave his form real strength.

In fact, except for the slight difference in accent and choice of words, Joe, as a Kauri, seemed just like Marge.

"All right," he said at last. "But we don't push it. If we can't get near, then we can't get near. Understood?"

They both nodded.

"And, in any event," he reminded them, "we'd better be back well before dawn."

Mia looked at the horizon. "But where do we look for them?" she asked.

"We follow the road, of course," he answered. "If they've got it blocked north, then it's got to lead where they don't want anyone going."

They hadn't flown on long before Mia said, "There's a slight fog of some kind. You can see all right, but it's like a thin, dark film over everything."

"That's been there since we entered this vile land," Marge responded. "It's just that you hadn't had anything to contrast it with before. Now it's getting more dense."

"What is it?" Mia asked, curious.

"It is evil," Marge told her. "It is the cloak of pure evil."

The Kauri felt no heat or cold, but Mia still felt a very real chill go through her. "It seems to come from the northwest," she noted.

"Yes," Joe agreed. "From Hypboreya."

They passed over some military roadblocks, Joe noting that all the guards were Bentar. Clearly, if you got this far, you weren't just going to be turned around with a warning. If you were lucky, the creatures from the dark side of faërie would kill you.

Beyond the roadblocks they flew low to the ground, hoping to avoid any faster and more efficient flying sentinels. Marge, who had all the experience in this sort of thing, took the lead, as the road and ground rose sharply in a series of switchbacks leading up the side of the great plateau. On a tiny ledge, Marge settled and the other two joined her.

"Well," she said, "there it is."

Below them were possibly the darkest forces in the service of Hypboreya, lined up as if for inspection, more immobile than any such armed force could possibly be. An army of the living dead.

"They look in a lot better shape than that crew Sugasto had around him the last time I had a run-in with him," Marge commented.

"Those were reanimated corpses," Joe reminded her. "Their value is as much psychological as anything, as you proved. Even a Kauri can kick their face in. I would doubt if they could handle the reanimation without a real expert sorcerer in the immediate neighborhood to keep them moving and direct their every action. These people below us are corpses, in a way, but they're not dead. These are people whose souls he's stolen and got bottled up somewhere, but whose bodies keep on. No souls, but with the rest of their brains keeping their bodies going, maybe even some of their skills, just no way to use them. They don't think, but they can obey even complex commands."

Mia was appalled. "There are *thousands* of them! Both men

and women, too! Even *children* in some of those brigades! How monstrous!"

Joe nodded. "That's why they're so confident. They can probably send small numbers of these, mixed by age and sex, into various parts of Marquewood and maybe beyond. They'd have to be fed, of course, but they wouldn't care what they ate. And, for whatever reason, their masters could send them anywhere, to do just about anything. There, Mia, is the step below slaves, doing whatever they're told, knowing nothing, feeling nothing."

"It's the sickest thing I ever saw!" Marge commented. "It's turning people into—*robots*. Machines."

"Will they do that to their whole army?" Mia asked, sickened. "Those boys . . ."

"No, I doubt it," Joe reassured her. "For one thing, a power like this is unique. The power to do this is also the power to pull the swaps. If you had that kind of power, would you let all your underlings know it? Who would you trust? Even Sugasto has to sleep sometime, have guards, servants. How would he know who to trust? Uh-uh. The Master of Dead would die himself before he'd let that secret out to *anybody*."

"Except the Dark Baron," Marge reminded him. "Remember, Boquillas pulled that trick, too, back on Earth."

"Yeah, but only with help. He has no real power of his own, remember. I don't know if Sugasto told him, or if he simply figured it out after seeing it done. He's that smart. And, remember, he had a way so that even Dacaro, who was working the thing for him, couldn't figure it out himself, and Ruddygore said the Baron purged his mind of the mechanism to prevent it getting out. So, it's Sugasto. That means our Master of the Dead did all that handiwork himself down there. Others can control and work them, of course, but only he can make a zombie."

"That's what your old body is or was like then," Marge noted.

He nodded. "But he'll need more than animation, more than programming, and more than just a good actor to pull off his scheme. The government knew we weren't coming back and was glad to get rid of us, I think. They couldn't oppose our return, but they'd assassinate both if they had the slightest suspicion they were being had."

"But what are they doing *here*?" Mia asked him.

Joe pointed to a small compound just beyond the lines of zombies. "There. That's the reason. This whole force is a bodyguard for whoever's in there. Dollars to doughnuts that's Sugasto in there with his commanders, and that the vast majority of these poor people were created on the spot, maybe over the last couple of days."

"Then those crates near the building there—see them?" Mia pointed. "They are commercial wine crates—but there is not much wine grown in Valisandra. Even *I* know that."

Marge gave a slight gasp. "That's because those bottles have no wine in them. They're the souls of these people!"

"We must do *something*," Mia said. "We can't just leave these poor people like this."

"Go to fairy sight," Marge told them. "Just concentrate and keep looking."

They did, and slowly a complex of huge multicolored strings, crisscrossing and knotting this way and that, formed like a bubble over the whole compound, including the crates. It was the largest, most complex protective spell even Marge could remember.

"We'd never get past *that*," she said firmly. "Even if we managed to evade the zombies, the Bentar, and whatever else is prowling about, there is just no way. We'd trigger something, get caught, and wind up in little bottles ourselves." The Kauri sighed in frustration. "Short of somebody like Ruddygore, the only one who might break in *there* would be Macore. He even broke into Ruddygore's vaults, remember."

"Macore, I'm afraid, is more likely down with the dead," Joe told her. "He passed through this region a couple of weeks ago. The innkeeper at the border remembered him."

"It's not much of a solution, in any event, I guess," Marge said. "If we smashed the bottles, we'd liberate the souls but that would just allow them to pass on. The only way to restore them would be to catch each one of them and stick the bottle down his or her throat, the way Ruddygore did with you. The trouble with that is, like Ruddygore, we'd have no way of knowing who was who, and the zombie we were trying to save would be trying to kill us for it. No, face it, it's back to back and belly to belly at the zombie jamboree and we got to run.''

"Huh?"

"You're too young. *Zombie Jamboree: The Song That Killed Calypso* by Lord Invader and his Three Penetrators. Never mind. It's just my grave sense of humor coming up in a hopeless situation.''

"Look!" Mia cried in an excited whisper. "Someone's coming out of the meeting place!''

Several figures, in fact. The distance was far enough that even with the Kauris' super nightsight and eaglelike telescopic vision it was hard to make them out.

"The big guy in black's got to be Sugasto, the old Master of the Dead himself!" Marge told them. "The others are probably his aides and military leaders—but who's that long-haired sexy broad with him? I can't quite get a fix on her.''

"I can't, either,'' Joe replied. "We need to get closer, and, right now, that would set off every alarm they have with them outside. Man! What I wouldn't give for a telescopic rifle right now! Just a couple of shots and it would all be over!''

Marge wasn't listening. "Whoever that girl is, she's hanging all over Sugasto. Funny, I never thought he'd be interested in that kind of thing. I—*oh, my God!*''

It was said so sharply that it almost triggered the other two's escape instincts. Joe calmed down, noting that a Kauri heart beat just as hard as a human one when scared. "What?'' he managed.

"That girl with Sugasto! It's Mahalo McMahon!''

"Can't be,'' Joe responded. "The Dark Baron was—'' It hit him. "—in the body of Ma— Oh, my God!''

"They *are* together!'' Marge added, stating the obvious. "For some reason, the Baron's still in her body!''

"Could be he no longer knows how to get out of it,'' Joe suggested, staring. It *was* the Hawaiian's body. That was clear now. "Maybe Sugasto thinks it's in his interest to keep the Baron like that, too. Who knows what Rules came into play?''

"Perhaps," Mia suggested, "the Dark Baron has found that he *likes* being a young and attractive woman."

"The Baron had as much interest in sex as a grapefruit does," Joe replied. "But if that's still him in that body, then it doesn't matter about the rest, just as it doesn't matter if the old bastard's a coequal, Sugasto's mistress, or his spiritual advisor. What it *does* mean is that the best mind in the history of sorcery is coupled with an incredibly powerful sorcerer. And our two most hated enemies are united and we're walking right into their lair!"

"Uh-oh! *Watch it!*" Marge yelled, and all three took off as suddenly a beam of blinding yellow light emerged from the black-robed sorcerer and headed right for them.

The ledge on which they'd been standing a fraction of a second earlier exploded with a loud bang, throwing fragments of rock all over the place.

They weren't waiting around to find out what came next, plunging rapidly over the other side toward the lowlands below.

"Look out behind and above!" Marge warned them, although they could barely hear her. From behind them, over the cliff wall, emerged a shimmering web of gold and crimson magic strings, woven tightly like a net, yet expanding like some gigantic firework. It descended rapidly now, continuing to fan out as it did so, and none of the three were sure they were going to make it when the thing finally got to their level.

Joe felt a burning sensation on his feet and legs but the thing barely brushed him, then dropped on past. Still, he felt suddenly terribly weakened, drained of energy, and was forced to the ground. He looked around, suddenly exhausted, and watched it drop just behind him and contract, singeing the ground a bit as it did so.

The other two were ahead of him; they had to have cleared it. But, man! What a *hell* of a piece of sorcery *that* was, and all extemporaneous! That guy has gotten *good!* he thought angrily. Too good. He looked down at the petite Kauri leg that had been just missed and saw an angry-looking welt, the kind he'd get from pressing his real leg against a hot stove.

That was the one trouble with the were curse, he thought

grumpily. Only silver could really kill you, but whatever was tried still felt like the real thing and hurt like hell.

He tried to fly, but made it only a few yards before coming down again. He just didn't have the energy. That *thing*, whatever it was, had drained him. He tested the leg, but even though it hurt like hell, he thought he was able to walk. How far was that place from town? Twenty miles, maybe, but that was air miles. And how far had they gotten away? He looked back at the cliff. Maybe four, five miles as the Kauri flies, tops. A long walk, and Kauris weren't built for walking. Worse, some kind of alarm would be raised, if only because the Bentar at the roadblocks and on patrol would have seen the net spell as well and guessed the rest.

It was a vast area and he was now quite small, but if they brought in some aerial patrols of those creatures near the army camp, his pale passionate pink glow wouldn't be hard to differentiate from the rest of the landscape. The best thing to do, he decided, was to find some cover and just lie low. Come sunup, he'd be himself again, stark naked and still grounded, but in much better shape to handle that kind of journey. He worried most about Marge and Mia. When he didn't show up, they might well assume he got captured in the net. That would impel Mia, at least, to try and find him. He hoped that Marge could keep her from doing *that*.

There was the sudden sound of leathery wings high overhead, and, despite the pain, he ran for the cover of a nearby small stand of trees. The same wings that made flying so wonderful were real inhibitors in a run, catching the air and nearly pulling him off balance, but he made it. The real question was whether or not he'd been spotted from the air before he did.

This is ridiculous! he thought to himself. *I'm a guy whose mortal flesh was changed by a curse into a Kauri and I have the fairy soul of a wood nymph! All that, and here I am huddling in the dark.*

Wait a minute! Was there something that one of those perverted oddities might give him? There were a ton of Kauri tricks, if he knew how to do them. Unfortunately, these bodies didn't come with owner's manuals.

Currently, he was all fairy, and wood nymphs and Kauris were closely related. If he still had the wood nymph part, then maybe he could mate with one of these trees. It was a perfect hiding place, but even if it were possible and he knew how to do it, there were real problems with it. Suppose it really worked and he was stuck forever as its nymph? Or worse, suppose he mistimed things and the sun came up and he changed back into Joe? Either thought was pretty ugly.

He heard horses and the shouts of men and Bentar, and there was still the sound of wings above, and they were coming closer. He tried to think, and realized that thinking what Joe would do was the wrong way to go. Joe was mortal and had quite different attributes. The real question was, what would *Marge* do if it were her here instead of him?

Marge, he realized suddenly, wouldn't do anything. She'd let go, relax, clear her mind completely and with discipline keep it that way, letting the fairy part take complete control.

"Check those trees!" a Bentar snapped to subordinates, who galloped toward him.

Go blank, go blank, let instinct take over . . . .

Slowly he pressed back into the nearest tree, backing up against the hard, tough bark.

Something gave, and the bark seemed almost spongelike, enveloping him just as the first Bentar reached the grove.

"Beat all the bushes and check those treetops!" the Bentar sergeant ordered.

"Uh—you mean *climb* 'em?" one of the soldiers asked.

"No, I mean flap your arms and go up and tweet like a bird!" their chief responded sarcastically. "Of *course* I mean climb 'em!"

Joe was enveloped in a cocoon of darkness, yet he could hear them clearly. Suddenly he felt little, painful pricks and felt a tremendous itch. With a shock, he realized that he was feeling what the tree was feeling, and the Bentar was using its clawed hands and feet and climbing! He could *feel* the creature on the branches above, but it was like a monkey on an elephant in comparison. The Bentar soldier poked and probed, but finally shouted down, "There's nothing up here, sergeant!"

"This one's clean, too!" someone else shouted from another point.

"Aw, we don't even know what we're lookin' for, Sarge, or whether there's anything to look for!" his soldier protested. "We can't climb and poke every damned tree and bush in the place!"

"Whatever it was, it was pale red and it flew," the sergeant responded. "I saw the aura briefly. But, yeah, you're right. Come on down, you two! Whatever it is, it isn't here or we'd have seen it or smelled it by now!" He snorted, then muttered, "This is no job for a soldier! If he thinks there's something here, he should send those brainless mortals he's got."

The Bentar clambered down from the trees and remounted. The leathery wing sound came close enough to rustle the leaves.

"Start a sweep west of here, and let us know if you spot anything," the sergeant shouted to the flyer. "If you do, we'll come running, but I'm not going to waste time with this. It's pointless!"

There was a gruff shouted response from above and then the wings flapped harder but grew swiftly fainter as it moved away. The Bentar turned on their horses and were soon gone as well.

In a few more minutes, it was as quiet as a grave again.

Joe, however, once more became a bit concerned about being trapped in the tree. *Okay, I got in, now how do I get out?*

And, after a moment, it came to him that you got out the same way you got in—by relaxing and willing yourself out. There was a gentle pushing, as if the matter at his back was firming up behind him and expanding, and he emerged from the tree.

He was relieved to find he was still a Kauri. That meant he was still a were and, therefore, still human, too. For all he knew, the wood nymph thing had nothing to do with it. This might well have been entirely a Kauri defense mechanism, since they were so close.

The leg no longer hurt very much. The were spell was repairing it, as it tended to repair almost anything except a silver wound.

If only that fairy soul business had been as a Kauri, he mused. Then he might have been able to accept it. Flying around, seeing the world, maybe even with Marge for company. But a *wood nymph*!

He was feeling better, even a bit stronger, but he didn't want to test out his wings yet. No telling what was still around. Best to wait a bit, even if it meant he didn't make it back before dawn. The object was to make it back at all. At least so long as he kept under cover here they were unlikely to come back and check this grove again, but it was a fair distance to the next cover.

Still, if he got back at all, it would have been worth it. The Baron in league with Sugasto again, and still in Mahalo's sexy body! He wondered what happened to the *real* Mahalo McMahon. He'd totally forgotten to ask. She was stuck in the Baron's nearly dead body the last he knew and being brought here, kept alive mostly by Ruddygore's magic. Of course, Ruddygore had still had the Lamp at the time, so she could be anything or anybody. She'd have made an ideal Kauri, that's for sure.

Make a wish. You can be anything and anybody you want to be. What would *he* do if offered that? He thought about it, and he had a lot more options than she had, because he knew Husaquahr and what was available here. There was a male counterpart to the Kauri someplace, he remembered hearing. It'd be nice to fly places and seduce all those troubled women, but as good as the Kauri life-style might be, it was, like most fairy lives, in the end, a pretty one-dimensional life that went on forever, never really adding new dimensions. That, more even than old friendship, was why Marge kept inviting herself along on these missions. It was a way, however limited, to do something a bit different.

The thing was, he realized that he'd just wish to be his old self again. He *liked* himself, his body, his image. He'd like to be smarter, or maybe wiser, and know a lot more, but, overall, he liked being Joe just fine.

Only he wasn't Joe right now, he was a Kauri who looked and felt more like Marge. That body and those Kauri instincts were telling him right now what he needed to do to get his energy back, but he was going to trust to dawn first.

Still, it was worth risking a bit at this point to see if he could make at least *most* of the way back the easy way. He looked out and looked around and saw nothing close that was threatening. The wings spread, and he was airborne.

He was pretty weak, but flying, even from cover to cover, was sure better and faster than walking. By dawn, though, he still wasn't back, and he was just too dead to go much farther. He felt sure he was beyond the first blockade, though, and knew it when he saw a ranch not far away. There was a barn there with a real hayloft, and he made for it, going in the top small door and collapsing on the hay stored there just as the first rays of the sun came over the horizon. Exhausted almost beyond endurance, he lay there, almost too tired to sleep, and watched the golden orb creep lazily up into the sky, its first warming rays coming right in the hayloft door and washing over him.

Suddenly he stirred himself up and looked down at himself. *Wait a minute! This isn't right!* Then he sank back, too tired to even think straight anymore.

The sun was up and it was a bright, new day, and he was still a Kauri.

Marge was tired, too, but she wasn't about to go to sleep yet. Mia had changed back to herself with the first rays of the sun, and she was frantic. "He is in the hands of those maniacs, I know it!" she wailed. "We must rescue him!"

Marge shook her head. "No, we can't. I sure can't do a damned thing now, even if I wanted to, and what the hell can *you* do? You go out there now, hollering that your master's gone, and lots of things are gonna happen. First, they'll all start checking to see if he's still alive by touching your ring. When it's established he is, they'll turn you over to the military camp. The camp will put two and two together—spies last night, a missing master this morning—and send you right up to Sugasto and the Baron. If they've got Joe, then they've got both of you, and that's the end of *that* and everybody else. You saw those poor mindless zombies. In fact, they might be able to milk *you* for enough information to do a great Tiana. Remember, they want the palace Ti, the demigoddess Ti, and that's the one you knew. You'd wind up plunging the whole world into darkness."

"What can I *do*, then?"

"Well, I, for one, have known Joe longer than anybody here, and I think that if they had him captured they'd already be here for us. Think about it. He's got no more resistance to common spells than you do, and about now he'd be in his human body again. He'd talk, and we'd be taken. You see any Bentar? Any soldiers coming up the stairs?"

"No."

"Then he's not captured. And, thanks to your ring, we know he's not dead. I think he got hurt, maybe badly, in that mess last night—he took that dive steeper than we did."

"But then—"

"Hear me out. He's a were. Folks around here, even bad folks, don't carry around silver-tipped arrows and they sure don't shoot them at Kauris. That means his wounds, no matter what they were, kept him down for the count but that he'll be good as new today. Look at you—not a bruise or sore spot on you! If he's got any sense, he'll hole up someplace, get some sleep, then start back. Since there's another moon tonight, goodness knows what he'll come back *as*, if it's after dark, but he'll be back."

"Then what—?"

"I'm gonna grab some sleep because I want to be fresh tonight in case we have to do a little looking. It won't be easy, since there'll be open season on Kauris, but I've got some experience in this. You'll stick close here because he might come back. If he's not back by *tomorrow* morning, then we start panicking."

"I—very well. But what should I do?"

"You can serve your master best today by convincing everybody that he's still here, and, perhaps, is a bit under the weather. You've got a sick master up here, but not *too* sick. Just a bug, no big deal. That'll keep people out and questions down to a minimum. Fetch meals as if for him—the kind of stuff he'd order, remember. You get the idea?"

She nodded. "I understand and will do as you say. For one day and night, anyway."

"Good girl. Do it right. I just hope nobody notices."

"Notices what?"

"We forgot in all the worry to slip on your bracelets and anklets, and you sure aren't gonna get them on now. Just hope nobody up here believes in were anythings any more than most folks do. Don't worry—I doubt if they will. Me, I'm gonna get some real sleep."

Mia felt momentary panic. The bracelets and anklets! Still there on the floor. The small earrings were still there, too, but she had those with a clasp to allow for full moon times. She moved to put them back in, then thought better of it. No, nothing but the collar and the nose ring. She looked at herself in the mirror. God! So very *plain*, sexless. But she would leave them off. If anybody asked, it would be that they were cut off by her master's orders, which she could not question.

Somehow, she knew, they would have to find a way to get a collar with a clasp, against the rules or not. Otherwise, what happened if she changed into something sometime with either too large a neck or, perhaps, an animal like a horse? She wouldn't strangle, but the collar would then fall through the reforming flesh and it wouldn't fit back on, either.

As ready as she could be, she took a deep breath, tried to stay calm, then opened the door and went down to see about keeping up the lie, wishing all the time that it was true.

It was a harrowing day for Mia, who was almost a nervous wreck by the time Marge awakened. She had tried getting some sleep, but what little came was fitful, and every noise woke her back up.

There was no problem taking some of the money they had and getting fake meals. Money was money, although most of the meals were dumped in the chamber pot and the mess, mixed with the usual contents of the chamber pot that she could hardly avoid adding, already attracting flies.

That worried her a bit. It would be just like the way things were going suddenly for a fly to land on her just at moonrise. *Everything* worried her, all of a sudden.

Only the cafe lady had noticed her lack of jewelry, and she'd lied and said it looked just fine. Coming back with the dinner had, in fact, caused her only problem; some of the troops were in town, and apparently word of her dance and extraperformance activities had gotten around fast. She was filled with requests, and feared she would be delayed too long and moonrise would occur right then and there, with her in the middle of the street surrounded by soldiers. She also knew that they'd come after her and maybe up to the room if she said she'd ask permission, but then she got the bright idea to note that her master was sick. *Real* sick. Some kind of flu. She didn't know if it was catching . . . *Kerchoo!*

She had a clear field.

Marge sat there, nervously waiting for her. "About time!"

"I had to get through a horde of lustful soldiers, my lady," she apologized. "I was not sure I would be here in time."

"Yeah, well, I kinda figured something like that. You still got a few minutes yet, and I'm still only *mildly* worried about Joe. After all, he'd be naked and on foot, with those patrols about, and it's a *long* way. I—"

There was a sudden figure at the window, that of a Kauri.

Joe climbed in, and Mia and Marge both frowned, then Mia looked down at her unchanged self and Marge at Mia's normality.

"I don't know what the hell's wrong with this crazy curse!" he grumbled. "This never happened before. Never."

Quickly he filled them in on what had happened—up to a point.

Marge, of course, caught it immediately. "Uh, Joe . . . You look *awfully* good and *awfully* fit and strong by Kauri standards for somebody who got drained by a spell that strong."

His eyes rolled heavenward, then to Mia, then back to her. "The curse must have restored it as I slept," he responded at last. "Maybe that's why I didn't change back."

Until that moment, Marge had never thought a Kauri could look embarrassed. She knew that there was only one way he could have gotten that kind of energy recharge, but she resisted the urgings of her Texas fairy soul to bring it up and rub it in. If he was as drained as he said, and then still made it that far, when he woke up it wouldn't have been an option but a compulsion.

"So what do we do now?" Marge asked instead. "The only way I know to go when you have a bent curse is to visit a witch doctor, but somehow I don't think we want a Kauri walking into any witch doctor in *these* parts and saying she's really a were and couldn't switch back because of a sorcerous jolt!"

"Perhaps it will repair itself now, Master," Mia said hopefully. "The moon will be up any moment."

"Jeez! That's a point!" Marge commented. "Maybe we should get into some kind of position . . ."

But it was too late. He saw Mia's form blur and twist, actually saw her very brief change into Kauri form. He, too, felt it, but he suddenly realized that he was out of position.

"Well, we've got two of us, anyway," Marge noted, looking at her twin where Mia had stood moments before. Joe, however, had been slightly closer not to Marge, but to Mia.

"I never realized that before," the Kauri went on, staring at the new Joe. "It even duplicated the nose ring! Holy smoke, Joe! You own yourself!"

Joe let out a long, exasperated sigh.

CHAPTER 9

FIFTY WAYS TO LEAVE YOUR LOVER

Black shall be the color of the forces of evil; gold or silver trim is optional. Good shall have use of any other appropriate color combinations. One of the few tangible benefits of good is that they shall be able to use the better clothing designers.
—The Books of Rules, II, 447(b)

JOE STOOD THERE, FEELING PRETTY STUPID. HE'D BEEN SO CONvinced, considering the day, that there would be *no* change at moonrise, that he'd been very sloppy.

"I have seen the objects transferred before, my lady," he responded, the title coming unbidden. Just as he'd inherited an entire duplicate set of Kauri powers and instincts, and, yes, compulsions, so, too, had the damned curse duplicated not only Mia, but the full deck of Rules governing her as well. "As weres are supposed to *exactly* duplicate what they are nearest, it can happen."

"This is madness!" Mia protested. "How can he own *himself*?"

"Because the ring's a fake, really part of him," Marge answered. "He's not *really* a slave, he's just duplicating, imitating one exactly." She sighed. "So *now* what do we do?"

"He surely cannot go out like that," Mia pointed out.

"And I can't stay in," Marge said. "After last night I need a recharge and a hotshot in spades, and, Mia, since you duplicated me exactly, so do you."

"I can do nothing but spend the night here, my ladies," Joe responded. "There is clearly nothing else I can do."

"Yeah, and hope that this at least means the curse is no longer out of whack," Marge responded. "Otherwise, tomorrow day-time, there'll be *two* slaves and *no* master."

Mia thought for a moment. "Uh, I would not leave this room all night in any case," she told him. "The town is filled with soldiers and they all have been pressing me to dance, and, you know."

"Besides," Marge noted, "you don't have the collar."

"I shall behave, my lady," he responded. *How odd to be doing that to Mia!* "I shall sit here and worry about the two of you."

Marge laughed. "Don't worry about us! We're not about to do any snooping tonight. Too hot out there for that! Come on, Mia! Let's blow this joint!"

Joe watched them go, then went over to the nightstand where there was some barely nibbled-on fruits and vegetables. *What a time!* he thought grumpily, finishing them off. While doing so, he was suddenly seized with the thought of how unkempt and messy it all was. By the time he was finished, he'd practically scrubbed the place down with the washbasin water and was checking for things to mend. The only thing he could do nothing about was the dishes and the festering food in the chamber pot.

The trouble was, he couldn't just throw it out the window as he had the dirty water.

It was quite late by this time; all the raucous noises of earlier in the evening had died down, and the town was basically closed. Maybe he could just sneak down . . .

No, that was madness. Suppose he ran into a bunch of drunken soldiers who wouldn't take no for an answer? He'd already been the victim of one compulsion he hadn't wanted to do; he sure as hell didn't want *that*.

Why couldn't I be standing next to Sugasto when a full moon comes up sometime? he wondered, frustrated and upset. Of course, he then would have Sugasto's potential, but it would be moot, since he wouldn't have all those years and years of train-ing, practice, and self-discipline to make any real use of it. Still, it certainly would be better than *this*.

That mess in the chamber pot kept bothering him, though. The accumulated buzzing of the flies alone was enough to drive him nuts. He went over to the window and stuck his head out and listened. Almost dead quiet. The hell with it. *I've done a lot of stupid things in my life. Maybe this is one of them,* he thought, but he picked up the trash can, gingerly, then, quietly, opened the door. The hall was dark, the only illumination coming from the reception area downstairs, which was just fine with him.

Quietly, he tiptoed down the hall to the stairs, then started down. The whole downstairs was dimly lit and looked empty. He continued down, feeling it was going to be fine, when suddenly a deep, rich male voice said, "You there! Come here!"

He jumped, turned, and saw, sitting at a table almost under the stairway . . . *Holy cats! It's Sugasto himself!*

At least he didn't have to stimulate a look of abject terror on his Mia-slave face.

"Come here! *Now!*" the sorcerer ordered, and he scampered over and knelt, head bowed.

"Yes, my lord?"

The Master of the Dead reached out a hand under the slave girl's chin and slowly raised the head, studying it. "Where are you going? Why are you up and about at this hour?" he demanded.

"M-my master has been ill," he managed, never feeling closer to doom than right this second. "I—I am throwing out what his stomach could not take."

Sugasto looked over at the chamber pot, but not too closely. *"Ick! Yuck!"* he exclaimed, disgusted. He reached out a hand and the chamber pot flew from Joe's hand. A bolt of blue-white light came from the sorcerer's fingers, enveloped the chamber pot, and the entire thing vanished in a puff of smoke.

Joe turned back to Sugasto, suitably impressed, and waited. The man had certainly aged since the last time he and Joe had seen one another. The face was pitted and puffy, the eyes surrounded with lines, the hair mostly gray, and he'd put on a fair amount of weight. Still, there was no mistaking the bastard. The worst part was, Joe realized, if he'd been there, as Joe, with his sword at his side, two inches from Sugasto's neck, he would have been just as helpless as he was now.

"Where's your collar, child?" the sorcerer asked, almost kindly.

"My lord, we came only a few days ago out of Marquewood. The collar which my master purchased did not seal and fell away and we have not yet had chance to get another."

When the only defense you had was your wits, you used what you had.

"Hmmm . . . Make a note of that, Quod," the sorcerer commented, and for the first time Joe saw that the sorcerer was not alone. With him was a Bentar officer, looking meaner and oilier than most of them already did.

"Of what, sir?" the officer asked.

"I think I made a mistake on the regulations. I like this plain, unadorned look. If restraints are needed, they can use shackles. No collars from now on. Get the word out. No jewelry or such of any kind."

"Yes, sir."

"Tell me, child," the sorcerer said, turning back to Joe, who had remained on one knee, "how do you like the new fashion in slaves?"

"My lord, it is not for such as I to like or dislike."

"Well said. Don't worry about returning thus to Marquewood. By this time next year, this will be the fashion there as well." He reached out suddenly and put his hand on the slave's bald pate. "Do you know that just by doing thus I could remove that which is you and put it in that little bottle there?"

"N-no, my lord."

"No?" The sorcerer seemed genuinely surprised. "Do you not know who I am?"

"No, my lord. I have no doubt you are the greatest of all sorcerers, but I concern myself only with serving my master."

He let go of the head and Joe had to suppress his feeling of intense relief. But the hand continued down the body, not missing what on any but a slave would be considered private parts.

Sugasto stopped that suddenly, then reached up and touched the nose ring. "Hmmm . . . Odd pattern. This is no common magician's product. The way it's done, it almost seems like . . . Who put this ring in your nose? And where?"

"My lord, I do not know the names. A big town in Marque-wood. The ring was purchased there."

"The one who put the ring in—was he a big, old man with a flowing white beard?"

"Yes, my lord."

"I *thought* so!" He took Joe's face by the chin and held it up, as if looking at a bust, and studied it. "I could almost . . . No, it would be inconceivable. Still—how ill is your master, girl?"

"He is recovering well, my lord. It appears to have been a touch of bad food. There is not much here. He was sleeping well when I left him."

Sugasto nodded. "Very well. If he's well enough to ride to-morrow, you tell him to come to the military camp outside of town. You tell him the Master of the Dead commands his presence. Can you remember that?"

"Yes, my lord."

"At midday tomorrow. They will be expecting him. You come, too."

"Yes, my lord. I will tell him." *Oh, great!*

"You get him there. Tell him that if he does not appear, ones will come for *him*, and he might well not have to worry about bad food again. Understand?"

"Y-yes, my lord."

"I like you, girl," the sorcerer commented, continuing in the gentle if patronizing tone of voice he'd used all along. "It would be child's play to alter that spell in the ring . . ."

Joe again fought momentary panic. What if Sugasto just took him, now, like this, and he changed back tomorrow morning? Worse, what if he *didn't* change back?

"Go on back up to your master, girl," the sorcerer said at last. "But don't forget to tell him when he wakens!"

"I swear I will tell him, my lord!"

"I know you will." He patted Joe on the rump. "Okay, now, off! I have work to do here!"

Joe didn't need any more urging. He was off and up the stairs as fast as possible and back into the room. His heart was pounding like mad, and he stood there, back against the door as if barring it with his body against intrusion, for quite some time.

* * *

"Sugasto? *Here?*" Marge could hardly believe it, and really didn't want to. "You don't suppose he's still in the place, do you?"

"I would doubt it, my lady," Joe responded. "I heard a large number of horses leave some time ago, although it was quite late. He would be riding with an honor guard, even if he needs no protection himself."

"Well, that's something," the Kauri commented. "You're sure he didn't suspect? Not that you were Joe, but that you might be Mia?"

"He saw some resemblance, my lady, that was clear, but he has never seen this body before and would be going on descriptions alone. Possibly, had I had hair and Marquewood slave dress he would have made the connection."

She chuckled. "Just like his kind to have their petty little perversions get in their own way. Still, you're lucky. With a wave of his hand, he could have put you in a trance and made you spill everything. It was a close call."

Joe nodded. "Still, my lady, he is not free of all suspicions, or else why would he command our presence later on? He saw Ruddygore's signature in the slave spell in the nose ring. I do not think he believes me to be anything other than I seemed, but he will be far more critical of the barbarian. Even worse, what if the curse does not lift at sunrise? Then his people will come later on and find *two* slave girls here. It is certain then that this would quickly become my permanent condition."

"Surely you aren't gonna keep that date anyway! Why, you'd be riding of your own free will right into the enemy camp! One slight misstep and he'll have the both of you!" She looked at the great sword Irving, hanging in its scabbard on the bedpost. "*You've* got a disguise, but what about that thing?"

"My lady, unless I had to call it by name to summon it to my hand, I could call it 'George' or 'Trenton,' for that matter. And if I needed to summon it, there would be little point in pretending anyway."

"What if the Baron is there?" Mia asked worriedly. "He, or

she, or whatever he is these days, has seen us. The disguises might not be good enough to fool him.''

''Well, my lady, he, or she, wasn't with Sugasto last night. I have thought of the possibility that this meeting is to do just that—let Boquillas have a look at us. It cannot be dismissed as a possibility. But doing anything but obeying is unthinkable. It is a day's ride over a single road to the border, if that would stop them. Otherwise, he has an army of men and fairies around here. We are as trapped as if we were in his Hypboreyan lair.''

''That's a point. Ah, sunrise!''

For a moment, Joe felt real fear when nothing happened, but Mia hadn't changed, either. Marge had seen the first light of dawn, but it was another two or three minutes before any part of the sun made it over the horizon.

Joe was Joe again. He let out an ecstatic ''Yippee!'' and banged one fist into the other. He turned to them and said, ''If I'm gonna go, I'd rather be as me. It looks like his snare spell just scrambled the curse for a night, which is a real relief.'' He looked over at Mia. ''First things first. I have to get some clothes on, and then we've got to find a bolt cutter.''

''Huh?''

''The spell gave me the ring but not the collar. Sugasto saw me—Mia—without it. In fact, he decreed them off right then and there. If she's got one on when we meet him, that'll be a tip-off right away.'' He turned to Mia. ''Remember, for some reason he took a real fancy to you. Play it cool but don't overdo it. I don't want him to order me to hand you over to him.''

The idea alarmed her. ''What would I do, Master, if he did?''

''Almost anything's possible this afternoon. If he does, then go. We'll find you. Hell, if I could get us both up there, on him, I'd do it and save us a real journey. But I'd rather we do it together, and not as prisoners of the enemy.''

''I'd think, once you get that collar off, you'd better try and get some sleep,'' Marge grumbled.

''The hell with sleep. He's expecting a man just getting over food poisoning anyway, and he knows Mia was up and about most of the night.''

''Yeah, but it seems to me that you need a clear head.''

"Very little sleep is needed during the were periods. It's as if you slept while the other form was awake. Don't ask me about it—look it up sometime."

"So what do you want *me* to do?"

"You'd best sleep outdoors today. Let them come in and do routine things in the room. They might well send somebody to search it anyway. If we don't come back, you can't do much. Return and tell Ruddygore. If we do, come again at dusk. We've still got one more night of the moon."

"Well, I don't like it, but okay. In case moonrise comes before you get all the way back, but it's clear, come to the back window as whatever you are. I'll figure it out. If they take you, they'll come and get all your things and I'll know. If nobody comes, not even the hotel people, I'll know that, too."

He nodded. "Good enough."

Getting the collar off was a hell of a lot harder than he thought it would be and took the better part of two hours and a lot of finagling to do it without cutting, burning, or strangling Mia.

He got ready in his new buckskin outfit, even though it was still mild out. It had the best image, and an image, with the beard and other disguises, different from the one they'd be looking for. Thanks to the Rules, all people here tended to categorize folks much stricter than they did even back on Earth.

As they rode out toward the camp, though, he was more worried about himself than about Mia. She'd shown time and again how cool she could be under pressure and she wasn't under the same kind of cloud that he was. Mia had proved herself last night; now Cochise was on trial.

Although he'd always thought of the Bentar as birds of prey, they looked more dinosaurlike in the full light of day. He presented his old pass to them from the entry station. They glanced at it, then nodded. "You are expected. Straight on to the flagpole, then the second building on your right."

And now, in the full light of day, they rode straight into the heart of the enemy force.

The building wasn't hard to find, and they were actually early. He thought it better to be early than late. A nervous-looking human officer told them to wait outside until called, and they did so.

Mia sat, looking at all the activity, then suddenly frowned, then got up, somewhat excited. "Look, Master! A flying horse with wings!"

He looked where she was pointing and, sure enough, there it was, all stately-looking, right out of the old myths and legend books. A huge, pastel pink stallion, not too different in coloration from Marge, with enormous birdlike wings, circling to land. Its rider appeared to use no bridle and, indeed, sat back a bit, almost tied on, feet straight out across its back so as not to interfere with the wings. It didn't look comfortable to Joe.

"Impressive," he said to her. "I've never seen one before, except in the picture books and on gas station signs, but I guess they *had* to exist somewhere around Husaquahr. Everything else does."

"That is the sort of steed we need for a journey such as ours, Master," she noted. "Far better to have wings, but if we cannot, that would do."

He agreed with that. He had actually considered making time by traveling during these three nights of the moon as a Kauri, but Kauris weren't very strong, and they could have taken little with them—nor, indeed, could any of them have so much as touched Irving. The iron in the great sword would have burned both him and Mia severely and would have killed Marge.

Still, he wondered how many of the flying horses were around here and if they served a primary military function. Many of the more experienced officers and noncoms here would have been on the losing side at Sorrow's Gorge, and he didn't remember any there.

The door opened behind them, and he and Mia arose and turned, expecting to see the office flunky calling them in. Instead, it was the Master of the Dead himself, followed by his Bentar flunky, the latter looking much the worse for wear. Joe knelt, and took his sword, still in its scabbard, and touched the hilt to his forehead in salute.

"Come, come! Get up, sir!" the sorcerer said, the wind catching and rippling his black robes. "I'm not the king, and it's a beautiful day." He breathed in and out several times. "Good, fresh air and sunshine. I get so little of it these days that I want to savor it when I can. You are . . . ?"

"Cochise, my lord," he responded. "Cochise of Tsipry."

"Ah! You are Valisandran by birth, then."

"Yes, my lord, by birth but not for a very long time. I was orphaned young. There was a sickness that went through my tribe, and many of the young children were sent south in hopes of avoiding it. Truly, I have not been back since, which is one of the reasons for this journey."

"Hmmm . . . Interesting." He turned to the aide. "Any Tsipry here?"

The Bentar shook its head negatively. "No, my lord."

"You seem certain of that."

"My people may be the sickness he recalls as a child. The *artu* of the Bentar had a bit of a disagreement with them fifteen or twenty years back. I remember it well; I was very young at the time. I would say that there are very few Tsipry *anywhere* now, sir, and most would be like this one."

Always nice to have your inquisitors back up your alibis, Joe thought.

Sugasto cleared his throat. "I see. Sorry to bring up old wounds on such a pretty day. Does the colonel's presence here trigger hostile feelings?"

"No, my lord," Joe responded smoothly. "It is a sad chapter because it was personal, but I have been in the position of his people in other cases, so I cannot judge. I fought for Valisandra and the Baron alongside his people as well as my own at Sorrow's Gorge."

"Indeed? I was there myself, but I don't recall you."

"Uh, pardon, sir, but I do not recall *you* there, either, but it was a very big battle."

"Uh, yes," Sugasto admitted. "And I was a horse of a different color there, at that."

A black stallion, if memory serves, Joe thought, but he said nothing.

"How is your health today?" the sorcerer asked him.

"Better, sir, but I am still being careful today while my full strength returns. Once my body expelled the offending food, I could sleep.''

"Come, walk with me a bit in this nice air," the sorcerer invited. "I was going to offer a complete cure, but it seems you don't need such services. The sun and fresh air aid recuperation better than most other things anyway. Stroll with me, and we'll reminisce a bit as two old comrades at arms meeting once again."

And that's exactly what he wanted to do. Joe knew, of course, that this was also a test, but he couldn't figure out why Sugasto was being both so friendly and so conventional in his interrogation. But, of course, he was a master sorcerer, and he would assume that anybody from Ruddygore had been as blocked as he'd block his own people from enemy powers.

Since Joe had indeed fought at Sorrow's Gorge, it was an easy test to pass.

They walked along, the Bentar, then Mia following, and Joe got almost as much of a kick out of the reactions of the folks they encountered as they walked as Sugasto obviously did.

"So, how come you aren't on our team now?" The sorcerer asked at last. "We can always use good men like you."

"I hope my lord doesn't take offense," Joe responded, "but I am a professional mercenary. I chose the Baron back then not out of old loyalties to king and country, but because I like the work and, if you are on the winning side, it pays well. The Baron lost."

"Only because of that damned dragon and some treachery on the part of the Council."

"Indeed, it looked to me at the time like a can't-lose situation. Since then, I have taken only small commissions from stable local authorities, and done, I admit, some less than honest work between jobs. The girl, there, for example, was booty from a little pirating I did downriver."

"And in spite of all this, you don't think we'll win?"

He shrugged. "It appears as impressive as before, and I have heard of your legion of the dead, which would have been quite useful in the old days, and your powers are legendary. But the Baron was the best in his day, yet not a good gambler in the end. His less than dependable political maneuverings, as you mention, were part of his undoing, and he allowed himself to be beaten by a lesser power who was better at psychology.''

Sugasto stopped and looked at the mercenary with some respect. ''That's an excellent analysis. It is a reason why Boquillas works for *me* now. Did you know that?''

''No, my lord. I thought he was dead.''

''Not dead, no. Different, I'll allow, but still with that amazing mind. I am not even certain that Boquillas *can* die. Consider, he has rejected and fought against Heaven, and he has betrayed Hell. When the soul has no refuge, it remains. The only relevant fact is that I have that mind and that knowledge at my disposal because there's nowhere else to go. As to the rest, we can fight if we have to, and Ruddygore, alone, won't find *me* the sort of ivory tower academic the Baron was—I know him far too well. But I prefer imagination first. I can say nothing more at this time, but if my plan works, we can conquer without war and perhaps without even a face-off, since the chilled livers of the Council would back any victory already won. There would be localized fighting, resistance, and pacification, of course, but no great war.''

''This interests me,'' Joe told him, ''but what if your plan fails?''

''Then tactics change. We lose nothing. That is the beauty of it. Uh—by the way, speaking of Ruddygore, how does it happen that your girl has one of his rings in her nose?''

He'd thought long and hard about that question. ''I haven't the vaguest idea,'' he responded. ''And I'm afraid you'd have to ask her original owner in Hell. I had no idea whose it was, only that she's mine now.''

''Ah, that explains it, then. The old fart always was a real hypocrite. Have you ever met him?''

''Once, my lord. He was an impressive sort of man, as I recall.''

''Indeed he can be that. He could have ruled all Husaquahr and probably would have, had he not that trick of escaping into the Other World for his pleasures. It diverted him from greatness

into moralizing and preaching, only it is *he* who determined
what is good or bad according to his present moods. To him,
this is all just a game, and everyone other than himself is just a
game piece, to be toyed with, played with, even sacrificed. He
is so ancient now and has played these games so long that he
plays now for the game's sake, without any goals or purposes in
mind. I could never accept that sort of thinking. One plays a
game to *win*. Don't you agree?''

"I do not fight to lose, my lord," he responded.

Sugasto laughed. "Well said! Ah—I know your stomach may
feel its bruises, but will you risk lunch with me?''

"In truth, sir, I feel like a starving man.''

They went to a huge tent pavilion where a galley had been set
up. It was full of officers when they arrived, but, to the mutual
amusement of Joe and Sugasto, almost all of them miraculously
finished eating and got out of there when they entered.

"Now *that's* the fun of it." The sorcerer chuckled. "If your
own side isn't terrified of you, what right have you to expect that
your enemies will be?" He paused, then stared straight at Joe.
"But you're not scared of me, are you?''

"There is fear, which is unreasoned, and that I do not have,"
Joe lied. "But there is also respect, which is both reasoned and
earned, and that I have for you in great abundance.''

The answer really pleased the man in black. "You are delightful! In truth, sir, you are the first nonmagical human being I
have been able to talk to like this in years! Ah, let us eat. Take
care, sir, that your stomach not rebel, but eat with confidence.
Either my armies eat only the best or they eat the cooks!''

"My stomach has survived worse than a bad piece of meat,"
Joe responded. "I will not let it cheat me of a decent meal.''

Sugasto laughed. He looked over at Mia. "Girl, come over
and sit on the ground beside me here a bit.''

Mia looked nervously at Joe, who nodded. "Go ahead.''

"Yes, Master," she responded, and went around to Sugasto's
side of the table.

It was unusual for a sorcerer, male or female, to take much
interest in sex except as another, sometimes required, tool of
the trade. Joe couldn't figure out whether that was it, or whether

it was the personal slave concept itself that turned the man on. It might just have been that, having had Boquillas around in Mahalo's body for so long, he just wanted a woman around who was always respectful, obeyed orders, and kept her mouth shut. Joe could see by Mia's eyes that she was far too terrified to have such thoughts herself.

The meal was not merely good, but excellent, and Joe had to wonder if this sort of fare was what the officers usually got. Somehow, the day the general showed up for inspection, you always got filet mignon instead of old army boot.

"So you are on your way to Tsipry," Sugasto said over wine. "A pilgrimage, of sorts, I take it?"

Joe nodded. "Yes, sir. I have funds at the moment, I have no pressing need of employment, and I always promised myself that I would do it. I have no memories of it that I can call true and I want to see it once."

"That's in the Upper Lakes district, if I remember," the sorcerer replied. "Cold up there, even this time of year. With summer waning, autumn on its way, and the need to divert resources, I've been playing with a little spell. Boquillas worked it out for our own people, but it's rather simple, once you know it. It insulates against weather, sort of in the same way much fairy flesh does it for them, yet, like them, you can't see it or know it's there. The only problem is, it seals *in* what is there as well, so you can't add much of anything, either, and it plays hob with hair. Not practical for most people, I fear, but slaves like your girl, here, are perfect. We're going to distribute it and have all the slaves treated this way. It dispenses with the need for those idiotic hafiids even in subzero cold and for sun protection in the tropics, reducing the cost to food alone. With your permission, I'll do you a favor."

Joe could hardly refuse in any event. He watched as the sorcerer turned the kneeling Mia toward him, then made a few hand passes and ran his hands over some of her body at a very slight distance.

"There," Sugasto said. "Now, within the normal extremes of nature, she's as protected as a nymph. Just keep her like this and all you'll need do is feed her. In fact, you'll have to. As our

experiments with this on some of our undead show, the spell
rejects anything not within its field. Otherwise, there are no side
effects. A little gift, in hopes that once you make your pilgrimage, you'll return and sign on with us.'' He snapped his fingers
and the Bentar aide, who had not eaten—they were, if Joe remembered right, eaters of carrion and sometimes freshly killed
prey—snapped to attention.

''Give me some paper and a stylus,'' the sorcerer instructed,
and it was quickly gotten. Sugasto scribbled something on the
paper, then made a pass over it. The writing, which, although
in the ideographic Husaquahrian alphabet, had been rather prim-
itive scrawls actually seemed to wriggle around on the page as
if composed of tiny snakes, forming then absolutely perfect
characters that looked like woodcuts. He made another pass,
and Joe recognized the seal of Hypboreya when it faded in in
sort of a gray color. The paper was then handed to Joe.

''Take that with you,'' the sorcerer told him. ''It is a safe
conduct good for sixty days throughout my realm. It should ease
problems in travel and make things easier. It will also get you
better food, I suspect. After that, I hope we will learn that you
have joined us completely. I believe we can offer a very high
commission to one like you. You could wind up a military gov-
ernor someday. I wish I could offer you quick passage to the
Lakes, but little goes to and from that area, and we have other
needs.''

''I thank you, my lord, for your extreme, unexpected, and
unwarranted generosity,'' he responded, hardly able to contain
himself. This was better than he could have hoped. ''I admit,
though, to looking longingly at one of the flying horses you
have. Why weren't *they* in our old battles?''

''The pegasus? They're tough to tame, hard to ride, and fragile as all hell. There's less there than meets the eye. They
wouldn't last minutes in a battle. We use them to speed orders
and maintain communications links around the empire. They're
not good for much more. Sorry—there's only two in this entire
military district.''

''I was not trying to impose, just commenting.''

''Well, I understand. It's a long, long way to Tsipry,'' he

noted. "Now, it has been a genuine pleasure, sir. I have much to attend to and you must excuse me, but I feel certain that we will meet again."

"As do I, sir," Joe responded, rising. He gestured to Mia, who got up and scampered after him.

As soon as they were away, a Bentar officer approached and bowed.

Sugasto looked at him. "Well?"

"A considerable number of coins, the usual clothing one would expect of one coming from the south, including loin-cloths, and the remains of what appeared to be bronze orna-mentations, a rather elaborate beltlike contraption that makes noises when moved or put together whose function we cannot fathom, although it appears innocuous, and the usual saddlebag materials. Nothing else, my lord."

"Hmmm . . ." the sorcerer said, thinking. "That man is one of the most dangerous nonmagical men I've ever met, but he does seem to be precisely what he claims."

"You had many ways to plumb his very soul and beyond, my lord. If you still have doubts, why didn't you use them?" the aide asked him.

"Partly because someone that strong has strong magical al-lies who could shield him, and partly because, to get through those, I would have most likely destroyed someone who might be extremely useful. There was also this very odd sense of fairy about him when I initially probed him that defied explanation. The girl had it, too, last night, which is why I found her so intriguing, but then she *didn't* have it today. It's the damndest thing . . . But he's a mercenary all right, and a good one, and she's definitely a properly bound slave, as both seem to be. Still . . ."

"If he passed all the conventional tests, why do you still doubt him?" the aide asked.

"Because, while I know I have never laid eyes on that man in my life, I could swear, after talking to him, that I've met him before, even spent some time with him. It's just a feeling; there's no rational basis for it, but I can't get it out of my mind. Perhaps it will come to me, sooner or later, or I'll find some good way to divine it without having to pay a price to a demon.''

''But you gave him safe conduct, my lord!''

''*Northbound*, yes. Where can he go that isn't ours? As I suspected, he was illiterate. He never even tried to read the safe conduct, which is a natural act of any literate person. It is valid, but it also states that, if he tries to leave the empire, he is to be arrested using all necessary force.''

''Still, my lord, you permit a potential spy of high capability to roam freely behind us?''

''Let him look. He won't be difficult to find. He has deep, genuine affection for that girl, perhaps even love of some kind, and she worships him as a dog worships her master. A big mercenary with a naked slave girl in the north won't exactly be unnoticed. The same spell that protects her binds her to me. If the spell is removed, she dies horribly. If it is not, then at any time I wish I can command her as easily as I work my will upon the dead. I can summon her soul to me, no matter where she is. No, gentlemen, I don't believe we have much to fear by giving him a little rope.''

Joe used his abilities of fairy sight to examine the pass and found nothing there. It was just what it said it was. Of course, he had no guarantee it was really a safe conduct, but that would be easy enough to test.

He breathed a sigh of relief. ''Well, *that* sure turned out better than it had a right to,'' he noted.

''Yes, Master.''

''But?''

''No, it is not that, Master. I have thoughts again of the flying horse.''

''Forget it. You heard what the man said. No use pushing our luck.''

''But there is one night of the full moon left, Master! The longest, just about all night! If one of us could somehow be next to that creature at moonrise . . .''

''Hmmm . . . I see what you mean. It might carry us and our supplies a pretty fair distance by dawn.''

"Then you will give me permission to do it?"

He looked around. "There's got to be thousands of lonely men on this base. I'm not gonna leave you here for hours and hours just on the off chance you might get in there. Too dangerous."

"Master, I am but your property, your tool. It is my function to try this if it is possible."

"No, if anybody tries it, it should be me. I can bluff my way around for a while if this pass is any good, and I weigh more than twice what you weigh, so more could be carried."

"Master, someone must get everything together and ready. I cannot leave without you. They would notice. Your safe conduct is nothing for me. And if I left carrying your sword, if I could, it would be noticed. But if you left, they would hardly remember the slave you came in with. I am the only one. And as you will change, too, probably to Kauri, you will be able to fly as well. But you must remember to wrap all things iron securely and only what we need and what the two of you together could lift."

He frowned. Damn it, it *did* seem worth a try, and since they wouldn't really be stealing anything, nothing would be missed. And, so long as she was not caught and managed to get away, two big "ifs," even if it proved impractical, it wouldn't be that much of a problem.

"You really think you can do it?"

"Master, the worst that happens is that I get caught and must be a tearful slave who lost her way. Otherwise, I shall simply become one of these men, or a Bentar, or something similar and nothing is lost. Yes, I believe I can do it."

"All right, then. Let's test out this safe conduct and go see the pegasus. If you can give everybody around the slip and hide nearby, it's on. Otherwise, you get on your horse, which will be left there, and you come out with me."

She nodded.

When you act like you have nothing to fear, it's amazing how easily you can move around restricted areas. They were stared at, now and again, but they reached the area where the flying horses—or, as they discovered when they got there, more properly flying horse—were kept before anybody even tentatively asked for their authorization.

Joe whipped out the safe conduct, and the man who made the challenge blanched and lost all his belligerence. Sugasto was right about one brag: his army was scared stiff of him.

The pegasus was grazing, much like any other horse, the huge wings folded up and at its sides. Joe stared and stared at it and couldn't for the life of him figure out how something this large could fly without a jet engine, but he'd had much the same feeling about Kauris, too. Not that the pegasus was a big animal; disregarding the wings it was actually a bit smaller than it looked when flying, perhaps more like a circus pony, complete with hairy hooves, although the legs looked impossibly thin, so thin that it was almost easier to believe it could fly than to believe it could stand up for long on them. Incredibly, aside from a long rope tied around its neck on one end and to a post on the other, there was no apparent stable or pen for it, and there seemed nobody around to ask.

"You really think you can do this?" he asked her, worried.

"Yes, Master, I do. There are plenty of shadowy places near the buildings there, and tall grass and rocks."

"Like as not the guy'll come back and fly it away. Then what?"

"Then I will return to you as something else."

They walked away from the pegasus and toward the shadows from the nearest building, which appeared to be some kind of livery supply or maintenance shed. In a moment, they were in back of it and out of possible sight against the back of a hill. After a minute or so, he knew they'd not been seen.

He stood there a moment, looking at her. She was hairless and naked and plain-looking, a hairless little eunuch . . .

He grabbed her suddenly, and kissed her the way neither he nor any other man had *ever* kissed her before, the kind of kiss you know only in your dreams. Suddenly, he released her, whispered, "Don't fail me," and walked back out into the open, leaving her standing there, totally speechless.

She would never fail him, she knew. She would die for him first.

* * *

"You left her *where* to do *what*?" Marge almost shouted at him. "How *could* you? Her life versus maybe two weeks time?"

"It was her idea. She came up with it and she just about pleaded to do it."

"With maybe twenty thousand horny guys around and *Sugasto*, for Christ's sake! Not to mention the Bentar!"

"I know, I know."

"Yeah? You ever thought that, if she actually *does* make the change, she's gonna need almost a runway to take off in, galloping the whole way? And when she gets up there in the dark she's gonna have some big, leather-winged goons just waiting to pounce? You think a *horse* can fly like a *Kauri*?"

"No, I hadn't thought about some of those things, and thanks for giving me more things to worry about," he responded.

"Then why in hell did you let her do it?"

He stared at his old friend and comrade. "Because I thought she could," he said simply.

She stared at him. "Holy cats! You're in *love* with her! Oh, great! What an odd couple you two make!"

He sighed. "You've been a fairy too long, Marge. You don't plan these things. Since we left Terindell, she's been a whole different person. And, no, I know what you're thinking—it's not the kinky bondage stuff. I'd do away with that in a minute if the Rules allowed it. It's beyond that sort of crap. Throw it away. Ignore the slave thing. She's been a partner, tough, has more guts than any *man* of *any* status I ever met, as smart as anybody I know, and in just a short week she's become my indispensable left arm. She's got all the qualities I loved in Ti, only more so, but without the qualities that kept us apart. I don't know another person who wouldn't have been *destroyed* by what's been done to her, yet the more she was stripped of everything, the stronger she's grown. The laws, the Rules, and the sorcerers took everything people think they desire from her, stripping her down to her core, and that core's proved already to be somebody remarkable."

She stared at him. "Boy, you got it bad." Still, she had to admit, he had a real point. That girl was beginning to look like somebody who, were it not for the slave business, would take Husaquahr by the tail and shake it.

The odd thing was, had she not been a slave, she probably would never have revealed or even known how good she was. She'd be somebody's wife, or maybe a political manipulator or something like that, depending on where she was, but she'd never have been forced to test herself and would never have been willing to take the kind of chances she took. When you had nothing, not even your dignity, you also had nothing to lose. With no inhibitions even possible, and with her brains and re- sourcefulness, Marge thought, she was probably more danger- ous than anybody, even Joe in a rage.

"She's not gonna look any better, either," Marge pointed out.

He shrugged. "I married my first wife because she had the most stunning looks of any woman I'd ever seen. She had the soul of a viper—if she has a soul at all. With Ti, it was not only her looks but her education, her background, her breed- ing—all the stuff neither I nor my first wife had. I may be slow and ignorant, but even I eventually learn. I guess it was because everybody always prejudged me by *my* looks. This is a primo lesson in how unimportant that crap really is. Boquillas was one of the best-looking, dashing, charismatic men I ever met. Su- gasto was kind of a pretty boy, too, when we first met him. It's what's *behind* the face and eyes that count."

"Well, okay, Lover Boy, we'll talk more about this some other time," the Kauri said at last. "If she's that good, and we don't have your iron wrapped, the money secure, and all the rest of the junk ready to go, and she gets here, we're gonna fail *her*."

"Good point," he admitted, and started work.

"You aren't even worried about her?"

"Worried sick," he admitted. "But if she wasn't my slave but my partner and equal, a mercenary or Amazon or something like that, I wouldn't have hesitated and you wouldn't have an- guished about it."

"Yeah, okay. You handle the sword, remember. And wrap it securely."

He nodded. "I'll do the iron first. The rest I'll let you get to, since I want to go down and settle the bill."

"Holy cats! You're gonna *pay* this dump?"

"Sure. I don't want any blemishes on the record. And if they know we intend to set out before dawn, they won't wonder why they never saw us leave."

"Well, I just hope your pegasus can carry everything. Us, too. We're great for sprinting and medium flights, but these wings won't match the kind a flying horse would have."

"The guy I saw flying the thing looked about average. What's a Kauri weigh, anyway?"

"Dunno. Haven't had to worry about a scale in years now. Fairy construction is very different from human, though. I'd say forty pounds, give or take. Just a wild guess. Still, it means not having to worry about straps and seat belts."

"Easily within limits, even with this stuff." He picked up the newly bought hafiid, then tossed it. "Won't have to worry about *that*, thanks to Sugasto. I wish we had a decent magician along, though. I'd love to know if he added anything nasty to that spell."

"I can read some of it," she told him, packing away. "Hey— you better take care of that bill now, or you're either gonna have to fly it down or she's gonna have to carry somebody the size of the manager."

"Good point," he admitted, took out some money, and left the room.

For Mia, the waiting was the worst part. Not because it was so boring in and of itself, but because she had nothing to do but think. Why had he kissed her like that? Why had he kissed her at *all*, let alone with such—such *passion*. They had made love, yes, but when they thought themselves married, it had been fun but, well, *ordinary*. And the last time, it was an act of kindness, she knew, to help her forget her shearing. This one kiss had been different, almost, well, *electric*. It had been hours now, and she still felt tingly and turned on. It wasn't the sort of thing that could be so convincingly faked—well, after living with him for months now, it wasn't something *he* could fake, she knew.

It couldn't be physical. The shearing and the removal of all adornments made her looked like an eleven-year-old eunuch.

She was finally snapped out of her confused thoughts by the appearance of a large red-bearded man in furs and horned helmet coming toward the pegasus. The man looked particularly odd because it was still fairly warm out, and he had to be sweltering in that outfit. The reason for his garb was apparent when he went to the shed and started assembling the gear and taking it over to the pegasus.

He's going to fly off! Too soon! Too soon! she thought, disappointed beyond words. This was all for nothing, just folly.

A soldier approached the man, saluted, and said, "Are you certain you want to risk it? You might not make it until after dark, and you know how bad the pegasus' night vision is."

She hadn't thought of that, *either!*

"Oh, ya, ya. No problem," the fur-clad man responded. "Ve only go little ways. Besides, is still full moon."

And, sure enough, he prepared to go. She watched with a mixture of sunken heart and total failure as the man created his strange saddle, strapped in, rode the pegasus, albeit uncomfortably, as a horse out to the main road, checked something—*the wind*, she realized, seeing a flag on the shed—waited, then kicked the steed into a gallop, going faster and faster down the road, and, suddenly, those great wings just spread out and the flying horse lifted, flapped a number of times, gained altitude, and then picked a direction and was off. The soldier, too, watched him go, then shut up the shed and secured it, then walked off.

Now what? she wondered to herself, looking around. The sun was very low on the horizon, the shadows long, but it had not yet set, and she would have close to an hour of darkness before moonrise. Some cover, yes, but there were a *lot* of people—and others—around. Where to go?

Even if she could evade these soldiers and make the front gate, it would matter little. It wasn't so much the distance, as taking total pot luck on what she'd become. A horse wouldn't do—it would be considered a stray or runaway and kept there, maybe tied up. She had thought soldier or Bentar, but now she remembered Sugasto's spell. The were curse usually didn't affect spells, which was why the ring remained. Sugasto had said that she not only didn't need to wear clothes, she *couldn't*. A naked soldier of whatever race, particularly with a ring in his nose, wouldn't be much of an improvement over now.

It had seemed so *simple* a few hours earlier. A *lot* had somehow seemed so simple a few hours earlier.

What around here could she become that would both allow her to escape this place and also be of some use? She had to find it fast, if it was here at all. The sun was setting, and the moon would surely follow. Not even a Sugasto could change that.

Joe and Marge both knew they'd have to allow some time after moonrise for Mia to make her escape, if, in fact, she had been successful.

Joe, once more a Kauri, waited with Marge for something, *anything* to appear.

"If she pulled it off, great," Joe said worriedly. "But, right now, I'd just settle for her getting back here as *anything*." He went over and stared out the window into the darkness.

Suddenly this huge face descended as if on a lift until it covered the entire window. Leathery nostrils flared, and two mean black eyes peered out from a skull that seemed made of molten rock.

Having no place to flee, Joe stepped back suddenly and did what he probably would have done even as Joe. He screamed.

Marge, literally on the back wall of the room, got hold of herself and looked at the monstrous face of the nazga.

"Hold it, Joe!" she shouted. "That damned thing's got a tiny little ring between the nostrils!"

CHAPTER 10

THE ROAD TO HYPBOREYA

When great quests slow and threaten to bore, something will always come along to speed it up. This is not to guarantee a successful or even more rapid end, but certainly a more interesting journey.
—The Books of Rules, XV, 251(d)

THE EERILY LIT LANDSCAPE SPED BY BELOW WITH STEADY AND impressive speed and power; huge, leathery wings beat in slow, steady rhythm like the drums of an oarsman. On the back of the creature, two small reddish figures reclined facing each other.

"Well, you've got to admit, there's plenty of room for our gear and us with no weight problems," Joe noted. "It hardly feels as if we're even moving."

"I feel like I'm riding bottom-side up on the *Titanic*," Marge responded. "And I hope that's the only analogy we have to that ship tonight."

"I'm just debating whether or not I even want to ask for the explanation of this," Joe said, getting to his feet. He walked forward, then looked down in front of the wing. "We're making incredible speed, though," he noted. "I thought you said these suckers were slow."

"Oh, they do all right once they get up to speed, and they have enormous endurance," Marge replied. "It's just that they take an hour to get up to speed, and a fair amount of time to slow down, too, unless they hit something. But we can outfly and outsprint them any day of the week."

Joe stared at the landscape. "I wonder where we are? It would be a real joke if we were headed south, wouldn't it? Wind up in the morning down in the City-States or over in the deserts of Leander?''

Marge looked around. ''No, we've been making north north-west pretty steadily. You can see the river down there still if you look closely, snaking through the highlands and gorges. Figure we started about eight o'clock, giving us eight or nine hours of darkness, then some margin to slow and land. Add an hour to gain this altitude and get up to speed, a fair tail wind, and, I'd say we'll make seven to eight hundred miles tonight. That's not bad.''

''You were totally against this idea,'' he reminded her.

She shrugged. ''Call it feminine pragmatism.''

''How's that?''

''If it had gone wrong, I would have been morally right and would have been the voice of reason over stupidity. Since it's worked, I'll take the eight hundred miles.''

''If we've got slowing and landing times, we'd better keep a lookout for any early signs of dawn,'' he said worriedly, ignor-ing the comment. ''I'd hate suddenly to become Joe, riding on Mia's back, at this altitude and with this dead weight.''

''Well, that's your worry, not mine,'' the Kauri reminded him.

''Thanks a lot,'' he said glumly. ''See if you can find the map in my saddlebags without having the rest of the stuff blown all over creation. It might be an idea if we tried to figure out where we were *before* we had to land.''

Marge fumbled with the straps as she struggled to get the map out without freeing the whole mess. Finally she managed it, unfolded the thing, and they tried using her figures and some landmarks to get their bearings. It wasn't as easy as it seemed, and for several minutes they couldn't find anything that matched, but, as Mia continued to fly pretty much up the river, had it been straight, they were finally able to come up with some points they *thought* might coincide.

''If that range over there is the Kossims,'' Joe said, pointing to a ragged line of jagged, glacier-scarred peaks, ''then those are the Scrunder range in Hypboreya. Just beyond them should be the Golden Lakes. If that's so, this will be mighty cold country even now. What sort of civilization is there, if any, in the Lakes area?''

"It shows a few villages with funny squiggles," she replied. "Who knows what this chicken-scratch really says? I know that the crossed swords symbol there is military—a northern guard-post area, probably, to help protect the royal retreat. And that shows the Kossims are dwarf territory and the Scrunder is crawling with gnomes.''

"I'd take the dwarfs, but the gnomes are where we're going,'' he noted. "They have a reputation of being pretty flaky to the point of overdoing a gag to homicidal proportions. If we put down anywhere in there, the only civilization that's marked is military, and I'm not sure I should use that safe conduct up here. Questions might be asked as to how a safe conduct probably dated yesterday wound up here today. The alternative is going around through gnome territory, right to the edge of the map. Then it's sixty miles of solid ice. Man! You sure the Hypboreyan kings are human? What kind of people would have a summer palace in the middle of an ice pack?''

"I admit to being puzzled by that myself,'' Marge admitted. "I know it's still a long way to the North Pole, but that place should do a real good imitation. Still, there's got to be some reason for all those soldiers scattered along there, and Ruddygore's information is always pretty reliable. It's off the map, though, and supposedly due north from that point there, just below the shaded area with the skull with its tongue stuck out disgustingly. I guess that's the so-called ancient battlefield. How far did he say it was from there to this palace?''

"Sixty miles over the ice.'' Joe sighed. "And no more full moons for a while.''

The creature they rode roared loudly, sounding very much like a cross between Godzilla and a train wreck. Joe turned, and saw what Mia was concerned about. The moon was low, half hidden in the haze below, and the sky was lightening up above.

"Uh-oh. Free ride's over.'' Joe sighed, feeling the beast already beginning to slow. "Looks hazy down there, but no snow except on the mountains.'' He walked forward, until he was almost behind the eyes of the nazga. "Come down anywhere flat where you think you have room," he shouted into what he hoped was an earhole. "If you see the lights of any settlements, come in near them but not so near as to be seen."

A snort answered, and he hoped that meant "message received and understood." He walked back to Marge and the packs.

"Marge, as soon as we untie this stuff, I want you to scout around for us," he told her. "I don't want any surprises, but we've got thirty or forty miles to the ice, then sixty on it. We'll do it on foot if we have to, but if there's any way to get any sort of transport, it would really help."

"I'll check for bus or train stations but I sincerely doubt I'll find any," she responded. "I'm also not too sure about horses, once we reach the ice. If it's relatively snow-free here, then the odds are that ice pack is water, like the Arctic Ocean, and that means that this time of year lots of cracks and crevices. You ever been on that kind of ice before?"

"No," he admitted, "but after coming face to face twice with Sugasto, I'm not going to let climate stop me."

Mia chose a broad, flat area closer to the mountains than the sea. To the northwest, perhaps ten or twelve miles, there appeared to be some man-made lights, and another couple of such signs of habitation scattered about. It was as good a choice as possible.

He and Marge decided not to chance a landing; they jumped off and flew, matching the enormous creature as it glided in. It proved a needless precaution; Mia settled down finally as gently as a feather.

It was hazy, though, making Joe wonder just what the temperature might be around here. He and Marge went to Mia and quickly unstrapped the packs, letting them fall to the ground. He looked at Marge. "Quick and thorough, before sunup," he told her. "Get going. We've got to decide what to take and what not to take."

The price now had to be paid for what they had saved in time. No horses, no pack animals, and still a fair way to go. Although it was difficult to tell just exactly where they were on the map, he knew roughly where the ice pack started, and Ruddygore had indicated that if he headed there and looked out, he'd have no problems figuring out where to go.

While getting the stuff together, it suddenly occurred to him that this couldn't be Arctic-style north; not only was it not far enough north from the subtropical regions for that, the sun wasn't already up. Since, this time of year, the sun wouldn't even go down, or not down much, it was clearly still a long way to the Pole, possibly a lot farther than they'd come. If that was the case, then why was it so cold here? And what kept the ice pack so frigid? Since he'd never before been out from between the tropic lines, at least not by much, he hadn't given it much thought. This would be the equivalent on Earth of Rome or St. Louis, not Anchorage or Stockholm. That was the only reason this were trick had worked.

In the true Arctic, the sun would never have gone down this time of year, full moon or not.

Suddenly Ruddygore's tale of the great battle, frozen in time in the ice by divine and not so divine intervention, came back to him. This was a place where natural law sort of worked almost all the time unless changed by something. If someone, sometime, had had sufficient power, there was no logic in Husaquahr that could stop him, her, or it from freezing the Equator and having palm trees at the poles. Or, it might just be that Husaquahr was in an Ice Age and nobody bothered to mention it before.

Very suddenly, the enormous creature that had brought them here shimmered and vanished, leaving a lone figure on all fours on the ground. He hardly noticed. He was suddenly Joe again, stark naked, and if the temperature was anywhere near freezing, it was on the wrong side of it.

He gave a holler as the shock hit him and started rummaging through the packs for his buckskin outfit and boots, praying that nothing had been left out. Mia, naked and hairless as before, ran over to him, puzzled. "Master, what is wrong? Did you step on something? Did something bite you?"

His teeth were already chattering as he found first the pants and got them on, then the shirt. She came to help him and he pushed her away, shouting, "Boots! Find me boots! And gloves, if we have them!"

"What is wrong?" she asked, looking through the other pack. "Here is your hat, Master. A bit flat, but—"

"Mia! I'm *freezing*! I need boots! And gloves!"

She rummaged around. "I did not know you were so sensitive, Master. It is a bit cool, but not terribly uncomfortable."

"Mia, it's the spell Sugasto gave you. You don't feel the weather; it's as if you have Marge's flesh or even some kind of spacesuit on you can't see, feel, or touch. I don't. Of the three of us, I'm the only one this weather can harm or even kill. Ah! The boots!"

"And here are your gloves, Master," she responded, still not quite following the reality of the situation. It just didn't feel, or even *look* cold. Oh, on the mountains nearby there was snow, yes, but there was grass here, and even some flowers.

Joe felt much better, but he still felt *damned* cold. This outfit would be uncomfortable around here but would allow him to survive; on the ice pack, though, where it was clearly going to be much colder yet, this would be no more good than a loincloth.

Of course, there were the blankets they had used to keep the stuff together. Irving, the sword, was wrapped in three of them! He knelt down and began unwrapping the great weapon, for the first time more interested in the container than the contents.

"We've got plenty of wool and cotton in these blankets," he told Mia. "You're gonna have to rig something from them that'll keep me *much* warmer."

"Yes, Master. I will do what I can. *Oh, look!* When we speak we spout steam like a dragon!"

"That's because it's cold," he told her again, trying to underline the concept. "We humans are always warm inside but the air is around freezing. Our breath, heated from inside us, gets blasted by the cold air and it turns to fog."

She nodded. "I knew that happened, Master, but it honestly does not feel to me as if it is more than you might feel on a cool, cloudy day in Marquewood. This will take some getting used to. I will not know your requirements."

"Don't worry, I'll tell you," he assured her. *The trouble is,*

I wish I knew if my requirements can be met, he added to himself.

He strapped on the sword and tested it out with the gloves. A bit awkward, but *this* Irving didn't need much in the way of feel—it did its own fighting.

He had finally warmed up to just chattering and looked around. The mountains were a couple of miles over there, and, from the map, he assumed they were now in Hypboreya and that those were the Scrunder. Since that range was essentially east-west, it put the Lakes to their east and a bit behind him. To the north was almost a tundra; grasslands, rocky outcrops, yet basically flat. Not a lot of cover, but at least nothing much was going to be hiding from them, either. Still, he knew he would have to try and bluff his way through whoever was in the nearest settlement. He needed furs, not leather, around here. Best to wait for Marge to give him the lay of the land.

Mia found some of the bread and vegetables he'd packed. Nothing to drink, though, right around here, unless they wanted to go mountain climbing.

"So how come you came as that thing?" he asked her.

"Well, Master, first the man came and flew the flying horse away, but not before he told his friend that the flying horses could not see well at night anyway, and so I had to think of what would best serve our needs and get me out of there and then I remembered us being chased—"

He laughed. "All right! All right! I figured it was something like that. It's done, it worked, and we're here." He looked around. "Why then do I suddenly long for that lousy cafe and that overpriced little room?"

He was suddenly convinced that they were being watched. That sixth sense that keeps men in his profession alive was tickling the back of his neck, and he suddenly whirled around.

He sensed—*something* getting out of the way fast, but where? And what? It was pretty flat here.

Mia saw him, tensed, and turned to look around as well. "What is it, Master?"

He shrugged. "I don't know. Probably nothing, but I'd swear that something was in the grass over there only a moment ago."

Before he could stop her, she ran over to where he was looking and looked around on the ground. She seemed to see something, because she suddenly crouched, as if waiting to pounce.

"Bunnies," said a tiny voice from somewhere behind her,
like the voice of a small child speaking through its nose. She
whirled, and a nearly identical voice said, *"Yes, bunny!"*

Suddenly Mia stiffened, then stood, knees bent, her arms out
in front of her and bent at the elbows so the hands hung down,
and twitched her nose. She looked stupid, bewildered—and
scared.

Joe reached down and pulled Irving from his scabbard. The
great sword hummed in anticipation.

In fact, it hummed *Melancholy Baby*.

Gnomes! he thought suddenly. He'd heard of their stupid
tricks. *"Mia!"* he shouted. *"Snap out of it! You are not a rabbit!*
It's gnomes! Gnomes playing tricks in your mind! Listen only
to me, not to them!"

She blinked, seemed to wilt for a moment, almost assuming
normal posture, when a chorus of the voices said, *"Horsey!
Horsey girl!"* and she was back somewhat in the same position,
only she was on tiptoes and actually whinnied!

In the meantime, Irving had finished *Melancholy Baby* with
a flourish and was starting on *God Bless America*.

Wait a minute! he told himself. *They can't possibly know
those songs! This is like a hypnotist's act. Shut them out! Ignore
them!*

Suddenly, out of the ground, rose a horrible, roaring monster,
all teeth and fangs, dinosaurlike and hungry. It roared, and Irving just about swung into action at his reflexive moves, now
humming the theme from *Rocky*.

He moved in toward it, the sword poised, and almost struck—
when the monster vanished, showing Mia there instead. *Another
split second . . . !*

"All right, you little monsters!" he growled. "That's pushing it too far! Irving—the next one you hear, anywhere, strike!"
He knew that the sword could not possibly be affected by these
creatures; its songs were strictly what was coming from his own
subconscious.

"Irving?" a tiny voice just behind him said with disbelief. The sword took control, whirling Joe around and striking something with the flat of its blade. There was a terrible screech, and suddenly Joe was looking down at a tiny, limp form, sort of greenish but dull, with flecks of gray. It was about a foot tall, if that, with an oval-shaped, sexless body, two short, stubby legs, and equally short arms with tiny hands. The face was a cartoon mask, with eyes five times too big, a nose that looked more like a hanging dill pickle, and a rubbery, oversized mouth.

It also was out cold, and a real goose-egg-sized lump was rising on the side of its head.

Suddenly the ground virtually erupted with clones of the little creature, all chattering excitedly and screaming, "Look what you've done! Look what you've done to him!"

"Nothing the rest of you don't deserve!" he shouted back. "That little bugger almost made me kill my companion! And the rest of you aren't any better!"

Mia stared openmouthed at the assemblage of little green something or others, but she repeated, "Companion?"

"Spoilsport!" they began muttering to one another.

"Spoilsport my ass!" he responded angrily. "You want me to instruct this sword, which is very sensitive about its very fine name, to whack each and every gnome it can? With the *blade* this time?"

There was a collective gasp.

"Not so funny when it's *your* neck on the line, is it?" he went on. "From the looks of it, your friend here is eventually gonna wake up. Maybe a day or two from now, but he'll wake up and just have a headache. But that's *iron* that struck him, and hard."

"Iron not hurt gnomes," one of the creatures said. "*Swords* hurt gnomes."

"Well, you deserve it," he told them. "We weren't doing anything to you and you scared that poor girl and almost made me kill her!"

"You not live here. Gnomes live here," another responded. "Gnomes no invite you two."

Well, they had a point there.

"We mean you no harm," he told them, calming down a little. "We want to cause you no harm and will not unless you do more things to us."

"What use live if gnomes no can have fun with mortals?" one of them asked, possibly rhetorically.

"You don't get many people out here, I bet. And the ones that do probably don't return."

The closest gnome shrugged. "Mortals come, be gnomes' toys. Gnomes play with toys till toys break. What wrong with that? *Gnomes* no go mortal places."

"I've heard differently," he told the creature.

The gnome shrugged. "Other gnomes might. Not me."

He gave an exasperated sigh, tempered only by the fact that they were talking, not torturing. "Look," he told them, "as soon as my other companion comes back, we are going to leave. We will not be back. If you leave us alone so we can do that, we will harm no more of you. Deal?"

They actually had to *discuss* it! During the mumbled and whispered debating, however, he caught strands of arguments concerning just how much gnomes had been suffering at the hands of bad mortals lately, and what bad times these were. It appeared that gnomes had been being killed off in large numbers by certain mortals with magic powers.

"We come from a good sorcerer with a charge to deal with those evil men," he told them.

They suddenly got even more excited. "You think you gon' kill bad men?" one asked.

He shrugged. "We are going to try to do what harm we can."

"You sorcerer?"

"No, but we have other secrets."

"Then you worse than dead already. Better off staying with gnomes."

Marge suddenly came in and landed in the middle of them, startling the gnomes. She looked tired, but resigned to the state. At her descent, the gnomes started screaming, "Hawk! Hawk!" and in a moment there seemed none of the little creatures around.

"Jeez! I've been a party pooper before, but I never had *that* kind of effect!" she said.

"Maybe we better get what supplies we can and get out of here," Joe suggested. "They're not much easier to deal with when you talk to them than when they're playing with you." He looked at Mia. "You okay?"

She nodded uncertainly. "I—I was *sure* I was a rabbit, then a horse," she commented uneasily. "I do not like these creatures, Master."

Mia repacked and rearranged and tore, cut, and tied, and with help from Joe managed to get a fair amount of it on her own back. Joe felt uncomfortable giving her that much of the supplies, but she insisted. At least, the gnomes laid off. Now and again they'd see one or two pop up gopherlike out of underground burrows, but they'd just as quickly vanish again.

"There's a settlement of sorts right near the ice pack," Marge told them. "It's not much, but it's something. It'll take you the better part of the day to reach it, though." She gave him the bearings. "There's not much else for a very long way. That ice pack is kinda weird, though. There's so much magic over it and even embedded in it that it looks as if a million two-year-olds got loose with the crayons. Beyond it, though, if I got high enough, I could almost make out your destination."

"Almost?"

"On the other side of that mess of spells there's a large area that seems almost covered in fog. On top of that, there's an almost evil cloud around it that seems nearly black as pitch, and, to top it all off, there's real smoke coming from there and reaching as high in the air as I could see. The thing would give me the creeps, except that the ice pack in front of it is even creepier."

He nodded. "I don't have any explanation for it, but at least it sounds as if we're in the right place and a lot quicker than we could have been otherwise, thanks to Mia."

"I assume from everything that you're gonna chance the settlement," she said rather than asked. "Looks military. I'd watch myself."

He shrugged. "Can't be helped. If I don't get some cold-weather clothes better than these and maybe some gear for the ice, I don't see how we can make it across anyway. You run ahead and find someplace to get some sleep. Check on us tonight. If we're in trouble, you might well have to try to spring us."

She nodded. "Will do. Uh—it just occurred to me why that high smoke rising in the air looked familiar, and if I'm right, it might explain something about this place."

"Yeah?"

"I think there's a volcano out there, either in the middle of or just the other side of the ice," she told him. "Remember, the center of the Kauri home is a lava pool. If that's another quiet-type volcanic region, it explains why folks might want to go there, and why it's shrouded in mist. Hot water, thermal pools—it's probably warm as toast and very pleasant inside there except for the company, like some kind of spa or hot springs type resort. And I'll say this—if you were gonna hide anything at all, that would be where *I'd* hide it."

"Makes sense. Now, go get some rest and don't sleep near any gnome burrows. No were business tonight, and we might well need you."

"Will do," she replied. "Gnomes don't bother me, though. They're not intrinsically evil, just, well, *gnomes*. You watch it yourself, though. No telling what else might be out there." She rose up into the air and was quickly gone.

"Well," Joe sighed, fixing his pack as best he could, "let's go the hard way." He was going to have some problems with Mia in this environment; although she was apparently quite comfortable, he got the chills just looking at her.

The walk was cold, dreary, and deathly dull. The scenery was all in back of them, but, then, with the scenery had come the gnomes, and he felt well rid of those. As the sun rose, the temperature got above freezing, although not tremendously so, and that proved a worse condition than the freeze itself, as the top part of the ground turned to mud and cold marsh, making the footing not only messy but treacherous. Worse, it seemed to have loosened every mosquito, blackfly, and nipping gnat in all creation and they all seemed headed right for meal Number One, which was him. The spell that insulated Mia, while not insulating her from the mud, also seemed to ward them off; she walked right through small swarms of them without once getting bitten, although there was maximum exposure, while he, with only a few exposed areas, nonetheless seemed like lunch to them all. He'd swear that some of them were large enough to have rotor blades and all seemed born with full-blown pneumatic drills on their mouths.

After only a few hours walk, they could see their eventual destination, although it was still going to be most of the rest of the day to reach it. It was that flat and that featureless. It stood out as a small grouping of dark blips against what looked like clouds below them, but which, in reality, was ice. They were still much too far away to see over the ice itself, but even from here there was a decided plume of black smoke across the horizon. Joe never so much wanted to get to a place that was probably going to be deadly or worse in his life. If he had to succumb to evil, it was damned well going to be at least *warm* there.

The slogging toward that far-off settlement was perhaps the most frustrating thing of all, since he walked and walked and walked for hours on end, the goal in sight, and for the longest time it simply didn't seem to be getting any closer.

These people, he decided, had to be supplied by air, just as the important ones who went out to that redoubt beyond the horizon had to come and go the same way. He couldn't help but imagine a fleet of the huge nazga with teeth that spelled out *Mack* and *Peterbilt* and *Kenworth* on them, and broad wings bearing *Rodeway* and *Yellow Freight* and *Preston* logos, flown by a team of tough-looking aerial truckers, and wonder what in hell their truck stops looked like.

Just because there was little else to do and not much even to think about, he allowed himself to slip into fairy sight, and what he saw gave him plenty to think about.

Not too much on "shore," as it were; the usual warm lifeform readings here and there of who knew what, and not a lot on the ice, either—until you looked toward that distant horizon. There, not immediately offshore but well out, in the direction they'd have to go, he saw just what Marge was talking about.

Just there, and going to the horizon, it was not white in fairy sight, but instead appeared to him as if some giant was collecting all the yarn in the world and dropped his savings in the Grand Canyon. Brilliant, glowing magical strings, so many of them, in every conceivable color, and so dense and overlapping, that no sense at all could be made of any of it. A shift back to normal sight showed only the continuing whiteness, deceptive in the extreme, but he understood why such legends about that place existed.

Supernatural phenomenon? Perhaps the dumping ground for the leftovers by those who designed Husaquahr? Or really the site of a frozen battleground between ancient forces back when those with power approached the status of angels and demons? It didn't matter. They had to cross *that*? Overland? Could anyone? He would bet almost anything that even Sugasto going out to the redoubt flew around that place. Ruddygore had almost shrugged it off, and yet Joe thought it might be the most dangerous part of the journey, perhaps more dangerous even than the summer palace.

What would happen if I died here? he couldn't help thinking. *Died in a place so barren and so cold, a place without trees?*

Mia broke his morbid train of thought with a more immediate worry. "Master, what will you tell people in those buildings when we reach them?" she asked him.

"Huh? Hadn't really thought of that. I guess I just thought I could rely on the safe conduct."

"But, Master, that won't explain anything about why we are here in this awful and desolate place, or where we are going, and why. After all, if we were allowed to this hideaway, we would have been entitled to fly there, would we not?"

She had an abnormal ability to shout at him when his brain was in park.

What *would* be a good explanation? Science? Not likely; even if that really meant something here, he could hardly fake that kind of education. Magic? No, not magic, since clearly neither of them had any. Besides, they were both rather clearly what they really were, even to the most ignorant.

"I think we're gonna have to fall back on the last refuge of the scoundrel in this sort of situation, particularly if they're really all or mostly military types up there," he told her.

"What do you mean, Master?"

"An insidious invention of bureaucrats and military personnel called the Top Secret gambit," he replied. "It means that only I, not even you, know why we are here, and I'm not supposed to tell."

"Do you think they will swallow that?"

He smiled grimly. "They might. After all, who but a lunatic, a sacrifice, or somebody really important would be up here in a place like this and going the place we're going?"

"But they will alert the palace!"

"Perhaps. Depends on just how scared of Sugasto the bastard has made his own people, even up here."

At least they didn't have a hostile reception to deal with. In fact, they didn't have *any* reception when they finally reached the place, perhaps an hour before sundown. The six buildings, all constructed of logs obviously brought overland or by air from somewhere else, looked incredibly weathered. Although none of the buildings were huge, all had two fireplaces and one had three. Nobody was on the lone street, and there wasn't much in the way of horses or other steeds, either, although there was the loud barking of dogs down at the end.

"Where are the people, Master?" Mia asked, looking around.

He pointed to the chimney tops. "There's smoke in all of them, so I assume they've got good sense and spend most of the time indoors."

"But which one do we pick?"

He looked at them. None of them even had signs on them. He guessed that the feeling was that you were only up here if you were assigned here, and if you lived here you knew.

"Three chimneys," he replied. "It's got to be some kind of office or mess or some kind of social center, being the largest."

He went up to the door, took a deep breath, grabbed the knob, opened the door, and went inside.

The first impression was of warmth. The place felt downright *comfortable*, but it only made certain parts of his body feel as if they were on fire from the contrast.

The place was something like a basic, small social club; it had a bar, a couple of tables, and one fireplace was being used to cook things on spits. Two slaves were in there, both males, one tending the cooking fire and the other wiping down the bar, both with rings in their noses, both as naked and hairless as Mia. They both turned and looked up at them. At a table, one of three, two of the toughest-looking women he'd seen since that truck stop in Wyoming ten years back looked at him in sheer amazement. Both were wearing fur-trimmed black uniforms and matching leather boots.

"Where the hell did *you* come from, Bub?" one asked in the kind of voice that matched her butch appearance exactly.

He hadn't expected women officers.

"I was dropped off by courier nazga quite a ways from here, back toward the mountains, this morning," he replied, trying to match their tough tone. "I've been freezing and getting bit since."

"Nobody told us that anybody was coming," she noted suspiciously.

"Nobody said to me that there was anybody here other than that there was some army personnel," he responded. "And I see that there are."

"We don't exactly get many people up here, you know." She got up, looking very irritated. "I think you ought to see security."

"Fine with me," he replied. "Can I leave my stuff here? The slave can help out yours. Just let me get some papers out."

"Sure, go ahead." She turned to the two slaves behind the counter. "You two better hadn't burn my dinner! I'll be back as soon as I can."

"It will be done, Mistress," one responded in a rather gentle tenor.

"It better be, or you'll sleep outside with the dogs tonight!"

Joe had just thawed enough to start feeling his bites when she led him outside again and down to the last small building in the settlement.

"Was this always a settlement or was it built for the army?" he asked, mostly trying to make conversation.

"I neither know nor care," she responded frostily. "In there."

He walked in after her and found himself in a smaller log house arranged into rooms like an office. Inside were two more women in the same uniforms as the first, looking as tough and weathered as the others. *Were there no men here?* he wondered.

"What have we here?" asked one of the security officers, a comparatively small woman with a loud, nasal soprano. She looked him over. "Where did *he* come from?" she asked the woman who'd brought him.

"Came waltzing into the club with a slave as if he owned the place," his guide replied. "*Female* slave, too."

"Go on back to dinner," the officer told the guide. "We'll handle this from this point." The guide clicked her heels together, turned, and left.

"So," said the security officer, "want to tell me what you're doing out here at the end of nowhere?"

"No," he responded.

She was almost as surprised as by his initial appearance. "No?"

"I have the same ultimate boss you do," he told her, removing the safe conduct and handing it over. "Don't worry—I *am* authorized to tell you that what I'm supposed to do has nothing at all to do with this place."

She handed the safe conduct back. "This means little when you're out of any beaten path and in a restricted military zone."

He shrugged. "What am I gonna do?" he asked her sarcastically. "Launch an all-out attack? Me and my slave? Spy on you? Tell them about the Ultimate Weapon you've got here? Steal your dogs?"

"Could be. The only reason for this outpost is to prevent people from going any farther, particularly out on the ice beyond this point," she told him. "If the reason you're here has nothing to do with us, I assume that's your objective. That makes you our primary mission right now."

He sighed. "Mind if I sit?"

"At the moment, stand."

"All right, all right. Yesterday I was invited to lunch by and with the Master of the Dead himself at an army camp just north of the Marquewood border. And you know exactly what I mean by 'invited.' "

"All right. Get to the point."

"It seems I impressed him on some other business, or maybe I pissed him off. Hard to say, but, since I'm still here, it was probably the former. For some reason he's convinced that enemies, perhaps spies, might get to the summer palace by land. I don't know what's going on out there and I don't want to know. He asked me if I would soothe his nerves by attempting an undetected overland trek to the palace and, if I made it, attempt to gain entry without their security and spells knowing. I have something of a reputation for doing what people believe is impossible along those lines. A nazga was told to divert north of the mountains miles from here and drop me off. If you want to check you can go up there and see where it came in and we landed. Nazgas make their marks on the land. I gather for some reason they didn't want to fly me closer in."

"I'll bet," she commented, and his spirit felt better. She was actually *buying* this crap!

"There wasn't much cold-weather gear that far south, so I was told I could get some here, since any spy would come equipped."

"So why didn't he put this in an order to us?"

He smiled dryly. "You obviously haven't met the Master of the Dead if you have to ask that."

"Perhaps. But, by definition, even his lapses aren't his fault. Why should I believe you?"

"Logic. Do I sound insane? No? That leaves me as either a spy or who I say I am, and I have to ask you, now, would a spy walk in here with a story like this and no cold-weather gear, leaving his slave with your people?"

"Maybe. If he were clever enough."

"Uh-huh. And even if I made it, how am I going to get back? How am I going to get messages out? The only way I have is via the palace and the Master of the Dead himself. Considering that, even if I *were* a spy, I wouldn't exactly be much of a threat, now would I?"

"Could be," she admitted. "But maybe not. We have one spy in custody right now from up around that area where you said you came from. He fell into the hands of the gnomes and is quite mad. The few who get away from the gnomes are always mad. Usually we have to bribe them to get people back at all; this one went so crazy the gnomes actually begged us to take him."

"You're sure he was a spy?"

"What else *could* he be? He's too crazy now even to make enough sense to create a story, but there's no other reason for coming here—unless your story is true, or unless he was someone who heard that there were only women on rear picket duty and thought he was going to have a field day."

His eyebrows rose. "There are only women here?"

"Women and slaves to do the drudge work, and by law the slaves are all eunuchs. Why? You getting any ideas?"

"Nothing personal, but not along those lines," he assured her, trying to sound both safe and not insulting. "When the Master of the Dead personally orders you to do something, you don't really think about much else."

"Maybe," she responded a bit suspiciously.

"I'd like to see that prisoner, though," he told her. "I'll leave my sword and stuff here. I just want to see what sort of person would come up here unauthorized. Having done a fair amount of spying in the south, I might have come across somebody that nervy."

She shrugged. "All he does is sit and sing this bizarre chant in some alien tongue. You can see him, but no tricks. All of us are experts with bow and crossbow and some of us are fine swordswomen. Not to mention that we have our own means of magical protections and can have the forces of true Darkness down on this place like a shot."

"I'm not the enemy, damn it!" He unbuckled his sword and left it on her desk, then followed her back. "Besides, if you have anybody who can read the signatures of spells, have them check my slave. One of her spells is from the Master of the Dead himself."

There was a small back area to the cabin, and she took a large set of keys on a master ring from a safe, then unlocked the rear door. Inside was a narrow outer area just wide enough to stand and not be grabbed by anybody inside, then a small single cell with thick bars.

Inside a small figure sat, stripped naked so that even if he could break out he'd freeze before getting very far. He was sitting on the bunk staring up at the ceiling in the semi-gloom and singing softly.

The man on the bunk looked over and saw Joe, and his eyes brightened. For a moment, Joe was afraid that his cover would be blown, but instead the little man yelled, "*Skipper!* You've come at last to rescue me! Take me back to the island, *please*! Otherwise the cannibals will *eat* me!"

His beard and hair were long and unkempt, and his eyes were wild and distant, but Macore was still clearly recognizable.

Joe ignored the little thief. "What will you do with him?"

"Standing instructions. Anyone who comes here as a spy, after his value for information and interrogation is done, is to be enslaved by spell, castrated, and fitted with a nose ring. As you can plainly see, he's of no interrogation value in any event now."

"You can do that here?"

She nodded. "We are not merely a military unit, we are a coven. We would have done it during the last three days of the full moon but we're short one right now. We can handle the rest of it, but that insulation spell is tricky. Complicated spells are best done during Black Sabbaths, and so he's got a few more days until Sergeant Murrah returns from presiding over the Serpent Goddess Virgin Sacrifice and Bake Sale at Magash."

He gulped. "Uh, yeah."

"Do you know him?"

He nodded. "I do, and he's no spy. He was as mad as this long ago. He probably had some strange-looking gadgets as well, if the gnomes didn't take and destroy them."

"No, they gave those back, too. We sent them on to the palace by courier, not knowing what they might be, but they looked to me like sophisticated spying gear of some foreign manufacture."

Yeah, Taiwan, most likely, he thought. Aloud he said, "He worked for no government or master. At one time he was the greatest thief in all Husaquahr. Apparently one day he stole those things and looked into them and went mad. He's been wandering all over since, but this is the last place I thought he'd be."

"Skipper! You've got to spring your little buddy!" Macore cried plaintively.

They walked back outside, leaving Macore to scream about being deserted, and shut the door.

"Thank the Demon Rastoroth for that door!" the security woman muttered. "At least it keeps his rantings in there!"

Joe scratched his chin through his beard and thought a moment. "You know, I might be able to use him."

"Sorry—the regulations are absolute," she told him. "If you stick around until we do the slave conversion, fine. Not otherwise."

"I don't want to delay all that long, but, what would be the harm? Consider—I'm heading *toward* the palace, not away from it. If he got away, he'd freeze or die on the ice. But I'm betting that somewhere in that scrambled brain of his is still the greatest thief in Husaquahr, the man who actually burglarized the Lamp of Lakash from the vaults of the enemy sorcerer Ruddygore himself."

"Really? *He* did that?"

Joe nodded. "Uh-huh. I'm pretty sure he could walk out of there any time he wanted to, only without warm clothes and provisions, he's stuck. If he had them, though, he'd head straight for his obsession, which is that gear you sent. If we told him it was in the palace, I'd wager he could make it there."

"So? I thought the idea was to see if *you* could make it."

He nodded. "But I'm on my own initiative as to how. If I set this little fellow out, and follow him, then if *he* makes it, *I* make it. And what is his reward if he does? He's sent right back here, and by that time your thirteenth member will have returned. If he doesn't, well, case closed."

"So? And what sort of route do you plan to take for this?"

He shrugged. "To go around is to invite tripping alarms.

You're not here to guard the castle; you're here to prevent anyone from going in a straight line toward it, across the part of the map marked 'deadly and forbidden.' If there is a weak spot in the palace defenses, it's from that direction."

"And with good reason!" she responded. "You can't see it, but *we* can. What looks like plain ice is a seething cauldron of the strongest and most complex sorcery imaginable. And it's coming from who knows how far beneath the ice? Imagine what might lie down there? No one wants to liberate *that*."

He didn't like the sound of it, but it was pretty much as he suspected. "Has anyone to your knowledge tried to cross it while you've been here?"

"No, but I've seen some of the results of the few who got back out. Whoever or whatever is imprisoned there is powerful beyond our imagination, and was frozen and trapped there by powers even greater."

"I've heard the legends. A fierce battle frozen in progress."

"That's right. We draw additional power for our coven from it, but we try and reject it. You can feel it coming, trying to seize control. Even our demon master appears to fear and respect it. It is why we do nothing in the Arts unless we are complete."

Which at least saves me from your witchcraft, he thought.

"You said you've seen people who were out there?"

She nodded. "Only you cannot call them 'people' anymore. Most are madder than that one back there, but with reason. I saw one with a goat's head, a woman's breasts, a fish tail, and the legs of a great bird. Some others were worse."

"That's just from *walking* on it?"

"From melting even a small amount. So much is buried there, in such chaos, that any heat, any digging, anything that disturbs and melts what is below, is liberated but undirected. It is miles away before it starts, and always we feel it here. It goes almost to the palace itself—over fifty miles. It cannot be crossed."

Joe felt very uneasy. "Well, that's what I was sent to do. I realize that now. All the more reason to give me the prisoner as well. Unless you absolutely need another slave around here, and the little guy isn't good for much except stealing stuff. Besides, you keep him, you won't make him sane. You'll still have to put up with that stuff.''

"Not if we cut out his tongue as well as the other," she responded, but clearly she was thinking it over. "You are really going to try it through the forbidden area?"

"I'm afraid that's the job. From what you say, maybe the Master of the Dead didn't like me, after all.''

"I would say so, too." She looked at him and sighed. "What a waste," she muttered, almost to herself.

She was so adamant and clearly so fearful of the place that he couldn't help harboring similar thoughts himself. For the first time, he began to doubt if he would ever see his son again.

CHAPTER 11

DANCING IN THE DARK

Any Company which shall survive to reach the Ultimate Obstacle to the attainment of their Quest shall be able to secure what they need to complete the Quest. However, successful completion is not guaranteed, and there are no warranties, expressed or implied, in these Rules.

—The Books of Rules, XV, 304(a)

"Macore!"

The sleeping figure in the cell snored, paused in midsnore for a moment, then turned over but kept sleeping.

"Macore!" came a louder, more insistent whisper. *"Wake up, damn it!"*

The snore turned into a sort of piglike grunting, and the little thief muttered, "Huh? What?"

"Over here at the window."

Sleepily he made his way up, grabbing his woolen blanket around him to ward off the chill of the night, and got to the window, standing then on tiptoes to see what was what. "Mary Ann?" he asked tentatively.

"No, you idiot! It's Marge! You remember Marge, don't you?"

He grew suddenly suspicious. "Yes, but I've been fooled before. There was a fellow in here today who reminded me of Joe, too. You might just be a dream sequence."

She floated up so that her face was framed in the window. "Dream sequence my ass! That *was* Joe, under heavy disguise."

233

"Well, if this is real, what the hell are you doing here?" He shivered. "Damn! It's too cold to be a dream."

"Ruddygore sent us on a quest to the palace out there on the ice. The same palace where they sent your tapes and video equipment."

He was suddenly very wide awake, but not quite following. "Ruddygore is interested in *Gilligan's Island*?"

"Afraid not. But your quest, at the moment, and ours come together. And if we do ours, Ruddygore will energize your equipment. Understand?"

"He wouldn't do it before. He's still mad because I beat his system on his vaults. That's why I had to suffer like this!"

"He didn't need something from you then."

"Good point," he admitted.

"Macore, how did *you* wind up here?"

"The gnomes tried playing all sorts of tricks on my head, but all they got were my memories of *Gilligan's Island* episodes. Exposure to this magically transformed them from gnomes into a band of hostile critics. They tossed me out to these people."

"No, no, I mean, what are you doing up here in the middle of nowhere to begin with?"

"I got a tip," he told her. "They said that up here was this vast sea full of magic with a tropical island in the middle of it. Nobody mentioned that the sea was frozen. Naturally, I had to find out, you see."

"Naturally," she responded, not really seeing at all. "Well, part of what you heard is true. That sea of ice *is* filled with incomprehensible magic. On the other side there *is* a volcanic island, with a great palace in the middle of it."

"That must be some powerful sorcerer," he noted.

"The Master of the Dead, Sugasto, lives there sometimes. And it's likely that's where the Dark Baron is as well."

He thought about it a moment. "Hold it! You're telling me that you want to cross a place of unbelievable magical powers so you can get to where the Dark Baron and the Master of the Dead are? And they say *I'm* crazy!"

"Yeah, well, after looking the place over, I can go along with you on that, but it *has* to be done, if it's possible. Surrounded by ice, patrolled in the clean areas by Bentar on nazgas, on the ground by an army of the dead, and by magical spells, the only way to reach it undetected is across that mean area. It's so powerful in and of itself that there's no way they'll fly across it or put anybody in it or maintain any sort of spell of their own in that area.''

''I'd rather take my chances with the zombies and the Bentar and the rest,'' he told her. ''I looked that other place over and it made me dizzy.''

''*You* looked it over? When?''

''Oh, I've got stuff—warm clothes, pikes, you name it—stashed all over this hick town.'' He suddenly went into a Cagney impression. ''They ain't never built the prison that can hold Cody Jarrett!''

''That's not *Gilligan's Island*.''

He shrugged. ''Would you believe that in the Disneyland Hotel that they only had one channel showing *Gilligan's Island* at all, and then only once a day? I had to watch *something*.''

''Yeah, well, I doubt if most people go to Disneyland to watch television. Never mind. You're telling me you can walk out of there whenever you feel like it?''

''Sure. But they've been feeding me here, and pretty decently, too, and I wanted to get some strength. Besides, I leave before I've mapped out everything, they hit the alarms like mad.''

''Macore, you pushed your fabled luck to the limit on this one.'' She told him their plans for him and the fact that the only reason it wasn't already done was just chance.

He stood there, thinking about her words for a moment, then said, ''Okay, you talked me into it. It probably wouldn't matter to Gilligan and the Professor—all that time on that island with Mary Ann and they never once made a move on her—but it matters to me.''

''Good. Joe's got them conned into believing he's checking Sugasto's security. He's gonna try and spring you to help. It's either get us to the palace or good-bye all that matters.''

''That would help. I'd like to look it over in daylight. You have any idea what any of that Fruit Loops spaghetti actually does?''

''I've gone as close as I dared to alone, and the only thing I can say is that the answer is, 'almost anything.' I think the old legend is true—this was a great battle between mighty forces of ancient times. But I don't think they're frozen in place down there, although that might have been the intent. I think everything and everyone in the battle was transformed into energy, magic energy, and then the whole mess was frozen in place. That's why it's so near the surface when it should be thousands of feet down in the ice. New snow and ice retain them in, but every once in a while melting of some kind liberates a spell which then turns back into whatever it was. That's why they feel things from there trying to get them once in a while. The trick is to cross that place without causing any melting of any kind.''

Macore whistled. ''Tough trick if they're close enough to melt out occasionally on their own. Let me sleep on it. But you make sure I get sprung before that last witch gets back!''

Even Joe suspected that it was the first surreptitious break-in to a major place in the world that had been performed before a live audience.

All thieves of Husaquahr had the power to see magic; those who did not generally were captured or died on their first job.

The witches of the station were more than convinced of his insanity when they watched the little man, bundled in furs, walk right out on the ice and then proceed for a good half an hour, until he was only a speck on the whiteness, right to the edge of what they called the Devastation.

They were prepared to counter him when he inevitably made his break for freedom; any sane man would. But even without his malady, Macore, once set upon a problem, became so absorbed in it that to flee simply wouldn't have entered his head.

''What's he *doing* out there?'' one of the women asked, more to herself than the others.

''Well, he took a measuring stick, a sharp saw, and leather thongs from the dog sled area,'' the security officer responded. ''*You* figure it out. I didn't like giving him the saw, which can be a weapon, but I had to admit to both personal and professional curiosity. If he can actually just walk into the Devastation and return, he will indeed be the genius the big man, here, says he is.''

"He's been out there in almost that spot for quite a long time," Joe noted a bit worriedly. "I hope he's all right. I really should have gone with him, but he insisted that for this sort of thing he worked best alone."

One witch was watching with a telescope. "He's doing *something* down on the ice. First he appeared to pack snowballs and throw them into the Devastation! Now he's working feverishly in the ice just this side of it. Now he seems to be lifting something—and now he's just sat down on the ice!"

"He's mad. All these are are the actions of a lunatic," the security officer said impatiently. "Best to haul him back."

"*You* go out there, right on the edge of *that*, and haul him back," somebody said. "This is as near as I want to get to it."

"He's up again!" the woman with the telescope said. "Now he's turned, facing the Devastation, just standing there. No, he just—he just took a step toward it! And another! He's walking very oddly, but—*he's inside!*"

Joe could use his second sight to see the massive collection of spells, but Macore was too far away and relatively too small to make out inside it.

"Can you see him?"

"No. He's been swallowed up in the mass. You couldn't see the Grand Altar of Stet if it were fifty feet inside. Not from *this* distance, anyway."

"It seems as if he's been in an awfully long time already," Joe said worriedly.

And it was even longer still, as they watched and waited, perhaps a half hour or forty minutes. Finally, the security officer said, "That's it. He's finished. If he comes out of there at all we'll not even recognize him as human. It can't be done."

"I wonder," Joe mused. "According to your own charts, it's about forty-two miles across to the palace at the narrowest crossing. If whatever he did worked, he'll want to do time tests."

"Wait! What's that over there?" someone shouted, pointing

to an area perhaps half a mile from where Macore had entered. The telescope swung, refocused.

"It's certainly a manlike shape," the woman said, peering through the eyepiece. "Too early to tell much more at this distance."

But, as the figure grew closer, it clearly *was* Macore, and he didn't seem to be any worse for the experience.

He got a cheering reception when he reached them, all but the security officer amazed at what the little man had done and forgetting his actual condemned prisoner status. The security officer cared not at all about the little thief, but she saw the potential if indeed someone had learned to cross the Devastation.

"Well," Macore sighed, "it works, but I'm not sure it'll do the job."

Joe was surprised. "You walked in and around for quite some time."

The thief nodded. "Sure I did—but I never went all *that* far in, and the kind of speed involved is very slow. I'd say two miles an hour if we're doing okay. And that's no rest, no sitting down on the job, for—what? Over twenty hours? That's a pretty long time not to stop or even sit down. I'm not sure I could do it. I'm not sure *anybody* human could do it."

Joe leaned close to his ear and whispered, "Consider the alternative."

He nodded. "The sanest way, the way any good spy would do it, would be to walk around just this side of it, always prepared. When anybody came along, or any spell was sighted, they could then duck in there and continue around the problem, then re-emerge. The trouble is, walking around the stuff by that route, even at the southern end, is like a hundred and eighty miles."

"I could make forty-two miles of relatively flat terrain, even with snow, in less than twenty hours, weather willing," Joe told him.

"Uh-huh. With a couple of pounds of ice strapped to your boots?"

Macore's solution, once given, was so obvious neither Joe

nor the others could imagine why they hadn't thought of it before.

"First, I saw that the spells were in fact below the ice. Not far, but below. Then I checked out how disturbed they could become by throwing ice balls into the area. Nothing happened. There's a layer of snow on top that's deep enough to give some traction and cushion weight. Then I cut blocks of ice out from the untouched section, strapped them to my feet with the thongs, and practiced a little walking. When I had it, I went in and walked around. No problem. It's really very pretty in there, if a little weird. So long as nothing actually melts, you're fine."

"What about dragging some blocks of ice along in a sledge?" Joe suggested. "They could serve as seats and replacement blocks just in case."

"Uh-uh. A sledge might not cause problems in and of itself, but it *will* cause friction," the thief reminded him. "And friction is heat and heat melts ice. Add to that the idea that a sledge would clear away some of the snow and you have a prescription for real disaster."

"We could travel pretty light," Joe told him. "So the real problem is where and how to rest."

"That's about it. Just sitting down on the ice, even with nice furs on, might well transfer just enough heat to attract one or more of those things to you the way lightning's attracted to the ground."

"If you've solved this much, we'll *have* to find a way to solve that other," Joe said. "For now, what about—inside there? Any bumps, mounds, ridges, or crevasses?"

"No, it's pretty smooth and level, at least on this side. No telling what it's like much farther in or on the other side. Every once in a while you hear this little click or pop and then some really weird noises, from screams to yells to sounds like lightning makes through the air, but that's about it."

Joe nodded. "Well, we're going to have to think this through today, that's all. We either have to figure out how to gain more speed or how to rest."

Macore nodded. "Somehow. I can't figure out why you can't fly into and over that, though, except that it's attracted to heat and motion. Maybe flying through it creates enough friction in the air to draw it. I dunno."

At the insistence of the security officer, Macore returned, was stripped and locked back in his cell, and it was there, in relative privacy, that they continued the conversation.

"What about Marge?" Joe asked. "Is she immune?"

"I doubt it. Not to the spells, anyway. Spells of that kind cover just about anything, even rocks and trees. I doubt if she'd need the blocks of ice, though. Anybody who can walk around here stark naked and jump into pools of lava back home isn't going to give off heat—so long as she doesn't fly. What about your girl?"

"Mia? I don't know. She *feels* warm, and I'm not sure I'd like to risk her without the ice sandals. But she doesn't feel the extremes. She walked barefoot on the ice pack! She *rolled* in the snow without effect!"

"Okay, that's a break, then. It means she has normal body heat only relative to other living things. She touches you, it's normal. She touches ice or snow or a hot poker, she's got instant protection. The odds are *very* good she wouldn't need the ice blocks, and also pretty good that she could carry ice. How strong is she?"

"Strong legs and back, fairly weak arms. Why?"

"If I'm right, she could carry a block of ice on her back." He snapped his fingers. "Yeah, that's part of it! We *all* carry ice with us. Except Marge, of course. A decent square would be enough to sit on and keep our warmth insulated." He paused. "Uh-oh."

"What's the matter?"

"Joe, you ever see a dog do his business in the snow? It comes out at body temperature. It's like pouring hot water or hot coal on the ice. We have to deal with that, too."

"Well, we better deal with that fast," he told the thief. "Their missing sergeant is due back in two days, and dear, sweet Lieutenant Quasa of security here doesn't see any reason why sentence shouldn't be carried out on you, pointing out that, as a slave, with Sugasto's protective spell, you would still have all your old skills for what we need."

Macore gulped. "Yeah, but I wouldn't have what *I* need. Let me work on it today and tonight. If anything, we probably should make our start at nightfall anyway. It's never warm enough on the ice out there to melt stuff of its own accord, but direct sunlight *has* to have an effect. Marge is better at night and you and I have the Sight, so it'll be lit up like a celebration in there anyway. Still, we're down to technical problems. We have the basic method."

"I hope," Joe replied, leaving him to his planning.

Mia had been spending most of her time helping the other slaves there. There were five in all for the detachment of thirteen women; all were native to Hypboreya, but, although slavery was an institution here, none had been born into it. They were all, effectively, political prisoners, sentenced to slavery for offenses against the interest of local sorcerers and high priests of cults, and, as such, had also been placed under spells of obedience, which she lacked. They were compelled to do exactly what they were told, and ask permission for just about anything else.

Mia thought them just a cut above the army of the living dead she had seen lined up on that plateau, and perhaps worse. They *knew* what had been done to them, and lived in daily humiliation with no hope of redemption.

She was down behind the bar helping with some cleaning and minor repair when the two women came in, and at first she paid them little attention and they, for their part, did not see her. She recognized one of the voices as that unpleasant and officious little witch of a security officer, Quasa.

"So what are you going to do?" the other woman with her asked the security chief. "That big man is dangerous."

"He must eat and drink," Quasa replied. "If we cannot make a decent potion that will put him out cold without his noticing, then we do not deserve membership in the Sisterhood."

"Why not just let them go off in the Devastation?"

"He and the mad one have done what he says he was sent here to do—find a security breach to the palace. I am certainly not about to let the mad one go, unless enslaved. A mind that can work out that sort of thing would be of even more danger, should he make it in, and, being mad, he might be uncontrollable. If that happened, we would be blamed. As for the big one, we have nothing but his word that he is official, and I have never seen anyone in the empire who operated without clearance. He had to acknowledge knowing the other one because the little one, being mad, might well recognize and spoil his cover. It is no more difficult and much more efficient to enslave two at one time."

"But what if he is truly working for the Master of the Dead?"

"Then we did our duty, and it is his fault for not insuring our cooperation. The man will have failed in his mission, thanks to us, and that will go well for our records, while he will have paid the price of failure. I would much rather answer for following procedure, in any event, than have to explain why and how I allowed possible spies to make it to the palace."

"All right, but do we have to cut him, too? It gets so lonely here sometimes, and he's so good looking . . ."

"Not only does the law mandate it, but it also would be taken wrongly if we did not, by those to whom we must report. I would rather follow regulations and do without a while longer rather than risk joining his status. As for his bitch, we'll drug her, too, so that she does not try and protect him. Once he is converted, she will be common property and we can bind her to the coven."

"When do you plan to do all this?"

"I told him our sister was due back the day after tomorrow. As you well know, she is due back any time now, and certainly by tomorrow. I say tomorrow night, moon or no moon."

Mia crouched there, hardly daring to breathe, hoping against hope that the staff slave would not betray her. She waited, pretending to keep working, until the two women finished their drinks and left, then got up and went out the door.

Finding Joe wasn't hard in that tiny place; finding him alone, when he was the only sane man around for hundreds of miles who was not in the palace, was more difficult. She had trouble unobtrusively separating him from the crowd, but finally managed.

"Master, in the bar, I overheard this Quasa woman saying

that they were going to drug both of us and enslave us both to them as well as Macore," she whispered excitedly to him.

He stiffened. "You're sure?"

She nodded.

"Did they see you or know you were there?"

"No, Master."

"When?"

"Tomorrow, Master. Their missing one arrives a day early. You are deceived."

He sighed, thinking. "Then we will have to go tonight. After dinner, I should think. They won't do it tonight, since they'd have both of us to take care of for a day and night. Get together the supplies, everything we've talked about. Meet me behind the security shack as soon as you can with what you can manage. Food, but only one small wine flagon. We'll use snow." He shook his head, thinking about what they were going to attempt. "I sure hope Macore worked out those details."

Marge had found a clever hiding place in the supplies building, where the slaves went to get what was needed. Now Joe headed there, knowing that he'd have to awaken her early, but she had to be ready.

He startled her so much when he shook her that she changed three shades of color before she realized it was him. Quickly, though, he outlined the changed situation.

"Joe, I'm not going to make it," she told him. "You know we aren't great walkers, and I haven't fed in two days."

"If you stay here, you'll die. Same reason."

"I know. Joe—we've been through a lot together. We've been as close as we could as comrades. I'm only alive and here in this world now due to your kindness long ago on a lonely road in West Texas. I've tried as much as possible to pay you back. Now I need something from you. Now. Right here. They won't be coming back in tonight; I know their routine and what they already got."

"Marge! Here? Now? I—"

She was changing, becoming a vision of an idealized Tiana, mixed with Mia, and now with every vision of every woman he'd ever loved or wanted to love. She was Venus, and Diana, and Lust herself.

"It is finally time, Joe," the vision whispered to him, those big eyes holding him. "Make love to me, Joe. Make love to me *now*."

Joe feigned an upset stomach at the end of the meal and excused himself, saying it was definitely *not* the food or the cooking, but rather an old ailment coming back.

Marge and Macore waited for him behind the security shack. He stared at the little thief, all dressed in thick furs, gloves, hat, and boots, although only the boots, being his originally, fit right.

"How'd *you* get out?" he asked the thief.

"I told you I could walk any time I wanted. That place couldn't hold a baby."

"Who told you about the advanced schedule?"

Macore looked positively rhapsodic. "*Mary Ann!* She came to me, Joe, as if in a vision, saying she loved me!"

Joe looked at Marge and gave a slight pig grunt. She smiled and shrugged sheepishly, but she sure wasn't weak anymore.

In point of fact, Joe felt damned good himself; wide awake, alert, excited, adrenaline flowing, the darker thoughts and fears that had been so close to the surface with him receding into the background. The Kauri were not true parasites; what they took from you was in the main stuff you wanted taken. Still, there was the present worry.

"I hope Mia's okay," he said. "We ought to get going."

"Here she comes," Marge noted. "You know, you're right. She makes *me* feel cold to look at her and I'm not wearing anything more than *she* is."

"Conditioning," he told her. "We feel what we expect. Ah! Mia! Any problems?"

"A little, Master. The dog harness was a problem. I have my own knife as well. My lord Macore, the best I could find for you was a butcher knife."

"It'll do," he replied. He stared at her in the semidarkness. "You know, I could almost swear you look familiar. I must say

I don't like the way they shave their slaves up here, though, although you look quite pleasant, my dear.''

"You remember her from Earth and the boat, Macore,'' Marge told him. "Don't worry about it. And the poor girl can't help the way she looks. Mia, you're gonna have to carry a real load out there and not drop with it. You think you can do it?''

"It is necessary, and so I must, my lady. I will not fail you all.''

"Grab all the gear and let's get away from here and well out on the ice fast,'' Joe ordered. "Sooner or later somebody is going to come looking for one of us and not find us. When they see Macore's gone, too, they'll put two and two together.''

"You think they'll come after us?'' Marge asked him. "I mean, you sort of showed them how it's done.''

"I doubt it, but even if they do, they won't be able to close on us, if we're well away,'' Joe replied. "And if they come in after us on their own ice blocks, they're not going to think about all the things we did, and it'll eat them alive.''

"One or two of 'em will come,'' Macore predicted. "They won't want to raise the alarm or report us missing, because it'll go against them that they let us escape. They'll want to bring us back, dead or alive.''

"Can't they catch us with the dogs, Master?'' Mia asked, concerned.

Macore chuckled. "Dogs won't go near *that* place. Dogs got more sense.''

"Let's go. We'll organize this stuff on the edge before we go into the Devastation,'' Joe told them. "Marge, since you're way too small and light to carry much of anything, stay behind and check on pursuit. We'll wait for you before we go in. Might as well make use of those fairy wings and all that excess energy while we can.''

She grinned. "Will do, boss. Now, in the words of my great grandpappy, *'Git!'* ''

They got.

The moon had risen just at dusk, and was slowly rising in the sky. It was still almost full, of course; not enough for wereing, but enough to give them some light across the dangerous ice pack.

"I kinda wished it would be a bit darker," Macore remarked. "I know we're damned hard to spot out here under these conditions, but I feel like a backlit target."

"Where do we go, Master?" Mia asked.

"Right where all those colors—" Suddenly he realized that, of all of them, she was the only one who couldn't see the place. "Do you see anything at all over there, where I'm pointing?"

"The ice seems to look a bit different, Master, a bit more moonlit as if it is glowing slightly."

"Good girl! That's enough. For now, just follow me."

They walked for quite some time, their boots crunching eerily in the dead silence of the cold. Joe turned back to Mia. "How are your feet feeling?"

"Sometimes it feels like hard, rocky ground, sometimes like walking on sand, Master," she responded. "But I do not feel this cold."

"Good. Not much farther to go."

"Are you sure this is the narrowest point, from here?" Macore asked him.

"There's not much to use for landmarks, but it's close. Four point two miles northwest of the town, if their map is right. The area's ragged, but basically oval in shape and pinched just above its middle. In the pinch, it's supposedly forty-two miles. It broadens to about sixty-five, so I *hope* we're right. The palace would be a mile north and about a quarter-mile in from the pinch on the other side."

"If we miss, we're gonna have everything from zombies to invader spells up the ass," Macore noted. "We better hit this one dead on."

Since the pinched oval of the Devastation was angled from the shore, he had been forced to guess on the pinch without being really able to see much of it, but he felt sure he was correct.

"Here," he told them, putting down the pack for a moment. "This is as good a guess as any. Better start cutting our ice blocks now. Mia, we'll cut your ice load large and heavy and then trim it down to something you can handle. You don't need to walk on this stuff, but we'll need what you carry to sit on.''

"Yes, girl, but even you must remember that, if you have to relieve yourself, it must go in the sack here,'' the thief put in, already starting to cut his own blocks. "It'll be as warm as ours. Once it's cold, and that won't take long, *then* we can dump it. We won't have to carry our crap, at least.''

The great sword Irving cut through the ice as if it were butter, and soon Joe was trimming a block into two smaller, lighter, slabs with flat faces.

"We might well not need these,'' the thief admitted, tying his own blocks on, "but we can't chance it unless we have to. If we lose the blocks, or they splinter, or prove too cumbersome, then we'll have to experiment. By that time the soles of our boots will be at ice temperature, anyway.''

Joe finished, and practiced a little walking. It was stiff, but he felt comfortable. He went over and helped Mia prepare his pack, then, after putting it on, they put together her harness and checked out progressively smaller rectangles of ice until she proclaimed that it was okay. What she could manage wasn't huge, but it would do.

She slipped off the harness for a moment and started doing some of her stretching exercises. Joe watched her, then went over to her. "Mia,'' he said gently "we've explained what's in there, just below the top. You know that nobody's ever been known to cross this thing and come out anything but a hideous monster.''

"Yes, Master. I know. But we will make it.''

"There are a couple of things I want to say before we go in there, just in case we don't. The first is, if, somehow, I don't make it, and you do, and Macore does as well, let him touch the ring and then finish what we set out to do. Understand?''

"Yes, Master.''

"If not, avoid anyone touching it and try and do it anyway if you can.''

"I will, Master.''

"Don't let anything stop you, not even regard for me. No matter what you feel, remember those living dead back there and your own slavery and the way the slaves were back at that camp and think of all Husaquahr under those people—and all in Tiana's name and mine. I swear I'll die before I let them do that. Will you swear it, too?''

''I will, Master.''

''In spite of that, and in spite of the fact that I'll sacrifice *any* life, including ours, to stop them, I want you to know something. I know you are just my slave, and that you were never my wife, and that you're Mia, not Ti. But I want you to know, truthfully, that, as yourself, just as you are, and here and now, I love you more than I've loved any other woman.'' And then he grabbed her and held her and gave her another of those kisses, only even deeper and more passionate than before.

Marge descended. ''Break it up, you two!'' she said sharply. ''The posse's hot on my tail and tryin' to head us off at the pass!''

The pair broke, reluctantly, and quickly helped each other with their packs.

''Okay, gang! Let's *do* it!'' Macore shouted. All of them took deep breaths, paused a moment, then stepped into the Devastation.

The first thing that hit them was that the Devastation was neither desolate nor even *quite* quiet.

''It sounds as if you were really way, way, aways, and yet . . .'' Marge said, fascinated.

''It sounds like Sorrow's Gorge,'' Joe completed. ''My god! How long has this been here? Thousands of years, perhaps?''

Marge nodded. ''And yet, somehow, you get the feeling that even the freezing didn't so much stop the battle as freeze it. It's as if the last second of that battle was being played, over and over again, like some broken record.''

''That was my impression when I was in here earlier,'' Macore admitted. ''I think the soundtrack changes a bit as we go, though. I think we *are* hearing the battle, or what was happening *here* on each spot, at that fatal moment back then. Kind of gives you the creeps, doesn't it?''

''I hear it, too, Master,'' Mia told Joe. ''The sounds of armor and horses and men yelling and screaming and even the sounds of magic. You could almost see the whole thing in your mind from those sounds.''

''Well, we'd better get a different part of the program,'' Marge noted, shaking herself out of it. ''We've got a very long way to go, and, right now I bet, there's at least a couple of Hypboreyan women's guards cutting out ice blocks not far behind us.''

''Oh, don't worry so much,'' Joe told her. ''We can take care of them in a fight.''

''Oh, really? And what good is even a great sword like yours against a crossbow? What's next? Bare hands against automatic rifles?'' Marge began walking, looking down at what to her was an incredible kaleidoscope of colors glowing just below the snow. ''Huh! Why do I feel that under this snow is the dance floor from *Saturday Night Fever*?''

''Put a little of your inborn fairy warmth on those spots and you'll do a dance, all right,'' Joe told her.

''Hey! Take it easy! I have to do three steps to your two, remember, and I wasn't built for forty mile hikes. I was *never* built for forty mile hikes. *Ai yi yi!* How do I get myself into these things?''

''You've had more rest than any of us,'' he pointed out. ''And probably a better meal, too.''

Macore looked around. ''I just wish we could erase these tracks in the snow. We're not gonna be real hard to track.''

Joe looked at Marge. ''You just remember that, no matter what, you've got to suppress that panic reaction of yours. No flying and no running.''

At that moment there was a sudden *pop!* near them and from the lighted ground under the snow quickly came a ghostly visage of a skeletallike horror mounted on a nightmare steed, rushing toward them, only the head and torso of the rider and the head and neck of the steed visible. It was transparent, but it screamed a ghastly scream and came toward them—and was gone.

''*What* was *that*?'' Joe asked.

Marge stood stock still. ''See? I didn't panic. I was too petrified. At least Husaquahr's now got a space program.''

''Huh?''

"My heart's in orbit."

"What *was* it, Master?" Mia asked. "It was—*horrible*."

"Oh, yeah," Macore said calmly, "I forgot to mention those. They happen every once in a while. I don't *think* they're anything to worry about, just something being liberated briefly because of the settling in the ice or whatever."

"Uh—Macore. Anything else you forgot to mention?" Marge asked dryly.

"Uh—not that I can think of. Say! This boring walk needs some livening up. Anybody want me to sing the entire *Gilligan's Island* theme song, complete with the end verse everybody forgets?"

"No," Joe and Marge responded in unison.

"Okay, okay. Sheesh! Everybody's turning into a critic on this damned world!"

They walked some more in silence. The cold was really getting to Joe in spite of the borrowed furs and fur lining stuffed in his boots. They couldn't really cover their faces very well, and, although there was no wind, it really did begin to bother him, and possibly Macore as well.

Equally troubling were the occasional manifestations that arose suddenly, each preceded by a cracking sound. They kept telling themselves and one another that they'd get used to it, but the farther in they went, the more horrible and gruesome the apparitions became. You just *didn't* get used to it; you merely dreaded the next *crack*!

"Jeez! Weren't there any good guys in this fight?" Marge asked.

"Probably. Almost certainly," Joe responded. "My best guess is that we're either on a lightly defended part of the field or we're inside the battle lines of one side. What's more interesting is that we haven't seen any human apparitions. Lots of dark fairy types, and some mean-looking monsters that might be fairy or mortal, a practical difference only to them, but no *people*."

"I also wonder just how long ago this battle *was*," Macore commented. "I mean, it's ancient enough to have passed into legend, and I've yet to recognize *any* creature as something I've met, but the armor and the weaponry and things like saddles and such look very up to date. In fact, a lot of it looks better than what we have now.''

"Some races might have died out right here," Marge noted. "Others might well have been transformed or scattered to the four corners of the world by any power strong enough to do *this*. As for the men, their souls might well be long gone and only their bodies remaining locked in the ice. We fairies, on the other hand, don't have that luxury. I think that what we're seeing are actual fairy souls, ancient ones, freed of their husks, unable to dissipate, rising in the cracks into the air and then dispersing to the air before a new husk can form. It's pretty depressing, if you're fairy.''

Joe sighed. "The only thing I can say is that everything I've seen so far is something I don't mind having dissipated. I keep thinking that we might not have it right, though. I keep remembering Quasa's tale of seeing the one-time humans turned into a collection of bestiary after being in here. I know there's even supposed to be frozen spells in this crap, but that wouldn't explain that sort of stuff. Nobody throws spells that give the enemy goat heads or fish tails.''

"Fairy blood was probably stronger then, like the magic," Marge guessed. "There are fairies even today with goatlike heads, and others with fishlike tails. Suppose you were standing right on one of those openings when the fairy spirit rose? The instinctive thing would be to find cover, to find a temporary husk. If pieces of those souls had time to get to mortal flesh, they might produce that sort of thing.''

"The odds of being on top of one of these cracks when it goes is pretty slim," Macore responded, thinking. "But if you added heat, you might get a whole bunch in full strength at once battling for the flesh. What do you bet that they peed themselves into monsters?''

After walking for what seemed like hours, at least, although there was no reliable way to tell time, they broke for a rest. The bag was well used, and they knew it would be a total discard by the time they were done, and the block of ice for a seat was barely big enough for Joe, with Macore almost sitting on his lap. The little thief looked up at the big man, grinned, and said, "Daddy."

"You be good or I'll throw you off!" Joe threatened.

Marge and Mia sat wearily in the snow, knowing that their body heat, at least, would not transfer without action on their part, and action was the last thing either of them wanted.

Mia looked back at their tracks. "Do you think they are still following us, Master?" she asked nervously.

"If they haven't peed their own selves into oblivion or worse by now, yeah," Macore answered before Joe could. "Most of 'em are kind of bored and not real energetic, but that Quasa is a tough, hard-nosed bitch who would pursue you to the City-States and beyond, if you forgot to fill out a form."

Joe looked around. "If there was any kind of cover I'd almost be tempted to wait for them. If they *do* catch up, Mia and I will handle them, understand? Just stay behind us and don't make yourselves targets."

"But the crossbows!" Marge objected. "And you don't dare run at them in here!"

"Don't have to," he told her. "It might be a little bloody and painful, but all the bolts I saw in there were wood or bronze-tipped."

"Whatever you do, don't bleed on the snow!" Macore warned. "Blood's *warm*."

"I'll try not to, if it's necessary. But if one of them goes down, it could be hairy."

"We may find out after all," Marge said. "If that's not two figures of flesh and blood coming, I don't know what they can be."

Joe sighed tiredly and got up. "And it was always my experience that women seemed to be *always* going to the bathroom. Bad luck."

"Perhaps not, Master," Mia responded, getting up as well and pulling her knife from the pack, then walking slowly away from him. "I, for one, would rather meet these two than an assemblage of those horrors we've been seeing."

Marge used her extraordinary vision. "Crossbows for sure. I

doubt if there's much hope of you not taking one in the chest, Joe.''

"Just remember where not to bleed!" Macore emphasized helpfully.

"And watch out for a chain reaction," Marge warned. "If you get one of them and she falls and bleeds, it's sure as hell gonna raise *something*."

The two women stopped about twenty or twenty-five yards from them, crossbows now at the ready. They weren't going to allow themselves to get close enough in to take a sword or knife.

"You're coming back!" Quasa told them in a firm, business-like tone. "All four of you. I don't know where you came from, nymph, but you can't fly here and you sure as hell can't run."

"*Nymph!* I'm a Kauri, you little broom-ridin' boot-lickin' daughter of a bitch!"

Joe drew his sword, which hummed in excitement of having its own feast. Below, the colored lights seemed to change and shift, as if reacting to the sword.

"Your crossbows won't save you," Joe told them flatly. "They'll cause us a little pain, but that's the way it goes. Your plan to amputate a part of me wouldn't have worked, either. It would have come back. The only thing you could have done to me physically was make my hair fall out, and I kind of like my hair."

Quasa seemed confused about the reply. Never before had she had someone in this position, where she could drop them with one well-placed shot but they couldn't possibly get to her, when they didn't surrender.

"What do you think you are? Demons? Sorcerers? You have no protective spells. I can see the spells you have. And the bitch is a slave. That's plain to see!"

He took a step toward the women, and Mia, to one side and presenting a separate target, started in, as well.

"But not even a sorcerer can see blood curses," he replied. "And even mercenaries and slaves can be werewolves." He'd long ago given up any idea of explaining the concept of just a were.

"Werewolves! You're bluffing!" But she didn't sound so confident, and actually retreated a step.

"So you can't kill us, you see," Joe kept on. "But *we* can kill you with these weapons. *You're* the ones who can't run or hide, not us. Better be sure before you shoot that thing. Blood's warm. You see the Devastation gathering around us? It senses battle, it senses *death*. Who knows what we'll raise by our fighting? Perhaps you'll have a pig's head and a duck's feet. How's *that* for explaining to superiors?"

"Stay back!" the other woman screamed. "We'll shoot!"

Joe and Mia kept their advances. Ten yards. Eight. Six. "We are already reconciled to that," he said.

The other woman, frightened and confused, raised her crossbow and trained it at Joe.

"No! Shiza! *Don't!*" Quasa screamed, but it was too late. Shiza fired her bolt.

It struck him with tremendous force right in his chest, the force of it almost bowling him over backward. It was only with an extreme will and the fact that he was wearing two flattened oversized ice blocks on his feet that kept him up at all. Even so, he bent over backward so much he was afraid he was going to touch the ground, and he did brush the snow slightly.

But, *boy!* That hurt like hell!

He straightened back up, looked down at the bolt buried deep in his chest, grabbed it with his left hand so Irving could remain in his right, and, gritting his teeth, he pulled the bloody thing out and away. It hurt more to remove the damned thing than it did to be shot by it.

"*Man!* Is that ever the worst case of *heartburn* I *ever* had!" Satisfied that the bloody thing had cooled, he threw it well away and continued forward.

It was too much for Shiza. She panicked, dropping the crossbow, then turned, kicked off the ice blocks on her own boots, and began running.

The display of color under them suddenly shifted and started chasing her. Puffs of electriclike energy bolts in a variety of colors seemed to come out of the snow, and the whole mess seemed to take on a life of its own. Joe, and even Quasa, stood frozen, watching what was going to happen.

The intensity of spells under the fleeing woman and following her was now blindingly bright and throbbing with energy. Even Marge watched with growing fascination. "I was right!" she muttered. "They're fighting themselves below to get out to that body."

Suddenly the place where the woman was now about thirty yards back erupted in the most complex pattern of magical strings any of them had ever seen, completely enveloping the woman. There was a crackling and suddenly the full volume sounds of fierce battle cries.

Where the woman had been caught by the forces below, there was now a mass of writhing, seething flesh in rapid motion under the furs, as the desperate fairy souls beneath struggled to get some sort of container, both to live and to prevent dissipation.

She was not one thing, or two, or five, but a hundred things, all competing inside her flesh for some sort of home. First an equine head, then one of some great lizard; a face, fleshy and fattened, had broadened lips, fangs, two broad noses and three eyes as well as a curly horn in the center.

The huge mouth opened, and it sounded as if she had the voice of hundreds, all speaking at once, and all speaking something different. But as none of them would yield, the flesh split, and from it came a horde of terrible, insane apparitions, all screaming in death agonies, then . . . gone.

"*That,*" said Joe, "is why it doesn't really pay in the end to be one of the bad guys."

Quasa turned and faced him and put down her crossbow. She tried a nervous chuckle. "All right. You win. I won't bother you anymore. Honest I won't. I'll just walk home now, *very* slowly . . ."

The wound in his chest still smarted and would for some time, but there was no more blood, and it was becoming a persistent ache, like a bruise that went right through him. He smiled back at the security officer. "I don't think so," he told her.

"I'll come with you, then, as your prisoner," she suggested.

"I've been to the palace. It's a neat place but *really* complicated. You need somebody to show you around."

"I'm afraid we just couldn't trust you," he responded. "Sorry, but our laws and procedures require that we deal rather harshly with soldiers of an enemy nation who try and turn us into slaves instead of treating us as soldiers. I'm afraid you broke the Convention with me, my dear. I truly wish I had the means of punishment—of making you like Mia, or, better, having you trade places with Mia, whose feet you aren't fit to lick. Unfortunately, I lack my magician, who's away doing things and won't be back until *much* too late."

The crossbow, which had been lowered to her side, had none the less remained cocked. It began to come up now.

"No, Mia!" he shouted. "Just get clear of her! This one is Irving's."

The crossbow stopped, not quite fully up to shoot him. "Irving?" Quasa said, disbelieving. "You named a sword like that *Irving*?"

The sword arm moved rapidly in a single motion, the edge of the shining blade swishing across her.

For a moment she just stood there, a stupid half-grin on her face. Then, in astonishingly slow motion, Quasa sunk to her knees, and, only at that time, did her head fall off.

Joe stepped back as quickly as he could without running or disturbing the magical elements below, many of which were now rushing up to engulf the headless body and even the head itself.

"*Coffee brown* strings?" Marge said in a puzzled tone. "I don't think I ever saw any that color before."

The head went through a terrible series of transformations and gyrations including growing tiny hooves before it exploded like the previous body, but Quasa's body, on the other hand, remained kneeling in the snow, frozen, as that massive coffee brown surge of strings rushed into it, easily forcing away strings of complex reds and violets.

The body twitched, then moved slightly. Joe continued backing away, and saw that Mia was safely back as well. They could do nothing now but watch.

The hands flexed, then went to the head and found only a bloody, spongy mass there, already cooling.

And then, to all of their complete astonishment, the headless body stood up.

"Don't worry! At least we can outthink it!" Macore said optimistically.

"Don't be so sure," Joe responded. "We don't know what shape or form it's taken under those clothes."

And then, slowly, something started to rise, almost ooze, out of the severed neck.

The head was somewhat bovine in appearance, but the eyes were huge, humanlike, and blazing with energy; when it opened its wide mouth, it showed, not a cow's flat cud-chewing teeth, but a nearly sharklike view of pointed ones.

"I'll lay ten-to-one odds to anybody that it doesn't say 'Moo'," Macore said.

"I, Saruwok, live again!" it cried in a deep, booming voice that seemed to echo from within. The words were Husaquahrian, but spoken with a thick accent and many differences in inflection.

"A minotaur!" Marge breathed. "Or whatever inspired the minotaur. A bit smaller than the legends, though. It had less to work with, I suppose."

"Particularly with its need to get a head," Macore added, almost inviting an unprecedented aggressive strike by a Kauri for the remark.

Joe faced the creature, sword still drawn, confident that iron would do the trick with one like this. The traditional eight foot tall minotaur might have been a challenge, but at four feet or so, it was hard to take this one quite so seriously.

The minotaur spotted Marge. "You! Nymph! How long?"

"Damn it, I'm not a nymph!" she responded, really irritated. "I'm a Kauri!"

"Who the hell cares?" it roared. "How long?"

"A few thousand years, give or take. You've been out a long time."

"A few . . . thousand . . ." The news seemed to shock Saruwok. Finally he asked, "How have my people fared since they were deprived of me?"

"Not well," Marge told him. "You're the first I've ever seen."

The minotaur gave a hollow, booming sigh. "I feared as much. But now that I have regained life, I may liberate some of my fellow *zlutas*. We shall rise again!"

"Uh—you can raise them?" Joe asked, not really decided upon his course of action yet.

"With three bodies like your own, I think I can."

"Yeah, you and who else?" Macore taunted.

"I am Saruwok, greatest warrior of my time!" he intoned. "I need no aid!"

Joe decided and approached the minotaur. "That may have been true a few thousand years ago, in your old husk," he told the creature. "Unfortunately for you, I'm afraid you came up a little short."

Dwarf steel came down with sudden swiftness, splitting the new head almost in two.

There was that crackling, electrical sound again, and this time it engulfed the body and was soon gone. The coat, pants, and boots stood there a moment, then collapsed into a heap.

"Score one for extinction," Joe said, sheathing the blade.

CHAPTER 12

THE MALICE FROM THE PALACE

No quest shall be fulfilled until all the logical possibilities have been exhausted.

—The Books of Rules, XV, 111(c)

AFTER A WHILE THEY BEGAN TO TELL THE WARNING SIGNS OF strain under the ice well in advance; they began to anticipate and avoid trouble, and became more confident of acting within the Devastation.

It continued to be a *very* dangerous place, of course, intolerant of all false moves, but it was no longer a place neither understood nor abnormally feared, if one respected its own unique Rules and powers.

No longer feeling the threat of pursuit, and with Macore leading a careful and meticulous examination of what was and was not possible within the eerie area, they actually grew confident enough to try a few things that made life much easier. The blocks of ice proved unnecessary in the end, although one still had to be very careful, and that alone improved both men's speed and comfort. Still, by sunrise, exhaustion was setting in. First it was Marge, already ill-suited for this journey and always having to force herself to work by day, then Mia, who'd had a full previous day, much of it strenuous, and Macore, who had earlier gone into the Devastation with his tests. Joe understood perfectly; he was going by force of will alone, determined that he would at least be the last to be seen failing.

"We aren't going to make it." Macore sighed wearily. "We're just too all in, and we're—what? Halfway, maybe, or a little more?"

259

"We can't exactly do much else but press on," Joe pointed out. "If we're on target, to our right and left this goes on for fifty to a hundred miles, and it's at least twenty back and maybe that forward."

"Then we're going to have to figure out some way to get some rest in here," the thief responded.

"What do you suggest? Spread blankets and nod off?" the mercenary asked. "Lie on a blanket and you'll draw Technicolor after a while, no matter what. Lie down in the snow and you might not, but the cold will transfer in through these furs and freeze our sweat."

Macore stopped, knelt down, and examined the snow. "Maybe not. It's very dry, powdery stuff, and there's absolutely no wind in here. I suggest we take turns. One of the girls and one of us. We might get frostbite or worse, but if one each of us is up, we can watch over the sleepers, both for signs of freezing or any magic buildups. A blanket roll can act as a pillow, keeping the head up and our breath heading upward. I think it's possible. On the other hand, it's *got* to be possible. Otherwise we're gonna drop one by one and get the full treatment anyway."

"I can keep myself awake," Joe told him, although he wasn't all that sure he really could. "You take it first, Macore."

"I will stay up with you, Master. I, too, can remain awake," Mia insisted.

He shook his head. "No, Mia. I want one of the two of us at least to be in some kind of shape, and Marge is going to be a lot easier forcing herself to stay up now than in midday. Most of all, I trust you totally to keep me out of trouble while I'm out, so I might actually be able to rest; I'm not sure I'd trust Macore."

It was a tough watch, although not particularly a boring one, as Mia would turn or shift, threatening to breathe down on the ice, only to have to be turned back, and Macore proved a fitful sleeper. Time and again there would be magical agitation starting, causing either Joe or Marge to have to make adjustments. In between, the two guardians had nothing to do but talk.

"Well," Marge sighed, "here we are again, in the middle of

it. It seems as if we keep doing it, theme and variation, over and over again. Same old challenges, same old enemies."

He nodded. "When we started off, it felt like old times, but it's grown old quickly," he told her. "I'm tired, Marge. Tired of being pushed around by forces over which I have no control, tired of being the only guy who can fight this or that villain, tired of playing the game. Sooner or later, my luck's got to run out. The worst part is, I'm almost afraid that it won't."

"Huh?"

He gave a long, mournful sigh. "I keep thinking of what Sugasto said about Ruddygore—that the old man was maybe the oldest living sorcerer, that he'd been playing the game so long that he was playing it on automatic, just to keep playing, with nothing but temporary objectives. Pushing pawns around the board like us, doing it again and again. Maybe Ruddygore loves the game for its own sake, but I don't. I know evil is always around and all that, but we small few *can't* be the only ones who can fight it. We *can't* be. Most heroes and heroines in the stories and legends get no more than three shots and they're gone, happily-ever-aftering or riding off into the sunset. We just seem to be going on and on and on."

"I know what you mean," she admitted to him. "I've been doing this to relieve the routine imposed on me, but it gets riskier and riskier each time, and I have more to lose. It would be nice just to have a break. A real long break to relax and smell the flowers and maybe see a little of this big world without having always to run for it or fake it. Even Macore—the old Macore would never have gotten so hung up on this stupid *Gilligan's Island* thing. He may have gone nuts over it, but it wouldn't have been his whole life or the focus of his dreams. I just wonder if we haven't shot our wad. The Rules tend to follow the story and legend requirements pretty well here. Usually, after great adventures, the grand epics go, there comes a time, almost always at the end of the third book, when the supervillain is vanquished, taken out. Forget that happily-ever-after stuff, though; that's fairy tales for kids, and even the Grimm tales really were grim until Walt Disney rewrote them."

"What are you getting at?" he asked her, feeling a bit uneasy.

"I think we're stuck, doing this over and over again, until we take the bastards out. And I mean *out*. Then it'll be some new class of villains to be set against some new set of heroes. There's really no end of it until we die or they do."

"Could be," he admitted. "But—how the hell are *we* gonna take out a world-class sorcerer like Sugasto? And the Baron just keeps slipping away more and more. We had him in our hands, under our complete control, and let him slip away."

"That's the point. It was supposed to happen then. If we'd taken the Baron completely out, then and there, no matter what plots Ruddygore came up with, it would have been over for us. Sugasto is Ruddygore's problem. He picked the S.O.B. to be an adept and then exiled him in the Lamp, rather than kill him in a wizard's duel; then, when he needed the Lamp, Sugasto was loosed again. The Baron's ours."

"You ever think maybe he *let* the Baron go? That is, made it possible?"

"Huh? *Why?*"

"To keep us in. To keep from having to go against Sugasto with a green crew. And, most important, because I am the only one the Rules will allow to meet this threat. I'm not going to make that mistake again, though. If I ever have another crack at the Baron, it's him or me."

"You'll get that crack. You'll both keep getting at each other until one of you goes. That's the system. The trouble is, even if we get him, it's not necessarily happy-ending time."

"What do you mean?"

"From King Arthur to Bilbo Baggins, when the ultimate evil in a world is vanquished, it's after the good guys have given all they can. Even the ones that pull through have had it. They always seem to wind up sleeping beneath a hill, like Barbarossa, or sailing off into the mists toward some Old Heroes Retirement Haven, whether they're human or fairy. They've done their bit, they're tired and worn, and they just want out. Isn't that what you were saying?"

He nodded. "Sort of. I don't necessarily want out of life, though—I've got a son, after all, and somebody I love. I just want out of the game."

She nodded. "I just wish I could shake the feeling I've had since Ruddygore's place that the buy-out is pretty damned heavy."

"You're Little Miss Gloom and Doom this morning, aren't you? Now I'm *really* not looking forward to this!"

The system *did* work, and when the sun was nearly overhead, they awoke the sleepers, detailed their own problems in watching over them, then tried it themselves. By dusk, all of them had at least some decent sleep and without real incident, although Mia had to admit quietly to Joe that it was well that she was a slave devoted to her master; otherwise, she would have killed Macore long before he got to recounting Episode Forty-One.

Although all of them still felt tired and physically wrecked, they made the other side shortly before dawn the next morning, to find that they were less than three miles south of the palace complex. Shrouded in clouds and mist, it was an imposing place, less a palace than a true island with a massive building at its center. It rose, black and forbidding, out of the ice, a massive volcanic cinder cone, with hissing fumaroles and geysers occasionally shooting from its flanks. It wasn't all *that* much above the ice pack—perhaps twenty or thirty feet—but it was a clear oasis.

"Odd. I always thought of volcanoes as two miles high and snow-capped," Marge remarked. "Still, Hawaii is a bunch of volcanoes and much of it seems fairly low. That's because you're only seeing the top of the volcano; the other couple of miles are underwater. It might be that much of that is really under the ice."

Macore nodded. "I keep wondering about its relation to the Devastation. It's so close, yet its great heat stops at the ice. It's as if all the heat that was removed from that great inland sea to freeze it was somehow stored up here."

Joe pointed through the mists of dawn at towers rising from the fog-shrouded island. "Well, there's the palace. Tons of magic in there. God! You try it with fairy sight and all you get is night time again!"

Mia looked around. "I am more curious as to why there are no guards, Master, or terrible traps."

Macore shrugged it off. "Nobody," he said, "is supposed to get this far. When you build a fortified wall and fill it with every defense imaginable, you don't also stick alarms and forts all over the inside. We've bypassed their impregnable defensive rings, which, I've no doubt, are nearly that. But the Rules always provide a blind spot. Don't get cocky, though! Joe's right—that place is black as pitch on the magical level. It'll have its own internal security staff and gimmicks. Trip one and it'll bring the full powers of both sword and sorcery down on us with nowhere to escape." He looked at the place. "I wonder where they'd put my video gear?"

"Gear second, Macore," Joe told him. "The bodies first. If we don't get the bodies, the rest, your gear, our necks, won't matter. The odds are, too, that those bodies will be inhabited by somebody and those bodies will have the capabilities we had, so they'll be excellent fighting machines and well-guarded to boot. Once we finish them, then we'll try for your gear."

"Uh-uh. *You* do your business, I do mine. Once you do in those bodies, all hell will literally break loose, and I'll have no chance. Once we're inside, we're no longer a company. You three go your way, I'll go mine. If I can help, I will, but that's as far as it goes."

There was no reasoning with him on that, and Joe was frozen stiff. Taking advantage of the clouds of steam and fog and the cover that the time just before dawn still gave, they moved toward the massive black region.

The moment they stepped onto it, they knew they were in a different realm. Surrounded by ice, the island, perhaps a half mile around, felt as warm and tropical as back home in a Marquewood summer. For the first time, Joe and Macore both felt the effects of painful frostbite on their faces. They forced themselves to ignore it as much as possible, and Joe, at least, knew that healing would be rapid, thanks to his were curse. He still had a bloody area in his coat and under it where the crossbow bolt had struck, but already there was no sign of a puncture at the skin.

"We're gonna have to stash these furs," Macore noted. "I'm starting toward 'well done' already, and they slow me down. I'd say we pick a spot in these rocks and try to conceal them. We may need them again, if we have to take the backdoor out of here."

Everyone was surprised to discover that, under it all, Macore wore his gun-metal gray thief's outfit. It was patched and well worn, but it looked like the old Macore once more.

"I stole it back, too," he explained. "I wouldn't feel exactly me without it, and it's a bit of a walk to the nearest tailor's."

"I wish I'd thought of that," Joe admitted. "It looks like I'm going to make my play wearing just a sword and swordbelt. I don't even think the boots are a good idea. For one thing, they're getting very soggy now that they're warm and, for another, they'll make noise and give little traction up here. Still, I'm gonna be pretty damned embarrassed if I get into a fight." He looked at Mia and grinned. "Now we *are* a pair, aren't we?"

Clothing secured, they began moving up the slope, quietly, low to the ground. Marge signaled a halt, then flexed and unflexed her wings. "Stay here a couple of minutes," she whispered. "Let me check out what's around."

"Be careful!" Joe warned. "They see or detect you and it's all over."

She nodded, then rose into the air, circled around, and was gone into the mist. She was gone only a minute or two, then came back beside them. "Feels like a Turkish bath on the top there. From the humidity, I can guess the heat. Up top are formal gardens of some kind all organized around thermal pools. It's very pretty, really. There's some statues of various Hypboreyan gods in the gardens and I'd watch out for 'em. They all felt magically 'hot,' as it were. The gardens lead to the palace itself, first to a kind of porch with some fancy pools that seem built like jacuzzis. Beyond those are arches that take you right inside the place."

"Any guards?" Joe asked.

"Two bored-looking Bentar. Not like soldiers—just sort of wandering around like night watchmen. Careful, though. They have swords on, and, remember, only iron can hurt them. I'd steer clear if I could, though. The sounds of a swordfight this early will bring lots of folks running, and the Bentar can screech like mad if they're hurt.''

Mia had her knife in her hand, but as they moved over the top and onto the gardens, she held it for a while in her teeth. The blade was an iron alloy; it would harm Bentar, but not easily.

The gardens truly were beautiful, a tropical Eden surrounded by the ice just beyond. Exotic trees and bushes were planted all over in a masterwork of royal gardening that obviously supplied the palace and also was in its own way a work of art.

If the gardens were Eden, then the statues placed here and there through them were Hell. Ugly, monstrous gods, on pedestals, each with its own small altar. Demonic figures, some reptilian, some ghastly distortions of the familiar, some with bat wings, and a few just indescribably loathsome. A statue for each main tribal god of any of the Hypboreyans, obviously, all gathered here for equal homage before the ruling family in a grotesque symbol of national unity.

Joe stared at one particularly vicious-looking doglike thing and thought, *Now at least I know where the Hypboreyans get their sunny dispositions.*

Still, Hypboreya was supposed to be a harsh land, requiring a particularly tough and ruthless breed to tame and keep tamed. Such people bred their own gods in their own images. They all felt what Marge had felt looking at the things. It was as if those grotesque miniatures were somehow alive, aware of them, and looking at them with malice. They gave them a wide berth.

There was the sudden sound of someone walking toward them from the direction of the palace, and they were immediately behind the hedges and in the bushes on both sides. Pretty soon a Bentar appeared, looking, as predicted, bored and sleepy. He was wearing a spiffier uniform than the regular troops, possibly a palace uniform, and wore a gold-encrusted sword and carried a bronze-tipped wooden pike, which he was using almost as an idle cane or walking stick.

Joe's hand went to Irving's hilt, but he did not draw. *One motion,* he thought, directing that thought to the sword. *There must be no unnecessary noise.*

The guard walked past Joe, then stopped and looked a bit puzzled, his reptilian nostrils flaring. He turned, more curious than alarmed, away from the swordsman toward the opposite low hedgerow where Joe knew that Marge and perhaps Macore were. Joe did not wait; he drew and pounced with a single motion.

The Bentar turned at the noise and reflexively put up the pike to ward off the inevitable blow, but the great sword sailed right through it, splintering the wood, and continued on through the guard's neck. There was that distinctive electrical crackling of fairy death, then the body, its head almost but not quite severed from the neck, sank to the path.

"Macore! Mia!" Joe cried. "Quickly! Help me with the body and stuff. We have to get rid of it! Marge—keep a watch!"

The inside of a Bentar both looked and smelled more foul than the living exterior did, but Joe and Macore got it, as well as the pieces of the pike, and Joe dragged the body by the feet well into the trees and against the bushes. Mia wasn't immediately to be seen, but there was too much to do to worry about her yet. There was no guarantee that the body wouldn't be found before it decomposed, although fairy bodies tended to decompose in a matter of hours, but it was at least completely out of sight of any of the paths. It would have to do, as usual, Joe thought sourly.

Mia ran up to him, looking pleased with herself. "The other's throat is cut and he is behind the hedges over there, Master," she told Joe. "It is so simple when they expect nothing."

Joe wasn't sure if he was pleased or not, but there wasn't much he could do about it, in any event. "Okay, let's get up there and inside as quickly as we can," he told them. "Marge, I'd ask you to fly up and peer in the windows up there, but I'd swear some of those gargoyles around the ledges just moved."

"I saw 'em," she told him. "I think they're night guardians, though, and likely going to sleep now, as I should be in normal circumstances. Let me take some care and see what I can see while you move up." Noting their looks of concern, she grinned.

"Relax. If worse comes to worse I can make them think I'm the sexiest female gargoyle they ever laid eyes on."

They moved up, bush by bush, hedge by hedge, toward the huge stone patio. It was hot, even the ground, making Marge's prediction true.

"I can't figure out where the zombies are," Macore whispered, puzzled.

"Huh?"

"Well, why use Bentar for duty like that when you're the Master of the Dead? This is the perfect place to program zombies to capture or kill anybody who doesn't have the password of the day. It doesn't make sense."

"I'm not going to complain," Joe answered, but he admitted that he had wondered the same thing.

Marge came down and joined them again. "Most everybody's still asleep, from the looks of it," she told them. "There are two big towers—this one and the one opposite—and then a big, almost circular level in between, with guard walks on top and two, maybe three storeys below. You'll never guess what's in the middle of the circle."

"A hole," Joe responded. "What?"

"The crater. The opening to the lava. A bubbling, hissing lake of the stuff maybe twenty feet down below ground level. Right in the center is a single column of very hard, shiny-looking rock that comes up a little above ground level. And right in the center of it is growing this tree! A weird-looking type I've never seen or heard of before. It's magic, all right."

"Any sign of what we're after?" Joe asked her.

"Uh-uh. This side looked strictly royal, anyway. I'd guess we came in on the wrong side. I couldn't get much of a look into the opposite tower, but I'll tell you that it's the center for this darkness. It's *got* to be the place."

Joe nodded. "Any way to go around?"

"Not that I saw. At the extremes of that circle I talked about, it actually juts out and away from the volcano on both sides. The drop looks sheer. Unless you want to go back down and onto the ice and around, you're stuck going through the building."

"The hell with the ice," Joe told her. "We came to break in here, so we might as well do it." And, with a cautious look around, they made their way up the stone stairs, past the two inviting-looking pools, and into the palace proper.

"Want to check out this tower just in case, Master?" Mia asked him.

"Uh-uh. We may blow it, but the other one looks most likely, and I'd hate to run into any watch here." He looked at two inner arches, each seeming to angle away from the tower hall. "Macore, you and Marge take that route, Mia and I will take this one. If Marge is right, we'll meet in a hall similar to this one on the other side. If we meet anyone or are discovered, though, they'll come to only one pair, not both."

Macore nodded. "Anything as vital as my gear would likely be in the magician's tower as well."

They went down their corridor, Joe with sword drawn, Mia with knife at the ready. Joe was still puzzled; by this point after dawn, this place should be crawling with servants—slaves, most likely, knowing these folks—and guards and maybe the living dead, so that, when the masters of the joint finally got up, they'd have breakfast prepared and everything cleaned and secured and ship-shape. Where in hell was everybody?

When they got closer to the outer part of the circle, there were arches and windows looking out on what would normally have been the inner courtyard. They crept to it, looked out, and saw the narrow stone walkway around the steaming, boiling pit whose tremendous heat even Mia could feel; in the center was the strange tree. It grew out of the top of a needle of pure obsidian, somehow immune to the forces churning around it; a massive trunk indicating great age, its bark an odd purplish color, its limbs spreading out almost all the way over the fire pit. The thick frondlike leaves appeared to be made of pure polished gold, catching the sulfurous fumes from the pit; from the limbs, under the leaves, the tree bore a pearlike fruit of shining, reflective silver.

Joe tried to use his inner self to sense what might be in the tree, whether nymph or demon or imprisoned god, but there was no sensation of any consciousness there. Yet, in fact, it was a living tree, although of what alien origins it was impossible to tell.

He seemed almost hypnotized by it, and Mia had to jolt him back to reality. "Hurry, Master! Before we are discovered!"

They went on, and were two-thirds of the way to the other tower, when Mia, who'd taken the lead, suddenly raised her hand for him to halt. "Listen, Master! Strange sounds from just below!"

Joe stopped, trying to tune out the rumbling and hissing from the fire pit, and he heard what Mia was hearing faintly, through the background—the song from *Gilligan's Island*.

"Macore?" he mused. No, that wasn't possible. First of all, it was coming from perhaps the floor above theirs, and, also, there were the voices, the background music . . .

The background music?

"There's an arch out there," he told her. "Keep a watch and out of sight. I've got to find out what's going on up there."

She didn't approve, but didn't have a say in the matter. A steep stone stair led up to the next level from each archway. Keeping close to the wall and hoping that nobody was looking out the other side, he went up, halted just before the top, then cautiously peered into a huge area and gasped.

Well, there was Macore's equipment, all of it. The tiny television had been recharged or was getting some kind of magical charge its transformer could handle, as was the small portable video tape recorder. The room was full, almost densely packed, with dozens, maybe many dozens, of the same sort of soulless, brainless living dead they'd seen on the plateau what seemed ages before.

Here, then, was the entire missing zombie staff, standing there, motionless, transfixed, watching *Gilligan's Island*.

He made his way back down to Mia and told her what he'd seen.

"But, Master—they have no souls or wills of their own! How can they *possibly* be watching a *show*?"

"I don't have an explanation for that, and I don't think I *want* an explanation for that," he told her. "Maybe there's some weird frequency in the thing that scrambles the spell. Maybe it's just that the show has finally found its perfect audience." He shook his head in wonder. "It's enough for now to know where those creatures are and not have to worry about them. Let's get going! People are going to start waking up and be all over here any time now, no matter what!"

Still, Joe was worried about just how easy it was to get in, and just how empty the passages were. True, here and there they had been required to flatten themselves to the wall or crouch behind something, or duck outside or in, but the place overall seemed ominously deserted, as if everything and everyone of importance had moved elsewhere, leaving nothing but a maintenance staff. That idea disturbed him more than a dozen sword-fights and magicians—that, after all they had gone through, they were too late or, almost as bad, were in the wrong place.

In the main hall of the second tower, Mia turned to him as if to say, *"Now what?"* and he motioned for her to go cautiously up the stairs.

The first tower level proved to be sleeping quarters, and in the halls were both Bentar guards and some female slaves going back and forth, all as naked and shorn as Mia. That gave her an idea.

"They won't know one female slave from another, particularly the Bentar, Master," she whispered. "Let me just see who's here by pretending to be one of the staff."

He nodded, figuring he could cover her, and also figuring that, at this point, they had little to lose. Again, he had to admire her guts, handing him her knife and simply walking brazenly down the hall. As she'd suspected, the Bentar gave her not a second glance, all humans probably looking alike to them, anyway, and if the handful of slaves there noticed a stranger they did not react. The odds were that there were a fair number of slaves here, if only to feed the egos of the masters, and quite often new ones would turn up these days.

Joe remained in the stairwell, nervous that someone would come down or come up, but Mia managed to make the circuit, looking as if she were on a real task for somebody, and come back before anyone did.

"All sleeping quarters, Master. They are simply cleaning up.

I do not like to say so, but this level does not look very used. At best, there was one or two rooms that appeared slept in."

He nodded. "Yeah, I'm beginning to get a real sinking feeling about this. Let's move up."

The second tower level seemed deserted, but there were only a few doors on either side, so they made their way cautiously down on both sides, then opened the doors. One proved to be a sort of sorcerer's laboratory, but with almost everything looking closed and put away, not used for some time. The other was some kind of meeting or briefing room. Joe was about to signal a move up again when there came the sounds of heavy boots ascending the stairs. He and Mia quickly ducked into the meeting room and shut the door, hoping that this wasn't the morning guard showing up for a briefing right there.

The bright light of day pouring through the windows along the far wall made Joe suddenly realize how late it was getting. "We might have to hide in here most of the day," he told her in a low tone. "Moving around until dusk is going to be more and more difficult, no matter how empty this place is."

"Uh—Master?"

"Yes?"

"Do you notice that the room seems to be getting darker?"

He turned and tensed. Sure enough, in spite of the light from outside, it *did* seem to be getting significantly darker inside.

There was a sudden sound from above and in back of them, metallic yet not like a sword, and suddenly, from overhead, an enormous bright light shone down, the product of a candle set inside an assemblage of mirrors to form a basic spotlight aimed at the small stage in front.

Tense, sword drawn, Joe turned back to where that spotlight shone.

"Ta tata, ta tata, ta ta dah dah dah dee!" a sexy woman's voice hummed playfully from the stage. From stage left, the spotlight caught just a leg, curved suggestively, and then, from behind, the woman stepped out.

The soul inside and the amount of time that had passed made the same body look far less like the old Mahalo McMahon; this was a gorgeous, sexy sex kitten, at once playful, sensuous, erotic as hell, and, for all that, dangerous. Then big brown eyes darted momentarily over in their direction, and just for a moment a wicked, playful smile came to her face, and Esmilio Boquillas shone through.

In a soft, sexy voice, she sang, "I enjoy bein' a guy bein' a girl like *me*."

She looked down at the pair, and the smile broadened. "Sorry, but I *do* so like a good entrance."

Joe didn't wait, starting a spring right toward the stage, but she lifted up a hand and a series of yellow magic strings sprang from it and held both him and Mia fast. He couldn't move forward. He stopped struggling and relaxed.

"You've got your powers back!" he said, amazed.

"A mere shadow of my former powers," she responded, "but enough for the likes of the two of you."

"How long have you known we were here?"

"Why, *darling*, I've been simply *mad* waiting for you to arrive! I *knew* the moment we discovered that the little thief had been captured over on the other side that you would have to follow. In fact, I've been waiting *ages*, ever since I let that little spy escape with the news that we had your old bodies here. Good old Ruddygore! I just *knew* he wouldn't fail me!"

"It will be Judgment Day before Ruddygore helps you, and you know it!"

"Oh, but he *has* helped. More than I could ever have done on my own. In fact, I owe it all to him. First, his silly little ego that made him think he could control Boquillas like a puppet and that a Boquillas with enough foresight to have prepared this soul transfer as a last resort into this *marvelous* body wouldn't also prepare defenses against the sort of control spells he'd use. Second, not realizing, as I would not have, that he'd done what the whole Council couldn't, given me some *power* again on my own. More than enough with my mind to unravel his leashes."

"How did you get those powers back?" Joe asked, testing occasionally the spell that kept him where he was and to no avail. "They said when the Council lifted somebody's power it was impossible ever to get it back."

"Oh, *do* struggle, my dears! The tighter you struggle, the

tighter it holds.'' She sat perched on the side of the stage, the smile on her lips impossible to erase.

"It *is* true, my old powers are gone," she admitted. "But you've heard it said that there's a little witchcraft in all us girls. I wouldn't have believed it myself until I became one, but once I realized there was real power there after becoming one myself, I knew instantly how to use it. Mahalo McMahon, as it turned out, was better than that. She was high priestess of the Neo-Primitive Hawaiian Church or some such thing. I also realized that I had it only so long as I remained female. That was no hardship; I decided I *liked* being a girl! I *liked* particularly the way men looked at me, the way they'd get all silly and fall all over themselves just because I batted an eye at them or swiveled a hip. It was a whole new level of power and control. And because I again had some power and the knowledge of how to use it, I could walk without fear, which is what keeps most women down. As a man, I'd never had much use for sex, except as a tool in my work, as powerful as it was. I began to discover how much I'd missed over all that time, how much *fun* it was to be a real person. The Rules decided that I was a witch, which was fine, but, thank the fates, I didn't have to be the Dark Baron or the Dark Anything anymore.''

"I'm glad to see you found your true calling," Joe responded sourly. "The Wicked Bimbo of the North."

She laughed. "I owe that to you and Ruddygore and the others, too," she said. "All those years, all that enormous effort, all for the *noblest* of ends. Then I was exiled to Earth, and saw so many political and economic systems, all launched for noble purposes, and I saw homelessness, starvation, misery, and despair. Some worked better than others, but not a one of them really worked any better than our own systems here. In disgust, the demoted demons and I decided to wipe it all away, but you stopped that, and I'm so *very* happy you did, my darlings. For the first time, I'm totally honest, even with myself, and totally free of those hang-ups. Now, for the first time, I can look myself in the mirror and know that I'm doing what I do and choosing what I choose for no other reason than because being bad is so much more fun!''

She frowned, staring suddenly at Mia, who was staring back, furious at Boquillas. "Why *darling*, that suits you just wonderfully, looking like that! One of my little ideas that's turned out so *nicely*. I never had much liking for women when I was a man and, now that I *am* a woman, I find I like other women even less than before. What a wonderful comeback, darling, and I had nothing to do with it! Ruddygore himself went to great lengths to insure you would sink to slavery."

"I have always been a slave, you witch! You should know! You killed Tiana, my mistress!" Mia shouted.

For a moment Boquillas looked genuinely puzzled and confused, but then she stared at Mia, then at Joe, reading the small spells Ruddygore had woven, and broke into laughter. "Oh, my! That *is* amusing!" she managed after a bit. "My dears, I didn't kill Tiana, let alone import some royal slave bimbo. How could I? *You* had the Lamp, which was the only way across at the time. Ruddygore wanted to insure that you would be lean, mean, and totally loyal and unwavering to the mission.

"You *are* Tiana, my sweet. You always have been."

"No!" Mia wailed. "It is not true!"

But Joe almost instantly realized that it *was* true. So many more things made sense if it was, and there was no getting around the transportation problem that Boquillas so neatly pointed out. There was no way that a Mia could have fooled him so thoroughly and for so long those first few months back. And, before they returned, Ti could read quite well, even English. Ruddygore again, playing with and manipulating everyone as pawns in his grand game. The Rules had not reduced her to this; Ruddygore had created the conditions so that upon landing this result was inevitable.

It became suddenly obvious, the whole plot. Her intuitive skills with weapons, for example. And what was it to Ruddygore, who could mess with both their memories and perceptions, to give her the dance, maybe taken from some strippers he'd seen in San Francisco, or some of the basic skills, like mending and tailoring? Why a slave? Because, otherwise, she could not be pared down to the tough essentials to get her to this point, and certainly not to aid in the destruction of the way back.

And all that so that they could stand there, captive of their worst enemy?

The "Mia" personality, so nicely adjusted by Ruddygore's spells, rebelled against the truth, but Boquillas was ready for that. "Let me simply disentangle those rather simple little spells that blinded you both. Won't take a second, and it clears away all that *messy* stuff."

Tiana stopped protesting and suddenly gasped. "Then it is true," she said simply.

Boquillas smiled. "Of *course* it is. And you will be very, very helpful to me. You see, as our palace slave, in reality the role you were handed by Ruddygore's fiction, compelled to obedience, you will be my closest advisor and critic. With you advising me, dressing me, prompting me, there will be no question in anyone's mind that I am the one and only original Tiana. And after I am in control and beyond threat, you will continue to be there to serve me and do whatever I command, living life at its lowest while watching me live yours."

"So you plan to be the one in Tiana's body," Joe said.

She nodded. "Of course. I can't be *you*, since I'd lose what powers I have regained, and, as I said, I rather *like* being this way. In fact, I shall be sad to leave this body for the more, ah, statuesque proportions of Tiana, but we can't have everything, can we?"

"I see. And what about me?"

She gave that wicked Boquillas smile once more. "But that's so *simple*, Joey baby! It's the most delicious part of all of it! We'll just slip little old you back into that *marvelous* body you had, whose statues don't do you justice, and you'll be right there, unimpeachable, convincing, truly returned, reinforcing my own image, with your great sword Irving as absolute proof that it's you. You'll leave the decisions to me, of course, but you mostly did that when you were reigning with her anyway."

"You bastard! What makes you think I'll do anything of the sort?"

"Oh, Joey *baby*! As a man who was just taken in by the simplest little old spell in Creation, you really don't think you have a choice, do you? If old Ruddypuss can convince you that this girl is *not* Tiana, how much simpler will it be to build a scenario in your mind that I *am*? And you'll be *much* too love-sick to do more than forgive and accept whatever I decide to do. Why, you have to create love potions and charms just to get into Witchcraft 101. Besides, if all else fails, there's always your son to hold you, isn't there? There are all *sorts* of possibilities with the boy!''

He knew at once that Boquillas was right and that they'd all been had, even Ruddygore. Boquillas had understood that in the critical first week they returned unannounced, they'd be under a microscope by politicians, courtiers, and top-ranked sorcerers. Sugasto couldn't exactly be around in the nearest closet to bail her out; with her powers still limited, she would at that point be as vulnerable as he would be. After consolidating power, though, and gathering it in, she'd be able progressively to eliminate anyone who might challenge, and Sugasto would take most of Husaquahr without even firing a shot.

Now *that* was a thought!

''You mean you'll spend all the time in the great palace as a puppet, doing what Sugasto wants,'' he noted. ''You *have* changed, Boquillas. This plot is up to your usual standards, but it's all so you can become somebody else's stooge.''

She waved a hand, and many of the yellow bands of magic flowed back into her. He could move again—but not toward her. He could not touch her or make a move in her direction.

''Come over to the window. Yes, that's it. Come here and look out and tell me what you see.''

He went to the window and looked. Just beyond the tower were other gardens, and, beyond them, the ice pack, and in the distance . . .

''The Devastation,'' he said.

She nodded. ''I think you understand some of it now, or you wouldn't have been able to cross it. A brilliant stoke, by the way, that I admit I didn't anticipate. You forget that I have the old bodies with many of your patterns. The moment you set foot on this ground, a standing spell informed me that you had arrived.''

''Yeah. So?''

She pointed a slender arm decked with jewels out at the far-off phenomenon. "They're still there, you know. The battle in full cry. Not just the souls, *everything*, perfectly preserved. Now, what do you think would happen if this volcano we're sitting on, a complementary phenomenon to the Devastation you might have guessed, went off? The flow would only reach the edges of the Devastation in most spots, but imagine the heat that would be given off—and the whole frozen valley would warm in proportion. On this world, it would be like the loosing of thousands of hydrogen bombs would be on Earth. An evil that even Hell fears would be loosed once more upon this world."

"Is that what you want? Still trying to bring about the final war between good and evil?"

"Oh, *darling*, of course not! Not anymore. I've outgrown that, as I told you! But if it's not me, then it's them. Sugasto is so conventional, you see. Power-crazed, yes, but his vision is so *boring*. You see, there is one way to restore *all* my powers. Only one way. The entire Council, which now includes dear Suggy, would have to reverse their combined spells. Even though not really on it anymore, it would require Ruddygore as well. With my powers back, in that situation, I would be both temporal and spiritual ruler. My powers would be near absolute. Did you see the tree in the middle of the lava pit?"

He nodded, sickened at her ambitions. "I saw it."

"It is one of *the* trees, the original trees, from the Origin of Humanity. Sugasto and the others believe it is the Tree of Knowledge which condemned humanity, as do others, but it is not. It is the Tree of Life. Eat of it, and nothing at all may harm you. With my powers and that fruit, I'll be a true goddess. I shall walk about my world, worshiped as the one who is truly divine. My reign shall be *forever*!"

He felt a cold chill. "How do you know which tree it is, or if it's really one of those?"

"Because, dear one, I've done my homework. It is what that battle was about out there. Two Powers, perhaps beyond anything we know, battling to become a third face, not Heaven, not Hell, but beyond and beside it, equal to both. That's why they got together to stop them, lest one side win and truly become a god." She shrugged. "I think even supreme beings have Rules, too."

"There's only one hole in your grand design," Joe argued. "Why would Ruddygore and the Council restore your powers? I think they'd rather die first."

"Indeed? Ruddygore, perhaps, but he knows that, if that were to happen, I'd be freed of the need for him. The others? Die for principle? How amusing you are! The only reason Ruddygore has remained so long is that he has never found a worthy successor, and he won't. But, you see, he has no choice, and neither will Sugasto. They will all do my bidding, since to toy with me or cast obedience spells upon me or try to do away with me is *genocide*! I have it rigged, you see—carefully placed mechanisms deep beneath this place, where even I at this point cannot find them. They will blow, this place will blow, the volcano will blow. The heat will melt the Devastation, and the world as we know it will end. Given a choice of that, or restoring me and being allowed to pass on, which do you think your old sorcerer will choose?"

"Aren't you afraid Sugasto will stop you? He might not be too pleased at this himself."

"Sugasto, at least, already knows that I've wired the place. Right now he thinks we're partners, destined to be a new god and goddess. He doesn't think much of women, you know. His own male ego, which I perfectly understand, blinds him to the possibilities."

Joe turned away from the windows, feeling a cold chill, and saw that heavily armed, mean-looking Bentar now filled the room.

A way out, he kept thinking. *The Rules require I have a way out!*

He turned back to Boquillas. "Can you answer me one simple question?"

"Of *course*, darling! A wife to be should have no secrets from her husband!"

"Why are all the zombies gathered around watching *Gilligan's Island*?"

She chuckled and shrugged. "Beats me. I, of course, recharged the batteries with a spell to see what someone had on those tapes. I was astonished when I saw what was on them, of course, and, even more, I was absolutely *stunned* to discover that it seemed to draw every zombie in the palace like a magnet. So far, I haven't worked out an effective method for turning it off. The spell provides continuous power, and, so far, the zombies will do nothing except prevent anyone from shutting it down. It *is* a fascinating thing, is it not? Sugasto will have to take care of it when he returns tomorrow. Inconvenient, but little else. It's even handy to have something to block Sugasto's powers a bit. I suspect it's some broadcast frequency interference that's acting like a drug to them, but it may be that a zombie retains just barely enough intelligence that it simply entrances them."

Joe hoped the technical explanation was right. Although he wasn't feeling all that smart right now, he'd watched the show in the old days now and then himself and found it occasionally funny. He didn't want to think about what that might say should the second explanation be true.

"Take his sword and lock him in the tower room!" Boquillas ordered the Bentar. "And watch him! He can be tricky and quite resourceful. The one who lets him escape shall feel my anger! The girl I will keep here. She has *much* to tell me."

The lead Bentar reached for the sword, then withdrew. "My lady, we cannot take *that* sword! It's iron! And so, too, is the belt lined with it!"

Boquillas sighed. "Details, details. Oh, very well." She withdrew the rest of her spells from him, then walked over to him and began playfully undoing the belt. *This is it!* he thought.

Joe struck the sorceress with a strong blow, knocking her senseless halfway across the room, then had Irving in his hand in moments. Mia—Tiana—struggled against her magical bonds, still in force, but could not help him.

Suddenly he was in the midst of roaring, howling Bentar and was in a fierce duel. In spite of their numbers and ferocity, the Bentar did not press in, facing the only thing that they were truly afraid of—*iron*!

He pressed them back and got to the open door, but now they

were between him and Mia—Tiana. "I'll be back!" he shouted and ducked out the door.

Boquillas struggled to get up from the floor, feeling her jaw. "After him, you idiots!" she screamed. "I want him *alive*! Better to risk iron than me later!"

Joe undid the swordbelt and let it drop. He was naked and exposed, with just Irving in his hand, but it gave him total freedom of movement. The bronze swords of the Bentar had cut him in several places, but he was beyond feeling pain. He tried to head up the stairway, hoping at least to get to the bodies, but the stairwell was filled with troopers armed with swords, knives, maces, and other unpleasant stuff. He'd never make it up through that mob, damn it! He had to get clear, wait until he could think!

He bounded down the stairs, leaping the railings, and came eventually to the main entry hall. All the forces he hadn't seen coming in seemed to be flowing out from all directions except the inner circle. *Slash! Hack! Cut!* Men and Bentar screamed, limbs flew. Although his body now bled from a hundred wounds, he was still on the go. He made the circle corridor and started to run, but, just past the first archway out to the crater, he faced a horde of men charging toward him. Turning back, he saw the others coming down the hall in a full rush.

He ducked back through the arch and down to the crater walk.

Man! It was *hot*! Even the stones around the narrow walkway burned his feet.

He started to run one way, then another, but soldiers of all kinds seemed to be popping out or blocking just about every exit he could see! The only possible exit was where those blank-eyed monsters were watching television, but he couldn't get to that! He suddenly felt like Dorothy at the end of *The Wizard of Oz*, trapped on the battlements with great forces all around and no bucket of water to throw.

Boquillas poked her head out of one of the upper tower windows. "You can't win, Joe! Those human soldiers there—see their lances and bolts? *Silver-coated*, Joe! I know the secret of your longevity! Give it up! Give one of them the sword and surrender! This time there is no way out! Who knows, you might always escape from the tower, right?"

He took his eyes off the closing forces for a moment and saw her up there, and suddenly from that tower window flew red and yellow magic strings, aimed right at him!

He jumped up on the side of the low crater wall, barely six inches thick, and watched the spells hit right where he'd been and explode with a big puff of smoke.

"Give it up, Joe, and come down from there!" Boquillas yelled to him. "There is no way out! There is no escape this time!"

He looked at all the forces around him, saw the silver tips, then saw that Boquillas was readying yet another bolt, while, behind him, the heat and terrible, almost choking sulfurous fumes rose from the bubbling and churning two-thousand-degree lava far below, and realized that Marge had been right, but that the Rules were often cruel.

Holding Irving almost like a javelin, he hurled it with full force into the mob of soldiers, where it penetrated and speared two Bentar and one human soldier before it came to rest.

Then, as Boquillas' new spell left her hands, he took a deep breath, and jumped backward into the pit.

Not trusting his sudden horrible scream of anguish, cut off in midsound, they all rushed to the edge of the pit and looked down.

There was nothing there. Nothing, and no one, except the bubbling, hissing lava.

CHAPTER 13

THE END OF THE WORLD BLUES

No conclusion of an epic saga is complete without a wizard's battle.
—The Books of Rules, XV, 397(a)

THE SMALL RING IN TIANA'S NOSE SUDDENLY CRACKLED A BIT, and she felt an irritating, slightly painful tingling there that soon passed.

Boquillas stared out the window at the sight she'd just witnessed, unable really to believe it. "He's dead," she muttered, amazed to her core. "He really killed himself."

"Noooo!" Tiana cried, even though she knew from the reaction in her nose ring that it was true, and tears began flowing down her face.

Boquillas sighed, turned away from the window, and came back to Tiana. "Somehow," the sorceress said, almost to herself, "I never thought he was the martyr type. Stupid! I would have made him a demigod."

"He'd already *been* a demigod," Tiana reminded her defiantly through her tears. "And he hated it."

Boquillas sighed. "Well, when Plan A goes a little off, you have to improvise a bit." She reached out and touched the slave ring in Tiana's nose in the same two-fingered manner Joe had used. "You're mine, now, and you're all I've got, so you're going to have to do, my dear. A bit of a letdown for me, but a considerable come-up for you. He's gone, so you'll have to replace him. Same script, just different parts, that's all. At least you won't blow it by killing yourself, too. The little bit I just added there compels obedience. You're *my* property now, all legal and proper, and you cannot act against my interests.''

It killed Tiana to call Boquillas by any term of respect, but she had no choice. ''Then, Mistress, you will restore me to my old body and rule as Joe?''

''No, no. Joe had no magical powers. Never did. Were I inside him, the whole Council, with Ruddygore leading the pack, couldn't give me what I need, and that cursed sword would never accept me in any event, which would queer everything. No, my dear, it's obvious. I shall still become Tiana; now it is *you* who will become Joe.''

''I? Joe? Mistress, it would be *obscene*!''

Boquillas grinned. ''I know. That's why I like it. At least you're easier to do. That protective spell Sugasto gave you includes what I call a soul-puller mechanism. My own powers aren't up to creating one, but since he's kindly provided one, it should be simple. We'll still need Sugasto to complete the process with me, of course. Until he returns, you shall attend me as my slave and not leave my side, and you shall begin telling me those details I need to know. And stop that confounded blubbering! You're going to have to learn to be a *man*, not a swishy wimp!''

Tiana obeyed, but she couldn't stop the tears. Joe was dead, and, no matter *who* she was, she loved him. Even now, knowing the truth, her memory fully restored, she knew that she'd remain this way forever if she could only have him back.

This wasn't the way things were supposed to work out, not at *all*. Joe was gone, she was a helpless captive of the powers of Darkness, the chief villain immune to harm or malignant sorcery herself by virtue of tying her fate to the survival of the world. This just wasn't the way things were supposed to be.

But hadn't Joe been *magnificent* in that final fight! If love meant anything, if sacrifice meant anything, and if evil could be that sloppy, there had to be *some* way, somehow, to stop this foul plan.

''I don't believe it!''

Macore nodded sadly. ''I saw it myself, from my perch in

the tower room. He went out fighting like the greatest heroes of old, and when hundreds of them surrounded him, he got a bunch more by hurling the sword and then jumped in. Even the villains will tell stories of that great fighter to their grandchildren!''

"I thought—somehow, this time, I had that feeling, but I thought it would be me,'' Marge said, feeling empty inside and fighting back tears.

Neither Macore nor Marge were caught yet and there was a question as to whether or not anyone even suspected they were there. Everybody had gone after Joe and Mia, as Joe had predicted, should one side be exposed.

Macore had spent the better part of the day asleep under one of the already made-up beds in the royal tower; Marge had used her own resources to do the same. Neither had abandoned his or her friends, although both felt as if they had. When it was clear that the other two had been caught, they retreated to the empty part of the palace and decided that there was no chance of their doing anything in the way of a rescue until nightfall. Macore had heard the commotion and wound up with a windowseat on the great fight and sacrifice. Marge had already been out somewhere and only now got the details.

"So what do we do now?'' Macore asked her. "Joe's dead, which means Mia's enslaved to somebody, probably the Baron, and beyond being just plucked out. We'd have to kill the Baron to free her now. There's nobody left now capable of destroying the bodies, either. And, to top it all off, I can't get my gear back because I'd have to fight off dozens of enraged zombies!''

"There's got to be something we can do for her,'' Marge told the little thief. "If I know Boquillas, he's vamping right now, picking her brains to get all the details he can. She still knows an awful lot about palace routine, palace personalities, and Tiana's own habits and quirks. Maybe enough.'' She started thinking furiously. "Where's his sword?''

"Still out there in the center court. It seems to have a life of its own for real. It won't let anybody pick it up. It's stuck partway into the rocks itself and just won't budge.''

"Excalibur,'' she responded.

"Huh?''

"The Sword in the Stone—an old Earth legend about another such sword. It won't budge until it accepts a new owner, and that's the only one who'd have the right and ability to pull it out."

"Who would that be?"

"Beats me. Irving, maybe. Poor kid. If it's true, he's not only gonna be stuck here with no dad, he's gonna wind up the great mercenary Irving with his great sword Irving." She sighed. "Normally I'd think that was humor; but under the circumstances, I don't feel all that funny."

"Neither do I. They almost certainly know how we got in here now, so I'm not at all sure how we get out," the thief commented. "One thing's for sure—we can't do anything, not to help her, not to help ourselves, unless we have a lot more information. Even if we somehow get out of this, which looks unlikely, what's the use, except temporarily to save our own necks? If there's any information that we could take with us, that would make at least *some* of this trip meaningful. Right now, the only thing we've got is bad news and worse news, and one of those items is that the Baron was throwing spells right and left out that window."

"Is that the bad or the worse?" she asked. "Wait a minute! I'm thinking!" She snapped her fingers. "Maybe there *is* a way. Suppose there's some way for me to talk to Mia."

"So what? You're now the enemy, right? She couldn't do anything against the Baron's interests, and that would include helping you. At least she doesn't have to volunteer information, or they'd be scouring this dump for us now."

Marge nodded. "Sure. But doing something against a master's interest is a knowing act. Suppose she didn't know she was giving us information?"

"How you gonna do that? Your mind-tricks work only on guys, right? And both the Baron and Mia are girls."

"No, for short periods I can make anyone see me as I wish, so long as I'm female in the illusion. Otherwise I wouldn't have been able to move around on Earth, let alone move around this place. You know that. I have no power over women, it's true, but if she thought she were talking to someone else, maybe unburdening herself, it might work.''

"Risky. If Boquillas has her powers back, it's not gonna fool him or her or, what the hell, I'm getting dizzy with all this!''

"You work on an exit,'' she told him, "and stay close to here and out of sight so I can find you again. I'm going to try something. It's better than just sitting here.''

It wasn't unusual to see the various female slaves who serviced the place at any point in the palace, day or night, and neither the human guards nor the Bentar gave a particularly small, very young-looking slave the slightest notice as she walked into the magician's tower and scampered up the stairs.

Boquillas had kept Mia close to her, but there were times when the slave was alone and miserable on the living quarters floor, told to wait while her mistress went to tend to something or other.

The very young slave waited, pretending to clean something in the hall, then went over to Mia, who sat, looking miserable in one corner of a sitting parlor.

"You are new here,'' the very young slave commented. "Do not take it so hard. After a while, you come to accept things, and you find it isn't so bad.''

Mia looked up at her, her eyes still red, but all cried out at this point. "It is for me. I was not born a slave, but high, and the master whom I loved and served is now burned in the fire pit.''

"High?''

She nodded. "I did not know myself until today. It was hidden from me. Once I was a mighty ruler, Queen to the one who is gone. Now I am less than you, for I am to become him in a mad scheme of my new mistress. Yet I would remain this way forever if I could but bring him back.''

I knew it! Marge thought triumphantly. *She* is *Tiana*!

"That is very strange,'' Marge responded. "You are to become the man who died today? How is that, if he is dead and his body burned?''

"There is another body above. Already my mistress commands me respond only to the name of Joe.''

Marge thought a moment, hoping to plant a thought. "But if you are put in this man's body, you will no longer be a slave."

"No. But I can do nothing or try nothing. To kill my mistress is to destroy the world."

"What? *How?*"

"I do not know. Somehow, if she dies, the volcano goes off, melts the horrible place out there, and unleashes an evil worse than she."

"When will you become him?"

"Tomorrow. When the Master of the Dead returns."

Marge sighed. "I must go now. I would not like your mistress to find me here and know you have told anyone so much."

"Yes, thank you. It helps to talk about such things to one who is as powerless as I, but I would not like you to suffer because of it."

Marge got up and quickly walked down the stairs again, hoping she could maintain the slave illusion long enough to get back in the clear.

So it *was* Tiana after all! That devil Ruddygore! Still, she stopped and looked out at the volcanic pit. No matter what had caused it, or what fed and maintained it, if it were for all intents and purposes no more than a volcano, she could go down into it. The Kauri cleansed themselves by lava swims in their native forest. There was always the risk of iron in that soup, of course, but if it were molten and liquid, and if she swam fast enough, it couldn't get in to poison her.

She made her way back up to Macore, who waited anxiously in the shadows of the empty room.

"I've got more than enough! She was in such an emotional state I was able to draw out precisely what we needed," she told the thief, proceeding to summarize the information.

Macore whistled. "Okay, now we know. That's Tiana so we're still in business, sort of."

"I thought you were only interested in your precious tapes."

"I am, I am," he responded, irritated. "But if they have that kind of effect on zombies, any world ruled by these people will be a world where all tapes will be forbidden. I'll never get to see them again!"

"Look," she told him, "I'm going to go into that volcano and see just what sort of trap is rigged down there. It's possible we may be able to pull off all of it yet!"

She zoomed out the window, went up at some speed, curved, and dove straight down into the crater in front of the lava tree, even to Macore's trained eyes nothing more than a reddish streak.

She was down quite some time, and he began to worry, but, eventually, the streak rose again, then angled and darted into the window. She looked *very* excited.

"Macore! I think I've got it! It's a series of simple, unstable spells that would cause moderate explosions around the edges of the lava pool nearest the Devastation. It wouldn't erupt as such, or I don't think so, but, rather, flow out toward the frozen valley. It's certainly bush-league spell stuff; Boquillas sure hasn't got all those powers back. Probably put there by some sort of fairy in her employ or some demonic-type who still owes her. The spells, though, would be impossible for Sugasto to divine or reach without using the same sort of stuff, and he can't take the chance that the act of doing just that wouldn't set it off—and it might! It's held to Boquillas by some very fragile magical threads. Break the threads, *boom*!"

"So where's that get us? Can you defuse it?"

"If I knew what I was doing, I could, but the only people around here likely to have the knowledge wouldn't be much better to deal with as winners than Boquillas. There's a flaw, though, because of its primitiveness. If Boquillas were to fall *into* that pit, the strings would not detach, they'd simply become embedded in the new rock. Later on, somebody with better motives could get some fairy, immune to it like me, to go down there with exact directions and untie the damned thing."

"Great. So all we have to do is to get Boquillas to stroll out there, where it's hot enough to burn your feet, and somehow ward off any spells she might throw, and push her in. Easy."

"Save the sarcasm. Now, look. The only way Boquillas can possibly pull this off is to convince Tiana, who will be Joe, that she's Joe and that Boquillas is really Tiana. Get it?"

"No. I got as far as Tiana as Joe, then my head started spinning."

"That sorcerous hypnosis, like what Ruddygore used, won't be possible. The magicians of Marquewood would read it in a moment. You can't have a demideity under an enchantment. Not right away. That means some kind of love potion. One that'll make her so giddy that she'll buy any kind of irrationality her so-called true love sells."

"So?"

"So we let them go through with it. All the way. But when Ti's in Joe's old body, she'll be a man. She might not feel totally at home, but her were experiences will have her adjust pretty quickly, like it or not. Macore, take it from me: there isn't a love potion ever made, or a love spell ever woven, that a Kauri can't manipulate, if the one who has it is a human mortal male. And if I can get through, then it's Ti's job to take a stroll with her love to see the lava tree. If Ti really loved Joe as much as I think she did, then we're gonna drive a Texas-sized truck through Esmilio Boquillas!"

"Uh—yeah. I'll take that. Sure," the little thief muttered. "And all that'll leave us with is Sugasto, currently one of the most powerful sorcerers in the world."

"Don't be such a grump! One thing at a time, damn it! Right now we just have to keep out of sight and undiscovered until tomorrow night."

"Don't they look *nice*? I've been putting them through exercises regularly and they are in tiptop shape."

"Yes, Mistress." Tiana looked at the two figures standing there in naked splendor before them. There she was—*her* body, just as it had always been. And there, too, was the Joe she'd met and loved, or the shell of him. Her heart ached just to see the shell.

A tall man dressed all in black robes entered and saw them. Boquillas turned and shouted, *"Suggy! Baby!"*

The Master of the Dead was in a foul mood and having none of it. "A bit sloppy as usual with that business, aren't you, Boquillas? And what the hell is that with all my zombies shorted out by that—that *abomination*?"

"Oh, calm down. We've got Tiana and we've got me and

you, so nothing's really changed. By spring, Joe and Tiana will *still* be perfect to the last detail. As for the zombies—well, *I* didn't cause it! I figured that, once you got here, you could figure out how to shut it off.''

''I'll blast those machines to the bottommost pits of Hell from whence they obviously came,'' he growled.

''Suggy! You have to stop worrying over unimportant things! After all, I look at the slave and what do I find but your own signature spell on her! You had them *both* in your hand! According to her, you had them to *lunch*! And then you handed them safe conduct and patted them on the head and sent them on their way! *None* of this would have happened if you'd just fingered them then and there!''

''It's that damned hair-shearing,'' Sugasto grumbled. ''Makes her look like a ten-year-old boy. Besides, who would have imagined that somebody that highborn could be reduced to *this*—and by her own people! As for the man, well, the beard threw me. You said he couldn't grow one!''

''And you, who can grow mustaches on tomatoes with a wave of your finger, got taken by a beard! Well, never mind. We can blame each other for our errors or we can say the hell with it and resolve to make no more. There is too much at stake for us to fall out now.''

The Master of the Dead calmed down, seeing her logic. ''All right. So when do you want to do this?''

She shrugged. ''No time like the present. We may as well start in. It will take a fair amount of time before everything is nailed down straight, you know.''

''Well, all right. What do you want me to do with the bodies? I can't get the slave ring out of that one, you know, and, as for yours, it would be almost wasted as a zombie.''

''Oh, preserve them, by all means. Particularly mine. It can be a zombie for the duration, until and unless we find someone suitable to stick in it. I've grown rather fond of it. As for the other . . .'' She went over to Sugasto, who bent down slightly as she whispered, ''There will come a time when we won't need her anymore. Then you can move into Joe, and she can return to what she is and serve us.''

Sugasto nodded. "I like it. Very well." He pointed to the body of the tall, muscular woman. "You! Come here!"

The body of Tiana the demigoddess moved, shuffling a bit, woodenly, more like a puppet than a real person, and stood, blankly staring, beside Boquillas.

"It's a good thing the sound of that crap in the courtyard doesn't reach up here or we'd have *them* down there, too!"

"Oh, I thought of that immediately," Boquillas told him. "That's why I put a cone of silence on this chamber."

Tiana watched with horror as the Master of the Dead stood facing both women's bodies, and placed one hand on Boquillas' head, the other, with a reach, on her old, original head. It hurt to see that body as much as it hurt to see Joe's; to be this close, to be in the same room, only a few feet away, with someone with the means to put her back, and know that she might as well have been on the moon. . . .

There was no sound, no magical pyrotechnics, no sensation at all, yet, suddenly, Mahalo McMahon's old body stiffened and the eyes glazed over, while, at the same time, the body of Tiana seemed to be filling up with life, animation, and motion.

It had taken Sugasto no more than thirty or forty seconds. No incantations, no nothing. That, perhaps, was the scariest thing of all.

At the same moment the Tiana body came fully to life, intelligence flooding the eyes and the movements becoming natural, the real Tiana felt her nose ring crackle once more. The body whose code the ring had borne, McMahon's body, was now technically dead. Suddenly, she realized, for just a fleeting moment, she wasn't anyone's property at all.

With a kick from her runner's legs and a leap from her dancer's skills, Tiana made the doorway almost as her old body shouted, "Stop her, you idiot!"

Sugasto whirled. Even though Tiana was already out of sight, he did not give chase. Instead, he simply raised his right hand, cupping it slightly, then pulled it back, as if grabbing a ball and pulling it toward him.

In the hall, Tiana suddenly stopped dead in her tracks, suffering tremendous vertigo. Then, slowly, she felt as if she were rising, going up, out and away from her body, then floating back down the hall. Yes, she could see her body! See it just standing there!

The pull continued, and she went right through the stone wall and back into the sorcerer's room. Sugasto smiled, hand now toward her, and she felt herself moving, being guided by an unseen but irresistible force. Now she saw it! Joe's body, standing there, wooden, lifeless yet alive! Something was drawing her toward it, and it was swallowing her, merging with her. . . .

She staggered, blinked, and shook her head which seemed full of cobwebs. She felt . . . *different*. Strange.

Sugasto chuckled. "You see, Boquillas? I wasn't the *total* fool when I first met them. She's always been mine any time I wanted her."

"What—?" Tiana managed, but the voice sounded low, deep, and hollow, alien to her. "You—you put me in Joe's body!" She didn't want to be in Joe's body—she wanted *Joe* in there.

"And in there you'll stay, until I say otherwise," the sorcerer told the new man. "And, remember, I can pull you out again at any moment, no matter where in Husaquahr you might be. And even as a soul, I can hold you and cause you unimaginable torment. Don't even *think* of moving until I tell you. You just saw what I can do!" He turned to the new Tiana. "You want to bind him temporarily with spells, or should I do it?"

"Eventually, yes," she told him. "We want him an objective critic of me and very well trained by the time we slip him the potions. *Uh!* This is such a different body! I think I'm taller, perhaps larger, than I was when I was a man! In heels, I'd be taller than *he* is!"

"So, what do you want to do, other than explore your new self?" the sorcerer asked her. "And, I assume, donning one of the outfits we had the slaves make up."

Boquillas turned to the new man. "All right—*Joe*. For the moment, we have to have an understanding. I've just thrown a spell on you, and I won't be careless enough again to remove it. You can move, you can walk and talk and get used to that body. But you cannot harm me, and you cannot harm anyone else, not even yourself. You could even make love to me, but you cannot harm me.''

"I would sooner make love to a horse,'' he responded. "It would be obscene to make love to you. Incestuous. It would be like making love to myself.''

"That will pass,'' Boquillas assured him. "Over time, the Rules will settle. You may always *wish* you were me, but you'll be you, as you are, and you'll operate normally like that, even naturally, as you became a dancer and a slave. And I, too, will assume the Rules regarding the blood royal, with which, of course, I was already comfortable, having been born into it.''

"Why go through all that?'' Sugasto grumbled. "Why not just stick a good hypnotic spell on him right now and be done with it?''

"Patience! Patience! *Dear* Suggy!'' She had a good four or five inches in height on him now, and it felt rather neat. "For one thing, at this moment, and for the first time outside that puny body, we have a relatively 'clean' Tiana in that body, unsullied by any spells other than the one I just put on and can thus factor out. I want to see how it moves, how it talks, how it *thinks*. The words he chooses, the manner of managing a large, muscular body. Those things will fade after a while as the old male mercenary prince pattern re-emerges and takes command. True, I could make him think he's Joe now and be a fair critic, but there are things even *we* are not aware of in our movements and actions. Little things. The major stuff can come later. There's no rush. But *this* education is *priceless*.''

"Why didn't you just put her in that body of yours, then, and observe?'' Sugasto asked her. "Then you'd have an exact model.''

"True, true, and I considered it, but I know the Rules all too well. Put her back in here and everything would return full almost immediately. Symmetry would be restored. I don't know her capabilities yet, and I won't risk losing our only other original. I can't explain it, but something just told me that if I put her in this body things would go wrong. Call it—women's intuition.''

Sugasto shrugged. "I never understood women and I doubt

if you do, either, for all your playacting at being one. But, as one with the Power myself, I've also learned that you don't easily ignore such feelings. Very well. But if anything happens to him, *anything*, I'll stick *you* in that damned slave body there, and you'll lick my feet and kiss my ass for a thousand years!" With that, he stalked out.

"He's always so cross when he's tired," Boquillas commented, seemingly unconcerned.

"It sounds to me as if you have to take as much care of me as you do of yourself," Tiana noted. "Your death threat against the world does not mean much if you are still alive, but in *that* body."

"Anything worthwhile involves risk. My! But you're the swishiest barbarian I've ever seen! Come, we should dress before doing much else, and I'm *starved*. We don't feed these bodies right." She walked out, and suddenly Tiana almost jerked forward, as if on a chain, and had to double-time it to catch up.

"Another of your ideas?" he asked.

"Just a part of the spell, dear. We're *such* a devoted couple now that we can't even bear to let each other out of our sight."

"That is going to be a lot of fun in the ladies' room," Tiana commented, and Boquillas laughed a very un-Tiana laugh.

They were passing the inside tower windows; outside, the inner courtyard glowed with the ever-present fire of the liquid rock. *Oh Joe! Joe! I'd join you now, if I could, and end this eternal torture*!

And somewhere, deep within her mind, came a voice, a thought, that she wasn't certain was hers or from some other, perhaps supernatural, origin.

"Bring her to my dying place," it said. *"Bring her there and it will end."*

Even compared to abject slavery, it was the worst evening Tiana ever spent. With Joe gone, nothing seemed to mean much anymore, but she might have been able to learn to live with it, sooner or later, if not for the fact that she was now in Joe's remaining body and almost umbilically attached to the body of her birth and the one in which she craved to live again.

Boquillas had dressed fit to kill, with about everything in the feminine arsenal of Husaquahr, including makeup, jewelry, and heels, which she negotiated quite well, but which made her tower over everyone else and even somewhat dominate his own large body. He had been given a rather deluxe loincloth, some sandals, and, most painfully of all, Joe's swordbelt and scabbard, minus the sword. It didn't really matter; the spell prevented him from using the sword anyway, although he had to wonder. That sword always had a curious fairylike life of its own, as if it were some sort of creature that fed upon those it killed. Joe had often spoken as if he had no control over it and that when it was in his hand, he seemed a mere observer.

Tiana had to wonder if the sword would respond to him in this body. If it did, would it be bound by this spell? Or, in fact, was that a moot point? Suppose he *could* kill Boquillas with the sword. What then? The volcano blows, the battle resumes, and that's it.

It would present one hell of a moral dilemma. Risk the destruction of the world or at best its enslavement by powers from a forgotten age; or allow Esmilio Boquillas to paint *Tiana*, not Boquillas, as the tyrant goddess?

And then, again, could he do it? Could he, in effect, destroy his own body?

He didn't particularly like being a man. Oh, there was nothing *horrible* about it, but it wasn't as much fun. It didn't feel right, and men carried such different mental baggage, such different interests and outlooks. He'd been a man during one of the early were episodes, just to see what it was like, and definitely decided that, at least for Tiana, girls had more fun. Hell, just look at how boring he dressed!

Dinner was a rather uncomfortable affair, with Boquillas constantly twitting him and making comments about the Tiana body as well, but the food was damned good. One of the serving slaves, who might or might not have been the one from the previous day who had listened so kindly, poured the wine and whispered in his ear, "Get her to the pit. If she dies there, we can stop the action."

Tiana stiffened. So he *wasn't* crazy. Who, then, was behind this?

With a start he realized that it had to be Marge. No mention had been made of either Marge or Macore since their capture, and it was another of Boquillas' lapses not to have asked about it when, as a slave, Tiana would have had to tell.

Marge was a Kauri. The goddess of Kauris, she'd said, lived in a volcano! *In a volcano!* Of course!

"Uh—Tiana?" The name stuck in his mouth and was hard to get out.

"Yes, Joe, darling?"

"Could I—could we—after eating, I mean—go down there for just a minute? I would like, just once, while I am still thinking straight, to see where he died."

Boquillas thought about it. "It wouldn't do any good, you know. You cannot do yourself any harm."

"No tricks. We *were* together a very long time, though."

"Hmmm . . . If I did, would you lie with me tonight? Would you lie there and pretend that you are Joe and that I am Tiana? Do it with me and make me believe it?"

"I—I don't know if I could. I can try."

"All right, let's try. If I'm pleased, we'll go down in the morning. If not, well, then, we'll see, won't we?"

"No. Let me at least say good-bye to him before I can do anything new."

Boquillas gave that wicked smile. "Joe, darling, we've got to start training you properly. In all cases, from now on, what I want comes first. There are no exceptions."

"All right," he sighed. "But bring me much stronger drink than this! I'll need quite a lot to forget who and what I was and who and what you are!"

It was fortunate that hangover cures were easier for witches than even love potions, because he needed one badly the next morning. He'd gotten himself so sloshed he could hardly remember the night, and he knew he didn't want to remember any more than he did.

Still, Boquillas seemed in very high spirits. "Come, my love, now that your head is clear and your stomach is settled, we will go down and honor your request.''

It was startling to see how Boquillas had changed just between night and morning. He hadn't had a truly accurate idea of how he looked and acted as Tiana—who did have that kind of self-image?—but the sorcerer's look and manner were far less exaggerated and more natural, the sort of way the original Tiana would do something, and her speech was changing as well, taking on more of Tiana's own speech patterns and even gaining a hint of the accent acquired by spending so much time growing up on Earth. Was he really *that* revealing, in spite of efforts to hide it, or was Boquillas really that good?

"I'd intended to go down there today, anyway," she told him. "The empty scabbard must be addressed, and we have an acid test to make while you are still relatively unencumbered. Come."

They walked down the stairs, across the lobby area, and into the left courtyard ring. At the first arch they went through, with him preceding her, and then down the steps to the narrow walkway around the boiling pit.

Both of them stopped suddenly at the sounds of *Gilligan's Island* and stared at that second level. "Hasn't Sugasto blown that thing to smithereens *yet*?" Boquillas said, irritated.

"Perhaps he's experimenting, now that he's got the situation," Tiana suggested. "I would say he is probably quite concerned that something exists that can negate his best spell."

"You may be right. If he goes on too long, though, *I* will want to trigger this volcano just to stop that moronic nonsense."

They walked around to almost the very spot where Joe had stood on the wall, taking on all comers. About twenty feet away, the sword Irving still stuck out halfway in blood-stained rock, although someone had at least cut free and hauled away the impaled bodies during the night.

Tiana went over and looked down at the bubbling mass. It looked like cooking pudding or an asphalt mixer and smelled of rotten eggs and worse. Only clever design kept that odor from permeating the palace—most of the time.

Joe's body was part of that now, burned, melted, to become one with the rock, the fluids boiled away in a flash.

He turned away, feeling sick.

"Listen," Boquillas said, "what is done is done. *You* are Joe now. You are all that is left of him. I did not want him dead, remember. We should never have been standing here like this, now. Cooperate with me. Become Joe willingly and accept me as I am. Help me to pull this off. You saw Sugasto's horrid vision, all those soulless bodies, shaved and mutilated slaves, police-state brutality. I don't want that. I would not *want* to be the goddess of a world like that. We need not be lovers, but we do not have to be enemies."

"Empty talk, empty promises," he responded. "Your slick tongue and fast mind have gotten you through everything, yet you still stand here, short of your ambitions. Against your talk, there is the certainty that Joe, the real Joe, jumped from here into *that*, rather than aid you. I cannot stop you from using me, from using magic, potions, whatever. But I can never surrender willingly, for to do that would be to spit on Joe's grave and call his sacrifice a lie. I would *never* do that. I could not."

She sighed. "Then we do it the hard way. In the end, it does not matter. It just means that instead of enjoying the benefits of being consort to a god, you will instead wind up sooner or later cleaning her toilets."

"There is no dishonor in being a slave," he said softly. "It is necessary work."

High above, from the window of the empty room, Macore and Marge looked down on the pair, and the little thief frowned. "You think you can get her in there?"

"If she'd just lean a little more against that low wall I bet I could deliver a sudden, flying kick."

"Yeah, from the front. She'll see you and stop you with a spell."

"It's a risk I have to take. There is no other way."

Macore looked out, gasped, and suddenly grabbed Marge's arm. "Look! Maybe there is!"

Marge stared down at the scene and gasped herself. The pair

stood there on the walk, facing away from the pit, and could not see it.

Slowly, carefully, but absolutely, a great golden limb of the lava tree was moving, almost like an excruciatingly slow tentacle, extending with every little movement. A new branch sprang out at its tip and seemed, as they watched, to grow smaller branches, almost like . . .

"Like a hand," Marge breathed.

"But it's too short and too slow!" Macore said. "There's no way it can reach her before they move!"

"Maybe, maybe," she breathed. *"Oh, remember it's iron!"*

Down on the courtyard, Boquillas sighed. "Well, try and get the sword, anyway. You cannot use it on me, and even if it tries on its own, I can numb your arm in plenty of time. Go ahead— call it. Call it the way *he* used to call it."

"All right," Tiana said wearily. Even if the sword responded, even if it flew to his hand, could he in fact will it to cut off the neck of his birth body?

The "hand" on the lava tree turned, lining up perfectly. There was the sword in the rock, then Tiana's stately body, then the "hand," all in a row. Just a tiny fraction more to the left . . .

Tiana held out his hand. "Irving! To me!" he called.

The sword remained in the rock.

"Irving! To me!" he tried again, and again the sword stayed put.

And then came a soft, sexy, deep female voice, as if from a great distance, and echoing all up and down the pit. *"Irving! To me!"* it said.

Boquillas, startled, turned slightly to her right and said, "Wha—?"

The sword flew from the rock like a rocket, striking Boquillas with tremendous force right in the chest, bowling her over on its unstoppable way to the limb. She was knocked back against the wall, stunned, and for a moment seemed to totter, but not fall back.

The sword struck the handlike end of the limb, crackling when it touched, but the limb pushed back with tremendous force, directing the sword, blade first, exactly back in the direction from which it had come at the moment Boquillas tried to straighten up. The great sword struck and penetrated right below the neck, knocking her slightly forward.

At that moment, Tiana suddenly felt all constraints lifted and acted almost without thinking, the emotions at Joe's loss and the hatred for Boquillas overwhelming any and all other thoughts but one.

"I will never fail you, Master."

With enormous strength, he seized the screaming Boquillas, lifted up that huge female body, and tossed it into the pit below.

"Yippee!" Macore cried from the window.

"Son of a bitch!" Marge swore. "I think she tore one of the strings loose on the way down! I gotta *fly!*" She leaped out, then down directly into the lava.

Tiana stood there, looking down at that same lava, and began shaking like a leaf, and then started to cry.

Macore suddenly felt the whole building start to shake a bit, and things began dancing around of their own accord. *Good grief!* he thought, suddenly panicking. *Earthquake! I gotta get out in the open! Com'on, Marge!*

Tiana was suddenly aware of the shaking as well, and looked around curiously, drained of emotion. Boquillas was dead. *Really* dead. And now someone else would inherit Husaquahr as a result.

He looked back down at the lava pool, oblivious of the shaking, oblivious of the cornices beginning to crack, of the crash as television, VCR, and stacks of videotapes went flying, leaving packs of suddenly enraged zombies loose.

The lava level was falling in the crater!

Tiana was still confused, stunned, and somewhat in shock by what had happened. Had the sword flown and killed Boquillas? What was that woman's voice? Marge? What had they rigged up?

It no longer mattered. Clearly, no matter what else happened, nothing was going to matter for anybody in this palace before long, and that included him. Oddly, that didn't disturb him, but he was seized with a sudden urge to see just what was happening out at the Devastation, and just what would emerge from that horrible place.

Just as suddenly as it had begun, the earthquake stopped. He turned again and saw, or thought he saw, the lava level stabilizing. Not really rising—it had lost a good fifteen or twenty feet—but it no longer seemed to be draining out.

Marge came shooting out of it, then landed on the wall. "Close call!" she exclaimed, sounding winded. "I got it tied off, but not before one tube flooded and blew. I'm not sure what's gonna happen, but I think the majority of them are still in the deep freeze. No guarantees about the closest point, though."

He looked at her, shaking his head. "Marge, I think we better get away from here anyway. Now that it's stopped shaking, Sugasto is going to be fit to be tied."

"Whoops! Forgot about him! Head for the royal side. Pick up a weapon if you can. Meet you on the garden porch!"

Tiana nodded. "At least we don't have to listen to *Gilligan's Island* anymore!"

"Yeah. Poor Macore. Watch out for the zombies!" And she was off.

He looked around, then made a run for the far stairs. There was pandemonium all over the place, and things were still falling and crumbling from the after-effects of the quake. Soldiers, Bentar, everybody was running all over the place, and nobody was paying the least bit of attention to him.

He looked back briefly across the center courtyard and saw why everybody was going his way. The topmost part of the main tower was cracked clean through, and seemed almost to be leaning precipitously. Even the gargoyles were leaving their perches there, flying around aimlessly and screeching obscenities.

He didn't see Marge on the porch, but the whole place was a mob scene as it was, and he couldn't blame her. At the moment, it was everybody for him or her or itself, and the safest place to be was out there, on the ice.

Suddenly there was the sound of doom, like horrible drums from the depths of the earth, beating an awful time. It seemed not to be coming from the Devastation, which now had its own jet of furious steam, but from *behind*, from the direction *away* from the battlefield. Kicking away some panicky people, Tiana climbed up on the wall and looked out, trying to see what was making the eerie, rhythmic sounds. And when he *did* see, he knew indeed that this was all some horrible nightmare, that he'd gone totally and completely insane.

Either that, or a Danish naval coast guard icebreaker was coming toward the palace, propelled by the furious slashing of massive oars sticking out of holes cut in the hull.

"*It's Ruddygore!*" Marge shouted in the air above Tiana with undisguised glee.

Sure enough, there was the huge sorcerer, resplendent in his Grand Master's robes, sitting in something like a throne right at the bow.

The ship stopped, and the entire thronelike chair rose into the air and deposited itself, and the sorcerer, gently onto the ice.

Throckmorton P. Ruddygore looked over at the smoking area of the Devastation and muttered, "Oh, my! This might well be ugly!" Then he got up and began walking regally over the snow and ice toward the black island and its palace.

The fleeing castle personnel, whether human, Bentar, or something else, soldier and slave alike, gave way before him, keeping a fearful distance. Tiana suddenly found himself alone atop the wall.

Ruddygore spotted him. "Hello! Where's Sugasto?"

"Haven't seen him since last night," Tiana called back.

"*Ruddygore!*" Marge screamed, practically flying into him and bowling him over. "Late, as usual!"

"Not at all," the sorcerer replied. "Until either the bodies were destroyed or Boquillas died, or both, I was powerless to alter events. Even I couldn't do them in, you see. But now, now that the Baron is ashes, it's no longer your business to close this affair, but mine. Mine—and Sugasto's."

"He's the new young gun, Pard," she responded. "You think you can take him?"

Ruddygore always looked to her like Santa Claus, but the expression on his face now was anything but cheery or merry. It was the kind of look that froze brave men, and sent everyone running.

"There's only one way to find out," he said softly. "The Baron is dead. The Council will back only one of us now."

He walked up the black slope and into the garden area. As he reached it, an idol like a great hooded cobra suddenly wriggled, as if coming to life, and hissed at him.

He hissed back at it, and it was engulfed in fire.

"*Sugasto!*" he called in his booming voice, the call echoing throughout the complex. "*Sugasto! Come! It is finally our time!*"

"Over here, fat man!" came a response, and they all looked and saw the Master of the Dead in his full black robes, standing on the far side of the porch.

"What say we meet on the ice?" Ruddygore suggested calmly. "Less chance of debris and more open space. Besides, we might have to tend to a bit of other business over there before we square off."

Sugasto nodded. "The ice it is. But I fear nothing coming from that pit. The horrors frozen there fought *my* sort of fight."

Marge felt exhausted, but she wasn't about to miss this. As the assembled soldiers and staff stepped back to watch, forming almost an audience, Tiana got down from his perch and walked up to Marge, now standing at the other end of the porch looking out at the ice.

"What are they going to do?" he asked the Kauri.

"Wizard's battle," she responded. "It's required by the Rules, I think, anyway, to end this sort of stuff."

"He will win, will he not? Ruddygore, I mean."

She shook her head. "I dunno. I keep looking at that steam over there. You can't see it—yet. But magical strings are forming shapes behind that mist, ugly shapes. And Ruddygore lacks the killer instinct. Remember Boquillas."

Between the wall of steam and the palace island was the broad expanse of ice. Now the two figures, both looking rather small against its plain backdrop, faced each other at a distance of about thirty feet, like two gunfighters in some bleak frontier showdown.

"I didn't teach you *everything*, Sugasto," Ruddygore noted. "All that time in the madness of the djinn where you sent me wasn't wasted, either, old man," the Master of the Dead responded. "As you have already seen."

"Your zombies are of little use to you now," the big man said. "And you'll not find *my* soul so easy to pluck."

Sugasto's hand went up, and an enormous ball of the blackest magic flew toward Ruddygore. Ruddygore responded with a massive, almost blinding flash of light that banished it.

"I saw *that*!" Tiana exclaimed.

"They're just warming up, feeling each other out," Marge told him. "I'm more worried about something else. I just figured out why Sugasto was so pleased to have this fight where it is. Every time they hurl something, either one, more power builds behind the mist, more incredible magic rushes in and solidifies."

Now both sorcerers let loose huge spells that met in the middle, and the entire area between them was awash in color, like a giant, jagged splotch of varicolored paints, the colors mixing and swirling and oozing around, forming *shapes*. Fierce, lionlike things, and things like some horrible nightmare of bears, against demonic shapes, ugly, serpentine, and gargoylelike, all roaring their fury and going at each other as the two men, like puppeteers, kept moving their hands and arms in fantastic, gyrating motions.

"I wonder what it seems like to them?" Tiana breathed.

Upon a vast plain of crackling, multicolored energy, the two protagonists stood not as people but as thoughts or expressions, each with his own distinctive colors. Thrust, parry, thrust again, done with the speed of thought, and with any of the weapons the imagination could supply; this was the plane of the wizard's battle.

"The djinn prepares you well for this, old man," Sugasto taunted. "Planes of madness, without rules, without form, until you give it thus."

An enormous demonic monster materialized, pouncing with a horrible roar upon Ruddygore. The big man became a massive mouth, all teeth and gullet, swallowing the creature and not resisting a very large *burp*!

"True, my boy, but I've been there since last you were!" Ruddygore responded.

Massive energy, all blues and greens and bright orange for strength, flashed out from the big man and took form; a great squidlike horror whose tentacles reached out and threatened to grab the brilliant will-o'-the-wisp that was Sugasto.

The man in black became a giant, whirling blade, cutting the tentacles like salami, stacking them up in uneven piles.

"You're every bit as good as the potential I saw in you when you were just a lad," Ruddygore noted. *"You still lack imagination, though."*

"Imagination! Fine talk from a man who plays the game so incessantly that he has forgotten why the game is played at all!"

"You never understood, Sugasto, and that was your tragedy," the big man responded. *"The lust for power, the god complex, has consumed you. You would be a god or the devil himself, yet those are the worst jobs in all Creation, for they are the loneliest. Let us stop this childish playing, Sugasto. Let me show you your victory! Let me give you your vision of the new world!"*

There was blackness, blackness all around, and the man in black was falling, falling down an endless hole. There was no top, no bottom, no sides, only blackness, falling forever. There was no one to catch him, no one to save him, no one even to sympathize. He was utterly, completely alone, falling forever.

No! There *were* others around him! Almost in terror, he reached out for them, drew them to him with his mighty power. Yes! Lots of people! They whirled with him, falling in the darkness, and he could see them, millions of them; men, women, children, all with glazed eyes and vacant stares, all without minds, without souls. . . .

Sugasto screamed.

From the porch, Marge pointed to the figure of the man in black. "He's staggering! He's *down*! Way to go, Ruddygore!"

But at the moment of victory, there came an ominous rumbling from the still steaming edge of the Devastation. Suddenly, the ice trembled, and huge fissures opened, coming outward in the direction of both sorcerers, the crack coming between them.

It was so unexpected that Ruddygore was knocked off his feet and off his concentration, allowing a weakened Sugasto some breathing room.

And then, suddenly, rising from the ice between the two wizards, emerged a monstrous head, with huge, glaring eyes, nostrils that snorted smoke and fire, and fangs dripping with the ichor of doom. Dragonlike, it was *more* than a dragon, it was the horrible face of all that was feared in dragons.

A second opening, then a *second* head, even more frightening and hideous than the first, appeared, snorted, and looked around. Now, yet a *third* appeared, and a small part of the body as well, showing the monster, fully thirty feet high, its three heads taking in the scene, looking as if it could devour them all. The castle crowd, once an audience, began running over the ice, away from the three-headed nightmare from the Devastation, but the sorcerers could not run.

Sugasto looked up and saw it, and smiled evilly. Getting to his feet as best he could, he pointed to Ruddygore who was still down, but struggling to get up.

"Creature of evil from times past, I charge thee destroy in the name of our same master whose reign from Hell is secure. Devour him who would stop our master's plan!" the man in black intoned, pointing at Ruddygore.

For a moment all three heads looked slightly puzzled, although they appeared to have understood; then, suddenly, long necks turned as one toward Ruddygore, just getting to his feet, and three sets of horrible, gaping jaws whose fangs were larger than the white-bearded sorcerer, came down for him.

CHAPTER 14

SWAN SONG FOR HEROES

*That is not dead
which can eternal lie;
And in strange eons,
even death may die.*
—The Necronomicon of Abdul Alhazred

SERPENTINE HEADS FROM THE THREE-HEADED GORGON LOOMED nightmarishly over the suddenly very small, frail figure of Ruddygore. One of the heads licked its chops with a horrendous forked tongue and made to go down for the figure. Suddenly, it stopped, its eyes wide.

"Why, it *can't* be!" the left head exclaimed. It swooped down and examined Ruddygore almost like a specimen in a jar. The right head followed.

"It is! It is!" the right head cried. "Look! It's young Muloch, all grown up and become a real sorcerer!"

"*No!*" the middle head exclaimed. "And yet—yes, you just might be right!"

The heads jerked around in rare unison until three sets of flaming, flaring nostrils were right in front of Ruddygore as he struggled to his feet.

"Hello, boys!" he managed. "Good to see you! It's Ruddygore these days."

Sugasto stood, wide-eyed, unable to comprehend what he was seeing. "Destroy him! Eat him!" he screamed.

"Who's that boorish little prick?" the left head roared.

"He's *very* loud," the center head noted.

"And *most* uncivil," the right head chimed in.

"An old student of mine who got ambitious," Ruddygore told it or them. "The sort who wonders too early why he should be taking lessons from an old fart when he knows, or thinks he knows, more than his teacher."

"Can we eat him?" the right head asked.

"Oooh! Let's!" the left head responded.

The center head looked at Ruddygore, who turned up his arms in an exaggerated "I-don't-care" shrug.

"All right, lads! At him, then!" the center head cried.

Sugasto unfroze and started running for the palace and solid ground.

"Oh, what fun!" the left head said.

"Yes, it's always *much* more fun when they run!" the right agreed.

Sugasto made it to the black, warm earth and scrambled up, the gorgon not far behind him. He reached the top not far from Marge and Tiana, and suddenly froze again.

Legions of blank-eyed zombies blocked his path.

Macore was singing the *Gilligan's Island* song to them from the wall. He pointed. "There he is! There's the one who broke it! Com'on, little buddies! At 'em!"

Sugasto stared and raised his hand. "Back! Back! I am the Master of the Dead! Obey me!"

But they continued to stare vacantly, blocking his way up, and, from behind him the center head of the gorgon came down and seized him in its jaws, then lifted him, screaming, by its mouth.

The other two heads started objecting and tearing into the sorcerer, who soon stopped struggling. The center head coiled, like a spring, then let go, tossing Sugasto high in the air, the heads jockeying for position as he came down.

"I've got him!"

"No you haven't! *I've* got him!"

But he went right down the center head's gullet, and that head suddenly had an incredibly pleased look about its grisly self.

"No fair! You cheated!" the right head complained.

"Yes, you were the one who threw him up, and you knew how hard and how far," the left head commiserated.

"Well, what do you want me to do?" the center head huffed. "Regurgitate him so you can have a second shot?"

"After all this time in this crazy world," Marge commented, "I thought I'd seen it all and couldn't be surprised by *anything* anymore." She shook her head in wonder. "Boy, was I wrong about that!"

Marge and Tiana turned from this argument to Macore, who was standing below before an audience of the living dead.

"Macore! How did you *do* it?" Tiana called to him.

He shrugged sheepishly. "I dunno. I made a run for it when the buildings started shaking, then decided to see if I could at least save some of the tapes. There they were, all staring at this busted television. When I came in, they turned on me. Surrounded by zombies, there was nothing else I could *think* to do, so I started singing, and they followed me out! Somehow, in their dim brains, I think they think I'm Gilligan!"

Out on the ice, Ruddygore approached the gorgon. "I always wondered what happened to you," he said to no head in particular.

"Oh, Gastorix called us from the High Mounts of Ris," the center head responded.

"We knew it was a doomed cause, but he was such a *nice* old fellow," the left head added.

"Played a positively *delightful* harp, too," the right head put in.

"Boys, that was three thousand years ago. You've been locked in that long. Things have changed."

The heads looked around. "Not all *that* much," the center head said.

"Still looks wizard eat wizard to me," the right head agreed.

"Same old story," the left head sighed. "Boy meets girl, boy loses girl, boy turns into hideous monster and eats her."

Ruddygore stopped for a moment, thinking about it. "Maybe you're right. Maybe it isn't all that different after all," he agreed. "Uh—but we have fewer and lesser types to contend with these days. What else is likely to come out of that meltdown? You and I know that in the old days you wouldn't have been able to nab someone of Sugasto's stature that easily."

The gorgon heads turned and looked back at the mist.

"Cooling down already," the center head said.

"Yes, indeed," the other two heads agreed in unison.

"Oh, I suspect you'll have quite an assemblage of demons, wicked fairies, that sort of thing stalking around," the center head told him, "if, of course, they can figure out how to get *out* of there before being swallowed back up. Most of them, though, were re-absorbed, what with everyone all crushing up to get out all at once."

"Not everyone is able to throw their weight around the way *we* can," the right head pointed out.

Ruddygore sighed. "Well, boys, the Lakes are that way and the River still flows. I'm over at Terindell now, right on the river. Let me know if you need anything, but I've still got a bit of the aftermath to deal with here. We've ended an entire epic today, and it's been a while since anyone did *that*. You know how many loose ends those leave."

"Oh, indeed, yes," the right head agreed.

The left head looked at the figures of soldiers and the rest still well away on the ice. "Can we eat them? After all this time, we're *starved*!"

"Well, the Bentar are all yours, and any fellows with the black and gold uniforms. Let the rest be. They're mostly innocent victims."

"Oh, thank you! Thank you!" the three heads cried together, and they sank beneath the ice once more, to come up, it was suspected, somewhere beyond the still fleeing forces.

Throckmorton P. Ruddygore sighed and made his way over to the porch area.

"Ruddygore! Are you okay?" Marge called.

"No!" he snorted. "When I fell on that ice I think I skinned my knee. Hurts like hell! Tore a perfectly good robe, too!"

"You'll live." She laughed.

He stopped halfway up the side, and Tiana gave him a mighty hand to assist him to the top.

"Good heavens! Is that *Tiana* in there?"

"I am afraid so," Tiana replied. "Boquillas decided to be me, and, well, planned on me teaching her how."

"Yes, I see." He looked down. "Macore! Will you stop playing with those poor unfortunates?"

"I can't!" the thief wailed. "They won't let me stop recounting the stories!"

Ruddygore laughed. "Let's leave him there awhile. I'm certain we can extricate him later, but it's about time he got what he deserved with that mania of his." He looked around. "Where is Joe?"

Tiana's face fell. "I think you had better hear the story from the start," he said.

"Yes, indeed. Tell you what—I'm going to soak this knee in that thermal bath over there. You can tell me while I do so."

Marge slipped away from them and walked back in through the now deserted and litter-strewn royal entry hall, then out to the crater. It and the lava tree were still there, although the sorcerer's tower still tottered precipitously, and there were cracks all over and chunks of rock here and there. It was already beginning to give the place something of the look of a ruin.

"It's all right, Joe," she said in a conversational tone. "There's nobody here but me."

The purplish trunk of the lava tree seemed suddenly to expand slightly, and from it emerged a small fairy form. "I had a hunch you'd get it," the figure now under the lava tree said. "I was hoping Tiana wouldn't."

"Well, she's not much happier than you are at the moment, you know," the Kauri pointed out. "Either one of you would be better off and happier as the other."

"Yeah, I know," Joe said. "Those damned Rules! You always have a way out, but when I stood there on that wall, surrounded, seeing those silver-tipped piles and bolts, I knew that there was only one way open, just what the Rules required. I looked at them, then I looked back at this tree, and I figured, hell, a tree's a tree, and it would free me of Boquillas' power and give me some freedom of action. It was surrender, die, or *this*. As much as I didn't want *this*, I have to tell you I would have taken death easily, even oblivion, except that it would have left my enemies victorious and Tiana in their hands. I remembered what we'd discussed about sacrifice and unhappy endings and all that. If this was to be the end of our great battles, then it was also somebody else's beginning, too. I hadn't taken Irving out of the mean streets of the inner city to have him grow up under Boquillas' or Sugasto's vision of Husaquahr. If that meant this, then it was a price I had to pay.''

"Hey! It's not so awful!" Marge responded. "I think you made a pretty good Kauri."

"Well, it's okay, but I didn't want a career out of it. Even so, Kauris fly, and very well, and can interact with regular society to a degree. Maybe I could take that. But wood nymphs—hell, I can't even figure out how to get *off* here! I could slide down, I guess, but even if I found some solid rock to stand on down there I'd never make it back up the outer wall. That's why I've been here all this time. I'm stuck!''

Marge smiled. "Well, let me see if I can find a rope or something and fly it out to you. Then I'll fill you in on all you missed. Ruddygore's here.''

"Yeah? Well, unless he's broken the secret code, that doesn't do *me* much good at all.''

"I fear the secret of such effortless soul-switching died with Boquillas and Sugasto.'' Ruddygore sighed.

They—the sorcerer, Macore, Marge, and Tiana—sat in Sugasto's old banquet room, sampling his wares. Since Ruddygore seemed unconcerned about the top of the tower falling down, they were at least less nervous about it themselves.

"You mean I am stuck like this,'' Tiana said.

"Well, not *exactly*, but there are few options. I can't fool around with that body, since I helped design it, as it were, with bound demons. The theory of the switching spell is easy enough to divine; the problem is that each and every individual is different. Thus, you need complementary mathematics to switch anyone that is unique to each individual. The question we have no answer for is, how did Sugasto and the Baron figure out the unique complementary equation for each and every individual they switched, therein detaching both soul and consciousness and placing it elsewhere? I don't know. Reattaching on other than a random basis provides the same problem for the host.

Thanks to Sugasto's easy lifting addendum, I know *your* code, and, of course, I know the codes for your slave body and for Mahalo McMahon, whom we had to care for after she was stuck in the Baron's wrecked body. We used the Lamp to cure Mahalo—she's the High Priest of an Amazon cult in the southern jungles right now and apparently loving every minute of it."

"You could use the Lamp on me, then."

"No." Ruddygore sighed. "I'm afraid not. You see, after Macore stole it the last time from a vault I would have said was the most secure in the whole of the universes, I realized that as long as it was accessible and known, it would be a magnet that could never be properly secured, as handy and seductive as its power was. I couldn't destroy it—it was of djinn manufacture—but I sent it flinging, out into space. I have no idea where it is now. Mars, possibly, if it hit anything."

Tiana sighed. "Then this is it?"

"That body gets you back an undisputed royal exalted position," he reminded her. "You were sort of deified, you know. We could easily sell you as Joe and Tiana merged, a single godhead, both male and female in one, and you could help provide stability to this land in these days of aftermath. The alternatives are that I can return you to the slave body from whence you were plucked, since I know that one, or to the empty shell previously used by the Baron, McMahon's body. It's not a bad body, but I have no idea of what you'd wind up as. You saw what the hormone levels in that body did even to such a staid fellow as Esmilio Boquillas. Most likely, whoever gets it will become a *very* sexy witch."

"What do you mean, 'whoever gets it'?" Marge asked.

"Well, we have all those zombies—thousands upon thousands of them. Not the reanimated dead, they collapsed with Sugasto's death, but the ones whose souls were taken and stored. Those souls are mostly stored here and almost all survived the quake. Alas, they are coded by a private spell, so there is no way of ever telling who's what. There could be faerie in there, as well as countless men, women, and children. We can put the souls back in the bodies, but we can't tell whose soul is which, so it's going to be totally random. You are by no means alone in your predicament, Tiana, and at least you have choices. But we'll use every body we have, I'm sure, saving, of course, the slaves for last. It'll be a mammoth job as it is.''

"I do not *like* being a man, even though I like men,'' Tiana replied. "It is different relating to them as a woman, instead of being one of them. I enjoyed being a woman, always have. I do not believe even the Rules cover this sort of thing, although, goodness knows, they cover almost everything else. Oh, I know the hormones will act, I will get used to it, more comfortable with it, but I am positive that the Baron was wrong. I think my own sense of who and what I am would keep me a woman trapped in a man's body no matter how much time passed. Joe, whom I saw as a Kauri, would be a much better woman than I will ever be a man.''

Marge said nothing.

"I agree,'' he said. "And since nobody voluntarily wishes to be a slave—I'm hoping, with some of the damage done in the quake making us a wee bit short on living souls, that we can eliminate restoring the slave bodies—you want the McMahon body, then.''

"I do,'' he said, "but you and I know full well that in spite of all this I am going to remain just as I am.''

Marge was so shocked she fell off her stool. *"What?''*

"Ruddygore said it. My return, now, as this, would stabilize first Marquewood and then the other regions. With my authority, I could insure that poor, suffering Valisandra and even Hypboreya gets the aid and assistance they need from the south to rebuild more stable and perhaps kinder governments. It is difficult to explain, Marge, but I was born of royal blood, and raised with a sense of duty and obligation. As a witch, I would be just another witch, counting for little, able to do very little. I would be happy within myself, but miserable at the things I would see that needed doing, that I *could* have done had I led instead of quit. I would honestly have been content to have remained Mia, slave to Joe, had that been an option, but it is not. Joe's sacrifice made victory possible. Now I, too, must sacrifice, in the name and interest of all those people who have no choices, and perhaps also to be an example and help those poor unfortunates who are going to revive as strangers, in the wrong bodies, perhaps the wrong sex, possibly the wrong age. I *have* to do it. It is my duty, and it is a big job I know I *can* do."

Ruddygore nodded. "I understand perfectly. For all these long years I have been looking for the one to whom I could hand over this heavy burden of mine, which I inherited but did not foresee, and pass on. I am quite weary of this life, I assure you. But look at what has arisen instead—the Boquillases and Sugastos and that hollow-souled Council."

Marge stared at him. "Were you *really* around when that battle was fought, as that creature said?"

"I am that old, anyway," he admitted. "I was much too young then, though, for such things; a mere junior adept. My master, the sorcerer Gastorix, whose power was so great that mine is but a pale shadow in comparison, was one of the guardians of the Eden Trees, which were placed here after that unpleasantness long before. I was *way* junior; he despaired that I would ever make sorcerer at all! His own prize pupil, whose name I will not even mention this close to the event, rebelled against *him* as well, and assembled a great multitude to seize first this tree, then the others, and become gods themselves. To gain allies to stop him, Gastorix had to promise many fairy and human chiefs that they would get to taste of the fruit. They marched off, and we never heard the details, although I always suspected that this place was the result. Since then, the Hypboreyans moved in and worshiped the tree as the one giving knowledge of good and evil, the source of torment and the strength of the devil, which is why they wound up such an unpleasant folk with even less pleasant gods. And now only we knew what it really is."

"Boquillas knew," Tiana commented. "She boasted of it."

Ruddygore nodded. "Yes, he would. He was the only other one who *could* have known. Back then, he wasn't even an adept, still trying to decide if he would go the royal line or attempt to become a sorcerer, being one of the most rare ones with both lines in his veins. So long as he worked for Hell, though, he was forbidden anywhere near here. When he betrayed Hell as well, he felt free to move."

The sorcerer looked over at Macore. "And what of you?"

The little thief shrugged. "I don't know. Nothing's much fun anymore. Stealing's too easy, I already got a fortune, and the thrill is gone. I been thinking maybe I oughta pack it in." Seeing their suddenly stricken looks he added, "No! No! I'm not gonna kill myself or anything like that! Relax! I mean take my money and go down south. Find somebody who loves little guys and looks like Mary Ann, or maybe Mahalo McMahon or somebody equally nice, and enjoy life for a change. With my money, even with my looks, attracting the girls won't be a problem, but attracting the right one will."

"And what will you do otherwise?" Tiana asked him.

"I thought maybe I'd have myself a big boat. Go out in the southern ocean, fish, laze around. Maybe give tours of the islands if I get bored."

Marge looked over at him. "Uh-huh. And how long an island tour?"

He smiled sheepishly. "Oh, maybe three hours."

Marge and Ruddygore walked across the central courtyard in the darkness. The crater was refilling nicely, already up to perhaps ninety percent of its old level, and things were calming down, both there and out in the region of the Devastation.

Sitting on the crater wall, idly swinging a leg back and forth, was the figure of a nymph, four feet tall with dark green hair and exaggeratedly endowed as were all nymphs.

"Hello, Joe," Ruddygore said. "How are you doing?"

"About as well as can be expected," the nymph replied in that soft, sexy voice they all had variations of. "It's still just sinking in, really. It's hard enough to accept that all my old enemies are dead, even if I *did* have a hand in it. Accepting *this* will be a lot harder. Right now it's okay—I mean, I've been a fairy before as a were and kept all my senses and personality and all that and adjusted pretty well, so it's been good training—but when the sun's up and it doesn't go away, or when it's a new moon and I'm still this way, well, after a while, it's gonna be hard."

"Oh, maybe not as hard as you think," the sorcerer consoled. "You have few physical needs, and you have powers that will come to you over time and will help you when needed. You have your wisdom and your experience. Not only are you unique in having your full self to call upon, you're also unique in a different way. Your first true tree was the lava tree. It accepted you, probably because of the genuineness of your sacrifice before it. You're not limited to it or stuck up here, but you are now, with me, a guardian of it, and of its secret. Because you mated with it first, its juices flow within you. It's as if you ate of it. You're invulnerable, Joe. Even iron will not hurt you. That's why the sword could be used and why you could throw it back. You can survive *anything*, just like this tree."

The nymph frowned. "You mean I could have picked up Irving and swung it?"

"You could if you could have picked it up, which I doubt. It weighed pretty much the same if not more than you do."

"There's that. But that means I'm stuck this way *forever*."

He nodded. "In a sense, you're sort of a minor deity. Other nymphs will sense that, by the way. You can heal them and their trees and groves and lend them power. I think that's a far better occupation in general than going around slicing people up."

"I never sliced anybody that didn't deserve slicing!" Joe protested. "But, yeah, it was kinda getting old. But this will get old even faster. I mean, I grew up tough, in a culture where the women had the kids and the guys worked three jobs to support 'em, fought hard, drank hard, drove hard. It's not just the sex. It might be a kick to be an Amazon. But I'm a four-foot-tall, automatically sexy, pale green bimbo!"

Ruddygore thought a moment, scratching his chin through his beard. "Well, there *are* minor true deities that rule each of the races of faërie, like Marge's Earth Mother. They have certain discretionary powers within their realm. Everyone's a little male and female, opposites in one. The yin and yang, the Oriental philosophers call it. If I asked politely, I might get you shifted over into the male side."

She looked up at him. "And what's a male nymph?"

"A satyr."

"Little guys with goat's legs and horns who dance around playing these big wide flutes?"

"That's them. Don't knock those flutes. We had a real artist among satyrs a few years back. We fed him a lot of Earth tunes, had him record them, got a fellow on Earth to front for him, and sold two million copies of pan flute records on late night television."

"No." She sighed. "Maybe I'll get desperate enough sooner or later to give it a try, but me dancing around with the chipmunks on goat's feet is an even wilder wrongness than this. At least I look like *something* here that wasn't put together by a committee."

"Your real problem," Ruddygore said, "isn't your form or nature, it's the fact that what you were destined to do is done; it's over, and while you're weary of all this and crave some stability, you also have suddenly been deprived of anything left to do."

"That is pretty much it," she admitted. "Things haven't exactly wound up as I imagined them, with me and Ti riding off into the glorious sunset."

"No, that's fairy tales. Sagas, on the other hand, are never without cost, and the principals rarely wind up truly happy when the evil is defeated. The constellations are filled with the shapes of creatures and personalities of myths and legends from hundreds of cultures, most of whom, it is alleged, wound up there because they came to unhappy conclusions."

"Yeah, tell me about it."

"It would never have worked with you and Tiana. Love does not conquer all and you know it. Ti is best at doing what he is going to be doing. Nobody can do that job as well or as faithfully. But that sort of role drove you insane once before and would again. It's simply not your element. She would have sacrificed it to remain your slave, but you would have been so guilty at the waste of her considerable talents and skills and intelligence locked in at that level. In the end, both of you would have been miserable."

"Did you tell her about me? Did she figure it out?"

"No. Sooner or later it might come to Tiana, but we decided

that it was your decision. I think you should, though. As a man and hating it, and as an absolute monarch of sorts, she's going to be very lonely. Just visits and talk—no permanence—would probably help her a great deal.''

"I'll think about it. I'm just not ready to handle that yet.''

"I understand. But it's part of the future. And, of course, you have a son.''

Her head shot up. "You think that isn't the number one thing on my mind? I had this vision, father and son, roaming Husa-quahr, showing him the sights and delights, watching at least the last half of his childhood. Doing things with him—fishing, hunting, all that. But he's here because his dad's a big, tough guy, with a sword that cuts through stone, and afraid of nothing at all. What am I gonna do? Walk into Terindell and say, 'Hi, Irving, I'm back, only I've been changed forever into a four-foot-tall, sexy, green nymph girl. Wanna go fishing?' "

"He might take it a lot better than his father being dead and him here alone,'' Marge put in. "He needs *somebody*.''

"He might not even be quite as put off as you think,'' Ruddy-gore added. "During his last exercise, he was trapped, inevitably, by the Circe, and turned into a pig. He's restored now, but it'll be some time before he lives that down. He's actually adapting quite well to the way things work here now. He's even showing some magical talents that I was quite unprepared for. From his mother, I suppose. It's a rather different sort of magic than mine, but he has great potential. Poquah has been giving him instruction in the same way Gorodo is teaching him the fighting skills. He's going to be *somebody* someday, Joe. He's got the talent and the will for it.''

Joe thought about it. "Maybe—maybe I *will* go back with you. Sure isn't any life sticking around *this* dump. Not as Joe—not right now. We'll pick a name. I'll be around, along with all the other fairies there, and I'll at least be able to be near, maybe help. Then, maybe, when I get a little more confident and maybe he's a little older . . .''

"I'll drop by for moral support any time,'' Marge assured Joe. "Maybe we'll go a few places together, two fairies out in the world. Poke in here and there. See old friends and a few new places. Maybe even take a trip on Macore's boat, remembering that I can fly for help if need be. It might be kinda fun to go a few places and do a few things without being on a wanted poster for a change."

Joe sighed and stood up. "Well, I guess it beats sitting through one hundred and eighty-nine episodes of *Gilligan's Island* all to hell, anyway." He looked back at the crater one last time. "Still, I sit here and I think of that conversation I had with Sugasto, and I wonder if it really *is* over, even now."

"Huh? What do you mean?" Marge asked a bit nervously. "Boquillas had no fairy soul. He's gone."

"Yeah, but *where*? He sure isn't going to Heaven, not any Heaven I could ever imagine, and he even betrayed Hell. Where *do* the great evil creatures of legend go when *they* die? Are they gone, or are they, perhaps, suspended somewhere, neither in Heaven nor Hell, looking like those poor souls in the Devastation for some reality, some way to loose themselves again upon the world?"

"I hadn't thought of that, Joe, but that may be a valid idea," Ruddygore told her. "If there *is* such a place, it must have such concentrated evil of such a magnitude that we must all pray that it *never* breaks out." He chuckled suddenly. "Of course, it would be unlikely in any event. Anyone who wound up in such a limbo would be such a power-mad egomaniac they'd always be at each other and never trouble us."

"I hope so." Joe sighed, turning for the last time from the crater. "I really hope so."

The last thing Esmilio Boquillas remembered clearly was the horrible, stabbing pain in the chest, and then someone lifting him into the air and throwing him down, down, until there was this horrible, searing pain that was suddenly cut off, leaving nothingness.

He had floated in this nothingness now for a very long time, although he had no concept of time. It was meaningless to him, without a body, without true form, without any boundaries or borders.

And yet, now, he was aware of others here, some having an

almost human feel, others giving a mental impression of something so hideous, so horrible, that were he still in human form he could not have beheld them without going mad. Somehow, they were blackness even within the total absence of light.

Finally, he could stand it no longer. "Who are you?" he asked in thought, for he had no mouth to form the words nor was there any true medium to carry them.

"I am Baal, who challenged even great Satan for the throne of Hell, little one," thundered back the response.

Another shape, another question.

"I am Sauron, the Eye of All, Darkest Lord of Middle-earth," the shape responded, and he had the distinct impression of some huge eye, near him, sightless but intelligent.

"I am great Cthulhu who sleeps forever beneath the Sea of Dreams until one day I shall waken once more and desolate the cosmos!" a third said.

And there were more, many more, existing together yet in splendid loneliness, each too powerful and too much a god even to acknowledge the others.

Esmilio Boquillas floated there, suspended between Heaven and Hell, between nightmare and reality, and thought about them all for a very, very long time. As powerful and as evil as he had been, he couldn't hold a candle to any of them, and they knew it. And that, oddly, placed him in a unique position, as he came to realize. As the lesser of all of them, he was the only one they would all acknowledge.

And, finally, he thought he had something.

"Hey, look, Cthulhu, baby! You're the greatest evil god of all, but we have to face it—we're stuck here. Now, if I can coordinate the others, get them to pull together with you, we might actually break out of this place. Once free, you could then easily deal with them, right?"

"I listen, little one."

And the next . . .

"Hey, look, Sauron, baby! You're the greatest evil god of all, but we have to face it . . ."

ABOUT THE AUTHOR

JACK L. CHALKER was born in Baltimore, Maryland, on December 17, 1944. He learned to read almost from the moment of entering school and, by working odd jobs ranging from engineering outdoor rock concerts in the sixties to computer typesetting, amassed a large SF/fantasy/horror book collection that today is ranked among the finest in private hands.

Chalker joined the Washington Science Fiction Association in 1958 and began publishing an amateur SF journal, *Mirage*, in 1960, and in 1963 founded the Baltimore Science Fiction Society. After high school, he set out to be a trial lawyer, but money problems caused him to switch to teaching as a career. He holds a bachelor's degree in history and English from Towson State College and an M.L.A. in the History of Ideas from Johns Hopkins University, and taught history and geography in the Baltimore city school system from 1966 until 1978 with time out for military service, until his writing career allowed him to become a full-time free-lance writer. Additionally, out of the amateur journals, he founded a publishing house, The Mirage Press, Ltd., producing over thirty books, mostly nonfiction, related to SF and fantasy, and, although no longer a major publisher, it still publishes an occasional book. His interests include computers, esoteric audio, travel, history and politics, lecturing on the SF field to private groups, universities, and such institutions as the Smithsonian. He is an active conservationist, a Sierra Club life member and National Parks supporter, and he has a passion for ferryboats, with the avowed goal of riding every one in the world. In fact, in 1978 he was married to Eva Whitley on an ancient ferryboat in mid-river, and they have lived ever since in the Catoctin Mountain region of Maryland with their son.